COMING BACK TO HOME

ELAINE STOCK

ALSO BY ELAINE STOCK

HISTORICAL FICTION

When Hope Calls Series

The Last Secret Kept

The Resilient Women of WWII

We Shall Not Shatter

Our Daughters' Last Hope

When We Disappeared

STAND-ALONE CONTEMPORARY

Her Good Girl

INSPIRATIONAL Romances

Always With You

The Kindred Lake Series

And You Came Along

Christmas Love Year Round

When Love Blossoms

COMING BACK TO HOME

First printing

ISBN-13: 9780999576359 (paperback)

ISBN-13: 9780999576366 (digital)

PUBLISHED BY GTG Publishing

Cover design by White Rabbit Arts at The Historical Fiction Company

For my readers—an author is
no one without her readers.

For my father, Charles H. Pakula,
who wanted another book.

For my personal cheerleaders:
My husband, Wally Stock,
and dear friends, Bonnie Lichak,
Megan Whitson Lee,
Bert Pearson,
Stephanie O'Connor,
and Susan Roberts.

A man travels the world over in search
of what he needs, and returns home to find it.
--George A. Moore

PROLOGUE

Atton, France, June 1946

She cannot move forward, backward, or sideways. Immobilized by the haunting truth creeping into her mind, her arms tingle with goosebumps. If it weren't for the panic gripping her, she probably would have burst into a near-hysterical laugh of denial. Still, it was time to face the reality she had chosen by leaving the only home she had ever known: she was alone, the world was vast, and ultimately, strangers could not be trusted.

An inner voice speaks to her in a gentle, reassuring tone, like a grandmother or aunt, full of wisdom. *You can take a chance. All you need to do is knock on the door. Put on a smile. Ask.*

A surreal image flashes in her mind. She sees a young woman hunched over, wearing threadbare black trousers she grabbed from a clothesline five villages ago, and a man's white shirt—smudged gray with dirt—hanging below her waist, with the sleeves rolled up high. Her hair is cut into a messy bob. Steeling herself against possible backlash, condescending looks, and unwanted advice to give up her search and live the life she once desired, she musters courage and keeps her best blank expression. This woman of yesterday is her—a person she can no longer relate to. No more. It's time to change her life, to prioritize others she cares about over herself.

She glances over her shoulder. Fool! No one is behind her; no one has joined her on this journey. Since she escaped the last man she trusted, others have kept their distance, and she's content with that. Other lonely and desperate women seeking validation, encouragement, and friendship—just like who she used to be—have also pulled away. Children, either abandoned or ignored, offer hesitant smiles before running off, leaving her alone.

She wishes she could blame her problems on the war that ended a year ago. At twenty years old, she sees this wish as a childish fantasy. They were all people living in a wild world, filled with brief moments of peace amid explosions of war, in need of essentials: food, shelter, and hope. Now that the war is over, the killing has stopped; however, everyone is trying to put the broken pieces back together. She is no different, having left her childhood home three years ago, dressed in the false armor of youthful self-righteousness, believing she would never falter and could achieve whatever she wanted.

Still damp and clammy from the morning rain, she brushes her stringy hair back from her eyes; a clump of gray strands entwines around her fingers. Only a few years ago, she would have never imagined her hair thinning and losing color, unlike her mother's dark tresses. A few older women she had met, also on the run, have tsk-tsked her, more as an admonishment for not knowing better than out of pity. "War and a lack of food age a woman, dear," said a white-haired woman, who had shocked her into silence. "Not having a man to keep you warm at night can also rob your youth." Her cheeks still burn with embarrassment and shame when she remembers the older woman's words.

She blinks away the images and cups her hands over her ears to block out the voices from the past. Commanding herself to function again, she squares her shoulders and looks ahead. Although she has made mistakes she regrets, now is not the time to dwell on them. Maybe there is never a perfect time. As she crosses the field of red poppies and tall grass, she moves forward, one step at a time.

Within seconds, she reaches the doorstep of the supposed safe house. The stone building is the oldest she has ever seen, dating back at least two or three centuries. How the structure withstood bombings and the ransacking of war is beyond her understanding. She cannot imagine the house having more than a kitchen, possibly a parlor, and one or two bedrooms—one for the caretaker and one for the children tucked under its roof, all waiting for the next shelter or perhaps a new home to open its doors. However, with the war's end, not all children in hiding were reunited with their families or placed with strangers willing to help orphans. This means she and her daughter still have a chance to reunite. A chance to heal the hearts broken by a separation that should never have happened. Unlike her healthier twin, this child might not grasp the complexities of family, but everyone, human or animal, at any age, understands love. As her mother, she wants to make up for the lost time with her precious child and shower her with endless love.

Hope, a long-lost feeling, warmed her heart. This must be the hiding place she has searched for more days than not over the past few years. She hesitates with her hand poised before the door covered in thick ivy.

She flexes her sweaty hands and then tightly clenches her fists. Instead of a polite knock, she pounds on the door. Words she hasn't spoken in years burst from her mouth. "I'm Rosa's mother. Let me in. Now."

1

LISELOTTE, BERLIN, GERMANY, DECEMBER 1943

Without a doubt, Liselotte knew as she fled her childhood home that she had just made the worst decision of her life. She brushed aside the ghostly chanting echoing in her mind. *Turn around. Go back. You made a huge mistake.* She had no choice but to silence the shadowy words.

Liselotte's heart raced, and her body went numb from the icy cold. Although it was foolish to stay still, she remained at the street corner of the only place she had ever called home. Caught in a whirlwind of second thoughts and fears, she mouthed, "Goodbye, my past. Hello, my future." It was now time to go to Gerhard, and together they would find Rosa—they owed it to their daughter.

All through the night, while icy pellets hammered down, she hurried down streets filled with tall snowdrifts. To avoid risks, she ducked for cover whenever others approached. Soon enough, she reached the outskirts of the city where Gerhard and his parents lived. The time she spent with him recently pushed all other thoughts from her mind and quickened her steps. Her first love, Gerhard, was meant to be her only love. He accepted her despite her faults and became her personal candle in this perpetually dark world. An SS deserter, his loving family hid him under the tool shed in their backyard. He would welcome her with open arms, no questions asked. Together, they would find a way to avoid the dangers of his coming out of hiding to search for Rosa, their daughter, whom her mother had given away to the Nazis.

She made a right turn. Three shops—a once-thriving butcher shop, pharmacy, and clothing store—now stood boarded up, creating a ghost town atmosphere—a common result of the ongoing war. Turning another right, the houses suddenly looked unfamiliar. How had she gotten lost after visiting Gerhard for the past several months? No matter. Knowing Gerhard would support her wishes made her decision to leave her home a little easier.

"You, child," came a shout from a house Liselotte was walking by. "What's all the fuss?"

Liselotte paused. Child? At almost seventeen, she was already a mother of two. Motherhood had made her an adult. But fuss? Had she even let out a moan? Heat flooded her face.

"Don't be rude," the stranger said. "I'm trying to help you."

She leaned against the broken fence in front of the house. A silver-haired woman stood on the steps of the house. She wore a black dress with a gray shawl draped loosely around her shoulders.

The older woman eyed Liselotte. "You're not wearing a coat. You shouldn't be out in this weather, dearie. You might catch pneumonia or something worse."

"Why do you care about me? I don't know you."

"I know these city streets well. They're dangerous for both of us."

"I can look out for myself."

"My daughter is about your age, and she says the same. She will still be my child when I'm eighty, and she's sixty."

Liselotte gulped. "Where is she now?"

"I don't know," the woman said as she walked down the shoveled path toward Liselotte. "I haven't seen her for a while."

Right or wrong, Liselotte could not bear to learn what happened to this stranger's daughter and knew she should not have asked. The last thing she needed was to hear a sad story and become discouraged. It was bad enough that she was trembling from the cold and fear, which stalked her like a wolf watching from the edge of the forest. To achieve her goals, she needed to strengthen her resolve. It was a fact of war—perhaps life, she was beginning to suspect—that heartache existed all around her. However, no one could afford to give up the happily ever after meant for them.

"Come in or don't," the woman said, tugging her coat tighter around her. She continued, "I won't extend my invitation any longer. We're in the middle of a war, not to mention a miserable winter, and it's too cold out here for small talk. Just watch—I'll slam the door in your face if you take too long."

Since leaving home the night before, Liselotte was so exhausted that she didn't know how to respond. She had been walking and avoiding others for nearly twenty-four hours, and the lack of sleep hadn't helped. The thought of staying on high alert for a few more hours or possibly another day threatened to drain what little strength she had left and her already fragile resolve.

"Put that way, how can I refuse?" She followed the woman inside.

"That's a good Fräulein." The woman pushed the door shut and bolted it securely. "Stomp the snow off your shoes. I have enough to do around here without having to keep after you."

The woman reminded Liselotte of her mother and the many times she had harped on her to stomp the snow off her boots. This ramped up her guilt for leaving her mother and her other daughter, Regina, behind. She looked into her host's blue eyes and asked, "What is your name?"

"Frau Bergman. And you are?"

"Gerda," Liselotte said. Wanting to maintain her privacy, she had rattled off the first name that came to her mind.

Frau Bergman crossed her arms. "The name suits you."

Liselotte remained quiet, relieved that the woman seemed to accept her false identity. For all she knew, the Frau's real name wasn't Bergman. With the war ongoing and the need to hide one's political views, as well as heritage and faith, fake names had become more common than ever.

"Sit, Gerda." The woman gestured toward a red upholstered chair in the small parlor. "I don't have much to offer, but I do have a pot of fresh root soup still warm on the burner. I'll fetch you a cup—it will chase away the chill from your scrawny bones."

"Thank you, but I don't want to take food from you or your daughter. Perhaps she's on her way home right now."

Frau Bergman stopped walking. "I wish I could say that it was a concern, dearie, but it isn't."

Liselotte's belly twisted. "You don't have a daughter, do you?"

Frau Bergman slowly turned around, her gaze fixed on the uneven floorboards. She began to tremble. "I didn't say anything like that."

Without hesitation, Liselotte grabbed a worn caramel-colored wool coat from a hook by the door, hurried toward the woman, and draped it over her shoulders.

"*Danke*, Gerda," the Frau said, a look of surprise widening her eyes.

Liselotte offered a soft smile. "Let me get the soup for you. Then I should be on my way."

Talking about my daughter upsets me. It shakes me more than the cold of winter. The Frau gestured outward. "Now, this house is mine, and I will tell you what happens here. My husband is a longtime party member working to serve the Führer's Reich." She lifted her head and smiled proudly. "Serving the Fatherland, Felix has been away for some time now, so there's no need to worry about him coming home and wondering who you are. I'm the one who manages this household."

What about her absent daughter? Had she left home in disgust over her Nazi-supporting parents, or was she serving the country elsewhere in some other capacity? Something told Liselotte that this daughter had left for reasons unrelated to political beliefs. Perhaps, like Liselotte, she was deeply in love with a man—her true partner in life—who brought her so much joy that her heart nearly stopped when they were apart. Gerhard was such a man, which is why she needed him by her side as soon as possible. Together, they would find Rosa, and one day, Regina would live with them, too. They might even add more children to their cherished family. Then life would be complete and wonderful, free from the condemnation of a mother who thought she knew everything. For now, it was a matter of timing.

She had to stay hopeful, patient, and considerate of others to avoid getting into more trouble.

The twilight sky, with its cobalt-blue hues blending with fading streaks of holly-berried red, would soon turn inky black. Since darkness offered some protection, she knew she had to leave, braving the frosty outdoors. Her thoughts once again turned to the absence of the Frau's daughter. Before she could reconsider, she blurted out, "I hope your daughter is managing to stay warm on a night like this."

"Stop obsessing over my daughter," the woman said. "It's none of your concern."

"You're right." Liselotte dropped her gaze to the floor. "I'm intruding. Pardon me."

"The war took her. End of discussion."

Surprise overtook Liselotte, and she lifted her attention back at the Frau. "I understand."

Frau Bergman narrowed her gaze. "How can you, Gerda? You're too young to be a mother, too young—"

"You're wrong," Liselotte said, using the same firm tone the Frau had used moments before. She carefully considered her next words. In need of a confidant, she wanted to open her heart and tell everything. Yet, she knew she had to guard her past like a sentry at a locked door. "I know well what the loss of family feels like. So yes, I can relate perfectly to what you're feeling. I'm sorry about your situation. I must go now."

The woman worried her bottom lip. "It will be a cold night. Stay—you can leave at first light."

"I have my reasons for leaving. Please understand that this isn't a reflection of your kindness."

"Dearie, at least let me fix you a satchel of food to sustain you on your journey."

Liselotte shook her head and began to step back toward the front door. The woman let out a shriek, almost worse than a rabbit being attacked by a predator, and placed both hands over her chest. Liselotte rushed to her side. "Is it your heart, your stomach, or your head? Do you have a fever?"

"I'm fine. But, like it or not, I'm preparing food for you to take. Please accept this small gesture. It's the least I can do after sending my daughter away. I'll be quick." The woman hurried into the kitchen before Liselotte could object.

Liselotte rubbed at the sudden chill crawling up her arms. Had she been naive enough to think she was the only one with family problems? Tears welled in her eyes as images of her twin babies spun through her mind. She tried to blink them away but couldn't. Regina was laughing while Rosa kept crying—always crying. Regina would call for her, saying, "Mama… Mama," the words slipping from her bowtie-red lips. Meanwhile, Rosa kept still, showing no sign of her feelings.

The floorboards creaked. Liselotte jumped, her heart pounding.

"I didn't mean to startle you," the Frau said. She lifted the package she was carrying. "Here's the food I promised."

A rich, tangy aroma made Liselotte's stomach growl. Was the food salty? Thick with gravy? Could she dare to imagine that she smelled meat? Another growl rumbled. She pressed her hand against her stomach, feeling her cheeks heat up.

"Now, now. Don't be embarrassed. It's not much." The woman handed her the small strapless canvas bag. "This is for the road. Just some leftover meat from yesterday's stew, a couple of day-old biscuits, and a chunk of cheese." She pushed a thermos toward her. "Oh, and this is the root soup I mentioned. You can either sip it now or take it with you. There's no need to return any of the containers."

"This is a feast," Liselotte said, her hands firmly at her sides. "One that I cannot take away from you during this time of food shortages."

The older woman winked. "Let's not start this nonsense again, or you'll never get out of here."

She was right. Liselotte needed to leave, especially since her chances of escaping Nazi scrutiny were better under the cover of darkness. "Thank you for your food and kindness. Will you be okay?"

"I've managed just fine, and I will keep doing so." She fixed her gaze on Liselotte. "Be careful where you walk and who you talk to, and keep using your false name. Gerda suits you, dearie."

"But—"

"Hush now. I was born in Germany, married a man devoted to this country, and know what to expect from people wandering the streets." Grasping the crook of Liselotte's left arm, Frau Bergman led her to the door. Instead of opening it, she slipped free from the tan coat with a wide tie belt—the one Liselotte had put on her before darting into the kitchen. She draped the coat around Liselotte's shoulders. "Take this old wraparound as well. I insist. No worries about me —I have another one."

"You're very generous."

"I appreciate your kind words. I hope you find who you're looking for quickly and easily."

Liselotte thanked her once more. Before the woman could notice the tears streaming down her cheeks, she slipped into the shadows of night. It was time to move forward and live it to the fullest. Soon, she would be with Gerhard, free from worrying about her mother's disapproval and harsh lectures questioning her judgment and sanity. She and Gerhard would ensure that their daughters would live with them, not their grandmother, as it should be.

Liselotte left the house, uncertain of her steps. When she reached the street corner, she stopped as if she had forgotten how to move her feet. A choking lump formed in her throat. Air escaped from her lungs. Unable to breathe or call for help, she clutched her throat in pure panic.

What was she thinking? She should never have left Regina behind. She was the child's mother and should have taken full responsibility for caring for and loving her. If she had to leave her home, instead of running to Gerhard, she should have sought out Rosa. She should have looked into the miserable eyes of every SS henchman, demanding the release of her little girl, who needed a lot of care to survive and see each and every new day.

So many *shoulds*.

She squeezed her eyes tightly, feeling the muscles around them pinch. With the world torn apart by war, marrying the father of her children was the right choice. Of course. She was confident the

Gestapo would stop their search for him. He could then support his family well, which was exactly what Rosa, a needy child, required. Unlike herself, her children would have a loving father, one who freely gave his love and time.

Liselotte trembled intensely. Was the ground shaking in Berlin? She looked around to see if tree branches were moving or if the doors to houses were swinging open with people rushing outside for safety. Nothing was happening. The quake was inside her.

Taking a deep breath, air filled her lungs and renewed her energy. Yes, she would find Gerhard. They would escape Berlin together and live safely under one roof, once and for all. The war would end, and life would go on.

Wary of police patrols on the streets at night, Liselotte managed to avoid the authorities and arrived at Gerhard's family home just as the early morning sun painted the sky with streaks of orange, pink, and red. Hidden behind the neighbor's tall fence, the sight before her caused tiny, dizzying lights to explode around her head. A smoldering fire. The remnants of a once fine house. Burned-out sheds and a garage. And what appeared to be three charred bodies piled in a heap beside one of the outbuildings.

She leaned forward and covered her mouth as a scream threatened to burst from her throat. Any moment now, she felt she would shatter under the weight of this horrifying reality her mind refused to accept as truth: She had been forever separated from Gerhard and his parents, who had become her surrogate family by welcoming her into their lives as a future daughter-in-law.

A gust of wind hit her face, causing Liselotte to sit up straight. A glint caught her eye. She wiped the tears streaming down her cheeks with the back of her hand and focused on what she was certain was the source of the flash of light: Gerhard's mother's diamond ring, the heirloom jewelry she always wore. Nausea twisted in Liselotte's stomach as she recalled visiting Gerhard's family home for the first time. His mother answered the door, pulled her inside quickly, and locked it behind her, though it was understood that if the Gestapo wanted to enter, no one could stop them.

"It's a pleasure to meet you, Liselotte. You're just as lovely as Gerhard described. Why didn't you bring my granddaughters to meet me?"

"They're at home with my mother. Next time, Frau Allenbach, I will bring my little sweethearts."

"Please call me Maria. Gerhard's father is Christoph to you. No formalities are necessary." Maria gently brushed a strand of Liselotte's hair from her eyes. "Gerhard told me all about Regina and Rosa. Don't worry or feel ashamed, sweetheart. In my mind and heart, each child is different yet perfect. We will love and cherish them for who they are."

Liselotte exhaled in relief, catching the woman's mention of Rosa. Just as she was about to speak, she turned as Maria lowered her hand. Her diamond ring brushed against Liselotte's chin, making her flinch.

"Oh, I'm so sorry," Maria said. "Let me see." Cupping Liselotte's face, she looked at the area. "Good. No bleeding, just a small nick. Again, I apologize. My mother gave me this ring years ago and warned me that her great-grandmother's ring was sharp like a weapon—a warning I should have listened to."

"Frau..." Liselotte began, then corrected herself. "Pardon, Maria. I'm fine. I'll be even better when I see Gerhard. Is he home? We arranged to meet today."

"*Ja*, he is here." Maria's brow furrowed. "He's out back, hidden away. I will give you instructions that you must follow precisely to meet him."

Liselotte listened closely to Maria's guidance as she followed her to the back door. They passed walls decorated with family portraits, elegant mahogany furniture, and plush carpeting underfoot. As a child, Liselotte dreamed of having these well-appointed features in her home. If only her family had been more traditional, like Gerhard's, she would have had more stability in her childhood despite her mother's strictness and her absent father. Now that her beloved Gerhard had returned to her after a separation, they could fix past wrongs and disappointments. After all, that is what husbands and wives do together.

"Gerhard," she said softly, opening the door to the tool shed and stepping into the small wooden building. The floor beneath her feet creaked.

"I'm right here," he said from below. "I counted on your visit today. Wait a moment while I get us some light."

It was a shame that he had to live in constant fear. She determined to brighten his days. He deserved joy just like anyone else.

Despite the risk of imprisonment for both Gerhard and herself—and her mother's constant disapproval—the memories of those early days with Gerhard and his family would always be precious to her. Now, as Liselotte's gaze drifted toward the remains of these loved ones, she fought back a pained moan. Leaning over, she vomited up what little she had eaten of Frau Bergman's meat, biscuits, and cheese. But her imagination gave her no rest.

She imagined two or three officers pounding on the Allenbachs' door, demanding entry and not stopping until either Herr or Frau Allenbach responded. Then, they were ordered to produce their son. To protect Gerhard, they denied his existence, claiming they had no idea where he was. Their response was dismissed as a calculated lie that betrayed the Fatherland, with a gun aimed at them for emphasis. The Herr and Frau were told to stay put while their house was searched, and anything deemed unacceptable along the way was damaged. Finally, when the search failed to find Gerhard, the officers took his parents outside to the other buildings, where he was found in the shed. All three were fatally punished. Every dream shared by Liselotte and Gerhard was shattered, leaving her hope for a wonderful life and family in ruins.

A shake rattled her shoulder. She shut her eyes tight, terrified of who she might see.

"Open your eyes and look at me," said a woman sharply.

Liselotte had no choice but to comply. In front of her stood a woman wearing a shabby blouse, baggy, dirt-stained men's trousers, and mismatched shoes. Silver strands of hair peeked out from a faded yellow kerchief.

"Who are you? What are you doing on my property?"

With her tongue heavy with unspoken words, Liselotte struggled to speak. Her sense of self was no longer about who she had become—an independent daughter, a new mother—but it now represented a journey she feared was over before it even began.

The disheveled woman nodded toward Gerhard and his parents' remains. "Not a pretty sight. Are you related to them?"

Still unable to speak, Liselotte wiped away the tears from her face.

"I understand. It's too difficult to talk about. I'm Gertrude," the woman said softly. She pointed behind her. "My husband and I live here, and we saw what happened to the Allenbachs."

At the mention of Gerhard's surname—the one she was afraid to share with her mother—Liselotte stiffened. Would her life have been different if she had been more forthcoming? Thinking back to how her mother often told Liselotte that they were living in Nazi Germany during a global war that might be worse than the Great War, it was probably better that her mother did not know Gerhard's full name. However, Liselotte had revealed Gerhard's father's position at the Fanta company. If her mother investigated further, she could trace Liselotte's location to this Berlin address, putting both her and Regina in serious danger. For all she knew, her mother might be on her way. Without wasting a moment, she struggled to her feet, ready to run.

Gertrude pressed a firm hand on Liselotte's shoulder. "Hold still."

No way. Yet with the woman now clamping a hand over Liselotte's mouth, she could not even scream.

"Hush. I believe they're all gone. Since crying and screaming will alert everyone, let's be careful, just in case. I will slowly remove my hand from your mouth, but you must promise not to make a sound. Do we agree?"

Liselotte wanted to say that crying was all she could manage, but she obliged with a nod.

"Good girl. You can trust me," the woman coaxed, slowly lowering her hand. "The Gestapo visited my husband and me, shoving open our door, storming through the house, and yelling at us to tell them where Gerhard Allenbach was, despite the fact that we told the truth—that we had no idea where Gerhard or his parents were. Their search came up empty. Eventually, they left and went next door to the Allenbach house. Minutes later, they set the place on fire. I'm ashamed to say that my husband and I hid, scared for our lives. At that time, we didn't realize they had also killed the poor souls." Gertrude looked away. "It's not safe outside—come with me to our house."

Thinking about nosy neighbors who might report them to the Nazis, Liselotte nodded.

Gertrude motioned forward. "It's best to stay hidden. Remain low to the ground—we'll crawl back to my house, where just my husband and I live."

At the back door of the house, a tall, lean man with thin white hair that hardly covered a large bald spot opened the door and extended his hand to Gertrude, then to Liselotte. He shut the door, double-bolted the locks, and motioned for them to follow him inside. After stepping into the kitchen, they moved down a hallway. Liselotte noticed a plain oak chair beside a table, sat down heavily, and leaned against the table for support.

"Come with us," the man said. "Every second counts."

"Let her be, Hugo. She has been through an ordeal."

"A word or two, Gertie?" He motioned for her to go into the next room.

"I'll be right back for you," Gertrude said, patting her on the shoulder. "You'll be fine."

Liselotte had her doubts.

"You don't know this girl," Hugo said, his tone loud and clear. "She's trouble." Gertrude's muffled response didn't reach Liselotte's ears. "I paid for our home," Hugo continued, "not you. I decide what happens here. Don't tell me to open our doors to strangers in need. I *need* to protect us. You don't want us to go up in flames like the worthless neighbors, do you?"

Liselotte jumped to her feet. Unwelcome and unsafe, and not wanting to hear what Gertrude and Hugo might say next, she hurried to the back door, unfastened the locks, and rushed outside. Without a clear plan for what to do next or where to go, she trusted her instincts, painfully aware that her life depended on escaping the area.

The roar of a car engine made her duck behind a tree. Hearing no voices, she peeked out and saw Gertrude and her husband speeding away in a black Volkswagen. They might be going to the police to report her. From what little Liselotte had overheard, she suspected they feared the authorities and would avoid any contact with officers. She was now convinced that, as a couple, Gertrude would ultimately obey her husband completely, and that they wouldn't give her real help. If anything, she felt threatened by them. She moved toward the remains of Gerhard's house but quickly stepped back behind the tree when she heard voices coming from the burnt house. Soldiers? The Gestapo?

"I heard it—it came from the east."

"*Nein*. It's coming from behind us."

Silence. Then came the words, "Must be the wind playing tricks on us. It's probably just the neighbors leaving." A loud laugh echoed around. "They acted like frightened field mice during our little cordial visit. I don't blame them for wanting to escape from you."

"Me? It doesn't matter. We followed orders. The *Ostubaf* will hunt us down if we don't report to him on time. Let's leave—no further delays. Hans has certainly taken off. I have a wife and three young children at home to worry about."

"You're right. My concerns lie elsewhere than these worthless—now dead—vermin. To think that they're one of us—Aryans—and not Jews."

"They might not be Jews, but they didn't show loyalty to the Third Reich, either, and that's why we got rid of them. Let's leave."

Liselotte pressed her right hand against her pounding heart, certain that the two soldiers—or whatever kind of henchmen they were—would hear it beating and come after her. She sank to the cold ground and wedged her knuckles into her mouth to suppress any screams. She forced herself to count: eins, zwei... zwanzig... einhundert...

Had thirty minutes passed? Or an hour? Despite the extra coat Frau Bergman had given her, cold seeped into her bones. If she stayed in her hiding spot, she would risk freezing to death. A dark voice whispered to her: "You wouldn't have to worry or feel sad about the cruelty of life if you gave in to the cold. Close your eyes and fall asleep; it won't take long."

"Go away, Death," she mumbled as she opened her eyes. At age seventeen, she still clung to her childhood belief that goodness awaited her.

Propped up on one elbow, she ignored the gust of wind hitting her cheek. Peering through the snow-covered evergreen branches, she saw no one. The two men must have retreated to their leader and fellow comrades, having completed their terrible mission. She brushed away a patch of snow and, finding a sizable rock, threw it over the fence, listening for a response.

Silence greeted her as she slowly dropped to her knees. Carefully avoiding making any noise, she stood up cautiously, looked around, then sprinted toward the remains of Gerhard's house. Once she was closer and could see better, she stopped at the spot where the door had been, knowing no further steps were needed. The second story had collapsed onto the first floor, making further investigation impossible and quite dangerous.

She pivoted and hurried toward the shed where Gerhard and his parents' lifeless bodies lay. Halfway there, the foul smell froze her in place. She remembered that rotten odor from her childhood when she watched leather being tanned over an open flame at a fair. She had gagged and vomited back then. Now, with nothing in her stomach, she dropped to the ground and dry-heaved until she couldn't anymore. Afterward, she crawled through the snow and over jagged rocks. She recognized Gerhard's parents' gold wedding bands, inscribed *love forever*, lying in a pile of ashes and bone fragments. Her throat worked as she fought again against her roiling stomach. Physically empty and emotionally drained, she rocked in place. After countless minutes, she called Gerhard's name.

"I know you're gone… I hope you can hear me." She crawled to the body, separate from his parents, who had clung to each other in death. Gerhard was the man who loved her—the one who was supposed to marry her and help raise her two little ones. Now, she was so alone in this upside-down world. Wanting to pay her respects to a mother who was not her own—a gentle, kind woman who had shown her gracious love when she needed it most, and to thank Christoph, who had stepped in for the father she had never known—she would have to come to terms—if possible—with her loss of Gerhard later.

After expressing her love for each of them aloud, she unsteadily stood and faced the bodies of the three dear people who, not long ago, had been as much a part of her life as she had been of theirs. "I will search for a shovel and bury you in the graves you deserve. And if I can't find one..." Fear gripped her. What would she do if new soldiers arrived? Could she protect herself? Was she capable of moving the winter-frozen earth three separate times? And if she only succeeded in digging one grave? Whose body would it hold?

Herself?

Liselotte had abandoned her family. Gerhard and his parents—her adoptive family—were no more. She may be young, but she had no future she wanted to meet.

With plenty of broken window glass around, she could pick up a jagged piece, lie down on the ground, and slit her wrists. No more worries. No more heartache. No more guilt. She reached out for a shimmering shard and pressed it against her right wrist, feeling its coldness and embracing its power.

Push. Cut flesh. End the anguish. No one would know. No one would care. Eternal sleep would call her name shortly. *Earth to earth, ashes to ashes, dust to dust.*

She opened her eyes, pushed away the darkness, and struggled to her feet. Glancing first at the remains of the house, she slowly turned to look at the three people she once loved. No, she thought, shaking her head with greater certainty. She knew what to do next.

2

AUDREY, 7 DECEMBER 1941

On December 7, exactly at 1:30 p.m., Audrey Wilson wished she were tuned into a radio comedy show instead of answering her mother's call for their Sunday post-church dinner. Dutifully—since complaining never helped—Audrey sat next to her ten-year-old sister, Caroline. They contrasted in color and personality. Audrey, who kept her shoulder-length reddish-brown hair free of clips and other restraints, preferred loose-fitting clothing. She enjoyed interests ranging from needlepoint and reading at home to singing at a semi-professional level. When she committed to a cause, she gave it her all. Caroline, a blond, always wore her long hair tied back and braided, and she preferred snug outfits, reflecting a strong personality and a need to be in control. Three weeks ago, poor Sis had broken her right arm while roller skating. Although she was a good sport about wearing a cast, she fussed over her meals as if she were five again. Audrey knew that Caroline just wanted the extra attention, and she couldn't blame her. Then there was her brother, Pete, who was a case all his own. At age fifteen, he still clung to his childish behavior. His latest dinner routine involved keeping score of how many times he could stick out his tongue—usually loaded with various chewed foods—at his sisters without their parents noticing.

This time, however, Pete refrained from making faces and instead reached for the radio sitting on the table, like a Thanksgiving centerpiece, and turned up the volume. Mom quickly turned down the radio. Audrey braced for the ongoing battle between her parents. Seated at the head of the table, Pop reached over, rotated the radio toward him, and increased the volume.

This was all typical of the Wilson family routine, which Audrey knew she should be grateful for. Instead, with the feeling that change —none of it good—was sweeping across the world, the effort to feel good had become overwhelming. It was hard to tell whether this was a reaction to the economic stagnation of the Great Depression years, which her parents still worried about, or to the world on edge after that madman dictator seized control of Poland just two years earlier and triggered the Second World War. In her social circles, what she once thought was the calm, pleasantly boring neighborhood of North Point, Milwaukee, had taken a nosedive. Her friends' parents, along with her own, were constantly arguing. Older brothers left their families behind to pursue their own wishes, ignoring what their families wanted. And good grief, three of her girlfriends were expecting babies out of wedlock while their parents pushed them into marriages they didn't want.

Aware that she had it better than others and shouldn't complain, Audrey practiced gratitude more often than not. Her father's shoe repair shop, downstairs from their spacious apartment above, provided enough income for the five of them to live comfortably in the building Pop inherited from his father. Her mother stayed home to care for her younger siblings. Best of all, Audrey got to pursue her love of singing not only in the church choir but also at a popular jazz café at night, three times a week, after waiting tables for the busy lunch crowd. When not working at the café, she volunteered at the local ARC—the American Red Cross Center—which offered a respite from the guilt of still living at home while yearning to live a truly independent adult life.

Mom, carrying a platter of meatloaf from the kitchen, frowned. "Hank, is it really necessary to have the radio so loud?"

"You bet! It's the Giants versus the Brooklyn Dodgers."

Her gaze darted between Pete and Caroline. "Don't talk gambling-talk."

In lieu of words, Pop raised his brows.

"Who's gonna win?" Pete asked around his gum. He blew a bubble and popped it loudly, a dimple quirking up, his dark hair framed his face with delight.

Mom placed the meat on the table. Without saying a word, she stepped beside Pete and put her hand under his mouth. The brat pulled his faded pink wad of gum from his mouth and surrendered it. She then reminded him to stop using the abbreviated term *gonna* for *going to.*

"Gross," Audrey said, eyeing her brother. Caroline echoed her sentiment.

Pop leaned into the radio, the cuff of his sleeve dipping into the mashed potatoes. "My money is on the Giants because of their SHO pitcher, though the guys at work are saying the Dodgers. Now, be quiet. Let me listen."

"So, you are betting," Mom said and sat across from Pop. She sighed. "What a fine way to talk after this morning's sermon about how little wrongs have big consequences."

"That's a laugh, Millie," Pop said. "I'm sure Reverend James is also keeping an eye on the game, hoping for a little green in his pocket." He narrowed his eyes at Audrey. "You turned twenty-one in the spring. Do you think you're old enough to help your mom?"

"Yeah, Sis," Pete said, a piece of chewed meat playing up his grin. "You're over the hill now. No one will want you anymore. Looks like you'll have to stay home and take care of us."

Audrey fought the urge to roll her eyes. Now that she was leaving her childhood behind and was finally old enough to vote, she was mature enough to know better than to retort to her brother or encourage one of her dad's hurtful comments.

"We interrupt this broadcast," a radio announcer said, with a deep, smooth voice that commanded attention.

"For crying out loud," Pop said. Pete called the announcer stupid for having the nerve to interrupt the game and ruin everything. They exchanged a sympathetic glance before turning their attention to Mom, who turned up the volume on the radio.

"Mom?" Audrey began. "What's wrong? You look scared stiff."

When Mom silenced her with a finger over her mouth, Audrey feared something was very wrong.

"Reporting live from Washington," the radio reporter continued. "The White House has just confirmed that the Japanese have attacked Pearl Harbor. Stay tuned for further details."

Audrey now had another important item to add to her list of concerns: she needed to find a way to help. With the country on the verge of entering the war, it was time to set aside her singing, weekend hobbies, and waitressing. Just days earlier, she had considered accepting her grandmother's offer of financial help to attend secretarial school at DePaul University in Chicago, only ninety miles from home. If the U.S. declared war on Japan, she envisioned countless thousands of men volunteering or being drafted. She was determined to do whatever it took to protect everyone's personal freedom. God help her objectors, whether family or friends. Without a marriage proposal or even a boyfriend, she had no worries about fulfilling a personal life. Most likely, she thought, she would step up her involvement with the Red Cross. After looking into this further, she would figure out how, where, and when to tell her parents.

Pop's mouth hung open while Mom's brows furrowed. Pete pulled out another stick of gum and popped it into his mouth. Caroline pushed the peas on her dinner plate from left to right and then back again.

Had any ships been hit in the strike? Did the explosions sound heavy and dull, like the thud of a wardrobe hitting a bare floor, or more like the sharp hiss of Fourth of July fireworks multiplied by some incredible number? Although Hawaii was not a state, Audrey had never considered that her fellow citizens, living in a place declared U.S. territory since 1900, could be attacked.

She dropped her fork onto her plate just as the announcer started speaking again. Wrapping her arms around her waist, she leaned toward the radio for better listening.

"This morning at 7:48 Hawaii Standard Time, the Japanese launched a surprise attack on the American naval base at Pearl Harbor in Honolulu." With sudden silence from the reporter, Audrey's family burst into conversation.

"Everyone, quiet down," Pop said as the newscaster continued.

"The attack occurred in two waves launched from six aircraft carriers. Eight U.S. battleships were damaged, and four were sunk, leading to hundreds, possibly thousands, of casualties and many wounded. Although Japan has not declared war..."

Pop turned off the radio, shook his head, then turned it back on and cranked the volume to the max. He swore, staring at his hands as if each finger had been burned.

"Let me see." Mom reached for his hands, but Pop pulled away.

With her parents absorbed in the breaking worldwide news, Audrey hushed her brother the moment he opened his mouth. She imagined the rest of the country glued to their radios or praying on their knees. She grasped her sister's hand and signaled to Pete that it was time to leave their parents for some quiet time.

"Thank you," Mom mouthed at Audrey, not bothering to put on a forced smile.

"I want dessert," Caroline said in her perfected irritable whine.

"Let's go," Audrey said, sweeping a stray blond lock off her sister's forehead. "If you're both good, I'll bring you a big slice of chocolate fudge cake soon."

Pete licked his lips and hurried down the hallway without arguing. Caroline looked longingly at Mom, who gave her a single nod. She took Audrey's hand, and they left the room.

"Audrey is a good kid," Pop told Mom, his words stopping Audrey in the hallway. "At her age, it's fortunate she's a girl and not a boy—she won't get into trouble if we go to war."

Audrey held still. Pop saw her as a useless girl—too young to assist their country in the war but old enough to help her mom with chores or, as he had recently been fond of saying, old enough to get a real job.

Her cheeks burned with heat, a mix of anger and irritation. She told her sister to catch up with Pete, and for once, Caroline didn't argue. Relieved, Audrey waited until her sister hurried down the hall toward her bedroom before refocusing on her parents.

"What do you think will happen next?" Mom asked Pop. "Do you think there will be a draft?"

"I'm afraid so, hon—Roosevelt already set a draft in place last year for all men between twenty-one and forty-five. Don't worry. When I turned forty-six last month, I felt like it was all downhill for me, but now it looks like my a*dvanced age* is coming in handy, after all. Looks like you'll have me and all three kids at home."

Oh, how wrong he was. Like her father, Audrey believed for months that the U.S. would get involved in this escalating war in some way. Contrary to what he said just a moment ago about her not contributing to her country because she was a girl—a young woman, pardon her—she was determined to help, regardless of her parents' likely objections. She would find a way.

3

LISELOTTE/ANNA, BERLIN, GERMANY, JANUARY 1944

Berlin was no longer safe. Herr Hitler—Liselotte struggled to think of him as her country's Führer—could not protect the city and its people, as many had once looked to him to safeguard them from harm. Despite this, everyone still feared him and the absolute power he wielded to change lives with just a single word. Since the major bombing raids last November, Berliners have lived cautiously. The attacks nearly killed Liselotte, her twin baby girls, and her mother, narrowly missing their home. Fortunately, they were spared. However, three thousand residents of the city lost their lives, either killed immediately or after suffering in the aftermath of the bombings. Thousands more were left homeless. These days, Liselotte made sure to blend in and avoid risks, even though no one paid her any attention. Mostly, she hid from others, scavenging for food like those who had lost their homes, happiness, and hope. While others were consumed by their daily struggles, she felt invisible to them. No one cared. This truth left a bitter taste in her mouth. Yet, her eyes were dry from tears she could not shed. Being closed off to emotion was her best way to cope and survive.

The evening of January 28 changed everything for everyone. First, six RAF Mosquitoes carried out a spoof raid, dropping Window—

aluminum foil strips to confuse German radar—and a few bombs. Four hours later, when the main force arrived and found broken clouds over the target area, they launched the most direct attack, which would lead to a two-day bombing campaign. This time, there was no warning from the illegal BBC radio broadcasts about when the strike would happen, nor did the brave civilians who usually stood outside banging pots and pans to alert others to seek safety in the nearest bunker have a chance to sound the alarm.

Liselotte heard the unmistakable whistle of a bomb and the air raid siren blare as she hurried out of the cellar of a beer hall that had been bombed during the November strike, the hiding place she had used since leaving behind the remains of Gerhard and his parents. She had only seconds to reach the nearest shelter. Wearing the warm clothes she had stolen just last week out of desperation beneath the coat given to her by Frau Bergman, she moved as quickly as possible through the crowd of countless others scrambling to survive despite the horrific circumstances. Reddish-brown fireballs lit up the night sky as people rushed from their apartment buildings. Strangers' elbows jabbed into her sides. Hysterical screams and commanding shouts fought for attention.

A man grabbed her arm and pulled her down the street, then suddenly vanished as they got swallowed up in the crowd, leaving her clueless about his identity. She struggled just to keep her balance and avoid falling while people shoved each other in the rush to find safety.

She was pushed through the shelter's entrance. The cries of women and children, along with the swearing of older men, assaulted her ears and nerves. Although this was not her first time hiding in this large building that could hold 250 people, as her eyes adjusted to the grayish light of the concrete-and-steel structure, the size of the place made her dizzy. They all faced potential destruction, capable of wiping out their lives with the press of a finger. While survival dominated everyone's concerns, the realization that they all shared a love for their Fatherland and heritage gave Liselotte pause: friend and foe were now equal.

"You're too distracted for safety's sake," came a man's voice from beside her. When she tried to step away, he grabbed her arm in a way that left no doubt he was the same man she had seen moments before. "*Ja,* it's me. Stop squirming before we both get hurt."

Liselotte swallowed hard, wishing she were kilometers away from the arrogant fool. How dare he handle her physically as if she were his property.

She yanked her arm back from his grip and looked at him sharply. "Who are you?"

"Klaus Agers." He tugged at his bottom lip, which wouldn't surprise her as a disguise for a smug grin. "You can thank me later for catching you when you nearly toppled over and would have pulled me down with you."

The sooner she could get away from this man, the better she would be able to think for herself and hold onto the little bit of individuality she had these days. Without saying a word, she turned toward the stairs to go to the second floor. He tightened his grip on her arm.

She groaned. "Pardon? I don't know you. You can't control me," she said, aware of how ridiculous it was to voice this protest while the Nazi regime waged war for control over the entire world, including its citizens.

Despite the seriousness of her situation, her cheeks flushed as she examined this self-appointed controller more closely. Klaus towered over her by a good twenty centimeters. Under his tan fedora, his dark hair looked disheveled, with strands tucked in one spot and others poking out unevenly. His right cheek was scratched with a dried trickle of blood, yet he did not act as if he were in pain from other injuries. Most mysterious was a black pullover sweater peeking out from the neckline of a neat gray trench coat, both of which appeared clean, along with his gray trousers and shiny black Oxford shoes that looked out of place.

He pointed to the Air Raid Warden—a boy who couldn't have been much older than her seventeen years, though she wasn't inclined to share her age with anyone, especially this stranger. "He's directing us downstairs," Klaus said.

Downstairs? The shelter was set up as a large communal room

with rows of bunk beds. The only exception was the private rooms downstairs, usually for dignitaries or others the wardens chose to isolate. Had they recognized Klaus?

The building shook. This time, she reached for him.

"That was close," Klaus said. His quick breaths punctuated his words as if each one were a complete sentence. For someone acting as her protector, he looked as unnerved as she felt. All she could do was stare at him as screams erupted all around them.

"Let's hurry," she said, leading the way down the dark stairwell as the warden had ordered.

"Have you been here before?"

"I'm afraid so, though I've never been in the lower section." She hesitated to tell him that, like many of the city's homeless, she had recently applied to stay full-time in the shelter. At registration, when asked if she had any family or friends she could move in with, she pressed her lips tightly to hold back the sobs as vivid images of her mother and baby girls flashed through her mind—the family she longed to hug. She yearned to smell the fresh scent of her mother's shampoo, the cookie-dough sweetness of Regina, and Rosa's applesauce breath.

Stay focused on the now, she ordered herself. But how?

Estranged from her mother and daughters, she was as much a part of the breakup as her mother. Whether right or wrong, the outcome was that she couldn't go back to her mother's side. Ironically, she wished she could be pressed into her mother's embrace, feeling safe and protected. Thinking about this for too long threatened to knot her insides with shame and anguish because, as much as she longed for nurturance from her mother, Helene was not a demonstrative person. Liselotte couldn't remember the last time her mother hugged her, let alone told her how much she was loved.

"Let's keep moving—we can't just stay halfway down the stairs," Klaus said.

When had she stopped moving?

"Take my arm if you're having trouble seeing," Klaus added, bringing her back to the present, a place where she needed to stay.

"*Nein*," she said, the word tumbling out in a rush. "Pardon. I didn't mean to sound abrupt. I can see fine. I'm just not familiar with..."

"Kindness?"

She nodded. Kindness, goodwill, and compassion—were these three qualities missing from his life too, and that's why he quickly recognized them in her?

"I'll do my best to ensure your safety," Klaus said. He spoke without a trace of emotion, whether good or bad, making it hard for Liselotte to interpret.

They continued downstairs, giving her more time to think. His actions in helping her conveyed everything she needed to know about him: a man who, in a life-or-death situation, focused on another person's well-being—in this case, her comfort. That alone spoke volumes about his character.

Downstairs, they approached another warden. The snowy-haired man did not ask about their relationship and directed them into a small room to share. Even though the ground and building remained still, Liselotte felt unsteady. Once inside, she sat on the lower bunk, wrapping her arms around her waist. She needed to distract her mind from herself. "I wasn't expecting a personal room. How about you? Have you taken shelter here before?"

"I thankfully haven't had any reason to," Klaus replied.

"I have, several times." She decided it was best not to ask about their luck in getting a private room. Sometimes, the less known, the better.

"Are you from Berlin?" he asked.

"Yes, I'm a Berliner—one without a family." Genuine tears welled in her eyes. "I lost them during the November bombings, while I was away. When I came back, my home was gone, and my family, too." Her breath caught; she was unsure whether her labored breathing was due to the twisted fib or the horrifying truth of her reality.

Klaus sat too close beside her. "Tell me your name."

Once the bombing ceased and he was able to leave the shelter, he would probably check on her. Without knowing anything about him —his job, dedication to the Reich, or personal connections—she decided it was best to share the name she used to register for living in the bunker. Hauntingly, she had taken the name two weeks ago by grabbing the identity papers from a young woman, close in age, whom she found lying dead on the street. "My name is Anna Bauer." She grew curious. "And you? Are you from Berlin?"

"Let's just say that the Reich has no issues with my bloodline or upbringing." He smiled, a mix of smugness and charm that was quite perplexing. "I'm in Berlin on behalf of the Führer. I have just returned from Poznań."

"Poland?"

"Of course. Germany is occupying the country—we have a lot to accomplish there."

She averted her gaze to the bare cement floor. She was sitting next to a Nazi, but why was she surprised by that? She had learned from Gerhard that everyone in Germany claimed to be a Nazi if they were Aryan by birth and, most importantly, wanted to see a new tomorrow. She guessed Klaus was in his mid-thirties; he seemed fit to serve his country. "Pardon me. I'm not finding fault."

"*Gut.*" A chuckle escaped his mouth. She glanced up at him. "I apologize for startling you, Anna. That wasn't my intention." He looked around their small room. "Now is not the best time to scare anyone."

The bunker trembled once more from another bomb. She cried out. He wrapped his arm around her and held her close.

"Make it stop... make it stop..." she called out.

"We'll get through this situation," he murmured into her ear. "It will be okay. Hush now."

Seconds later, or maybe minutes—who knew, since time moved differently in a bomb shelter—they faced each other and then pulled apart. She brushed off her clothes. He glanced sideways, then looked back at her, cleared his throat, swore, and muttered an apology.

Wanting to think about something beyond her immediate situation or family, she asked Klaus to tell her about Poznań.

He pulled back and sat up straighter. A chill passed between them. She glanced at him then quickly looked away.

"Have you ever visited Poland, Anna?"

"Honestly, I've never left Berlin. I never had a reason to until now." She slowly glanced at him and wished she had kept her focus anywhere but on him, but she didn't have much choice in the cramped room. His brown eyes—more coal-black than brown in the dim light—were especially captivating. The way he carried himself radiated confidence, a quality she could appreciate right now, all things considered.

Anna—Liselotte—tensed. She wasn't over Gerhard, and she didn't want to let him go. Plus, she and Klaus were strangers. It was best to keep it that way.

"Berlin has everything we good Germans need," Klaus said.

She appreciated his direct, nonjudgmental attitude and began to relax. Well, as much as anyone could in a bomb shelter. It was almost like they were meeting at a café for lunch, getting to know each other better. However, this chance encounter wouldn't have happened during peacetime. She had already told him more lies than a stranger should accept, and she didn't need to make this meeting more than it was: two strangers helping each other as bombs rain down from the sky.

She ran her tongue over her lips. Every word he spoke could also be a lie.

She paid closer attention to his words and avoided reacting emotionally. The less he knew about her, the safer it was. "I'm all ears about Poznań." She looked around the dull room. "Please, take me far away from here, at least in my mind."

"Poznań is a great city. It will be beautifully restored and possibly modernized for the glory of the Fatherland once we finish with the country—or what's left of it, that is." He flicked his fingers as if shooing away a pesky insect. "Poland will soon no longer be its own country, but rather, part of Germany. Poznań is already designated as the capital of Reichsgau Wartheland—a German administrative region."

She nodded, understanding it would be unwise to oppose or

dispute him. He had expressed what any good German citizen would say.

"It is located in the northwestern part of Poland, about 274 kilometers from Berlin," he continued. "It is the fifth-largest city and one of the oldest, offering a rich history to explore."

Anna wondered about the rich history that Klaus hinted at. Did he mean historical artifacts or other cultural treasures that could improve life for many, or was it about those in power working on behalf of Hitler to enrich themselves? Even though she was curious about Klaus, she had to admit that it was best to stay guarded without knowing more about him right now. The last thing she wanted was to show her fear and give him control over her. She needed to choose her words carefully. "What an honor for you that the Reich chose you to continue important work in Poznań."

He raised an eyebrow. "Tell me, do you have children?"

"Herr Agers," she said, nearly gasping. "Must I answer that question?"

"I always have reasons for the questions I ask."

She chose to share another half-truth, her specialty lately. "I have no boyfriend or husband. Like many others, this war has kept me… occupied." She shrugged. "Perhaps after the war, I can meet and marry a fine German man."

"Call me Klaus." He patted her arm. "You will have opportunities in the future to contribute good German stock to the Fatherland. No need to worry for now."

A wave of ice ran down her spine. "Pardon?"

He examined her from head to toe, his gaze slow and purposeful. "To bear children for the Führer." He gestured for her to stand. When she did, he rolled down the rough gray wool blanket and patted the thin white sheet.

She hurried to the door, willing to risk running through the city streets targeted by bombs, anything rather than being in a room with him.

He grabbed her arm. She planted her feet firmly. Then he covered her mouth with his hand, perhaps sensing a scream rising from inside her.

"*Nein*… *nein*. I would never take advantage of you, Anna. We've both been through a lot. I was just trying to make you more comfortable so we could sleep—in the purest sense of the word. It's especially unwise to leave this shelter right now." He glanced at her bunk, then at the upper one, then back at her. "I'm exhausted, and I'm sure you are too. We will sleep separately—you can trust me."

She trusted no one. "I'm tired too, but I doubt I can sleep. I've never been a good sleeper, and when…" She hesitated, nearly revealing that after her twins were born, she settled into a routine of sleeping only four hours a night. "When the war began, my sleep only worsened."

"I think that's true for all of us," he said. "Berlin is a large city, and I'm not sure the enemy has calculated the number of attacks needed to destroy this great city of ours. If it is any comfort, Berlin is also the most heavily defended industrial area in all of Europe."

"Do you think the Allied countries are planning to strike multiple times?"

"Yes, they will keep attacking us until they suffer more losses than they anticipated in both equipment and personnel." He tugged at his clean-shaven chin.

"What is it?" she asked.

"I can tell you one thing: this evil force trying to work against us has never faced an opponent as strong and determined as Germany. We will conquer and thrive."

"That's good news," Anna said, certain it was the expected answer. Chills ran down her arms as she envisioned a prosperous country, successful only by the number of casualties from all the bloodshed.

"Germany will not surrender," Klaus continued. "Neither will I. I love my country too much to give up. What about you, Anna?"

"Nor am I giving up," she said, hoping he did not hear her insincerity.

"Well, then. Let's get as much rest as possible. Tomorrow—a new day for new chances—will come soon enough." He hoisted himself onto the top bunk, stretched out, and with his shoes still on, pulled the small blanket over himself. Within seconds, a lone snore escaped his lips.

She had nowhere else to go, no one to return to, and no place to call home. Caught between the desire to sleep and the fear of surrendering to recurring nightmares of Gerhard and his parents' death, she sat in the corner of her bunk next to her pillow, hugging her knees to her chest. Leaning against the cold wall, she pushed away thoughts of wanting a blanket. It was best to focus on the present and not think about the possible disasters the next day might bring.

WHEN ANNA AWOKE, her eyes were dry, her mouth was soggy, and her neck muscles felt stiff. The bunker's gray, reinforced concrete walls had no windows to let in daylight, so she couldn't tell if it was day or night. The silence inside the shelter suggested that many of the other occupants were probably still asleep. Disoriented, she stretched, swung her legs over the side of the mattress, and sat up, startled to see someone's arm draped over the upper bunk.

Klaus.

Do not utter a sound, she ordered herself. *Remember, I'm now Anna, not Liselotte.*

Having slept in the same clothes—the two sweaters, gray trousers, and coat she arrived at the shelter in—she was already dressed and ready to slip out of the room and the shelter entirely. The sooner she could get away from Klaus, the happier she would be, since it meant a possible step closer to finding Rosa. The fear of an enemy attack, being stopped on the street, interrogation, or arrest felt minor compared to the risks posed by the stranger sleeping above her. Although Klaus had treated her civilly, her instincts told her to keep her distance from him—and from anyone else.

Klaus suddenly jumped down from the top bunk and leaned against the bunk beds, smiling. "*Guten Morgen,* Anna. I trust you slept well, as much as one can in a bomb shelter."

With her heart pounding, she took a deep breath to steady her nerves. Although she knew she should respond to his polite greeting, the right words escaped her. Despite the risk of sounding young and foolish, she said, "It's so dark in here. How can you tell if it's morning or the middle of the night?"

He rolled up his jacket's left sleeve and looked at his wrist. "My watch hasn't failed me yet. If you're curious, it's four in the morning. Besides, my internal clock never lets me sleep past this early hour that others swear at."

Chatty, wasn't he? "I slept reasonably well, considering the circumstances."

"Living with war fatigue is challenging," he said, pressing his lips together firmly and appearing concerned. If he expected her to reveal her emotional state, she would not say a word.

"I'm sure there is a kitchen in this shelter," Klaus continued. "Multiple kitchens, in fact. Let's raid one before we head outdoors and see the damage."

Driven by the harsh reality that she had nothing to lose, she hardened her resolve. She had her own life to live—the best she could in Nazi Germany—and she was determined not to become anyone's prisoner, on any level. While her heart told her she still mourned Gerhard, she was learning that allowing someone to shape her had consequences. With Gerhard, the result was that she had borne two children, from whom she was now separated. Additionally, her romance with him had widened the divide in her relationship with her mother.

She stood with her arms crossed. "The two of us? Why do you think I'm leaving this place with you?" Without waiting for his reply, she headed for the door.

He grabbed her arm, spun her around, and pressed her against the wall. Her coat shifted, and her sweater rode up. The concrete wall scraped her lower back. Still, she didn't flinch; she refused to reveal the growing fear tearing through her inside.

"I'm an excellent judge of character, Anna."

She suppressed a smirk. "Not with me."

"Oh?" His brows lifted. "Are you saying you are not who you claim to be—a young woman without a family or home? Are you hiding in plain sight from the Reich, someone I should be suspicious of?"

"Of course not," she said quickly, hoping her uneven breathing wouldn't give her away. "I haven't lied about who I am."

"Good, then," he said. "I see that you desperately need help, and I want to assist you." He looked around the small room. "Before I continue with my assignments, I will visit my parents, who live in Halle. It's only 170 kilometers from Berlin and usually a two-hour drive, but it might take us twice as long because of the poor road conditions I expect to face. If we can get through the nearby debris and reach the Berlin office, a car should be waiting to take us there. You will find my family to be friendly and welcoming. Unless you have a better option, you'll come with me." He smiled charmingly. She wished he looked anything but pleasant.

"Anna," Klaus continued. "Does leaving bombed Berlin appeal to you?"

While she had no desire to leave Berlin until she found Rosa, let alone leave with a seemingly high-ranking Nazi, she might be able to use the fact that this man, with all his connections, could help her locate her baby. What she needed was to figure out how to get Klaus interested enough to assist in her search—without revealing Rosa's developmental concerns and thus risking her child at greater risk. "It certainly does."

4

AUDREY, DECEMBER 1941

Her country was at war. On December 8, the US declared war on Japan. Today, December 11, at 3 p.m. EST, just hours after Germany declared war on the US, Congress voted unanimously to declare war against Germany as well.

Audrey pushed open the always-unlocked door to her family's second-floor apartment above her father's shop. A surge of excitement and nerves flooded her, leaving her unsure whether to shout hello or quietly slip into her bedroom. The last thing she wanted was to feel guilty for refusing to stay within the strict boundaries of her parents' watchful eyes. It was so frustrating: in Wisconsin, she was old enough to marry, vote, and drink alcohol. Yet, all the men and women she knew—including her mom and her lady friends—saw women only as caretakers for their husbands and children. Women were expected to stay at home, their proper place. What would happen as more men enlisted or were drafted to fight in this growing war? Women would have no choice but to fill the necessary roles in the workforce. And after the war, when men returned—those lucky enough to survive—they would all need to find jobs. Were the women supposed to give up their positions? Audrey's own uncertain position in American society as a single woman without children had made her nearly anxious as she approached her twenty-first birthday in June. Now that she had crossed that societal milestone, she hoped her country would see her as capable of making a meaningful contribution to the war effort.

"Audrey, hon," her mom called. "You're home already? Is everything okay?"

The partial railroad-style layout of the six-room apartment stretched from the living room into the dining area and then the kitchen. From there, a hallway led toward her parents' bedroom, her brother's small room, and the larger room Audrey shared with Caroline. The apartment's setup was perfect for her parents to keep a close eye on their kids' comings and goings, though it had some downsides, especially when it came to privacy. Needing some time to think and enjoy a little alone time before Caroline got home from school, Audrey wanted to go to her room. However, she couldn't avoid her mom's radar, even though she gave herself an A-minus for trying. Giving in to her mom's greeting, she went into the kitchen, forcing a smile into her voice.

"Hi, Mom." The way her mother was wringing a red-and-white-checkered dishrag told Audrey everything she needed to know. "I guess you heard the news."

"Oh, I heard, all right. Our trusty radio told me about the government's decision." Mom glanced at the clock above the kitchen sink. "By now, I'm sure every American knows what's happening."

Go gently, Audrey's inner voice advised. *Coax the news out of her without triggering her panic buttons.* "Where are Pete and Caroline?"

"They both had after-school activities, but Martha phoned to say the children had all been sent home. They should be home by now—it's just a five-minute walk for each of them. That's also why I'm nervous."

"It's early—just twenty past three. I'm sure they're hanging out with their friends and have lost track of time. If they aren't back soon, would you like me to go find them?"

"No," her mom said so quickly that Audrey's neck pinched as she looked away from the clock and toward her mom. "If they're not back soon, I'll have your father search for them. I want you to stay here, right where I can see you." She set a cornflower-blue platter of brownies on the table. "Have a seat, Audrey."

Audrey blinked. Had her mother baked? Usually, when Millie Wilson wore her lucky yellow apron—signaling she'd baked a lot—she would have caught Audrey's attention immediately upon entering the kitchen. But Audrey missed that big clue. Life had changed for all of them. Like everyone else she knew, she had started and finished the past four days since Pearl Harbor was bombed with a dry mouth and a fearful curiosity about how much her life was about to change. It was as if she were holding her breath while waiting for a medical diagnosis. Today marked another day of change, not just for America but for herself—she had decided to take action to help spread cheer during the war, especially to American servicemen overseas. For now, she was more nervous about how her family would react when she told them she was leaving.

Mom sat at the table and reached for the dessert dish, offering Audrey the chocolaty treat. "I just took these out of the oven right before you walked in, so they're still warm—just how you like them."

"Thanks," Audrey said, thinking about how eating warm, fudgy chocolate suddenly ranked high on her list of revolting foods. Although she should at least try a bite of the treat to appease her mom, she couldn't bring herself to sample one, let alone produce a satisfied moan from her lips. "I'm sure it's scrumptious, as always. And I smell a hint of caramel in it, which you know is my favorite—not that Pete will praise anything that isn't purely chocolate, but..." She was talking too much, revealing her anxiety. Not good.

Mom sat down beside her. "You can't eat." A statement, not a question. "Honestly, I understand. I could barely bring myself to bake this afternoon, but I did it for you kids."

Audrey nodded her appreciation. "I'm sure Pete will eat it, despite the caramel." She managed a chuckle. "He eats anything you bake—never refuses sugar. And Caroline, too."

"Let's set aside the topic of brownies. I know something's bothering you. Tell me."

"Actually, Mom, let's start with you," Audrey said. "Of course, you're anxious about the country going to war, but there's more to it, isn't there?"

"You're right, sweetie." However, instead of continuing, Mom sighed and looked away.

Audrey touched her mother's arm. "Now you're really scaring me. Is Pop okay? Did something happen—"

"Pop's fine," Mom said. She looked toward the white-painted archway that separated the dining room from the kitchen. "He's still downstairs in the shop, so we have a few minutes to ourselves before he comes up expecting a late lunch—I give him lots of credit for putting business first before feeding his belly."

"Mom? You were saying?"

"It's time we have this overdue conversation, especially with what just happened at Pearl Harbor." She again paused.

The silence between them threw Audrey off balance. Reaching for a small bit of humor to steady her nerves, and hopefully her mother's as well, she was about to share the joke Pop had told her last night about what happens when a sailor, a lawyer, and a dog warden bring bad news into a bar, but her mom sighed loudly, catching Audrey's attention.

"I admit I've been upset, Audrey. Not only was our country threatened and our servicemen harmed and killed at Pearl Harbor, but we Americans are now more vulnerable than ever before."

"Understood. That's a given, but with the government positioning us to join the fight, the US has a good, watchful eye out for its citizens."

"Hush," Mom said softly. "When did you become the comforting parent, and I the scared child?"

Audrey smiled, knowing her mom would keep going if she had a moment to gather her thoughts. She waited quietly.

"What I mean... what I'm more concerned about now that this war involves us, is that our family has also become a target, even if unintentionally." With a blank look, Mom tossed her napkin toward the center of the table, and a corner landed on the dish of brownies.

Oddly, she left the napkin on the dish, not bothering to wipe up the icing that dripped onto the apple-green oiled tablecloth.

Having never seen her mother so rattled before, a new wave of panic swept over Audrey. She pressed her hands against the side of the table to steady herself. "What do you mean? Is there something I don't know, but should?"

"I'm sure everything will be fine."

"Mom, there's a global war going on, and this country is now involved. I understand if you're not okay with what might come."

"Although your father has never wanted to discuss his family or his past, secrets tend to catch up with people eventually."

This shifted the conversation unexpectedly. "Is this about my grandparents? They passed away the same year you got married, right?"

"Yes, sadly, from the Spanish influenza that was spreading rapidly. They were such loving parents to your father and so kind to me."

"I'm sure they could see how smitten Pop was with you."

"I think so, though we were so young, in our teens," Mom said. "They came from Odesa, in Ukraine… well, back then, it was part of the Russian Empire. That area had seen horrors during the pogroms, which were attacks on the Jews."

Vaguely, over the years, Audrey had heard about these attacks. "Why were the Jews blamed?"

Mom sighed. "They were blamed for all the wrongs non-Jews were enduring, giving new meaning to the term *scapegoat*."

Blaming others has been part of human history since the beginning. The poor, immigrants, and those facing social hardship due to physical challenges, unforeseen difficulties, and often bad luck have been seen as threats by wealthier and more powerful groups. There was also the inhumane judgment by some who considered others of certain races or faiths as inferior, labeling them as non-people, similar to what was currently spreading throughout Europe. It was tragic that these targeted individuals struggled for basic needs while the wealthy and officials had plenty but still wanted more. Although issues like civil rights, slavery, wars, and dehumanization of groups as depraved and subhuman were not new phenomena, one must stand in solidarity with fellow human beings.

Didn't they?

Yet history showed that, time and again, mutual support was overlooked.

And Audrey possibly had family members who had suffered from this prejudicial hatred?

It was all madness.

She shook her head to clear her thoughts. Although she could talk for hours about the wrongs and travesties that have happened century after century, she needed to focus on what upset her mother.

"Wait a second, Mom. Our last name is Wilson—that sounds all-American to me. Are you saying that Pop's parents were Jewish? And why has this been kept from me?" Suddenly needing some space, she pushed back from the table but stayed by her mother's side. "We've attended church as long as I can remember, not synagogue. I don't understand."

"Pavlo Babenko, your grandfather, and Olena, your grandmother, came from the same neighborhood in Odesa. They were the same age —born in 1878—and went to school together until the government banned their instruction."

Audrey struggled to keep up with the unfolding story of her hidden heritage. Her mind felt like it was plummeting into a nosedive, ready to crash. At the same time, she experienced a surge of adrenaline at the thought of having more relatives still alive, let alone a whole new, richer heritage. What hurt, though, was the unknown reason why she was just now hearing about this. Had her parents not trusted her with this news? Were they ashamed of these relatives? She searched her mind for anything she might have done, or that she had done when she was younger, that could have caused this lack of confidence in her parents. Nothing came to mind. Her neck and shoulders tensed with an odd annoyance that bordered on anger. Anger at her mother for not telling her years ago? Anger at world leaders for mistreating people?

"I can see you're upset—"

"Mom—"

"Hold on, Audrey. Let me explain before you jump to conclusions, okay?"

Audrey hesitantly nodded.

"Pavlo was Catholic. Olena was Jewish. As a girl, Olena was only allowed to attend school for a short time—probably through her elementary years, though I'm not entirely sure. Because of the danger of pogroms, her family faced many hardships. Olena's father's butcher shop was repeatedly attacked by police and local residents. She and her four brothers often had to hide with their parents and extended family. When the couple turned seventeen and clearly loved each other and wanted to marry—something strictly forbidden for a Jew and a Catholic—it became clear that Pavlo's family was now also in danger. His family arranged for the two to travel to Warsaw to stay with Pavlo's aunt and uncle, which was also risky for the young couple. You see, Audrey, it was also becoming increasingly unsafe for anyone in Poland suspected of being Jewish. From what I understand, Pavlo and Olena stopped mentioning their religions, likely talking about what remained of their faith in hushed whispers between themselves."

Audrey looked at her mother, whose brows lifted as her forehead furrowed. "Just as it's happening again in Poland—well, what's left of the country after Germany seized and destroyed it. It sure seems like bad never leaves, and good sure as hell doesn't stick around." Audrey hadn't meant to say such strong words, let alone use the h-word. A rush of heat flooded her cheeks.

"I agree," Mom said, surprising Audrey. "To help matters, Olena converted to Catholicism, and they married. With help from other Babenko family members, they sailed to the United States. They settled here in Milwaukee, changed their last name to Wilson, and opened Pavlo—now Paul's—shoe repair shop, where we've lived ever since they passed, and your father took over the business."

"Jiminy," Audrey murmured, awestruck to discover the truth about her being a second-generation American in her family, at least on her father's side. All those years lost, she should have asked for details about her paternal relatives, but instead, she embraced her loving family, including her mother's parents, and never thought to ask. Oh, she had asked casual questions about her paternal grandparents, all right. What did they look like? What did they do for fun? And do you have pleasant memories of them? Consequently, she easily accepted the simple answers: Grandma had dark hair, and the sound of her knitting needles filled this very home you're sitting in; your granddad was bald and played a fierce game of checkers.

Audrey inhaled deeply and then asked her next question. "What happened to the family left behind in Odesa?"

"I'm unsure. Communication between your grandparents and their family stopped." Mom sniffled as she excused herself to grab a handkerchief from her purse on the kitchen counter. She then returned to the table. "From what little Olena shared with me, not hearing from relatives troubled her and her husband. While I don't think they ever easily shrugged it off, your father's birth kept them busy and joyful. They did the best they could. Between establishing Paul's business, family matters, community activities, and attending church, they moved forward despite their heartache."

"So, I have family in Poland and Ukraine?"

"Possibly, if they're alive. Who knows what's happened to your relatives in Warsaw since the German occupation in '39? Or if there are any remaining relatives in Odesa. On one hand, it's a shame that your father's side of the family hasn't stayed in touch, but then again, with all the struggles they've faced, I imagine they must have been busy just trying to stay alive. Right or wrong, that daily fight for survival became their normal way of life."

"Do you mean not crossing the line of what they've been told to do or not to do?"

Mom nodded. "Perhaps they sought comfort in knowing the given and found some safety in not exploring the unknown."

"And the relatives here in Milwaukee?"

"It was an elderly aunt and uncle. They passed away when you were a baby. Their only daughter moved to Texas. I'm sorry to say that we haven't kept in touch over the years."

Audrey's palms and the back of her neck broke out in sweat. "In trying to understand all of this, please explain why you're telling me all this just now?"

Mom fixed her gaze on her. "Your brother and sister are still young. They need to experience as much of their childhood as possible. Can you promise me not to tell them about this family news?"

So, her parents wanted to give Pete and Caroline extra protection because they were so young, which meant keeping the secrecy game going? Was there something more? Considering the ongoing war and the country's new involvement, she could see this line of thinking, but only to a point. "Don't you think keeping secrets from each other about one another has already gone too far? We have a heritage we should be proud of, not one to hide out of fear of repercussions."

"Audrey, just a few days ago, our country was attacked by a foreign entity—it's all too new for us to fully understand right now." Mom fixed her gaze on Audrey so sharply that she squirmed. "You, missy, have had it pretty easy your whole childhood. You don't know what it's like to face prejudice and hatred… of repercussions, as you said."

Audrey wiped her palms on her slacks. She had never seen this side of her mother before. Sure, she could understand how her mom was being protective of her little ducklings—as she fondly called her children—but her mom had always had it fairly easy, too. As an only child, she was raised by a father who had become a postmaster and started working at the new South Milwaukee branch on 10th Avenue when it opened in 1931. Sadly, he suffered a fatal heart attack two years later. Her mother was ahead of her time, always working outside the home. To this day, Audrey's grandmother still chuckles when criticized about why she had not retired from nursing, claiming she would stop when she dropped. She had used those overused words so often that, when Audrey was younger, she believed her grandmother had coined the cliché. Truth be told, Gram had too much nervous energy to stay home and bake cookies or host Mahjong parties. Ironically, Gram discouraged her daughter from working hard. Instead, Mom was encouraged to believe that good girls should become women who prioritize their husbands and children, making a house a true home. With all that in mind, as much as Audrey enjoyed relying on her mother being home, thinking about the decision she made earlier today—and had yet to share with her—did not make things any easier.

She squared her shoulders. "Please explain where you're going with all you've just shared with me."

"Your father and I believe that the country going to war is enough for Pete and Caroline to handle, at least for now. They don't need to know the drama of our family history. Understand?"

"Somewhat," Audrey replied, though it was far from enough. "We're facing uncertain times right now, so I do understand where you're coming from regarding Pete and Caroline, especially considering their ages."

"One more thing about your brother and sister." Mom took a deep breath. "I would appreciate it if you kept your judgments about your dad and my decisions to yourself because I can't believe there's one family in this whole world that doesn't keep secrets hidden—"

"Mom—"

Mom raised her hand. "Let me finish. I just wanted to say that there could be many explanations for the decisions that Paul and Olena made, explanations we might never understand, explanations that brought them a lot of mixed feelings."

"Like embarrassment or shame?" Audrey suggested.

"I'm not sure if I like your tone." Mom wrapped her arms around her middle. "That's beside the point, though. Now that Japan has bombed Pearl Harbor and we're at war, who knows if President Roosevelt will round up American-born citizens of Japanese and German descent and put them in camps—like the Germans are doing with the Jews? Will there be a rebellion among the non-Jews in this country—or a German takeover of the U.S.? And will Americans of Jewish heritage be rounded up and sent to camps, even if they don't follow the faith and traditions of their ancestors, like this family? Who is safe in this country? I don't have an answer, but I will do what any mother should do to protect her children. Do you understand any better now? Do you see where your father and I are coming from and why we must keep up appearances and blend in with our fellow Milwaukeeans? Why the five of us must stick together?"

"I don't mean to be contrary, but I have two different thoughts," Audrey said. "On one hand, yes, I understand what you're saying. With anger and fears rising in this country, suddenly lurching into a war, and with a heritage that—if we were in Europe—could get us removed from our home and deported to a camp, I can see the need to be vigilant and protective. Honestly, though, I can't help but wonder if our American relatives had extended their helping hands further, our remaining family members in Europe might have escaped the pogroms and emigrated to the U.S. before Hitler intensified his actions." Filled with too much nervous energy and fighting the ghostly images of relatives being assaulted, and unable to stay seated, Audrey jumped up from her chair so quickly that if she had not righted the chair in time, it would have fallen over. She started pacing the small kitchen, raking her fingers through her hair without caring what her mother might think of her frantic behavior. "We might have sponsored them to come here when leaving was more likely and practical, like the time between the Great War and this global conflict that has now reached us."

"Audrey, I don't understand why you suddenly have the gumption to lecture me, but let's drop this for now." Her mom stood up, leaning against the counter, briefly burying her hands in her apron before straightening up. "You've never told me about your news. This might be a good time—before your brother and sister get home."

"I... uh... let's forget my news for now."

"No way. Tell me."

"What's going on here?" her father said, startling both of them. He stood at the kitchen entrance, his brows raised and deeply wrinkled, showing the disbelief and anger he always struggled to hide. "I came up from the shop for a quick bite to eat, and instead, I heard my wife and daughter yelling at each other. Someone has some explaining to do, and make it fast."

Audrey's heart pounded so hard that all she could do was resist the urge to rub it and draw more attention to herself. "Maybe now is not the best of times."

Both of her parents stood apart, staring at her with wide eyes. She had no choice but to tell them.

"I'm leaving in two days." Recognizing that this was definitely not the response they wanted, it made it even harder to gauge their reaction.

"Let's back up so I can understand." Pop stuffed his hands into his black trousers' pockets. I expected to see your mom smiling prettily for me, with a sandwich or soup in the making, but instead, I hear her rattling off information about my family that isn't your concern."

"Of course, it's my concern," Audrey said, unable to hide her anxious tone. This conversation shifted from tense to full-blown crisis-management mode in seconds, fueling fresh doubts. She should have slipped away in the middle of the night as she had considered the other day, leaving a cryptic I'll write-more-when-I-can and don't-worry note. "Pop, your family is my family—people worth not forgetting... the reason I'm about to get more involved with the Red Cross."

"Pardon?" Mom said.

Audrey licked her dry lips. "As I just said, I'm leaving in two days. I head out to the Washington, D.C. headquarters for training."

"Training for what?" Pop asked. "You already know how to serve coffee and doughnuts, and you can certainly do that here in Wisconsin."

"The Red Cross is an international organization—"

"Can the lecture," Pop said, his gray eyes darkening.

Audrey's chest tightened. She urged herself to speak calmly. Adult to adult, even if the other adults in the room—the ones she had always looked up to throughout her life—were acting anything but that. She willed her body to cooperate and breathed in deeply, pushing aside her father's warning. "It does far more than serve coffee and doughnuts, but if I were appointed to serve snacks, you bet I would do so. My regional Red Cross officer holds me in high regard and believes in my potential. When I told her I wanted to do my patriotic duty, she said she'd put in a good word for me and that I could be trained to go overseas. Our men need our support."

Pop leaned a few inches closer to her; his frown made her step back against the counter, whose edge dug into her lower back. "You are not going anywhere."

Sidestepping from her father, Audrey added, "If I were another son of yours, at my current age of twenty-one, I doubt you would say these things about me. I imagine you would be proud that I want to serve my country. Sure, you'd be anxious about my fate, but you wouldn't be bossing me around like a ten-year-old girl."

Pop shook his head. "We won't give our consent for this foolishness."

A surprising blend of sadness and anger twisted Audrey's heart. Was this really the father who always encouraged her to chase her dreams, try new things boldly, not be afraid, and help others? "You need to trust me and—"

"This has nothing to do with trusting you, Audrey," Pop said suddenly, so composed that she wondered if he was reconsidering his words. "It's not that I don't trust you, but I do not, under any circumstances, trust anyone when it comes to your life. And certainly not those who are on a killing spree in a war zone."

Her breath hitched. Was this his love surfacing again?

"You're just being downright stupid." Pop looked at Mom, then back at her. "I know I'm speaking for both your mother and me."

Stupid? That's what her dear father thought of her? And he claimed he was speaking on behalf of her mother, too... and Mom hadn't corrected him? Her insides clenched tightly like a fist. All her energy drained away, and she collapsed onto a kitchen chair.

"Audrey," Mom said. "When you become a mother, you'll understand why your father and I are worried and want to keep a close eye on you. There's nothing wrong with us wanting you to be safe."

In the calmest tone she could muster, Audrey said, "If we don't win this war, I may never get the chance to become a mother in the good ol' USA if our country ceases to be an independent nation. I will do whatever it takes to help win this war."

"You want to help?" Pop said. "Very good—then help here. Help your family. Help your state. There's plenty for you to do for your let's-help-the-boys' cause without getting yourself killed."

"You know, I could easily get killed walking down a Milwaukee street."

Mom gasped. "Don't say that—ever!"

"There you go, kiddo," Pop said. "Now you're upsetting your mother even more."

"Here's the thing... I'm a legal adult now. I don't need your permission. I will be leaving in two days."

"Two days?" Mom and Pop said in unison. Mom brought her hand to her throat as if she were being strangled. Pop's face turned a deep red. Were they finally understanding what she'd told them to be the truth?

"You need to think this over more carefully," Pop said. "After dinner, once your brother and sister are in bed, the three of us will talk further."

In her heart and mind, Audrey knew she had made the right choice. She was contributing goodness to a struggling world and would lift the spirits of others risking their lives for their country. "My mind is made up—there's nothing more to talk about. Our servicemen need our support. They need good cheer. It's the very least I can do."

The sound of pounding footsteps approaching echoed through the kitchen. Out of the corner of Audrey's eye, she saw her father's quick, narrow-eyed glare as a warning not to speak.

"Mom... Pop?" Pete called. "What's all the shouting about?"

Mom pushed the air down to hush them. "Enough. No more discussion—for now—with Pete and Caroline home."

"What aren't you telling us?" Pete asked as he entered the room.

Pop frowned. "Nothing you need to know."

"I'll tell you later," Audrey said, then hurried out of the room toward her bedroom. Much later, she thought. When you and Caroline are old enough to understand the madness of war—that is, if she herself can understand... if her family remains together and doesn't fall apart anymore, or suffer like what her poor grandparents did.

Halfway down the hallway, she stopped, feeling more unsteady than just moments before. She leaned against the wall, grateful for a moment of solitude. Was she the one destroying her family in the name of serving her country? She took one step forward, then another, and yet another. She had a mission to complete, no matter how long the war lasted.

5

LISELOTTE/ANNA, GERMANY, JANUARY 1944

The Wehrmacht officer driving the Kübelwagen swerved, narrowly missing the body of yet another person who did not reach a bomb shelter after last night's attack. The front tire hit a rut in the road. He navigated the dip and kept going, but the front passenger door swung open. Anna, as if caught in a tornado, was pulled toward the open door.

"*Guter Gott!*" Klaus yelled as he wrapped his right arm around Anna's shoulder and his left around her waist, pulling her back inside the vehicle. Reaching across her to close the door, he told her to hold onto the back of the driver's seat.

With one arm, she obeyed the command, and with the other, she grabbed the driver's right arm. The young man, who was probably no older than her seventeen years or maybe even younger, cursed and fought to free himself from her grip. After a few frantic turns of the wheel, he carefully steered the German jeep away from nearby bomb craters, abandoned vehicles, and the dead.

Klaus pulled her back onto the rear bench seat, not quite firmly but not gingerly either. She rubbed her arm where he accidentally pinched her; at least, she believed it was an unintentional move by him.

"Settle down. This is just the beginning of our journey."

Dreading a long, monotonous trip, Anna looked at Klaus. "I'm not sure if I can compose myself." Not that she had any other option. She was out of viable choices. Looking around the vehicle, she remembered when Klaus first mentioned at the shelter that a car was waiting for him. Images of a nice, comfortable Mercedes or BMW flashed through her mind, not this disgusting army vehicle that made her stomach churn with nausea. Riding in such a luxury car might have eased the pain of fleeing a bombed city, but that was the core issue: escaping not only from the fallout of a war, but also from Berlin. This city was the only place she ever called home, in Germany, the only country she ever lived in. It fought to survive, even though her Fatherland had started the ugliness the world was now facing.

A gentle touch brushed her knee. She looked up at Klaus, feeling more confused. Was he making a pass at her, perhaps taking advantage of the frightening moment they had just gone through, or was she overreacting? Flirting with women might be typical for him, a man bolstered by his higher status in the government. Still, she didn't have to go along with his wishes.

A moment later, Klaus withdrew his hand and looked at the back of the driver's head. That was fine with her. From what she could tell from the little he had revealed about himself, he was constantly on the move due to his service to the Reich, though he lived with his parents when not traveling. The more she thought about it, Klaus, who wore no wedding band, could still be married and have a home with his wife, kept secret from others. At his age, he might even be a father to several children, perhaps from various romantic encounters. She sighed, wishing her imagination were more controlled. Victims of a bomb attack, they both needed to focus on escaping the city quickly.

"That was too much excitement, yes, Anna?"

She nodded, confused by his sudden empathetic tone.

"It appears you're still shaken up. I don't blame you."

"You aren't upset by what just happened?" she asked, regretting how childish and defensive she sounded. She had to be careful at all times with this Nazi stranger, or her ruse would end suddenly, leading to consequences that could be severe. Most importantly, she would never see Rosa again.

He faced her. "Are you afraid of me?"

A crucial question. She hesitated, unsure how to phrase her response.

"By taking you away from Berlin, the place you call home," Klaus continued, "I promise to protect you as best as I can during this time of war. No harm will come to you under my watch."

While his words—his promise—should have comforted her, her instincts advised caution. She searched her mind for a topic to steer their conversation elsewhere. "Since we have plenty of time before arriving in Halle, tell me about the first time you traveled away from home."

"Where do I start?" he said, amusement evident in his voice. He tugged at his stubbly chin. "Ah. 'Know thyself? If I knew—'"

"'...myself I would run away.' Johann Wolfgang von Goethe. He's a favorite of mine, though my grandmother detested the novelist and playwright."

"Then it's a good thing she's not here, or I would get into a scrap with her."

She noticed his sneaky grin and chuckled. "Well, knowing her, I guess it's a good thing you can't go back in time and meet her." In reality, she had never met any of her grandparents, but she wanted to hide those details from him. A sudden wave of sadness threatened to overwhelm her with feelings of an intimate family life she had never experienced. Still, she couldn't allow herself to fall into that emotional state, and she searched her mind for other topics to talk about.

A few minutes later, as they crossed the Glienicke Bridge over the Havel River into Potsdam, they made small talk about the scenery, and her mood brightened. Grateful for the easing tension between them, Anna leaned toward the passenger window, still gripping the back of the driver's seat, giving a cautious nod to safety this time. "Just like I learned in school, there are many lakes and rivers in this capital city of Brandenburg. Even with the winter wonderland of snow and bare trees, it looks more like a park than a city. And to think my childhood home wasn't far from this area." She wondered how long Potsdam would stay safe from bombing. Was it just a matter of time before Germany faced total destruction, or would it keep defeating its enemies and rise triumphantly from the smoke-filled sky? "What a shame that circumstances weren't different so I could have traveled this short distance to see such beauty back then."

"I can tell your education has taught you a lot about places beyond Berlin, your native city," Klaus said. He patted her shoulder, and although she did not flinch at his touch, she moved closer to the window and stayed quiet. "Including the Havel River," Klaus continued, "there are about twenty waterways in this city." He pointed to two boys chasing each other across a snow-covered field. "For their safety's sake, they should be careful, but it's nice to see children having fun."

She nodded, surprised by the joy he expressed at the thought of children. Unless it was an act. She hoped not.

At the end of the bridge, the driver slowed down. Anna sat up straighter.

"A checkpoint," Klaus said in a calm, steady voice as the driver rolled down his window, letting the cold air rush in. "Have your papers ready."

From her coat pocket, she pulled out the identity papers she had shown at the government office, where they picked up the driver and the car. Hopefully, the document would also pass inspection by the guard at this checkpoint. *Remember, I am Anna Bauer, and as per Klaus Agers, I am his cousin. Herr Agers will provide any other details—the less said, the better.*

Aside from a slight smile she offered to the SS guard, Anna mimicked how Klaus presented his identity papers and responded to the question about where she was heading. When Klaus was asked a more detailed question, Anna drifted into a daydream...

If life had been different when the twins were three months old—just last August, hard to believe—she would have tucked them into a stroller to gently push them through a neighborhood park. Regina and Rosa would have felt the warmth of the orange-red sun on their faces, breathed in the clean, fresh air, and heard the sweet birdsong and the laughter of other children playing in the grassy areas while their dogs chased after them. If life had been different, there would not have been this cruel war—or any war at all—where the ruling power believed that *Untermensch,* like Rosa, born with physical deformities and lesser intelligence, did not deserve to live and thought she was polluting the purity of the Aryan race. Her poor baby. Rosa. The thought that the Nazis had labeled Rosa as a life unworthy of living brought tears to Anna's eyes. Surely, among all the German babies born—and those born in occupied countries—there must, unfortunately, be babies like Rosa, who need to be freed from such harsh restrictions and death sentences. Could she do something like this? Could she find Rosa and help unite other parents and their needy children?

"Reichsführer Himmler is the person I report to," Klaus said, pulling Anna back into the present moment inside the dingy, still terribly bumpy Kübelwagen. "I'm on a short break from my work in Poland to visit my ill mother. I had just picked up my cousin, Anna, in Berlin when the bombs struck last night, and we had to take shelter." Then, Klaus leaned toward his open passenger window and spoke to the guard, only for his ears. They were signaled to pass through the checkpoint.

"Are you okay, Anna?" Klaus asked.

"As much as one can be lying at a checkpoint."

He huffed. "I did not tell one falsehood, *cousin.*"

Speaking of untruths, she was about to do something she hoped she would not regret. Patting his arm, she said, "Then I'm glad I'm with you." Knowing full well that it was best not to inquire about what was exchanged in confidence between Klaus and the guard, she returned to her original question from a few minutes earlier. "And the first time you traveled away from home, my cousin?"

A sly grin spread across his face upon her last word of *cousin.* "Would you appreciate hearing about the inconsequential visit to some sort of fair when I was a five-year-old *kleiner Schrecken* bent on destroying my older sisters' lives or the more meaningful trip in '33?"

Out of the corner of her eye, she saw a tree branch fall into the river. Once again, she wondered how nature went about its daily routines while savage beasts roamed the earth on two legs, tearing at each other's throats. "Since it is common for five-year-old boys to terrorize their sisters, tell me about the trip in 1933—back in the prehistoric days."

"If that's what satisfies your curiosity. Fine. I was about to turn twenty-three that month, far from being prehistoric."

She quickly calculated their age difference and realized she was six that year, but she kept that information to herself.

"My Vater, an economics professor, was quite intrigued by the new Chancellor Adolf Hitler."

"Oh, right. I knew 1933 was significant for a reason."

"Vater was hoping to align politically with Hitler. From what Vater read and heard, he agreed with Hitler's economic viewpoint on why the German economy was so weak and who should rightly take the blame."

Anna swallowed hard. Although she was not a fan of Hitler, she was a German-born woman, Aryan in heritage, and she understood whom she needed to publicly show her loyalty to. Otherwise, there would be consequences she wanted to avoid. She ignored the sudden wave of queasiness swirling in her stomach. "I can understand your father's position. Did you have to travel far to see the new Chancellor?"

"*Nein*. It was right here in Potsdam. Maybe I should have traveled more outside of Halle, but with everything the city offered and my time at Martin Luther University, along with all that Vater prepared me for, I instinctively knew I would serve the Fatherland, and my travels would soon become widespread and nonstop. I wasn't wrong. Going back to your question—Vater built a strong connection with a friend who arranged an overnight trip for us to Potsdam. I was lucky to see the ceremonial handshake firsthand between President Paul von Hindenburg and the new Chancellor—Adolf Hitler."

"Where did this happen?" Anna looked out the window. "Will we pass this notable site?"

"Not today. The meeting took place at Garrison Church. What was so important about it was that it marked a union between the military and Nazism."

She considered how impressionable young adult Klaus probably was at that time. Witnessing the changing of the guard—so to speak—and realizing how essential Hitler had become to Germany, such that no one who wanted to survive dared question his authority, must have been remarkable for Klaus. "Well, I appreciate your thoughtful reply to my question. Now, tell me more about your family. You've mentioned your sisters and, of course, your father, but you haven't said anything about your mother. Are you estranged from each other?"

"First, let's start with you and your family."

She folded her hands in hopes he wouldn't notice her slight tremble. Should she start with the truth or with lies? She remembered receiving wise advice from a classmate who had learned the hard way about the ugly consequences: when lying, keep it simple, because you have to remember what was originally said, or it will come back to trap you like a wild animal. She also disliked him taking back control of the conversation—of anything—but if she stayed one step ahead of him, maybe she would be okay.

"As I mentioned when we first met yesterday, I lost my family in November—well, the little family I had. Mutter. Oma. Oma's other daughter—Tante Anna, whom I'm named after." Tamp down the wordage, she cautioned herself. At least, by using her new name, she would be able to remember her fictional aunt.

"No siblings?" Klaus asked, eyeing her knees. She leaned away. "That could be lonely."

"No siblings. I had plenty of friends to keep me company, though." *And two babies to keep me busy*. "And before you ask, if you must know, no father to speak of."

"That's sad. You have a fighting spirit, I'm learning. Surrounded by a few older women, you managed to do okay."

She pursed her lips. What nerve. Just about to confront this, she stopped herself and remembered to redirect their conversation to him, away from herself. "Now, tell me about your family." She forced a smile. "From what I've heard so far, your splendid family."

"Vater and I are close—always have been. I think that his not being able to relate well to females made him closer to me, not my two sisters."

She could not resist. "He got close to your mother."

He pressed against her right side. "That's one way of putting it."

She stiffened. She and her big mouth. "And your sisters?"

He straightened. "Maude, the eldest, is happily married to a charming but no-nonsense man currently serving in the SS. They have five children."

"I can't imagine having…" She was about to say she couldn't imagine having more than the two children she already had, but she kept her lips sealed. Klaus fixed his gaze intently on her face. Had he set a verbal trap for her?

"Yes, Anna?" he prompted.

"That's a big family—in my opinion. As long as everyone is happy, that is what really matters."

He nodded. "And healthy. Five strapping boys. Not one damaged with defects."

"Damaged?" she said aloud, as the word *defects* replayed over and over in her mind like a needle stuck in a record groove.

His narrowed eyes communicated his unspoken message: she was being unreasonable for not understanding.

Realizing her mistake, she masked her feelings with a hollow laugh and prepared insincere words. Her mother's warning about the Nazis pursuing her daughter, Rosa, echoed in her mind. She struggled to avoid flinching or groaning. "Relax, Klaus. I'm just joking—I understand fully well about the imperfections of the mind and body, especially at its cost to Germany." Her body recoiled in reaction to her harsh words, even though they masked her foolish question about being *damaged*. She took a deep, silent breath to steady herself as she nearly collapsed from guilt and disgust. "Germany doesn't need to weaken itself by providing welfare to those who can't care for themselves, much less give back to the Fatherland."

Klaus gave an indecipherable nod. "My sister's sons are a tribute to Germany."

"How does Maude handle five boys?"

"Three of them are now teens, all well-behaved. The younger two are five and eight. Mutter sometimes helps, but believe me, Maude keeps them all in line."

"What about the other sister?"

"Helga was newly married a year ago. She's already expecting—any day now. For all I know, by the time we arrive in Halle, she may already have given birth to them."

"Them? Is she expecting twins?"

"That is what the good doctor believes. We shall see. For the greater good of Germany, Helga and Oswald are hoping for boys."

Twins. Anna's eyes quickly welled up with tears, and she looked away from Klaus. She could only hope, for Helga's sake, that her twins were born healthy.

She wanted to sigh. She wanted to scream. She wanted to ask why everything had to serve Germany's *greater good*. The world was made up of many countries, filled with people who, day after day, failed to care for each other, leading to catastrophic destruction. If only everyone across the globe could genuinely care for the *greater good* of one another, the planet might have a better chance of spinning smoothly through time.

Again, her mother's words haunted her. *'Damaged is how the Nazis see people like Rosa. I tried to tell you—never take her outside while this war is going on, or it will be all over for her. You wouldn't listen to a single word of caution because you had to see your lover.'*

Liselotte had ignored her mother's advice back then, refusing to believe she could be right. Now, she saw things differently. She had only thought of herself and wanted to be with her lover, Gerhard, the father of her children. If she had focused on her daughters instead of herself, she might have saved Rosa from the Nazis and kept her family together. This was all her fault. Her mother had been right, after all.

"Anna?" Klaus said, jolting her back to her new identity. "You've grown pale. Are you ill?"

"I'm sorry." She leaned against the window, resting her head against the cold glass. "I have a headache coming on, that's all." She glanced at the driver, who peered at her in the rearview mirror. "No worries. Nothing for you or the driver to catch."

"I'm sorry to say, but even for us Nazis, aspirin is scarce, and I have none to give you. Klaus gently touched her arm, holding his hand there a little longer than she liked. "Close your eyes and rest. I'll wake you when we arrive in Halle."

"I'm not sleepy," she said. "Just not in the mood to talk much. I'm willing, though, to listen to whatever you'd like to share."

"How do I know you aren't a spy against the Führer and waiting for me to reveal top secrets?"

"You will have to take my word for it—that you can trust me." She rubbed the throbbing spot between her eyes. "Besides, forget Nazi secrets—I'm more interested in *your* secrets, especially on the personal side."

He put on a serious look. "And you talk about me being a tease?"

She mentally scolded herself for sounding like she was flirting with him. She waited for him to continue.

"Okay, then. I'll tell you about the town we're about to drive through—Luckenwalde."

"You have my attention."

"I was hoping to hear that." He smiled that irresistibly charming smile, and she cleared her mind to listen to what he had to say, already considering it as cheap entertainment.

A sudden noise sounded, followed by a thump from beneath the vehicle on the right side. The driver started to oversteer, swore, and shouted, "Flat tire."

Klaus pulled a pistol from under the seat. Anna gasped. It had been years since she last saw a Luger up close, but she recognized it instantly.

"Precaution," he said, ordering the driver to pull over as if he was considering another option. When the driver stopped the vehicle, the two men jumped out. Anna was about to follow, but Klaus shot her a disapproving frown. "Stay here. Much safer. Let's see if this is an ambush or plain bad luck."

A shot rang through the air. The driver fell to the ground. Silence.

"Klaus—"

"Stay inside the car, Anna," Klaus shouted. "Squeeze onto the floor. *Schnell.*"

She could not obey and slipped out of the vehicle. "Man—on your right."

Klaus fired twice. The man, now about 4.5 meters away, collapsed to the ground. Klaus, still holding his pistol ready, rushed to the fallen man dressed in torn civilian clothes. His tan shirt and black trousers were quickly soaked with blood. He wore no coat to shield himself from the cold and the howling winds.

Klaus kicked the crumpled man, who raised his arms in surrender and groaned. "Anyone else with you?"

"No. Need money. Food." The man's hands were dark red from clutching his wounded gut. "Wife and babies at home. Help."

"Sure. I like helping good folks." With a single pull of the trigger, Klaus fired at the man's temple. "There you go. Now you're out of your misery."

Anna slapped her hand over her mouth and began to step back, but not before a groan escaped her lips.

"You," Klaus said, more like a bark than a voice of concern. "I told you to stay in the car. Don't need two wounded on my watch." Without waiting for her reply, he grabbed her arm with his left hand, holding his gun with his right, and forced her back to the vehicle.

She started to squirm. "I can walk on my own."

"Not in your shaky condition." He glanced at her, his now softer eyes catching her by surprise. "I promised to take care of you, and that's what I'm doing. Let's see how our driver is."

Before she could even respond, they were already back at the Kübelwagen.

Klaus shoved his pistol into her hands and dropped to the ground beside the driver. "Shoot at anyone approaching."

"But I... don't know..."

"Sometimes, no one needs to know the facts."

If this were any other time, country, or lifetime, Anna, who would be Liselotte, would cross-stitch Klaus's last haunting words, frame them, and hang them on a wall like her mother's old motto samplers inherited from her grandmother. Ironically, they were *Home Sweet Home* and *Bless Our Family*—phrases that were as unfamiliar to Liselotte's home life as peace was in Germany.

"Soldier," Klaus said as he shook the driver.

Pity, Anna thought. Neither she nor Klaus ever bothered to ask the young man's name. That troubled her more than not knowing.

"Just a graze on my side... I have another side. I'll live."

"Hold on," Klaus said to the driver. "I'm going to help you sit up, then, if you can, to stand up."

"Are there others?" the driver asked.

"Doesn't seem to be. We're in a flat area—I don't see any houses or buildings. Where this scum was hiding is a mystery that I'm not concerned with since I'm not bothering to find his supposed family and tell them the news." He called Anna over and asked her to stay by the driver's side while he changed the tire. "Keep my gun ready, and keep an eye on the area for any activity, including an approaching vehicle. I'll change the tire, and then we'll continue."

"I'll drive us to the nearest base," Klaus told the driver. "Or camp, or command office—whichever comes first. We'll get you medical help soon." He helped the driver to his feet and guided him a few meters away, telling Anna to follow. He nodded toward his gun in her hands. "Keep alert." He turned toward the vehicle.

"Klaus, do you have experience changing a tire on a Kübelwagen, let alone driving one?"

He squinted in a way that clearly showed he was not someone to be challenged. "I have expertise in many things," he said. "It's time you must trust me."

Why? She had no intention to stay with him much longer. Like him, she had also gained a variety of skills over the past few months in the name of survival. Disappearing when it suited her was one of those skills.

BACK ON THE ROAD, Anna was continually amazed at Klaus, who managed to steer around ruts, icy patches, and several dead animals. They traveled in relative quiet until he cleared his throat and looked toward the passenger seat where she sat. The driver was stretched out on the back passenger bench.

"How's your headache, Anna? With all the excitement, I forgot to ask since we left that worthless lost cause."

"Still lingering," she said dismissively. Cranky, she warred with herself to stay quiet, but her tongue got the best of her, something her mother always said would be her downfall. Maybe because of what her mother had cautioned, to be on the safe side, Anna aimed for a saccharine tone. "And I forgot to praise your driving skills in maneuvering this monstrous vehicle. I'm impressed."

"I told you to trust me." Before she could reply, Klaus looked at the rearview mirror. "Driver?"

"His name is Karl," Anna said. "He appreciates it being used."

She looked at Klaus to gauge his expected reaction to what she was sure he would call insolence, but all she saw were expressionless eyes and an unflushed face. He was skilled at maintaining a neutral demeanor, even better than she was. This made her curious about the experiences he had faced in which such a countenance would be advantageous. Perhaps she needed to learn from him.

No. She needed to get away from him. Pronto.

Karl, sitting upright, leaned toward the driver's seat. He batted his eyes several times. "Yes, sir?"

"Your condition?"

"A little pain."

"How much longer until we reach the nearest place where we can leave you?"

"Stalag III A is about four to five kilometers ahead, sir. Oberst Lutter, the camp commander, is stationed there. I've reported to him several times—a dependable man."

"Good to know."

Karl smiled in appreciation at Anna as she helped him lean back into his seat. She noticed Klaus watching her. Thankfully, a comfortable silence settled once again among the three of them. The sky grew darker and heavier, making her wonder if it would blanket the dull, barren flatland stretching endlessly around them with snow.

"Turn right, then left," Karl said. "The camp's gate will be on your right side."

"What kind of camp is this?" Anna asked as they drove past several tents and large one-story buildings. She suddenly was unsure whether she wanted to know the answer.

"POW," Karl said. "Have you been here before, Herr Agers?" Karl asked.

"*Nein*, though a few colleagues stopped by on business and relayed matters to me."

"The prisoners are from all over," Karl replied in a strong, excited tone, one he hadn't used since he was shot. "We even have Americans, Italians, and Russians. The camp follows the Geneva Convention and the Hague Regulations, but not when it comes to the Russians."

"Why is that?" Anna asked.

Klaus grunted. "The idiot *Moskali* never signed the Geneva Convention. Guess they thought they never would be caught." He pulled up to the wrought iron gate framed by two buildings. "Driver, I trust this is the guardroom and transit building?"

"Yes, sir. We will stop here until we are approved to proceed to the Administration Building."

For Karl's well-being, Anna hoped the security checks would finish quickly. About ten minutes later, they signaled them to proceed. A medic took Karl away. Anna waved goodbye while Klaus spoke with the second-in-command to arrange for another car, this time without a driver.

Anna took advantage of the extra minutes and visited the washroom. As she stepped out, she saw a boy who looked to be no more than fourteen or fifteen, wearing a gray-blue striped shirt, gray trousers, and a dingy cap of an unclear color. He carried a tray with a small loaf of brown bread and a covered pot—probably soup—

heading toward the spot where she had left Klaus. His gaunt frame indicated he needed the food; his grim expression made it clear: the food was not meant for him to enjoy.

Uncertain whether he spoke German, she had to try. "*Sprichst du Deutsch?*"

The boy paused, glancing over his shoulder then ahead. "*Ja*. But I'm Polish."

"You're a prisoner here?"

He nodded. Two male voices echoed from down the hall. Without acknowledging her even for a second longer, he continued walking. She wanted to ask him why someone so young was a POW. What crime could a person that age possibly be guilty of? Was he a Pole who had lived in Poland, was imprisoned, and then taken to Germany without explanation? Although he had identified himself as Polish, he might have been of Polish heritage but a German citizen. *Citizen*? What did that strange, elusive term mean these days?

She gulped, understanding the harsh truth that it didn't matter. The boy was born at the wrong time, in the wrong place, and now faced a government that owed him no explanation. How long had he been in this camp? Had he been imprisoned elsewhere? What about his poor parents, who were probably overwhelmed with worry, anger, or both? That was, if his parents were even alive. If they were alive, did they have any say in the matter, or was that forfeited because of their Polish blood?

Rosa. Her little girl was taken from her family and lost her human rights to a decent, fair life because the German government did not see her as normal or deserving to live.

Rosa, I will find you. I won't give up until I know what has happened to you.

Upon hearing the click-clack of footsteps, she jerked back against the wall. A tall, expressionless man stared at her.

"You must be Anna. Herr Agers asked me to find you. A quick bite to eat and a drink are waiting for you. The Herr is eager to leave."

She was, too. "*Danke*." Without delay, she hurried back.

"Next town is Dessau," Klaus said after driving five kilometers from the POW camp.

"The concentration camp?"

Klaus glanced at her before refocusing on the road. With no driver, it was just the two of them alone in the vehicle, and Anna sat beside him. "No. That's the Dachau Camp you're thinking about, located outside of Munich. Dessau is a city on the way to Halle." After a moment, he added, "Are you okay? You've been awfully quiet since we left the Stalag."

He would be quiet too if he had a missing child. She looked directly at him. Then again, for all she knew, he might have an unaccounted-for child. She knew little about him. "It's the young boy," she said delicately, emotionally shaken from the Stalag visit. "The one who brought us something to eat."

"That *boy* is not in the camp out of charity. Whatever his crime, believe me, he deserves to be imprisoned. At least he's not in one of the extermination centers. No need to pity him."

His blunt response wasn't what she expected to hear. An inner voice warned her not to show any emotion, possibly stoking a rage she hadn't seen from him before. "Do you have any children, Herr Agers?"

"*Nein.*" He grinned, making Anna suspect that what he really meant was that he had none, as far as he knew. He was, after all, a decent-looking man and must have had his share of nighttime company. As she well knew, war not only separates people but also brings them together for both right and wrong reasons. "And you?"

Was he trying to trick her? She despised lying, but she had to safeguard her daughters and herself. She let out a heavy sigh. "I've already told you—I have no children."

"Would you like to?"

"That's a very complex question," she said honestly. "Let alone personal."

"In my line of work, I can arrange for that to happen, for the greater good of the Fatherland."

"Pardon?" she said, struggling to keep a note of disgust and shock out of her voice. Her insides grew cold. "I don't need anyone to set up a romantic rendezvous for me."

Much to her relief, he remained silent for a long, tedious stretch of minutes, but like all good things ending, he finally spoke again. "It doesn't need to involve romance."

What was his obsession with procreating? And, in the name of the Fatherland? If she were to have children again, she would want to do so willingly and for her own sake—and for a committed husband's—not to make any nation more prosperous through wealth or control. If there was a difference between those two.

About to demand that he stop the vehicle and let her out—she would walk the rest of her supposed destination alone, war or no war—he suddenly pressed down on the clutch and then stomped on the brake. He raised a protective hand across her to stop her from flying toward the windshield. Two army vehicles blocked the road ahead. Klaus swore. Anna sank lower into the bucket seat, wishing she could disappear entirely. Wishing for the end of this bloody war, where the two sides only seem to be evil versus evil.

"Take your identity papers out immediately," Klaus said, even though she had already pulled them from her pocket before he finished speaking. Three Wehrmacht soldiers in gray uniforms and steel helmets stormed their vehicle. The driver's door was yanked open, and Klaus was pulled out.

A thick-mustached man pointed a pistol at Anna. "Out. *Schnell.*"

6

AUDREY, TRINIDAD, APRIL 1944

"Mail call," Audrey shouted. This call signaled personnel to assemble for the distribution of mail to the wounded, volunteers, and those in command, which usually caused heads to turn in the hope of hearing from family and friends. Approaching eleven in the morning, the temperature was already sweltering, leaving most everyone perspiring from the humidity, irritable, and dreaming of diving into a swimming pool and never leaving. Audrey pulled the collar of her Red Cross uniform, a navy blue dress cinched with a wide black belt, away from her damp neck and again wished she had been sent to the Aleutian Islands like her training pal Catherine.

Audrey blinked, but no one looked her way. Left alone to sort and distribute the mail, she headed toward the mail tent, hoping her coworkers had a good reason for not answering the call of duty.

"There she is, our very own birthday girl," came a shout from behind her. Betty?

Audrey looked back and saw two more women workers following Betty into the tent.

"Surprise!"

"Happy Birthday."

Just as Audrey wondered what the three ladies were up to, another woman and a man entered the tent. Dorothy was holding a pitcher with a sleeve of paper cups tucked under one arm, while Fred beamed proudly at the tray he carried, which held a chocolate-frosted cake that tilted dramatically to one side.

Audrey cupped her face with her hands, her cheeks hot under her fingertips. "Please tell me that's a pitcher of an exotic Caribbean cocktail. I could use one right now—poured over my head, ice cubes and all."

Fred laughed. "Plain old water, but one can certainly pretend."

"There's no way we were going to let you stay droopy and skip celebrating your special day," Betty said.

"Here I was, thinking I had done an amazing job of concealing my woes of…" Audrey trailed off. Of what? That she was turning another year older while surrounded by brave soldiers wounded in this horrible war? She inhaled deeply and thanked her friends for remembering her special day, especially when she felt far from special. "If we didn't have to show for mail call right now, I'd really grab that pitcher and pour it over my head—that's how hot I am."

"Babe, you're hot, all right," Fred said, setting down the cake. If Audrey didn't know about his commitment to his wife back home, she might think he was flirting rather than just teasing harmlessly. Instead, like with the other men on this island base, she saw Fred as more of a brother than anything else.

"I don't mean to be a party-pooper," Candace began, "but we'll celebrate after mail and lunch."

"I have another obligation right afterward," Audrey said. "Tonight?"

"Gosh," Dorothy said. "By then, you'll be almost a day closer to your next birthday."

"You're something else—something wonderful." Audrey headed for the exit. "You're aging me already… and to think I won't be officially twenty-three until four in the afternoon."

Fred cast a pitiful look at the cake. "Hope the flies don't find this." He followed Audrey to the exit.

Audrey glanced over her shoulder at Fred and smiled. He was in his early thirties. Fred, from the UK town of Falmouth, had been disqualified from serving in the British Armed Forces because of significant hearing loss. Refusing to stay home during the war, he volunteered for the International Committee of the Red Cross and had no regrets. An affable guy, many quickly adjusted to his presence, facing him so he could easily see them and read their facial cues to understand better. That's how they truly were—coming together as a team to support each other, often saying that if they had to be in the middle of a war, at least fate brought them there for a worthwhile reason.

Halfway to the mail tent, Audrey again fought to push away the sense of gloom that seemed to haunt each of her birthdays as they approached, reminding herself to put life into perspective. She began to mentally list what she was thankful for. This assignment, to a camp mainly for men suffering from torpedo-related injuries, had given her an open window to see how fragile the human body and mind could become. It helped her focus on her health and well-being, making her feel more positive and grateful. She had built strong friendships here at the Trinidad base — reliable people she could depend on after the war, whenever that day finally arrived. She had climbed the proverbial ladder from volunteer to a paid position. And despite the heat, humidity, and more months of rain than not, she at least avoided being in the middle of a combat zone. However, if she was needed and assigned to a more challenging situation, so be it. She was always prepared to help and offer compassionate support to those in need, whether for the troops or civilians.

She quickened her pace to catch up with her friends.

"Audrey? Got a moment?"

Audrey glanced toward the hospital ward tent she was passing and recognized one of the nurses. "Yes? Do you need my help?"

"It's Joseph. He's asking for you."

Without hesitation, Audrey hurried over. "Has he taken a turn for—"

The nurse raised her hand to soothe Audrey's increasing fears.

"No, hon. He's fine—well, as good as he can be, all things considered. He's been asking for you all morning."

"That might be a good sign." It had been touch and go for Private Joseph Campanili—Joe to her—who was on a troop transport hit by a torpedo. She had personally delivered his mail several times, always offering a sincere smile and words of encouragement. "I haven't picked up today's mail—just got the call out to the others. I hope he's not disappointed."

The nurse winked. "I don't think that matters to Private Campanili." They headed to the private's bed, which he had been in since arriving on the island three months ago after losing his left foot in combat. It has been a slow and difficult recovery, which he endured stoically.

"He's a strong guy, all right," Audrey replied, aware of her all-business tone, contradicting the feelings of her insides twisting in an unusual mix of elation and guilt. Sure, that was it. Dedicated to putting the wounded first—doing so by ignoring her wishes and desires—guilt controlled her each time she visited Joe because, gosh darn it, she liked him. Hmm. Maybe a little more than just liking.

The nurse was called away, and Audrey turned the corner toward Joe's curtained bay. Noticing the privacy curtain left open like a doorway, she paused there. "Knock knock." For a moment, she debated whether to address him by his official rank or his first name, which he had insisted she use when they first met. Familiarity won. Wartime had a peculiar way of demanding either enmity or camaraderie—no in-between—and the former was certainly not why she had joined the Red Cross. "Joe?"

"Come on into my castle, Audrey." She stepped inside as Joe propped himself up into a sitting position and broke into a smile.

"Well," Audrey said, unable and unwilling to suppress a smile in her voice, "judging by your expression, it seems you're the only one who doesn't mind this blasted heat, soldier."

"In the grand scheme of things, I can handle this weather, especially since I'm counting my lucky stars that the rainy season is starting late."

She looked around the small bay. "I don't have the mail yet. Sorry about that. I was unexpectedly delayed."

"That chocolate cake must have been super delicious to keep you from visiting with me."

She laughed. "Word does get around fast here."

"Happy birthday, Audrey."

"Thanks. But really, what can I do for you? I understand that you requested to see me."

"Are you always so business-like? Can't a fella just want to chat?"

She playfully pointed to herself. "With me?"

"Yeah, I want to talk to you," he said. "Only the two of us birthday kids are here—until a doctor or nurse shows up. Pull up a chair before you're called away."

She darted out of the bay to grab the only available chair she had passed on her way to him and set it beside his bed. "I didn't know it was your birthday today. It's kind of nice having somebody to celebrate with."

"You can say that again. Especially since no one back home writes to me."

"You too?" she blurted, then shook her head. "Sorry. I have no right to bring up my personal situation to you."

"Stop, right there." He looked at his left leg, then at hers. "Just because I'm lounging comfortably in a hospital bed, far from home, in the middle of a war that makes me want to swear if it weren't for you sitting in my presence, doesn't erase that you're human too, in the same situation as me, minus an injury."

She fought to shift her focus from herself to him, where it belonged. She swept her gaze over his sandy-colored hair and brown eyes, recalling how those eyes always appeared cheerful, no matter the physical or emotional pain she'd seen him go through. How he managed to stay so strong was beyond her understanding. "Put that way, yes. You're right. So, what's this about no one back home writing to you? From what you've told me about the small-town feel of Rochester, New York—despite it being a city—I'm surprised everyone there hasn't picked up pen and paper to write to you."

"Yes, they knew I was shipping out to fight, but nah, they're too busy to write. A few high school gals who had puppy-dog crushes on me wrote to me when I was first drafted. You know… *Dear Joe, I hope this finds you well… hurry home to me, and we'll pick up where we left off.*"

"Aww, that's sweet."

Joe frowned. "No, it's not—not when you get the same basic letter from the few girls who went out of their way to ignore me in school but suddenly found themselves without their boyfriends at home. It's the same letter, just signed by someone else." After a few moments of silence, he continued. "And family? My father's been gone for years—took off, not deceased, you know. My mom's been working seven days a week for years to support me and my little sister, who can be a handful without me since she has some quirks."

"That's a tough situation for your mom; nothing to envy, really, but I understand." Audrey cringed. "Sorry. I have no right to say such a judgmental thing."

"That's just it, Audrey. I believe you have the right to feel this way. Considering you've told me that you also haven't received a sack full of mail and that it's both our birthdays today, we can spend a minute or two being miserable together."

He made a sulky, sad-eyed face.

She frowned.

He sputtered a laugh.

She exploded in a near howl.

When they both calmed down, she stood. "I must get to the mailroom—have a job to do."

"They're talking about shipping me home."

That made her pause. "When?" she asked, unsure if she wanted to hear the answer.

"Next week. Doc thinks I can get better rehab back in New York—maybe even get a prosthetic faster than if I stay here. I can't say Mom won't be anything but happy that I can relieve her by looking out for my sis."

"How do you feel about that?"

"Mixed." He tugged at his whiskered chin. "I'll tell you straight up, I want to give you my address. I'd really like us to stay in touch. You know, like real mail that you can look forward to receiving. Well, as best as possible, considering you're still stationed away from home. Maybe you can meet up with me after the war." He looked away. "If my lack of a foot doesn't bother you."

She tsk-tsked him. "You know better than that."

He met her gaze. "You're right, and I'm glad I do." He reached for the small notepad on his bedside table and jotted down what she assumed was his address and phone number. "Here you go. Don't lose it."

"I'll be quite protective of it… actually, I'll also commit it to memory." She slipped the paper into her pocket. "Happy birthday once again. I have to go now, but maybe I can swing by later."

"Hope so, Audrey."

She left the small bay area she had enjoyed visiting since Joe was brought to Trinidad. Although she wouldn't admit to anyone that she had favorites, he was her top patient in the two years she was here. She had started to see him as more than just a friend. Maybe this was unprofessional, but that's simply how it was.

Her strides were quick, and within seconds, she stepped into the hot, sticky outdoors. This distraction from her loneliness and the pain of not hearing from her family since leaving home brought her relief.

Just as she was about to step into the mail tent, where she knew piles of stacked bags waited to be sorted and letters to be distributed, someone grabbed her arm. She looked up. "Fred? You have alarm scrawled all over your face."

"Forget the mail—we have it under control. Director Neal wants to talk to you right now."

"Trouble?"

Fred shrugged. "One way to find out."

7

LISELOTTE/ANNA, GERMANY, JANUARY 1944

Anna and Klaus were ordered to stand two vehicle lengths apart, raise their hands in the air, and kneel on the cold ground covered with patches of ice. Asking why was as pointless as asking what would happen next—whatever these armed soldiers wanted. She obeyed, keeping her eyes on the soldier who aimed his gun directly at her. Now that he moved closer, his mustache looked like a smudge, emphasizing his ugliness. To her surprise, he started firing questions at her, not Klaus.

"Point of origin? Destination?" Just as she was about to answer, he shot off more questions at a clipped pace that made her flinch with each one, as if each was a bullet. "Reason? What is your relationship with each other? German or Jew?"

Her mouth dropped open at the last question... or was that an accusation? Could a Jew not be a German? Were Jews no longer allowed to claim a German heritage?

"My name is Anna..." She almost let her real last name, Kellerman, slip out, but then remembered the name she told Klaus, which matched her identity papers. "Anna Bauer."

With the tip of his gun, the soldier gently touched her cheek as if using his fingertips. Disgust surged through her, and she fought off a sudden numbness—a mental state promising her emotional escape where no one could hurt her.

"Get on your feet, whore," the soldier barked. He aimed his gun at the brush behind them, shouting confidently to his fellow comrades that he would be gone for only a few minutes. His foul implication did not escape Anna.

"Get the hell away from her!" Klaus yelled. He stood up quickly and ran toward the winter-gray-uniformed man in front of Anna.

Believing Klaus was about to be shot, Anna screamed. The other two soldiers were upon him in an instant; the smaller one hit Klaus on the side of his head with the butt of his rifle. He collapsed to the ground, so silent that she wondered whether he was still alive.

"You," said the soldier, who again spoke directly to her. "On your feet. Off with the clothes." He jutted his chin toward one of their vehicles. "Over there. Move it."

A quick movement flashed past Anna. Klaus. He was alive, healthy enough to move, and brave enough to come to her rescue.

He lunged at the soldier, wrapping his arm around his neck. "One move and I'll choke the life out of you."

Klaus thrust his gun at Anna. "Keep it aimed at this beast." He drew another gun and pointed it at the other two, instructing them to lie face down on the ground and put their hands behind their backs. Then he yanked the rifles off their shoulders, tore off the shoulder straps, and used them to bind their hands.

Klaus, ignoring his injury, spoke firmly. "As my identity papers state, I am Klaus Agers. As the other identity paper of Anna Bauer states, she is who she is. She's also my cousin. I will be reporting you to the one I take orders from—Reichsführer Heinrich Himmler—for not only assaulting the two of us but also for your attempt to rape Fräulein Bauer. Get up and get going."

"*Nein*. We're stationed here."

"That's not our concern. Do I have to repeat myself?"

Without saying another word, the two men on the ground squirmed like worms and managed to get to their feet. They began moving toward their vehicles.

"Halt," Klaus ordered. He aimed his Luger across the road at the empty field. "Go that way. No delays. No excuses."

Once the three soldiers vanished, Klaus grabbed Anna's arm. They quickly headed to their jeep.

"Can you drive with your wound?" Anna asked.

"Watch." He got into the driver's seat and started the vehicle.

She hurried to the passenger side, pushed by a gust of wind. "Before, I was amazed you had one gun. Now I learn—the hard way—that you have two. What else don't I know about you that I should?"

"There's plenty to know about me." He kept his focus on the road, avoiding her gaze. "It's a matter of whether you should."

She kept her gaze fixed on him, ignoring his rudeness. Maybe if she modeled kindness and concern, he would consider returning it. "You're still bleeding—you must be hurting."

"I'm fine," he mumbled, mentioning that this road would take them straight to his hometown of Halle. His omission of the journey's duration unsettled Anna more.

Noticing another trickle of blood from his head running toward his throat, she pulled a handkerchief from her pocket. "This may look second-hand and dirty, but I assure you it's clean." Before he could object, she pressed the folded cloth to his wound.

"You have a gentle touch." Klaus surprised her by taking the shabby cloth from her hand. Their fingers brushed briefly, giving a hint of warmth against the January cold. He held it to his head for a moment longer before pressing it back into her hand. "I have to drive," he added as if justifying his dismissing her attention.

He continued down the same road they had taken to what Anna now thought of as the ambush. He drove more slowly than before. Whether it was due to extra caution or because he was having trouble with his head wound, she couldn't tell. Still, his driving was steady enough that she didn't worry.

"You were wonderfully brave back there."

He shrugged one shoulder and winced. So much for her not worrying.

"I can drive if you want." She could do no such thing, but on this open stretch of road, how much trouble could she get them into? Never mind that this road was in Germany during one of the most horrific wars the world has ever seen, with an overwhelming number of guards, soldiers, and desperate people ready to strike at the next target, which very well could be them.

"I'm fine. Don't ask again. I told you I'd watch over you." He shook his head slightly, making her wonder if he regretted sounding harsh. "Besides, driving distracts me from what just happened… from wanting to turn around, find those bastards, and snuff the life out of them."

With his gaze now on her, she gave him a sideways smirk. "After what you warned them about, I doubt they're even in Germany."

"You might be right."

Klaus's slow driving since leaving Dessau had nearly become a crawl. Tempted to gently shake his shoulder to check on him, she held back, not wanting to face another reprimand. Instead, she chose to talk to him more, hoping that conversation would keep him alert.

"Tell me about Heinrich Himmler. Is he your direct commander? I wasn't aware that you were in combat."

"Yes, Heinrich is the one…" His brow furrowed deeply.

"Yes?" she prompted, even more curious about his connection to the infamous Himmler. Then again, Klaus's unpredictable behavior might very well be because of his head wound, which could cause trouble for both of them, after all.

"I follow his orders. He's the one I report to. And if you're curious, I do so with honor."

"Were you ever in active combat?"

He shook his head and grimaced. "Not combat. Active, though."

No more details? "How so?"

"Heinrich caught my attention with Vo…vols… I mean, *Volksliste*."

His words were slurring. If she kept him talking, would it help? "Meaning?"

"It's the classification… of people… with pure German blood. An easy enough definition for the masses to understand, don't you think?"

Compared to everyone else without such blood? Anna's head

began to throb. That was the vaguest explanation she had ever heard. How far back in history did the Nazi Party need to go to distinguish white Aryans from others, like Jews, Roma, or any other groups they considered unimportant and a threat to Aryans? Decades or centuries? What about people who, due to the hardships of birth or social circumstances—such as alcoholism, mental illness, or physical disabilities—were considered by the Nazis to have tainted German blood?

Rosa. Her daughter.

Vomit surged up her throat, and she swallowed it quickly. She remembered arguing not long ago with her mother about her over-concern regarding the Nazis' interest in Rosa. When the Gestapo arrived while she was with Gerhard and took her baby, all she could do was blame her mother and leave, ultimately abandoning her other twin daughter, Regina, along with her mother.

"Anna?" Klaus asked softly, his tone gentler now. He steadied her sudden trembling with a firm grip. "Are you feeling sick? Should I pull over?"

"Just a wave of sad thoughts. I'm fine." She pushed herself to continue. "Do you usually travel with your commander or other health agents who perform blood tests?" She had no idea what to ask and hoped she wouldn't sound like a babbling fool. She wanted to learn more about this mysterious program without accidentally revealing Rosa's health situation and possibly making things worse.

When he gave a blank look, she tried again. "You mention pure German blood—do you seek out and arrest those who fail a test?"

"If only it were that easy." He swayed toward her, blinking rapidly, then swayed back.

"Klaus? Are you dizzy?"

"Told you, I'm fine," he said through gritted teeth. "No more questions about... how I'm feeling."

"All right, then," she said, relieved that focusing on him at least eased her queasiness. Maybe if she kept him talking, whatever was bothering him would fade away. Then, once they reached Halle, she planned to find a way to distract him and escape once and for all. "You fascinate me."

Klaus opened his mouth, but no words came out.

"Oh, come on, now. This will be a long ride if we don't talk."

"It's only about… about fifty-five… kilometers…" His eyes crossed. One brow shot up. "Between Dessau and Halle. Fifty-five. Not long at all."

"Well, it's going to feel a lot longer, and I'm already bored. You, Klaus, have a golden opportunity to impress me with your work for Reichsführer Himmler."

He stared at her for several seconds too long as a lopsided grin spread across his face.

"Eyes on the road, please."

He faced forward but swayed again. She touched his arm. He shook her off, tsk-tsking like the old biddy who lived next door to her mother's house and never minded her own business. Did she still live there? Had a bomb targeted their street? Were her mother and Regina alive and well?

Nein… nein. She had to stop dwelling on her not-so-distant past. Again, she swallowed her nausea. She had to stop thinking about the family she had abandoned.

"Anna, why are you groaning? What's wrong?"

Had she made a noise? "Just awful thoughts again storming my mind. War doesn't bring out the best in me." Or anyone, she thought to herself.

"Try to relax," he said. "Yes, we're at war—with the whole insufferable world. Sometimes, you just have to ride it through to the very end. We will win."

She nodded in concession. "This is pretty bad—one second, I'm asking if you're okay, and the next, you're showing concern about me. What a pair we are."

For a long moment, he remained silent. If luck favored her, he would stay that way. Then he cleared his throat, and she quietly sighed her displeasure. She humored him by glancing his way.

"Returning to the topic of my work, let me say that, because of the nature of war, many children are suddenly left without a family, or even a home. This is especially true in Poland. Thanks to Himmler's insight, he has created effective policies to address these unfortunate situations that benefit the Fatherland. My role as a liaison is to place these children with reliable, loving German families."

She resisted the urge to cross her arms and instead folded her hands on her lap. "For the preservation of good Aryan blood, then?"

"Indeed. That's why I'm often on the road."

"What about your safety when traveling and out of war zones?"

"I have means of safeguarding myself and my men."

Were others assisting Klaus? How extensive was this Volksliste operation?

Klaus hit the brake and leaned against the steering wheel. Anna scanned the area for another group of men causing trouble. There was no one in sight. Just as she was about to ask Klaus if he had seen anything suspicious, she stopped short. His face was pale, and beads of sweat dotted his forehead. His eyes were squeezed shut. Without a word, she pushed her way out of the passenger door, ducked around to his side, and opened the door.

"Do as I say and do not argue," she demanded in the firmest tone she had ever used on him.

He cracked his eyes open for a moment. His brown eyes, usually reminding her of wheat, now looked like muddy water. "You sound like a mother."

She refused to respond to that comment. "I'm going to help you move to the rear seat where you can stretch out and, hopefully, be more comfortable. I'll drive."

He blinked his eyes open and looked at her as if she were the one suffering. "Have you ever driven an army vehicle—or any vehicle? Yes or no?"

"Yes," she said, regretting how timid her voice sounded. Behind her mother's back, she took a few driving lessons from a boy in her class she liked and hoped to see more of. Their lessons ended after five sessions. She eventually met Gerhard, and the idea of this other boy became a joke.

"You don't sound sure. I'll drive… give me a…" He leaned against the back of his seat, closed his eyes, and looked even paler.

She looked both ways on the road. Why wasn't anyone driving past them? "And now he has to pass out on me," she muttered.

"I'm awake," he said. "And very alert."

"Right. And I'm a British spy arresting you." When he didn't reply, she shook him until he stirred. "Stay with me, Klaus. Open your eyes and look at me."

"That's what all the women say."

Good grief. She wanted to elbow him in the gut, but she took pity on him. "Put your arm around me. I'll help you to the back seat where you can stretch out and relax."

"*Nein,*" he said. "To the passenger seat. I'll help you."

"To drive? Only one person can drive a vehicle."

"I'll direct. Help with the clutch."

Unless he passed out completely, or worse—which she truly did not want to happen since she, despite herself, was dependent on him, at least for now—she knew this was also pointless to argue. She followed his instructions. Within minutes, they were on their way down the road, though not at the speed she preferred. She hoped her next stop would be Halle. She felt sorry for the poor stranger who might get in their way.

8

LISELOTTE/ANNA, HALLE, GERMANY, JANUARY-FEBRUARY 1944

With Klaus flickering in and out of consciousness as they entered Halle, Anna had to stop several times to ask for directions to his family's home despite having the address he provided. Each time she slowed down or braked, he would jolt awake, bark out the command to continue, and then doze off again. Although she was worried that a serious health problem was behind his inability to stay awake, there was only so much of his complaints she could tolerate. Fortunately for both of them, she was a quick learner and managed to drive the jeep well enough to get them to his parents' place safely.

She held her breath as she navigated through old, brick-lined, narrow streets, trying to avoid women wearing ragged overcoats and kerchiefs tied under their chins, bent forward against the howling wind. Children darted across the road, making the drive even more challenging. Young men were nowhere in sight—only white-haired ones, well over their fifties or sixties. While driving through the Old Town section of the city, just past St. Mary's Church in the market square, it suddenly hit her: all the younger men were fighting for Germany in the war, in one capacity or another. And here she was, with one of Halle's younger men, on leave to visit his family but wounded by a German soldier.

A little beyond the city center, the architecture shifted from Gothic to Wilhelminian-style buildings, reflecting—as she had learned in school—the German equivalent of the Victorian era, between 1888 and 1918, compared to the British period of 1837 to 1901. Anna caught sight of a few grand houses, but it was the number of apartment buildings that sparked her curiosity, as she wondered if there had ever been a large migration from rural areas to the city. And why? She imagined that behind the large wrought iron entranceways, with their luxurious stucco decorations and small windows protruding from the buildings, there were grand stairwells leading to elegant living quarters. These buildings also must have had magnificent courtyards that undoubtedly offered needed respite from the war. Who had once lived in these fine accommodations? Who, after the war, would be able to afford such splendor? For a moment, she wished she could study history more deeply. She wished for many things besides being a nursemaid and driver to the man she only wanted to escape.

Before her, two gray-haired women walked up the boulevard, one pushing a cart while the other leaned on a cane. With the houses and buildings poorly numbered, Anna slowed down.

Klaus stirred and struggled to sit upright. "This is not the address —what are you doing?"

"I'm in need of further direction and didn't want to disturb your sleep."

"Well, I'm awake now." Klaus looked around and pointed ahead. "Proceed."

"Are you sure?"

"Move over. I'll drive."

"I'll continue," she said firmly, but without saying another word, she followed his instructions and shifted the jeep into gear. Less than three minutes later, she turned right and arrived at his family's home.

"What are your parents' names? How should I explain myself?" she asked, pushing past her embarrassment for not asking this basic question earlier. Considering that they had been shot at and she had faced the threat of rape, she had been rightfully distracted.

Klaus leaned back heavily. "Heinz and Gretchen, but it would be best to observe formalities, or you won't make it past the doorway. Regarding your unexpected presence with me, you're my new secretary, coping with the loss of your family in Berlin, so please act distraught."

"Trust me, that's not a problem."

He pointed to a white-brick, standalone house with dark green shutters and trim. A quick glance showed a slate roof in excellent condition. "You can pull into the driveway to the right of the house."

Less than a minute after Anna turned off the engine, a woman of average height stepped out of the house. With bobbed white hair streaked with hints of faded brown and her lips brightened with red lipstick, she wore a dark plum high-neck sweater paired with a black skirt that reached her mid-calf. Her rosy cheeks paled as she stared at the passenger-side window. She hurried down the steps, crossing a snow-covered patch of lawn that Anna imagined blooming with flowers in the spring.

"Mutti," Klaus murmured as his mother opened the passenger door.

"*Sohn, Sohn,*" the woman said, ignoring Anna. "What is wrong with you?"

"Frau Agers?" Anna said firmly to get her attention. "Your son needs a doctor."

"Who are you?" Gretchen Agers shot Anna an icy stare. "What have you done to him?"

Beyond possibly saving his life? "I'm Anna Bauer, Klaus. Herr Agers' new secretary. On the way here from Berlin—"

"Berlin?" Klaus's mother's eyes widened. "The city was bombed."

"*Ja*, but we managed." Anna hoped she sounded genuine. "We took safety in a bomb shelter. The condition of the roads caused by the bombs delayed our arrival."

"How were you hurt?" Frau Agers asked Klaus directly. She reached out to touch his head, but Klaus pulled away. Anna wondered if his reaction was due to manly pride or physical sensitivity. Probably both, she concluded.

"Debris fell on top of him," Anna said, stepping in for Klaus when he took too long. His mother covered her mouth with her hand, but not before Anna noticed a look of panic. "He hit his head and hasn't been well since."

"Why are you here with him?"

"Fräulein Bauer had nowhere to go," Klaus said, still with his eyes closed. "I invited her here—she had to drive me. I couldn't."

"Klaus, are you blinded? Why..."

"No more questions." Klaus opened his eyes, his glassy gaze visible. "I can still see. Anna says I need medical care." Wincing, he added, "She may be right."

Anna needed to exercise caution regarding the challenges and further delays posed by his mother. "May I assist you in moving your son indoors?"

When Frau Agers nodded, Anna hurried to the passenger side. She grabbed his left elbow while his mother supported his right side.

"Where's Vater?" Klaus asked.

Worry creased Frau Agers' face. "It's only four in the afternoon."

Anna imagined her silent words: You know your father works long hours for the Führer and arrives home after dinner time... *Mein Gott,* Sohn! Do we need to take you to the hospital?

The poor woman needed her help. Anna patted Klaus's arm to get his attention. "Herr Agers, there are two steps for you to climb. Let's go slowly."

Without argument—from either son or mother—they entered a formal foyer featuring a large wooden floor medallion, a white marble stand at its center, and a red glass bowl filled with several calling cards. Although it was empty of garments, an ornate oak coat rack stood to the left of the door. To her right, a narrow-framed painting of a winding river from a hillside viewpoint hung, making Anna wish she were there—or, really, any bucolic setting. A wave of surprise washed over her when the Frau asked for her help in assisting Klaus to the sofa in the parlor, the room straight ahead. She then excused herself to call for the doctor.

Anna, too self-conscious for her own good and too tired to worry about etiquette despite the Frau's imminent return, sat on the cozy wing chair directly opposite Klaus, grateful for the plush seat compared to the hard seats of the jeep. Besides a faint ticking from the mantle clock, the house was quiet, though she expected numerous questions from the Frau and Klaus's father when he returned from work.

"Anna?"

She glanced at Klaus. "You should be resting, not chitchatting with your secretary."

He grimaced. Or was that a grin? He patted the sofa. "Come here."

When she looked around and saw they were the only ones there, she took three steps and sat beside him. "Make it quick before your mother comes back and causes a fuss."

"I doubt that. She hasn't seen me—the son who can do no wrong—for a long time. And she likes you too."

Not wanting to fall into the trap of asking why the older, dour woman supposedly liked her, she decided to play it safe. "Is there something you need me to do?"

"Yes... and no. I just like your company."

"Business-wise, Herr Agers, how can I assist you?"

"You will find the listings of my contact numbers in a wallet in my coat pocket."

Anna gasped. "*Nein*. I will not talk with Himmler."

"Easy there. He doesn't have time to stay in an office. You need to leave a message with his assistant, mention my injury, and say I will be delayed in returning to work."

"But you have yet to see the doctor." A fool with half a brain could see the obvious: Klaus was suffering from an ailment that would keep him confined for a while. However, exhausted and weak, as if she were the one who was ill or injured, she lacked the energy to argue. "Fine. When your mother returns, I'll—"

"What will you do?" Frau Agers asked as she entered the room. Her narrowed gaze at Anna's closeness to her dear son radiated disapproval.

Anna jumped to her feet. Focusing entirely on Klaus, she said, "Herr Agers, your mother has returned. Yes, I will contact the office and let them know about your situation. First, let me see if your mother needs my help."

"That's unnecessary, Fräulein Bauer," Frau Agers said, sounding neither overly harsh nor warm. "I called my husband. He is bringing the good doctor and should arrive soon. You can leave now—I can have my daughters stop by."

"Not today," Klaus said, oddly clear and steady on this subject. "There's only so much I can handle."

"And that's why I need them by my side."

Klaus tried to stand. He would have fallen over if Anna hadn't grabbed his arm and helped him sit back down. "Mutti," he said. "I'll miraculously recover and walk out of here if you threaten to bring my sisters on me."

"Stubborn boy," Frau Agers murmured, but smiled kindly at him. "Let me get you a comfortable pillow and—"

"No need to fuss over me," Klaus said.

"Why not?" Frau Agers bent over her son, catching Anna's attention. "You know I can't do this when your father's here."

The sound of the front door opening was heard, followed by footsteps. Two men entered the parlor. The older one resembled Klaus closely, while the other was chubby and younger.

"You made it home quickly," Frau Agers said.

"Of course. I need to help my son get back on his feet and on his way for the great work he's doing for Germany," Herr Agers said, then stepped behind the sofa and patted his son's shoulder. "Klaus, my boy, there are better ways to visit with us."

Klaus looked at his father's hand and waved him off. "Pardon me, Vater. The slightest movement makes me dizzy."

"I'm sorry to hear that. I've brought the good doctor to examine you."

The doctor placed a large black bag on the coffee table in front of the sofa and asked Frau and Anna to leave the room. Always feeling awkward at unfamiliar social gatherings, Anna, as she followed Klaus's mother, found it frustrating that this woman seemed to look down on her. Unsure whether to stay by the doorway until she was invited elsewhere, she relied on a familiar tactic, trusting that this beautiful house would have a convenient place for her to freshen up. "Frau Agers, may I use your toilet? It's been a long trip, and I must be a sorry sight."

Without saying a word, the Frau led her to a door at the end of the hallway. "Meet me in the kitchen when you are done. I would like to talk to you."

Anna offered a polite smile. Once inside, she leaned against the door until the click of the woman's low-heeled shoes on the wooden floor faded into the distance. She washed her face at the sink, splashing cold water on it to calm her nerves. Nonsense, she told herself. She did nothing wrong. There was nothing to feel guilty about. If she were asked to leave, she would do so gladly, somehow finding her next place to shelter.

When she entered the surprisingly modest kitchen, with its black-and-white tiled floors and simple white-painted cabinets, she was surprised to find Frau Agers sitting at the small round table in the center of the room, an Art Deco red-and-black-striped teapot resting on a crocheted trivet. It reminded Anna of the few Bavarian china pieces her mother had inherited from her mother's collection.

Frau Agers pointed to a chair next to her. "Have a seat, Anna. Would you care for some tea?"

"*Danke*. A hot drink would be good."

The woman poured her tea into a cup with a matching saucer. She invited her to add sugar and cream if she liked. Absent was her offer to call her by her first name.

"I have no treats to offer you with your tea. These days, we don't get much company, and my husband and I tend not to indulge in sweets." She wrung her hands, looked at them for a moment, and then slid them under the table. "It's rare even for Klaus to visit, but he serves the Fatherland, and that is the main concern of my husband and me, as well as any good German citizen."

From what little Anna observed between the mother and son, she could tell Klaus's mother was also quite worried about her son's overall well-being. Still, strangely, she seemed unable—or maybe not permitted—to voice her concerns to her husband. "I'm sorry for the intrusion, Frau Agers, but I followed your son's instructions."

The Frau leaned into the table. "The household hasn't been the same since our help took off on us last year. They were Jewish, of course. Not that we knew it until afterward. Fled in the middle of the night, as expected of vermin. Of course, now it's not easy to find a replacement."

"Took off?" Anna echoed. Despite growing up during the years when Hitler came to power, spreading hatred and blame against the Jewish population, among other groups, she felt sick to her stomach every time she heard Jews labeled as vermin. One look at Klaus's mother's stern face made her hold back her burning question about how she had the right to dismiss another's life as unworthy of respect. Then, a memory surfaced… She had been talking to her mother and remarked that she could not imagine dating a Jew. Now, as she sat across from Klaus's mother, who couldn't hide her disgust and prejudice, Anna's face heated with a little disgust and a lot of shame. What other groups of people did this woman not approve of?

"It was no shock they fled, especially working here," the Frau continued. "A couple and their three young daughters—imagine subjecting children to such risk of facing German streets with heavily armed soldiers hunting for runaways like them."

Anna thought it would be a real surprise if the Jewish family had stayed in the Agers' home. She felt sorry for the children and hoped this family found a safe place and avoided being caught. If they were discovered, it would surely mean a one-way trip to one of the horrible camps in Germany, Poland, and maybe even other countries by now. It always came down to the children. Adults, caught up in their own struggles to improve their lives, often overlook the consequences for their children and…

White dots burst in front of Anna, swirling clockwise around her as she leaned counterclockwise to regain her balance.

She was guilty of the very accusation she had pinned on the woman sitting beside her. Not long ago, she only cared about herself. All she wanted was the love of one man, and pursuing this desire came at a terrible cost to her twin babies, a price she was all too willing to pay. Her mother understood this better and had tried to warn her.

She would not listen.

She had lost everything. Family. Her home. Even her true name.

Anna glanced up to see the Frau with an alarmed expression.

The woman reached for Anna's untouched tea and lifted the cup to her lips. "Drink. I suspect you haven't had any food or drink in some time." She touched Anna's forehead, likely to check for a fever. "Shall I ask the doctor to examine you?"

"That's not necessary." Anna offered a small smile to emphasize her words, even though she felt far from having a reason to smile. "I'll be fine. This tea will be a big help. I appreciate it. Please, no worries."

"All right, then," Frau Agers said. "Tell me the real story of why you're here with my son and how he got hurt."

Caught between betraying Klaus's wishes not to tell his parents how he was hit on the head by Nazi soldiers or lying—again—to his mother, which might lead her to discover the truth on her own and face her inevitable anger, Anna wrestled with the dilemma in her mind. She decided to stick with the story that Klaus had started and which she would embellish.

"Frau Agers, I want to emphasize that I am forever grateful to your kind son. Not only did he hire me—a woman committed to the Nazi Party and everything it represents—but if it weren't for Herr Agers, I likely would have died in the bombing raid. He's a true hero." Relieved to see the woman's facial features soften, Anna leaned back more comfortably. "After meeting to discuss the details of working for him, the air raid siren blared. We had no choice but to take shelter for the night." She dropped her gaze and sincerely sniffled.

"If it becomes too difficult to continue, I'll ask my son to tell me when he's feeling better."

Anna took a deep breath. She would stick with the story she told Klaus, one that was quite understandable and unfortunately common during wartime, and one that was close enough to her own reality. "Because of the bombs, I lost my family right before Christmas. I was born in Berlin and have lived there all these years, but I have no extended family and no close friends, just a few acquaintances. Now, I have nowhere to live. I've moved from shelter to shelter, trying to find work. It was by chance that I overheard two women talking about how your son needed a new secretary. One thing led to another, and we agreed to meet. Just when Herr Agers hired me, the sirens went off. We planned to leave early the next morning, but on the way to one of his command offices in Berlin, metal debris fell and hit his head. I wanted to take him to a doctor, but he refused, insisting that I drive him here instead."

She glanced at the Frau for guidance on what to say or do next. Her thoughts briefly drifted to the idea of sneaking out of the house in the middle of the night and escaping—escaping like the Jews who had once worked here until they were considered non-human enemies of the Aryan race.

"Gretchen?" Klaus's father called, entering the room.

Both Anna and the Frau looked up.

"I've seen the doctor out," Herr Agers said. His eyes darted between the two of them. "Let's talk privately, shall we?"

"It's fine, Heinz. After speaking with Anna, she should also be aware of what's going on."

Herr Agers removed his black-rimmed glasses, revealing his suddenly wrinkled brow. "Well then, I have good news about Klaus. The doctor has diagnosed him with a concussion, thankfully, one he will recover from without complications. That is, if he follows the advice of prolonged bed rest in a dark, quiet room."

"Our son, confined to a bed and holding still? For how long?"

"For several days, possibly weeks. The doctor will visit again at the end of this week to do another appraisal."

"This does not sound good."

"That's enough, Gretchen. Our son is a strong man. If I say there's nothing to worry about, then that's enough."

Frau Agers looked at Anna. "Well, Fräulein Bauer, it looks like you will be our guest for a while. You can settle in the carriage house where those Jews lived, though I trust you won't be fleeing like they did."

"*Danke.*" Anna smiled, hiding her true intentions. "I don't plan on leaving."

9

AUDREY, AETOLIA, GREECE, MAY 1944

Audrey expected—and welcomed—the less humid spring climate compared to Trinidad, along with the view of the mountains north of Aetolia. However, despite her efforts to emotionally prepare for the tragic reality she had been warned about, she was unprepared for the sight of countless people of all ages lying dead in the streets from starvation. Greece had not experienced a famine of such massive proportions since ancient times. The suffering, caused by humans rather than a naturally occurring blight or epidemic, resulted from the naval blockade between the Axis and Allied forces, as well as the Axis control of Greece. A concise letter from Hermann Göring to Reich military leaders, stating that Germans must be fed at the expense of non-Germans who were starving and perishing, fueled the situation.

"How do you get used to this?" she asked Ruth, another Red Cross worker assigned to introduce Audrey to the camp and her responsibilities of preparing and transporting the remaining supplies they had left in reserve to children and other civilians living off the premises. They were on their way to grab some chow, an irony that kept replaying in Audrey's mind and made her feel guilty for having something to eat.

"Right there, that's the number one mistake you're making," Ruth said.

Audrey looked at Ruth, who was two years older. Although a sweet person, her tough attitude, dark circles under her eyes, streaks of silver in her hair, and her habit of smoking cigarettes whenever possible made her appear more like someone in her fifties than twenty-seven. "What do you mean?"

Ruth stopped and crossed her arms. "You don't get used to it. The longer you expect to adjust to seeing either those who are walking skeletons or the victims of starvation, the rougher it's going to be for you. Did I ever tell you about my first week here a year ago?"

Audrey shook her head, tense about what Ruth was about to say.

Ruth withdrew a metal case from her shirt pocket and took out a smoke. "Want one?"

Thinking about how the Aetolia camp also sheltered many homeless people because of the crowding on the mainland, Audrey said, "I don't smoke—maybe I should."

"Finally, you're right about something," Ruth said, but when she offered Audrey a cigarette, and Audrey declined with a wave of her hand, Ruth lit one for herself, held the smoke in for a few seconds, then blew it out and sighed contentedly. "While Lisa was showing me around the joint, we came across the first dead person I've ever seen. Well, outside of a combat hospital when I was stationed in Belgium. Anyway, the little boy..." She swallowed hard several times. "We named him Alexander—every child deserves a name. He couldn't have been more than ten years old." She took a deep drag of her cig. "Alexander was lying dead in the road, his eyes wide open as if in shock that no one cared to feed him. Lisa believed he was crawling to our camp looking for a scrap of food."

Ruth suddenly pivoted. Audrey, thinking the woman was about to be sick or cry, reached out to her but then pulled back when Ruth shouted a string of angry curses. She then faced Audrey. "If it weren't for this stinking war, this place would be paradise."

"What's your advice, then, regarding continuing the good fight?"

"Expect your entire body and mind to want to shut down from the horrors. So, girl, when you feel this way—believe me, you will, and often—ask yourself why you accepted this mission to come here because I'm sure your director informed you about what you were getting into."

Audrey reflected on her meeting with Director Neal, noting how he had been candid about what she would face in Greece. Based on his observations, he believed she was the strongest member of his team to answer the call of duty in this country. *"Humanity,"* the director stated, confidently yet with admiration, *"is the driving force that inspires the Red Cross to prevent and alleviate human suffering."* These words reflected the ideology of the International Red Cross's founder, Henry Dunant, which Audrey embraced and practiced every day since dedicating herself to the organization. *"You will also collaborate with the Turkish Red Crescent Society, a large and robust group of dedicated humanitarians. I believe you are equipped for this task, but I want to hear an affirmation directly from you."*

During the private meeting with the director, Audrey reflected on her strengths and vulnerabilities. When it came to her strengths, she had to admit that she was not easily intimidated and was willing to support those whom society had marginalized. She also had her share of vulnerabilities, especially feeling unappreciated and unwanted, which, if anything, increased her ability to empathize with others.

She was surprised when Director Neal asked her about the personal support she received from family and friends back home. For a while, her friends had corresponded with her, sending long letters about how they were contributing to the home front effort and supporting their country during this time of war. They shared the latest updates from their boyfriends fighting overseas or filled her in on the latest gossip from their high school social circle. Whether it was because the mail was having trouble reaching her after she started taking on new assignments following her departure in '41, or because their interest in her was waning, their communication stopped—as if Audrey's friendship had never existed. What hurt the most, though, was the complete silence from her family. The night after her mother revealed her extended paternal heritage and explained why her grandparents came to America, her parents threatened to cut off contact if she left home to join the Red Cross. So, did she understand vulnerability? You bet. And she faced it, head-on, anyway? Yes, definitely. She looked the director in the eye and said, "I fully understand the human need to rise above one's circumstances and to press on to thrive and not simply to survive. More importantly, human beings must care for one another, not cause suffering, and not contribute to the evil of inhumanity. This is why, sir, I believe I'm qualified for the Greece assignment."

Director Neil agreed that she was more than qualified, and she was determined not to disappoint him.

Audrey saw Ruth as a fellow woman whose raw strength and energy enabled her to work for others. "Ruth, I committed to the Red Cross during this terrible time of war because I believe in helping others overcome human suffering. I know this fight won't be easy, but I'm not one to chicken out."

Ruth grinned. "That's what I was hoping to hear from your scrawny lips."

"Hey," Audrey said, matching Ruth's playful tone. "My lips aren't—"

Ruth didn't stay to hear what she had to say. In long, deliberate steps, she walked toward the mess tent, signaling for Audrey to follow.

WITH ONE HAND on the steering wheel and the other pointing at the church spires of Aetolia, Roger acted as both driver and tour guide for Audrey. She had never seen such a mix of ancient ruins and modern buildings set against breathtaking mountain scenery.

He whistled. "Some view, huh? You might even call it stunning if it weren't for the cursed destruction from all the fighting and looting."

They drove past a line of houses with broken windows and belongings piled up in the front yards, serving as a warning that more would follow if not given freely. Audrey cringed. "I've heard about the looting, but I didn't realize it was that bad."

"That's just one horrible result of war, among many others. Another is the extensive—no exaggeration—damage to the infrastructure. Why do you think it's taking us more than an hour to drive to a place that should only take twenty minutes at most?"

"I had heard about the power supply being damaged, but I never imagined the roads would be this torn up."

Not for the first time since they left the camp, Roger swore. "Honey, welcome to war. Not a pretty reality at all."

Definitely not. The cozy Wisconsin town she left behind had made her so naïve, blinding her to the terrible consequences of war. Aetolia was a clear example of how people struggle to survive when outsiders take over their country and drastically change their lives. It was shocking to think this was just a preview of what was happening across Europe. Moreover, it was almost unthinkable to imagine such a scenario in the United States if the Axis powers were to win and take control.

Roger pointed to the spirals of smoke drifting from a group of houses nestled at the foot of a hill. "At all times, ma'am, be careful—the most you've ever been. We're Red Cross, all right, with a flag attached to our vehicle and badges and identification coming out of our butts—excuse me, ma'am… whoa, Nellie. Brace yourself for…" Their jeep dipped so low in a rut that, for a brief moment, Audrey wasn't sure if they would surface or be caught in the ditch.

"Ooo-wee," Roger called out after navigating the vehicle back onto the road… what was left of the road. "Whew. My backside needs a rub, but I'm not pulling over now."

"Good idea," Audrey said through clenched teeth. "You were saying, though?"

Roger stared ahead blankly, rubbing the back of his neck. "Right. I was trying to warn you. Be cautious at all times. This place is crawling with Italians and Germans, with the Greek Resistance right behind them. And if that doesn't spell regular military fighting mixed with guerrilla warfare, I don't know what does. You should be okay, though."

"I'm not sure if I like the sound of the word *should*. It's ambiguous, for sure."

"If you say so." Roger scratched his head. "Listen, let's do what we came to do and get back to the ranch, as they say where I'm from."

"No argument from me," Audrey said, her eyes scanning the area as Roger eased the jeep to a stop and pulled up in front of a boarded-up house. "Does someone live here, or are they just meeting us?"

"Lives here, all right. A family of six—a mom and her five kids. Don't mention her man, or you'll get non-stop waterworks. Got that?"

Unfortunately, Audrey understood. Like most fathers, husbands, and sons, the men of Greece were either fighting the Axis powers in the Resistance, imprisoned, thrown into a shallow grave, or wishing they had been buried long ago. What they were not was at home with their families, kissing their wives or girlfriends, laughing with their children, or enjoying meals without worrying about what the next day would bring.

Audrey stepped out of the vehicle and pulled out two navy blue duffels filled with rice, beans, other food staples, blankets, a few toiletries, and one sad-looking doll. Since shipping was blocked, it was a miracle that the Red Cross had managed—and was allowed—to enter the occupied country, let alone stock supplies to share with starving civilians. Sadly, their supply level was running low quickly. No amount of contact with their leaders outside Greece could confirm whether there would be any additional deliveries. Every worker she knew feared that if their own supplies became any scarcer, they would be shipped out. Undoubtedly, the death toll across Greece would increase dramatically.

A bony teen approached. At first, with hair cut short, tattered trousers cinched around the waist with a rope for a belt, and a plain white shirt stained in many spots, Audrey couldn't tell whether this child was a boy or a girl. As she moved closer, the shape of the child's round, smooth forehead indicated she was a girl.

The girl waved her hand, then said a word that sounded like *neh*.

Audrey had learned some basics of Greek and recognized the word for hello, even though the spelling was more complex. She felt relieved that Roger spoke the language fluently and acted as a translator. "Red Cross," she said in Greek. When Roger did not correct her, she breathed a little easier. She lifted one of the duffels. "Food. For you and your family." She had said the words in English, and when Roger translated, the girl smiled.

The door to the house slowly creaked open, and the sound was carried away by the breeze. A woman in a black skirt and blouse, with her stringy hair loosely falling over her shoulders, stood watching the scene and scanning the small yard for others—or so Audrey thought. Was she dressed for mourning, or was this her only outfit?

"Eliana," the woman called and waited. The girl hurried to her mother's side.

"Red Cross." Audrey handed the woman one of the bags. "For you —food, blankets, toothpaste."

The mother bent down to whisper to her daughter, who then ran into the house calling out two different names. Two boys appeared at the door: one, judging by his height, slightly older than Eliana, and the other, around seven years old. With his beady eyes and small frame, it was hard to tell their exact ages. They picked up the two duffels and went inside.

"Come in," the woman said, surprising Audrey in English. "Drink?"

Audrey looked to Roger for direction.

"For a moment or two, ma'am," he replied.

They entered the dark house. Immediately, Audrey saw two younger children sitting on the bare floor, rocking back and forth. She did the one thing she wanted to do for them. The one thing she needed to do for herself. She unzipped the smaller of the duffels, plunged her hand inside, and felt around for the soft stuffed critter. "Here he is." She sang a ta-da as she pulled the bear out. "This is Teddy."

"Teddy," the older of the two seated children repeated and looked at his sibling, who smiled.

"For you." Audrey knelt before them. "Teddy is yours. To play."

Their mother spoke in Greek. The two children squealed with joy.

Remotely, Audrey sensed the silence around them but was too busy entertaining the children. "Let's unpack the bags," she said, then stood. Other than the two children taking turns cuddling the stuffed toy, only Roger was in the room. Had the others left the house? Were soldiers standing outside, ready to attack? The sound of many footsteps suddenly surrounded them.

The mother re-entered the room and placed a rickety bamboo tray with a teapot and two cups on a narrow table. The other children gathered around her. "*Tsái?*"

"Tea," Roger confirmed Audrey's guess.

The thought of this woman offering what must have been from her limited food supply brought tears to Audrey's eyes. She blinked rapidly to clear them, then forced a smile onto her face. She shook her head, hoping not to appear rude. In Greek, she said, "Use for you and your children—not me."

"Time to head to the next stop," Roger said, speaking English for Audrey and Greek for the others. He unpacked the two duffels and apologized for having to take them, though the woman waved off any concerns. A chorus of thanks echoed through the small house.

Once outside, Roger offered to drive, which Audrey was fine with. As she climbed into the jeep, a wave of awkwardness came over her. She mumbled an apology.

"For what?" Roger asked as he pulled away from the house.

Audrey cast one last glance over her shoulder at the woman standing outside the house. Her five children were tightly gathered around her, their arms linked, smiles spread across their faces. The youngest held the stuffed bear. That was the last straw! She wiped her eyes and turned away. "For being way too emotional when I know I shouldn't be."

"Give yourself a break—we're in the middle of a war, people are starving to death, and we just visited a woman who I'm willing to bet my life on that she's barely hanging on, holding herself together for her children's sakes. I'd question you if you didn't shed a tear. Ah, hell." He sniffled. "I might just cry, too."

"Don't you dare." She touched his arm. In the most serious tone she could muster, yet with a smile, she added, "I need you to drive us safely to the next stop, then to the next, and back to base. Understand, pal?"

Roger nodded. "You did well with those kids. Do you want any? Our two little boys keep Wanda and me plenty busy, but we can't imagine life without them."

"Children are nice, for sure." She chuckled. "First, I'll work on meeting the right man, and then…" Her mind filled with a particular man's face, but she quickly dismissed it since it wasn't likely to happen.

"Audrey? Are you going to cry on me again?"

"Oh, stop, Roger," she teased back. "Like I said, first things first. For now, I definitely have a lot to focus on rather than getting all swoony over a fictional Mr. Right."

They drove for another fifteen minutes in comfortable silence. Roger resumed his role as tour guide. "See over there?" he said, pointing to a stretch of open land before a hillside. "I know you won't believe this, but it's the God's honest truth. When I first came to Greece two years ago in '42, I saw a man and woman, spread out on a makeshift picnic blanket, enjoying a bite to eat… maybe something else afterward." He laughed. "Who knows? War does make for interesting companions at the oddest times."

"Yes, I can imagine. Especially with the threat of losing one's life."

"It's a nice spot, isn't it? Right at the base of the mountain, there's a little creek." He made a right turn and pointed upward. "I hear there's an ancient church on the other side of the mountain—you can't see it at all from the road. I'd love to hike up there someday to check it out and explore all the other historic sites across Greece. That is, when I don't have to worry about getting shot at or stepping on a mine."

"Don't laugh," Audrey said, "but I swear, when the camp is quiet, especially at night and there's a soft breeze, I hear the strumming of a lyre and the bright rattle of a tambourine."

"It's possible. Considering all the history of this country, I wouldn't be surprised if certain things—sounds, scents, maybe a ghost or two—have gotten trapped right where our camp is. Well, at least I'd like to believe that. Somehow, that makes me less afraid to face tomorrow."

"Less afraid? How's that?"

"I like to believe that life—in all its greater glory—goes on. You know, like when someone dies, their spirit keeps living." Roger swept his hand from left to right. "That humanity isn't in vain, that one person, one force of evil, can never wipe out goodness."

Audrey reflected on the possibilities that could be. Like the boy Ruth had mentioned, dying of starvation, his eyes wide with shock and despair at the thought that no one would feed him. Of all those taken by cancer and other cruel illnesses far too soon. Of the losses that accidents and unforeseen tragedies claimed. She turned away from Roger for a moment. *Do not cry,* she ordered herself. *Hold it together.* She faced him again. "Yes, I can see how believing that certain aspects of life remain, even when we can't see them with our eyes, would make it easier to start each new day knowing it wasn't in vain."

He straightened in his seat. "Before we reach our next stop, let me ask you something else."

"Sure, as long as it's not my weight." When he narrowed his eyes, she grinned. "Sorry. I guess I needed to joke. Ask away."

"Although the Red Cross has traditionally focused on comforting those in mental anguish, it is now also heading in a new direction—one that supports families in searching for children separated during a war. After seeing how you interacted with those children at the last house, helping them feel at ease, I believe you would be perfect for this kind of aid. I know the small group of men and women running this service in Greece—they could really use your help."

"Me? I just did what any other person would do—try to soothe a child. Besides, why would you say that? I wasn't at that house for long."

"I saw enough to tell me that you would be perfect for the job." He leaned toward her as if to share a secret. "I know what I saw, lady. I have no doubts about your capabilities. I can put in a good word for you. Just say when."

10

LISELOTTE/ANNA, GERMANY, 1944

The clock on the bedside stand struck five o'clock, and Anna immediately growled at it, flipped it face down, swept the blanket off herself, and slid out of bed. She nearly tripped on her borrowed bathrobe from the Frau. In her rush to reach the kitchen and free Frau Agers from bringing her son's breakfast tray, she splashed water on her face, brushed her hair and teeth, got dressed, and hurried from the carriage house to the main house. In the past, she often played a mental game linking gray clouds or bad weather to a warning to be cautious. This morning, she chose to ignore the still-dark sky with its full moon. Whether it was an omen or not, she was determined to make each day of her life unfold as she wished. She would have no one to blame but herself if she didn't at least try. With a plan to slip away from controlling Klaus and his standoffish parents, she needed to stay in the present, not dwell on her haunting past or worry about what tomorrow might bring.

Despite the wartime conditions, the back kitchen door to the Agers' home was usually unlocked. It wouldn't have mattered—if the SS or Gestapo wanted to enter a house or any other building, they definitely wouldn't have waited for an invitation. Quietly entering, Anna was relieved not to see the Frau. She blinked. Maybe Klaus's mother had an early start, already cooking and bringing her son his breakfast. The absence of pots on the stovetop or mixing bowls on the table eased her breathing. "May I help you, Fräulein Bauer?"

Anna flinched at the Frau's icy tone, then steadied herself. "*Guten Morgen.* Today is the day Herr Agers wanted to review some essential paperwork." She remembered how Klaus was fully awake the morning she hoped to sneak out of the bomb shelter, away from him. "Since Herr Agers is an early riser who prefers to get work done right away, I didn't want to disappoint him and thought I could bring him breakfast and coffee to start the day." She averted her gaze to the floor to appear modest, leaving a strand of hair shadowing her face. "May I do so, Frau Agers? I'm so new to this job, which honors the Reich, that I'm trying my best to do everything just right. I figured that after not seeing Herr Agers for—"

The woman raised a hand to stop her. "Tired of eggs, my son requested last evening that he would like toast and jam. You know where those ingredients are, so go ahead and make it, why don't you? I'll put up a pot of coffee and bring it to his room later."

Oh, I'll have my eggs scrambled this morning, Frau. Thanks for asking. No toast, though. "*Danke,* Frau Agers." Without delay, Anna pulled out a loaf of rye bread from the built-in wooden bread box on the kitchen counter, its aroma of caraway seeds reminding her of the licorice she enjoyed as a rare treat in her childhood. She quickly sliced a couple of thick pieces on a wooden cutting board and put them in the electric toaster, then added an apple from a nearby basket to his tray. Next, she grabbed a jar of homemade raspberry jam from the refrigerator, wincing at the memory of telling her mother she was tired of eating rice and beans. How many other Germans were enjoying the luxury of delicious food that filled the Agers' home? Then another, more recent memory flooded her mind and stopped her in her tracks: the POW camp that she and Klaus visited. Those men—and boys—certainly were not eating half as well as in this household. Fully aware that the Frau's gaze was on her, Anna grasped the tray and headed toward the stairs.

"That's a perfectly sized serving you've prepared," Frau Agers said, making Anna feel as if she were cornered prey. "And you two haven't known each other long?"

"Correct," Anna replied, her mouth dry. Reflecting on the many meals she had once enjoyed with Gerhard and how he always had a ready appetite, she stretched the truth about Klaus and hoped she was right. "From what I've seen of your son eating, I know he usually has a good appetite."

"*Ja,* that he does," the Frau said, surprising Anna with a warm smile. "He can outdo his sisters and father any day."

"Herr Agers speaks fondly of his sisters. He has no brothers, right?"

"Two girls and one boy are plenty for me."

"Pardon, I didn't mean to imply—"

The woman waved her hand to stop Anna from speaking. "You're fine. Do not repeat this, but it was my pleasure to spoil my son."

Amazed by Frau Ager's unexpected confession, Anna nodded and stayed silent. So, Klaus was his mother's little prince. All right, then. Noticing that, it's likely he couldn't do any wrong, at least in his mother's eyes.

Frau Agers pointed to the stairwell at the back of the kitchen. "You can take the tray to my son using those stairs—it's more direct. His room is the second on the right."

Anna thanked the woman she suspected cared deeply for her family, as she should, and proceeded. A quarter of the way up, she stopped when she heard a loud sigh from the Frau, still in the kitchen.

"He's my little prince," the Frau said, using the exact description Anna had thought moments ago. However, she had spoken so softly that Anna decided she was probably talking to herself. "A shame," the woman added, "that it's only when Klaus and I are away from his father."

Anna gripped the handrail so tightly that her palm pinched. Clearly, some friction existed in Klaus's family despite the rosy illusion of togetherness he had painted for her in his description. Did they have more in common than not? This little insight into Klaus might just be the start of bringing them closer. The thing was, she wasn't sure she wanted a man in her life anytime soon. He was handsome, she had to admit. He seemed to be a hard worker and came from a good family, though she really did not have a clear grasp of what defined a loving family.

The upstairs hall walls featured bright yellow-painted wainscoting on the bottom half, topped with wallpaper decorated with red and brown flowers. Its cheerfulness did not help her increasing agitation. Her hands began to shake. To stop the tray from rattling further, she pressed against the wall, steadying her nerves. What was wrong with her? Most of her time with Klaus was spent wanting to get away from him. Was this a crush? Was she so lonely or afraid that she needed Klaus Agers in her life, forever and ever? No. There would be no Klaus in her personal life. She continued to his room out of duty, and nothing else.

Following the Frau's instructions, she quickly found Klaus's room. After knocking and announcing her name, she felt relieved when Klaus invited her inside. If she had expected to find a pale man lying in bed, eyes closed and barely able to gesture for her to set down the tray, she could not have been more wrong. She was also mistaken in thinking he would be confined to a single bedroom. Instead, he occupied a spacious room with a visible arch leading to two other rooms. The pinkish morning light streaming in through large six-over-six paned windows made the place quite pleasant.

Klaus, fully dressed in a forest green pullover sweater, black trousers, and comfortable shoes, groomed with a shave and brushed hair, stepped confidently out of what must have been a private water closet. "I'm glad you're here."

"You must be hungry." Noticing a cherry side table next to an armchair, she walked toward it to set the tray down, but was taken aback when he grasped the tray and set it down himself.

"I've never been much of a breakfast eater, so let's get out of this chicken coop and go for a walk. I have a lot to talk to you about."

Well, clearly, she was mistaken about him enjoying hearty breakfasts. "I'm glad to see you're up and about. I was under the impression that the doctor wants you to rest for a week or possibly longer."

"Nonsense. All I have is a constant headache and fatigue."

"You experienced a major blow to your head, which the doctor said—"

"I know what he said, and I know how I feel."

"You'll worry your mother if she brings the coffee pot up here like she said she would, and you—and I—are not present."

"Doesn't matter. I need to get out of here—want to feel the fresh air on my face."

She glanced around the suite. "This house—and your rooms—hardly resemble a chicken coop, as you've described. Besides, your mother will personally escort me to one of those prisoner camps if I let you out of this… this palace."

He chuckled. "I knew it. You're not concerned for me. Rather, you're terrified of my mother."

She was about to argue, but as soon as she opened her mouth, he continued.

"No worries, Anna. I'll make sure that Frau Extraordinaire doesn't baste you for dinner." Klaus gently touched her chin, lifting it with his finger so their eyes met. His familiar, tender tone surprised her. He loosened her arms, which she had unknowingly wrapped around herself. Then he did the one thing she would not have expected: he pulled her against his chest and ran his fingers through her hair. "It will be fine—I'll make sure of that for you."

Dazed by her desire to stay tucked in his protective arms but driven by the instinct to resist, she stepped back. She forced herself to meet his gaze. "Let's go outside, as you suggested. The cool winter air will be good for both of us."

"All right." He moved to the closet, grabbed a jacket, and tossed it to her. "This should keep you plenty warm." Then he mouthed, "Follow me."

"Can you walk okay?" she whispered.

Instead of replying, he opened the door to the hallway. Rather than turning left—the direction she had come from—he turned right and led them to another stairwell she had never seen before. She followed him outside, straight into the side yard, which was opposite the wing that housed the kitchen and parlor. This exit plan would likely keep them out of his mother's sight.

After a few minutes of walking, she glanced at Klaus to see if he was having trouble breathing, swaying with dizziness, or squinting from the bright sunlight. He seemed to pass each of those checks. She decided to ask, just to be safe.

"Are you managing well enough to continue?" Still feeling self-conscious after being in his embrace a moment ago and unsure how that made her feel, she struggled to find humor. "I don't think I could pick you up if you fainted on me, let alone carry you back to the house."

"No worries." He gestured to the left. "At the end of this path, there's a thicket that leads to the Saale River—a pleasant, short walk, though we won't go all the way to the water. I have an important proposal to discuss with you, and this walk should give us the privacy we need."

With no practical alternative to suggest, she nodded in agreement. They continued walking in silence for about five more minutes, following a straight path that carried them farther from the neighboring houses. It was just the two of them; not even a red deer foraged in the wooded vegetation for breakfast. With every step, she grew more tense, unable to tolerate the silence any longer.

"May we talk now about what is so urgent that we need to sneak away from your mother? Surely, she must be suspicious by now and might be right at our heels."

"This again? Do I come across as a man who can't handle his own parents?"

His abrupt, growly tone caught Anna off guard, freezing her in place.

He stopped walking and stared at her, his eyes narrow and intense. Hypnotic. She wasn't sure if that was good, bad, or just plain wrong.

"If it makes you feel better, I left a note on my bedroom desk saying I felt well enough for a walk and asked for your company. Mutter knows better than to argue or follow me. Vater, the dedicated man he is to the Reich, is already at work."

Anna suspected that many of Klaus's acquaintances knew better than to question him. She swallowed hard. If his own mother couldn't challenge him, it also meant that Anna shouldn't dare to find out what might happen if she pressed him with more questions. She waited for him to continue.

He gestured toward a low stone wall, likely an old farmer's wall once built to divide a pasture. He leaned against it, placing his palms on each side of his hips. A look of exhaustion clouded his eyes. Contrary to what he said, he had suffered a serious injury that he was cautioned about and should have taken more seriously than his casual brush-off. It was bad enough that, out of fear of another reprimand, she held back from voicing her concerns further.

"Sit beside me," Klaus said, waiting until she did. "Back when we first met and took cover at the shelter, you seemed flustered when I asked if you had children, and more so when I commented that at your age, there would be plenty of time to bear children for the Fatherland."

She had felt more than just flustered, but knew better than to risk irritating someone she was starting to see as having a short fuse. "Yes," she said simply.

"There are many orphaned children in need of a good German home. We may have introduced you to my parents as my new secretary, but I want to do more for you."

She held her breath.

"Especially because I know you can do more for Germany." He reached for her hand, his touch warm despite the morning's coolness. She might not be a professional anything, but she knew that, especially in a business relationship, they shouldn't be holding hands. But if she moved hers away, would that send the right or wrong message and cause her more problems? She might fake a sneeze or a cough, but he would probably see through her act, and then what?

He squeezed her hand and gently brushed his fingers across her cheek. Before she could reply, he softly hushed her. "Anna, you act overprotectively of someone—maybe a few someones. And, as much as you try to appear mature, I think you're actually younger than you claim."

She remembered telling him that, after the war, she hoped to find the man who would be the right husband and father of her children. What she left out was that she had already met that man, and was still suffering the trouble and heartache it caused her—and ultimately, him.

"You know, Herr Agers, war has an awful way of aging a person."

"When it's just the two of us, it's Klaus," he reminded her, a twitch pulling at the corner of his mouth. He leaned toward her ear, even though no one else seemed to be within hearing distance. "I can easily uncover the facts about you, Anna," he whispered, his breath a caress she did not appreciate. He leaned back slightly. "I can find out what you're hiding—or is it whom you're hiding? And why."

All she needed was to stand up and run. Given his condition, she could easily outpace him. As for where to go, she would decide as she went, taking it one minute at a time. With no time to waste, she stood. He grabbed her wrist, his fingers like handcuffs, and yanked her down to the stone wall, the cold stones scraping her back.

He pressed a hand to each of her shoulders, pinning her down and leaving her helpless and speechless. With his mouth near hers, he said, "Don't test me again. You and I can—will—make an excellent team. Think of it as a partnership. You do what I say on behalf of the Reich, and you'll live. Even better, someday you'll be free to keep fleeing the miserable life you seem eager to escape and start fresh. If not, I will investigate you and uncover everything the Reich needs to know about you—and any loved ones you might have. Trust me, you won't want to live another day." He pulled back, sweeping his hand under her chin to meet her gaze. "Also, keep in mind, I have already started preliminary investigations on you."

"You... what?" While there was a slight chance he was bluffing to force her cooperation, there was a greater chance he was not. She would be a fool to think that he hadn't looked into who she was this whole time, whether when he first grabbed their getaway car at the POW camp or, more recently, from his parents' house. He gave the word *incapacitation* a new meaning. She held back the urge to question further, argue, or tell him he had no right to control how she should live, much less assume how she had lived in the past or what she wanted for the future. He was evidently a high-ranking Nazi with ties to all the wrong people she knew to avoid.

"Tell me…" His sudden blinking and swaying surprised her.

She pushed him back. Aware that she could leave and escape without him following, she also knew she had to help him. Sure, there was a chance he was pretending his injury was acting up to get her to cooperate, but she needed to behave humanely despite his threats.

"Klaus, let me help you get home. You need to rest."

He raised his hand. "Let me catch my breath. I'll be fine."

"But—"

"Don't make me swear at you," he said more forcefully than he behaved.

She crossed her arms. "Why not? Is swearing somehow worse than threatening my life?"

"I need to finish our conversation before heading back."

"Hurry, then."

He nodded, then winced. "I want you to come with me when I try to move the children to Germany. You'll be safe—guards will be with us at all times."

What was he talking about? Which children? Where were they? Although he had supposedly started an investigation into her past, she needed to learn a few more things.

"None of this makes sense. Start from the beginning—and leave out the threats."

"It benefits the greater good of the Reich. You want to do everything you can for the betterment of Germany, right?"

Despite his condition, refusing him would trigger immediate anger and likely cause her death. If she wanted to survive and keep searching for Rosa, she had no choice. "Of course, I do."

"But?"

She licked her dry bottom lip. "What would I have to do?"

"Let's start our walk back to the house."

"Are you up for that? We can sit here longer if you wish."

Klaus stood up. Without wobbling, he continued walking down the path they started on, not bothering to glance back at her.

"That's the trouble between us," she shouted, painfully aware that she should keep her thoughts to herself but couldn't. She followed after him. "I'm not sure if I'm more disgusted by your arrogance or by myself for obliging you."

He snickered. "That's one of the things I like about you, Anna. You can be unexpectedly funny. Okay, this is the start you insist on learning: We're increasing our Germanization of Poland."

"What exactly does that mean?" she asked, quickening her pace until she was beside him.

"We're eliminating Polish culture and its people."

She froze, breathless, wishing she could block out all the chaos of life until after the war ended and everything was at least halfway right with the world again. "How can Germany do that? Invade a country and erase its people's culture?" She gasped, slapping her hand over her mouth.

"Come, come, Anna. We are Germany, and we aim to set this tilted world right."

Eliminating. Klaus used that purging word in the same sentence that ended with the phrase *its people*.

"But... how—"

"By doing what all countries or groups of people have done since humans first roamed the Earth—we conquer, control, and decide what is best."

"Regarding who will live and who will die?" she said quietly, the awful words leaving a bitter taste in her mouth.

"You're absolutely correct." He glared at her sideways. "Why the sudden naivety? Germany is handling matters, one country at a time. The Reich will reign for the next thousand years—if the Holy Roman Empire could do it, then Germany can and will as well. It's acting in the best interest of the world and its people. As you know, those outside the Aryan race can be detrimental to leading a good and proper life by bringing down the strong, superior ones. These outsiders must be eliminated."

There was that cursed e-word again—eliminate. "And the Polish children? My role?"

"There is no such thing as Polish children—remove that term immediately from your vocabulary. In that former country, there are those sub-humans born to Jews and other non-Aryans. Fortunately, there are superb children born to noble Aryan parents. We seek out the latter children—orphans and often homeless—who are suitable for Germany and make them German by removing anything of Polish origin, including names, language, education, schools, seminaries, and town and city names, and replacing them with German ones. On behalf of Heinrich Himmler, I've been working to remove *racially* good children and relocate them here in the Fatherland."

On behalf? That was an odd way to phrase this type of work, where one group of people forced another, but she would not question his choice of words right now. With each word Klaus uttered, her stomach lurched. She could not understand—never would be able to grasp this concept of hatred spewing from his or any Nazi's mouth. Anna fought the urge to wrap her arms around her middle.

"Why the look of dismay?" Klaus asked.

Evidently, her facial features must have given her away. "Because you are making it sound like these children are separated from their families, kidnapped, and dragged back here like animals tossed into a zoo cage—that they're commodities. I must have misunderstood."

He shook his head slowly, resembling a teacher showing disapproval. "Not quite. This plan—*Generalphan Ost*—GPO—aims to prioritize the well-being of the right children by giving them a much better home than their families could have ever imagined. As I mentioned a moment ago, these children are orphans, and often, they're homeless, living on the streets. This is a kind and compassionate act."

Since mentioning that it seemed to her these children would have thrived in a stable family if Germany had never invaded and occupied Poland, she kept silent because it would have been pointless with

Klaus and might have caused her serious trouble or harm. "And the well-being of the wrong children?"

He made a clucking noise. "Anna—what am I going to do with you? As a German, you should know better than to play the do-gooder to those who are weakening the German race." He narrowed his gaze at her, his usual warning. Sensing his growing anger and disgust, she looked away. "You don't want me—or others—to think that you care for those we've taken the time to sort out, declaring them unworthy of Germanization, do you?"

Did Klaus mean that the German government had the authority to decide who was a valuable human being? Maybe she came from a strong family line, rich with pure German blood running through her veins, but if she agreed with him, she would become the very lesser human who did not deserve respect—the ones the Nazi party aimed to *eliminate*.

"Several locations," Klaus continued before she could reply, "have been established in Polish cities to house the children when we… find them. Sometimes, the children come from as far as Yugoslavia and Hungary. They are given new German names—both first and last—and are forbidden to speak Polish, which helps them learn German. They learn everything about being German to the point of believing they *are* German. Unless they become difficult and resistant. Usually, this happens with the older children, especially if they discover the truth. Because of that, the younger ones are the most desirable."

Although Anna didn't expect the truth from Klaus, ironically, she asked, "What is this truth you mentioned?"

"That their parents have abandoned them, or sometimes, realizing that they can help their families financially by living with others who have better means to support them. Then, we bring them here to Germany to enjoy a splendid life."

Living in a war-torn country, at the mercy of those who destroy lives in other occupied nations just because Germany considers other options unviable? To Anna, it definitely sounded like kidnapping and indoctrination, not parental abandonment.

"Klaus, I'm not sure how much I can contribute to this operation."

He gently lifted her chin again so she could look him in the eye. His tall presence looming over her didn't help soothe her shattered nerves.

"Of course, you have a lot to offer—you'll be a great addition to the GPO. I wouldn't have asked otherwise. If you want me to stop investigating you, you'll need to agree to help us."

Another direct threat? If he was that unsure about her, then why was he even bothering with her? Surely, there were better candidates than her—someone he had just met during a bomb raid—and someone who would clearly show full Nazi Party loyalty. "What would I do?" she asked in an attempt to steer the conversation in a way he would see as positive.

"Once the children are located, they need to be processed. That's where I believe you will be especially helpful. With your soft, welcoming features and gentle way of speaking, you will put the children at ease, calming their fears." He narrowed the distance between them, weaving his fingers through her hair. "You've certainly shown your tender side to me, helping me relax. I can't imagine you not having a positive impact on our efforts to improve Germany."

Her breath felt like it had frozen inside her. One moment, he threatened her; the next, he praised her as if he had fallen in love with her, like a schoolboy acting on a crush, and she could do no wrong in his eyes.

She stepped back from Klaus. He was seriously mistaken. An unloving mother, who cared more about her boyfriend than her two daughters, she had abandoned her remaining twin after learning that the Nazis had taken Rosa. She was the worst person to help a scared child. But since it was clear that he would ignore her and instead tell her how to act, she decided to take control. For now, she told him she would consider his offer. Tonight, though, she would do what she should have done days earlier.

11

LISELOTTE/ANNA

Contradicting Klaus's expectations, Anna was right that Frau Agers would be worried about her son going for a walk—with his secretary, no less—despite the doctor's orders to stay in bed in a quiet room. When his mother hurried out to greet Klaus, Anna stepped aside to give them privacy. The farther she was from him, both physically and emotionally, the easier she found it to breathe. It was challenging enough to listen to Klaus outline the GPO Nazi plan that glorified reprogramming innocent children, all supposedly to increase Germany's Aryan population—a notion she increasingly doubted was not just kidnapping those children. However, with Frau standing at the house entrance, watching them closely and looking adoringly at her son, Anna couldn't help but wonder if his mother was completely unaware of what her son was doing. Or was she, like many other parents of Nazi children and members of the Nazi Party, proud of their child?

"*Sohn*, once again, you prove your mastery of making me worry."

"I've just taken a walk, and I'm no worse for it," Klaus replied, despite a slight sway in his step as he and his mother approached the door. "I just need a little rest, that's all. Fräulein Bauer and I will leave right after breakfast tomorrow, and it's wise for both of us to rest, considering our journey."

The woman, seemingly forgetting or ignoring Anna completely, was about to close the door on her, but Anna managed to grip the doorknob and follow them inside. Instead of going into another room, mother and her son stayed by the door and kept talking, leaving Anna to overhear every word.

"Ridiculous, Klaus. You just got home, and you're already planning to leave again? In your condition? I contacted your sisters, and they're coming for a family dinner on Saturday. Won't that be nice? You can—"

"Mutti, we're at war. Trust me, many other men are in worse shape than I am. We need to return to Poland. I'm sure my sisters will understand. I just wanted to check on you and Vater."

His mother shuddered. "I've heard about what's happening in that occupied land."

"Then you understand the terrible situation of the former country, which is exactly why my visit here has to be cut short."

The Frau cast a sideways glance at Anna. "And you must bring her?"

"Of course. She has now been promoted to Operations Assistant."

It was bad enough that the Frau talked about her as if she weren't there, but now Klaus was doing the same.

"Pardon me. I feel a headache coming on. Now it's my turn to rest." Anna walked toward the kitchen door to leave and go back to her guest bedroom in the carriage house, fully aware that neither Klaus nor his mother offered her assistance. Perfect.

"One moment, Fräulein Bauer." Frau Agers waited for her to turn and face her. "There is aspirin in your bathroom. Dinner is served at six. We'll be enjoying a nice ham, and I hope you will be well enough by then to join us."

"That would be nice," Klaus added.

He sounded too charming, and his mother expressed genuine sincerity, for Anna to wiggle out of the invitation. Without a real headache, as she had claimed, she planned to fine-tune her escape route, especially since she had walked around the area with Klaus that morning. Also, she wanted to pack her belongings—the little she had. However, she figured she could do this after dinner. Besides, she would need a good meal in her stomach to make a run from Klaus.

"*Danke*, Frau Agers." She turned to open the door, but, glancing over her shoulder, she said, "I'll rest now and see you at six."

ANNA VISUALIZED the dinner table in the dining room as it once was, maintained to the standards of a more formal decor. Now, the overall atmosphere felt subdued, but she could still appreciate its faded elegance, especially given the current worldwide war. A lacy white tablecloth draped over a solid white linen cloth, with two lit silver candlesticks, created a cozier arrangement of the eight thick, upholstered chairs around the table than she would have expected in the Agers' household. Less elegant was the worn carpet beneath her feet, a chipped flower pot on a fireplace mantle darkened by what she suspected was a film of dust, and a nearby window curtain with its right section sporting a hole.

"Come join us, Fräulein Bauer," the senior Herr said, standing up and greeting her from his seat at the far end of the table. Anna hesitated for a moment to recall his first name—Heinz—just as she noticed his brows furrow. "Has your headache subsided yet?"

Goodness. Anna hoped she hadn't frowned or, worse, revealed other nervous feelings. The Frau sat on the left side of the table, her hair pulled back tightly in a braided bun, her facial features tense. Klaus, sitting across from his mother, also stood to greet her. With an unreadable expression, he gestured toward the remaining seat beside him.

"I'm fine, Herr Agers," Anna said. "I appreciate your concern, but I assure you my headache has thankfully eased. I believe the room's cheerful lighting just now played tricks on my senses for a moment." It was a flimsy excuse, but hopefully it distracted him from her well-being, which mattered little to him—or any of them.

Frau Agers apologized for not having any help to cook or serve the dinner, but assured everyone that the meal would be tasty. She headed toward the kitchen.

"Would you like my help?" Anna asked, trying to put some distance between herself and the father and son. The Frau thanked her but declined the offer and quickly exited the dining room, as if she also wanted to create more space between herself and her family.

"Tell me, Klaus, how work is progressing," Herr Agers asked his son.

Klaus turned pale and tapped his head. "Aside from my physical mishap, very well." He avoided eye contact with Anna. "With the Red Army chasing us, we're working hard to move the orphans as fast as possible to Germany."

His father leaned into the table. Behind him, framed antique paintings of military scenes, showing uniformed men on horseback with swords and guns raised in full charge against an unseen enemy, all seemed to coordinate with the Herr to make sure he did not slip in words or actions. "If you had done what I last advised, Germany would be in a much better position than it is now. But listening to advice has never been a talent of yours."

Anna flinched as if the Herr had spoken to her directly. She glanced sideways at Klaus to see his reaction, surprised by his nonchalance. When his father reached for his wine glass, she noticed Klaus looking toward the kitchen. She wondered if he was nervous about his mother entering the room and hearing her husband verbally lashing out at their son, maybe demanding to leave Klaus alone. They have a guest. What's wrong with him that he has to air family issues openly? Yet, when she peeked at Klaus again and saw how he seemed unfazed by his father's ridicule, she began to believe that poor Klaus was used to a father who might never think he did enough.

Poor Klaus? Since when did she start feeling sorry for him? He was a Nazi who followed Hitler's orders, not someone showing kindness. His father was no different.

Klaus got up and excused himself, saying he wanted to check on his mother. Anna suspected he was trying to get away from his father, after all.

"Anna, if I'm understanding correctly, my son now has you to work with?" Herr Agers asked.

The odd, most unexpected question made her lean back in her chair for support. "*Ja*, Herr Agers. I'm fortunate he wants me to work for him in bettering the Fatherland."

The Herr brushed his knuckles against his chin. "You are quite young. What did you do for work before you two met?"

She sat taller and smiled, prepared with a practiced reply. "A woman always appreciates a generous compliment like yours regarding her age, especially when she's older than she looks. As for—"

"I'm well aware of Anna's work experience," Klaus said as he re-entered the dining room carrying a tray of sliced ham and potatoes, his mother trailing behind with a bowl heaped with what looked like sauerkraut and cooked carrots. "However, that confidential information is only for me to know, Vater."

Frau Agers placed the vegetables on the table in front of her husband. "Heinz, Klaus was just telling me some very interesting news about his work. Would you like to hear it?"

Herr Agers looked up at his wife, his narrowed eyes displaying his disapproval. "You're covering up and coddling him again. Our son will never become the man he needs to be."

"Vater," Klaus interjected, "do you mean the man that *you* want me to be?" Without giving his father a chance to reply, Klaus got to his feet. "Once again, my appetite is gone. Pardon me, but I'm going for a smoke and a walk."

"Since when do you smoke?" Herr Agers asked, echoing Anna's thoughts.

"When the occasion calls for it."

"I'll bring a tray up to your room," Frau Herr said. "You have a long drive tomorrow."

Every family had its version of discord. Anna stood quickly and excused herself to return to her room.

12

LISELOTTE/ANNA

Anna had only a few toiletries to pack, and then she was ready to leave. *Leave.* What a wonderful, liberating word. She set the jacket Klaus had lent her for their earlier walk by the chair next to the door. March in Germany still felt far from springtime. She could not worry about whether this handful of items was enough. She had to escape from Klaus, who was more shocking by the second. And if she got caught? It was a huge risk, one she probably would pay with her life. Taking a chance, though, was worth it, especially if the alternative meant that she had to commit Nazi atrocities against children.

Having no home or family to return to, a job that could support her, and living in a country under attack, she struggled against the fear that her life was essentially over. Oh, she wanted to live. She would be turning eighteen this July. There was still time to improve her life. She might find Rosa, or maybe even Regina... and she might persuade her mother to let her have custody of Regina. Could her mother forgive her? Maybe it depended on her making the first effort and forgiving her mother. Good grief. She hadn't had a headache when she claimed to have one after returning from the walk with Klaus, but if she kept dwelling on these thoughts, she would only invite a nasty pounding in her temples—an ailment that would slow her down... Fleeing from a situation she shouldn't be in to begin with? Bolting from a reality she didn't have the courage to face? She had her children to be concerned about, not casting blame for Rosa's disappearance. But what did she do? She ran off. As for Klaus, she should be more concerned about innocent children being separated from their families and countries. Not that she could single-handedly combat the Nazis and stop the war, but perhaps if she remained by Klaus's side, she could be more productive for the greater good. Instead, was she about to run away again? Could it be time to break free from her faulty tendency of escaping when things get tough, to grow up and stop only thinking of herself? A knock came at the door.

About to shove the *Seesack* under the bed, she glanced at the antique pedestal mirror in the corner. The irony of how comfortable she felt in this very room, in what could be a charming residence if it were another time and circumstances were far different, did not make her feel more at ease.

Another knock. "Anna?" Klaus called. "May I come in?"

She very likely could not say no. She opened the door just a crack, enough for their gazes to meet. For a moment, she could not move. Did not want to. Then, all that Klaus had told her—the children forcibly taken from their families and their native country of Poland—rushed through her mind. She gripped the door frame so tightly that her hand hurt.

"I hope I'm not disturbing you," he said. "Sorry you had to witness the Agers-circus tonight."

While his apology on behalf of his family was unexpected, she was unsure of her role. Should she dare to comment as a guest—one who was about to leave soon—that although she could be sensitive to him, his father's actions did not affect her? Or, as his new assistant, was it her responsibility to stay neutral regarding her employer's personal issues? Should she be a friend, a confidant, telling him he can feel free to share anything he wishes because she has supportive shoulders to lean on? Just as she decided it was best not to take on any role other than being herself—a person with her own life to straighten out—he pushed the door open and walked into the room.

"What you've observed about my father's behavior is typical. He competes with me as if whoever can do the most for Germany wins the greatest prize in heaven."

"Does he always put you down whenever he can?"

Klaus nodded. "And Mutti picks me up, but never in front of him." He snorted. "My sisters—older and wiser—stay away as much as they can."

"All this time, I believed you had an enviable family." She stepped back against the chest of drawers and lowered her chin to avoid looking at him.

"Enviable?"

She knew she should have remained quiet. At best, she needed to take control of the situation, especially to steer him away from the topic of family, her greatest vulnerability and, clearly, his weakness as well. She didn't need to bond with Klaus Agers over anything. "I have my own troubled family ghosts that haunt me."

"You must be hungry. Would you like me to bring you a tray of toast, maybe a couple of eggs, and some tea? I don't cook often, but I can manage that."

His shift of focus from his family did not go unnoticed by her. "No, thank you," she replied, hoping her stomach wouldn't betray her with a growl. She usually moved faster when she had less food in her system.

He walked to the door and pulled it open, then paused. "Well, if you change your mind, you're more than welcome to help yourself. My parents have already retired for the night. We leave at six in the morning. I'll knock on your door at five—will that be enough time?"

"That's plenty of time. Thank you." She was tired of this polite little chat and was relieved when he stepped into the hallway. "*Gute Nacht.*" Just as she was about to close the door, she nearly gasped when he stuck his hand in the gap between the door and the frame. "My goodness, Klaus. I could have hurt you."

He smiled. "Good. You're again calling me by my first name, which I appreciate, especially from you. No worries, Anna. You didn't hurt me, just as I won't hurt you. Don't trouble yourself as we enter Poland —what's left of it. I'll look out for your safety. Always."

Unsure of what to do or say, she nodded slightly. This time, she did close the door, but he pushed it open again.

She stepped back, clutching the V of her burgundy sweater.

"One more thing—actually, a quick reminder—and then I'll leave you for the night."

Although she could predict what he would say, feeling silly, she stood there like a loyal soldier and waited.

"I trust you will stay put tonight."

She tilted her head. "Of course I will. What an odd thing to say."

He shook his head without showing any signs of dizziness, unlike how he had experienced his concussion over the past few days. The corners of his eyes crinkled as a grin played on his lips. "Not when it comes to you, Anna," he said, then left the room without saying another word.

Always eager for a challenge, Anna was now more determined than ever to escape. With her bare feet, she padded across the thick rug to the window. Relief washed over her at the sight of only a sliver of moonlight, and excitement surged through her. The darkness had never stopped her before. She had clearly improved her traveling skills after sneaking out of her house in the middle of the night to meet Gerhard. Now, with Klaus, it was just a matter of minutes before she would be on the move again.

Anna was running for her life. Eager to move as fast as possible, she left the Seesack behind in the guest bedroom, thinking it would be bulky and slow her down. Ready to stretch the truth if confronted by soldiers or anyone, she would rely on her quick, on-the-spot creativity that hadn't failed her yet. She also made sure to keep her identity papers in the pocket of the trousers Frau Agers had given her. For now, her main goal was to reach the Saale River that Klaus had mentioned during their walk yesterday. She prayed that by then, she would have the wisdom to decide whether to head north toward Berlin—to find her remaining family, if they had survived the recent bombings—or to go south, to whatever place offered a new beginning for her.

Without natural light to see by, the first sensation that washed over her was silence. All she could think about as she hurried away from the house was how beautiful and peaceful the quiet sounded. No one to scold her, no one to tell her how they thought she should live her life, no one to say she was too young to make adult decisions. Even better, her own conscience left her alone, especially regarding whether or not she had made the right choice to leave Klaus. With each step, she realized how sharp her sense of smell had become. Relaxed and free from daytime restrictions, she took a deep breath of the crisp late-winter air, letting her lungs enjoy the scent of pine, wet leaves, and the thick smoke billowing from chimneys that always conjured the image of reading a book while cuddled under quilts beside a fireplace on a cold winter night.

The intensity of her escape caused her to push aside her vulnerability, freeing herself in the process. As she moved deeper into the dense cluster of trees, she slowed down and began to use her hands in front of her to feel her way. She forced herself not to think of her mother and daughters, the people she met while searching for Gerhard and his family, and the strangers she encountered while living homeless on Berlin's streets. A tall, young, and far too thin man. A woman of unknown age carrying—and constantly dropping—three duffel bags. Another woman, heavily pregnant, clutching her belly as if already holding her baby. Two old, ragged men sharing a cigarette on a street corner. Eyes peering out from a stack of crates, with scars under their once-bright blue irises that had seen better days. Like her, they were victims of the war. This wasn't the first time—and probably not the last—that people paid the price for brutal fighting.

After walking for about twenty minutes, a roaring sound ahead made her stop—finally, the river. This signaled she had reached a critical decision point: either return to her past to make amends or move toward a new beginning, as is often said during wartime.

Movement came from behind her. She moved forward and heard the sharp snap of twigs from behind. She paused, and the cracking sound stopped as well. She kept going, but once again, she sensed movement behind. Her heart hammered in her chest. She paused again. The sound of whoever was following receded. Deer? Stone marten? She swallowed hard. A person? The feeling of being followed felt incredibly real. She wasn't nervous about an animal but worried it was a person—especially Klaus—and what he might do to her. Without calling out to inquire further, she raced ahead.

Despite the darkness, she leapt over fallen branches, dodged a suspicious-looking snow pile hiding who knows what beneath, and narrowly avoided getting slapped in the face by a low branch. Unable—and not wanting to block thoughts of her family as she had moments ago—she sprinted with determination, driven by her desire to reunite with her daughters and live a fulfilling life. She burst out of the thick woods. Everything seemed quiet.

A shove to the ground silenced her scream. She landed face down but quickly rolled over, ready to fight back. She opened her mouth to try another scream, but a hand covered her lips, blocking her cry for help. The attacker pressed down on her chest, pinning her to the cold ground.

"Stop fighting me," a deep male voice demanded.

This was not Klaus. The wooded darkness hid his features, but his paunchy stomach leaning against her and his rough voice indicated he was a few decades older than Klaus. Suddenly, he yanked her pants down. Cold dampness whipped around and through her, causing her to start trembling.

"Be quiet. Stay still. Once I finish, you can leave." He laughed. "Maybe."

She bit his fingers. Something or someone shoved him away.

She turned around. Klaus.

Using a knife, Klaus sliced the attacker's throat and kicked the louse away from her. He helped Anna to her feet, then grabbed her arm and pulled her into his embrace.

She stepped back. "No. Don't touch me... hurt me."

"I would never hurt you, Anna." He turned to spit at her assailant. "I'm the one who saved you. I'm the one who will always protect you." Before she could protest, he took a step forward and, this time, pulled her into his embrace more firmly. "What are you doing out here?"

Warmth enveloped her, not quite like when her mother covered her with an afghan during an illness, but more like the feeling of a personal protector forming a barrier between her and a storm. Feeling his strong grip holding her firmly against him, she realized struggling was pointless. She also admitted to herself that she did not want to break free from his hold. Still, she was unwilling to reveal the truth about her nighttime walk.

She pulled back. "Fresh air does wonders for my headaches. Knowing about the long trip ahead, I wanted to come back here, hoping to find the river. I thought I could finally shake the throbbing in my head and enjoy the sights between here and Poland." Hearing how ridiculous her own words sounded, she held her breath.

"Instead, you found trouble."

"Well, I wasn't looking for any," she said, hearing the defensiveness in her tone. She cast her gaze downward. Despite the darkness surrounding them like a heavy cloak, she doubted he could see her expression, but it felt right not to give him too much attention, even if he had just saved her from a heinous situation. She wrapped her arms around her middle. "I don't even have my bag, proving I wasn't running away." She cringed, reminding herself that the less said, the better. "Just needed air."

Had she said too much? Was he now even more suspicious of her? His silence only unsettled her further.

"*Ja*," he said after a stretch of seconds that felt more like hours. "I know that because your belongings are in the back seat of our vehicle. Feeling better than I have in days, I decided to start for Poland earlier than planned and went to get you from your room. Seeing the packed Seesack, I suspected you might have returned along the trail we walked earlier this afternoon and went to search for you." She felt his eyes on her and looked up. "My jacket I loaned you is also there—I can't believe you aren't dressed better for the winter cold."

Thinking it was best not to address his comments about the left-behind pack and outer garment, she looked at the dead man—the one who might very well have killed her after he violated her. So much blood. On the ground, on Klaus, on herself. On the collective hands of Germany. She jerked her head away so quickly that her neck spasmed. Fiery pain erupted along her neck and head. "Are you going to just leave that no-good monster there?"

"I can't think of a better place for him. Do you believe he's worth more of our time and consideration?"

He might have been a human being, but right now, she couldn't see him as anything more than a bastard ready to hurt her. Whether he had a family, was a devoted Nazi, or was the opposite and was wanted by the SS, she cleared her mind of concern for him and shook her head. "You're right," she said softly, painfully.

Klaus extended his hand to her, but she did not take it. With a sigh, he grasped her hand and, holding it firmly, led her back to the house. "My mother packed us breakfast for the road. Both my parents extend their farewells and good wishes to you. No reason to go back inside unless you need to use the toilet."

She couldn't bolt easily. Not now. Pushing back the fleeting feeling of how much she enjoyed being in his arms moments ago, and reminding herself of the revulsion she now felt, she relied on the hope that the right moment to escape would come. "Then, it's onward to Poland."

"Indeed, onward. It's time to go, Anna. I'm glad you're coming with me. You have my word that you have nothing to fear."

The one thing she could count on, to her advantage, was her refusal to rely on his promise.

13

AUDREY, LONDON, SEPTEMBER 1944

The door to Audrey's small—and that was being polite—office swung open. Audrey looked up just in time to see her coworker and friend, Shannon, shushing her with a finger pressed to her lips, signaling her not to acknowledge her.

Audrey leaned over the desk to close the gap between herself and her young client. Nine-year-old Jordan visited her at least once every two weeks at 14 Grosvenor Crescent in South West London. Starting on September 1, 1939, the British government evacuated millions of children, mothers, teachers, and those considered infirm during Operation Pied Piper to rural areas and even overseas to Canada and the United States before the danger of torpedoes hitting ships made crossing impossible. The date was no coincidence; it marked the exact day Germany advanced into Poland to occupy and terrorize the country in a way the world had never seen before, just two days before Britain declared war on Germany. Jordy, an only child, was brought to the train station by his mother along with other children from their neighborhood. His mother stayed behind because of her job as a nurse at one of London's hospitals.

Jordy was a determined boy, full of grit that would be admirable if not for the tragic circumstances that made him an orphan. Like many other children called back by their parents, Jordy went willingly and happily into his mother's waiting arms. However, during another wave of evacuations, he was not among those escaping danger. Miraculously, there were no bombings on Christmas Day of 1940, but during the first week of January, two bombs hit the apartment building where Jordy lived with his mother. She threw herself over Jordy but died in the blast. His dad, serving in the Royal Navy, had been missing in action for an entire year before the bombing. Jordy was the only survivor from the entire building, which had four other flats. Fortunate enough to have an aunt on the outskirts of London, he went to live with her, though her never marrying or having children meant many lonely hours for Jordy. With one in five London schools severely damaged and other school properties requisitioned during the Blitz, he spent the immediate post-bombing period helping his aunt, clearing rubble, and befriending a few homeless children.

Jordy often visited Audrey's office to ask for help finding his father. He insisted that people did not disappear without a trace, and he wouldn't fully accept the term *orphan* unless he knew his father was also dead.

Audrey held back words he couldn't hear, words he wasn't ready to face. Without official documentation, she refused to crush the child's hope. "Jordy, the good news is that there is no bad news about your father."

"You said those exact words the last time I asked."

She offered the same patient, caring smile she always had ready for him. "You're absolutely correct. And I do so because there's a lot to hope for in a strong man, like your father, who bravely has been at sea fighting to protect England—and the rest of the world—from evil countries so that you will never know what harm is about."

A frown curled Jordy's lips. "Of course, I know all about harm, Audrey. I've lost my mum. Auntie Bea's okay, but you know she's not the same as one's mum. I just want to know about my dad, that's all. The truth, I mean. I can handle it."

Audrey had encouraged Jordy to call her by her first name ever since they met. However, she still found it hard to look this child in the eye and tell him the harsh truth that sometimes families are torn apart by war, and ultimately, never for a good reason.

"Yes, I know you're a brave lad." She pulled a handful of index cards from her top desk drawer and stood. "Just like when we first met, when I filled out cards about your dad to start the tracing process, I have some fieldwork to do today. Would you like to help me?"

"You bet."

"Splendid. Why don't you wait in the hallway? I'll be right with you."

Shannon, still standing at the door, rapped on the frosted glass window. "Hello to the two best people in the world."

Although Audrey and Shannon were friends rather than just colleagues and had known each other for some time, Shannon's charming British accent still delighted Audrey and made her smile. "Come on in."

Jordy jumped to his feet. "Hi, Miss Shannon. You look nice… I mean, you look just as nice as last week." His cheeks turned red, and he quickly left the small room.

"He's such a darling," Shannon said as she entered the room and took Jordy's seat. "I want to marry him when he grows up."

Audrey playfully tapped her palm against her cheek. "There's a thirty-one-year difference between your ages. Even if you waited until he was twenty, you would be fifty-one."

"What are you trying to say, sweetie? That I'll be an old hen by then? I'll age like all human beings, but…" Shannon gave herself a quick glance. "But this chick is never going to be an old bird." After a playful sigh, she added, in a more serious tone, "Jordy seems extra sad today."

"You noticed that, too. Now that you've mentioned it, I think today is his mum's birthday."

"No wonder he's upset."

Audrey nodded. "I was thinking of taking him to the neighborhood park… Well, what's left of it. Maybe he can help me gather information about the missing relatives of any children—or adults—

we meet there. Sometimes, when we help others and shift our focus away from ourselves, we can exorcise the sorrow demon."

"I agree. I see it all the time in our line of work."

"Would you like to join us? The weather's cooperating—no rain nor chill."

"Yes, there's plenty of both on the way, all beginning next month." Shannon glanced at her wristwatch. "All right, then. I just finished with my last scheduled client for the day. First, I want to talk with you and find out what's been weighing on your shoulders."

Audrey tapped her chest. "Me? I'm fine."

"Yes, and I'm the world's richest woman."

Audrey looked out the window at a young girl and a boy playing catch. "Do you think they're brother and sister?"

"Based on their facial similarities, I would say so. They might be about a couple of years apart in age. Do you think they have a home, or are they living on the street like too many children?"

Audrey faced her friend and shrugged. "I sure hope they have a home… one with two healthy parents." She ignored her eyes watering.

Shannon patted Audrey's arm. "Oh, dear. I'm sorry. I must have rubbed a sore spot."

Audrey sniffled. "You're fine."

"Well, you aren't." Shannon sat up straighter and pointed at the window. "Look at Jordy—he's talking to an older man who was sitting all by himself until our boy decided to keep him company. See, that's a prime example of what you were just talking about when it comes to exorcising one's sorrow demons. Now, talk. It's time for you to shed those stubborn tears of yours."

"I'm not teary-eyed." In direct contradiction to her words, Audrey wiped at her eyes with her fingertips. As a caring friend, Shannon held back from teasing her and stayed silent, giving Audrey space to gather herself. Like steam rushing through a pipe in need of relief, she gave in to her low spirits. "Sorry. I admit, I'm throwing myself a pity party."

"We all do, at times."

"I joined the Red Cross shortly after Pearl Harbor was bombed.

You know—young, brave, and eager to fight for the noble cause. I believed I was doing the right thing. My parents said otherwise."

"Ouch."

Audrey nodded. "It was like I said I volunteered to join the navy and was heading to serve on a ship with torpedoes or become a female spy and might not see them for a long time, if ever again—not that any of that was wrong when it comes to defending one's country. They pointed out that I could just volunteer for the war effort at home. Safe and sound."

"Remaining under their radar?"

"You got that right, Shan."

"What happened?"

"I left. They stopped talking to me. No phone calls. No mail."

Shannon looked at the boy and girl tossing the ball back and forth. "You've mentioned a brother and sister, I believe."

Audrey sniffled again. "Yes. My bratty but lovable brother, Pete, and my precious sister, Caroline. He's now eighteen—hard for me to believe. If he hasn't been drafted or enlisted, he's probably in college, making our folks proud. I guess someone has to because I—"

Shannon squeezed Audrey's hand. "Now, now. None of that. And your sister?"

"Caroline is… Oh, my. She's thirteen this year. She's probably gorgeous with her blond, wavy hair that reaches halfway down her back. Such a good girl—sweet as an apple and kind-hearted. She probably has the boys at school lining up to ask her out, whenever Mom and Pop give her the okay." Audrey surprised herself with a chuckle. "Knowing Pop, he'll cross his arms at any boy who approaches him about dating his youngest daughter, scowl his face into one of his scary don't-mess-with-me expressions, and tell the poor boy to come back in twenty years."

"You miss them."

This was clearly not a question but more of an obvious statement. "Yes," Audrey breathed, relieved to voice her honesty aloud.

"All right, then. I'll ask you a tough question. Are you ready?"

Audrey rubbed her arms against the sudden chill. Since starting what was becoming a career with the Red Cross, she had witnessed incredible beauty. A soldier walking after being told he would never take another step again. POWs smiling in a prisoner camp upon receiving a Red Cross care package. Delivering good news in the form of a letter to those who were not expecting any. Assisting in the birth of a healthy baby in Greece. She had also seen many people suffering from heartbreak. Orphaned children. Children and the elderly made homeless by the war and living on the streets. Various workers having to travel home due to family tragedies. A couple in France smiling after their wedding, only to lose their lives in a bomb raid. And now, in England, so many people were lost and separated from each other because of the Blitz that still held the country in its grip afterward.

She looked up at her friend.

"Are you feeling guilty for not listening to your parents because you think you ruined your family by growing up and choosing independence?"

Audrey leaned back from the challenging, spot-on question. "That's a reflective question and a half. This month I've been especially focused on thinking about them—I believe because both my mother and brother have September birthdays. My memories came to me this morning... of singing happy birthday to Mom and slicing a generous piece of homemade chocolate cake for Pete." She wrapped her arms around herself. "I never imagined that wanting to help my country would lead to breaking up my family. It's not like I called them names, hurt them in any way, or became a hideous criminal they should be ashamed of."

"And yet, they treat you as if you've never existed, right?"

"Yes. I've tried writing letters from each of my Red Cross posts, and if they were received, I wouldn't know because they never replied."

"Have you phoned?"

"Yes, I've tried." Audrey lowered her chin and squeezed her eyes shut to block out the flashes of her parents' faces, as well as her brother's and sister's. "Once, I heard someone pick up. I said hello—it's me. Ha. I even said my name, just in case they didn't recognize my voice for any reason. Then I heard him… Pop. He told me to never call again. It was all too much for me and drained me for weeks. So, I never called again." After a moment, she added, "Do you know the worst part?"

Shannon shook her head.

"Here I am, helping to bring families and loved ones together, yet I can't even bring my own back from brokenness. Lately, I feel like the biggest failure of all time. I'm unsure if I should continue in this kind of work."

"That's a heavy load to bear on your shoulders. I wonder—"

"Miss Audrey… Miss Shannon…" Jordy called out as he ran toward them.

Without considering social or business propriety, Audrey stood and opened her arms to the young boy, who was without a mother and possibly a father. "What is it?" she asked as he ran into her arms. "Has something bad happened?"

"Nothing like bombs or Nazis."

"Thank God," Shannon murmured.

"But that old man I was talking to needs your help. He says he hasn't found his grandson since the Blitz. He believes he must still be alive. I told him that if anyone could help, it would be you, Audrey."

"How… me? But I haven't even…" Audrey hadn't found Jordy's father. She also hadn't found each of the missing persons among those who had filed requests.

"Yes, you," Jordy said. "You're the only person I know who has so much hope and who doesn't give up. That's why I keep coming back to your office. Maybe no one else will find my dad, but I know you will." He glanced over his shoulder. "Oh, oh. George is standing. I'd better make sure he stays there until you can speak with him. Hurry, please." He ran back outdoors.

"Nothing like pressure," Audrey said as she watched Jordy.

"He has confidence in you." Shannon patted her arm. "You're not about to give up on him, are you?"

"Of course not. I'll keep looking for Jordy's father until I get an answer—hoping it's a good one for both of their sakes."

"That's what I was counting on hearing from you." Shannon grasped Audrey's elbow. "You're no loser, Audrey Wilson, when you can give a nine-year-old boy so much hope that he wants you to do the same for a stranger he just met."

"And he just gave me hope, as well." Audrey nodded slightly, took a deep breath, and proceeded toward the boy and the man. She had work to do, including phoning her family.

14

LISELOTTE/ANNA 1944

When someone touched Anna's arm, trying to wake her, she struggled to stay in the house she had been dreaming about. The line between reality and sleep was that, in her dreams, her home became a place she yearned to return to. Her twin daughters and Helene, her Mutti, were there, welcoming her with open arms.

"Liselotte," Mutti called as Liselotte entered the house. "Welcome back. It's never too late to come home."

"Oh, Mutti, I'm glad to be home too. It hasn't been that long, though. Not even a year." There she was—being disagreeable again. The last thing Liselotte wanted was to spark misunderstandings that would surely lead to more disagreements. She lowered her chin and looked at the braided green-and-red rug. "Pardon me, Mutti. I didn't mean to correct you."

Mutti swept her hand through the air. Liselotte remembered when she had done the same in the past, as if shooing away a pesky fly. This time, however, it was as if her mother pushed away the last bit of stale air between them, refreshing and sweetening the life-giving oxygen with a Christmas-like aroma of cinnamon, ginger, and cloves.

Mutti grasped Liselotte's arms and pulled her into a hug. "Goodness, my darling daughter. No worries," she murmured lovingly into Liselotte's ear before stepping back to look her in the eyes. "Now, come. It's time to see your sweet daughters."

Liselotte, suddenly nervous about this significant moment, wrapped her arms around her waist. "How are they, Mutti?"

"See for yourself." Helene called her granddaughters downstairs. Two sets of footsteps thundered down the stairs from the second floor. "Your ten-year-old girls are not babies anymore—they're growing into fine little ladies."

Liselotte's breath caught; something felt terribly wrong. First, two pairs of healthy, young legs energetically descended the narrow, creaky stairs. According to Mutti, the girls were ten. How could that be? She had only left them behind in December 1943.

Left them behind. She could no longer deny the truth. She was the one who had abandoned Regina and Rosa. She had walked away from her mother, a mother she had always called *Mutter,* not the more affectionate term *Mutti* as she was calling her now.

"Mama!" came a chorus of the sweetest musical notes she had ever heard. Instantly, Liselotte was wrapped in a forgotten warmth. Tears welled in her eyes. Both girls stood before her, each with an identical smile, brown eyes the color of honey, plaited chestnut hair, and matching yellow skirts with white blouses. For the life of her, she could not tell which child was which.

"Regina?"

The girl on the right nodded with a big smile. "*Hallo,* Mutti. I missed you."

Liselotte slowly fixed her gaze on the other child. "Rosa?" Her voice was barely a whisper.

"*Ja,* Mutter. It's me... Rosa," she said clearly in German. She started jumping in place. "I'm Rosa. I'm healthy and fine, and you weren't home to see me grow into a big, good girl. I can talk. I can walk. I see and hear perfectly."

"My darling, Rosa... you were always fine with me, even back then..." Liselotte could not finish the lie. As she walked away from her daughters, she was overwhelmed by how much care her little Rosa required—every hour of every day—because of her physical and mental health challenges. Perhaps she—as Rosa's mother and protector—was the one who truly had an abnormality.

"You're wrong, Mutter," Rosa said, each word coming out stronger than the one before. She kept jumping up and down, each jump higher than the last. "Bad Mutter... bad Mutter... you're a bad Mutter..."

"Anna," a stern male voice said. "Wake up now. I've had enough of your whimpering and yelling."

She cracked one eye open. No daughters. No mother. No welcome home.

Klaus.

"Pardon," she said, unsure why she was apologizing. Whimpering? Yelling? She sat up straighter in the passenger seat of the car. "Klaus, are you upset with me for having a bad dream?"

He gripped the steering wheel so tightly that his knuckles turned a pale, grayish-white. "It's just that you came close to shouting as we went through the last security check. The last thing we need is to be questioned to the point of being delayed. It's already bad enough that my return to Poland has been pushed back by a few days."

The setback in his return to work was not her fault. If she wanted to be fair, it wasn't his fault either that he suffered a concussion from the blow to his head delivered by that miserable soldier. She wouldn't take any blame, but it was better for her not to dwell on or extend this topic. He was in a bad mood, whether because of problems he dreaded facing or people he needed to report to. But this wasn't her concern.

"Who is Rosa?" he asked.

She gulped. "Did I shout her name in my sleep?"

"*Ja*, as well as others I couldn't easily recognize."

Anna shrugged, hoping her guilt didn't show on her face. She refused to look away. "I'm not sure who Rosa is. Perhaps someone my mind conjured up in a dream."

"Are you sure?"

"Of course." She glanced around and again swallowed hard. Houses and businesses with missing walls were scattered everywhere —destroyed by bombs and flames, a sight she was all too familiar with from living in Berlin. Craters in the road caused Klaus to jerk the wheel several times. Stray dogs roamed the area, but people were absent from everyday routines like going to school, visiting shops, or sitting on park benches chatting with friends. In fact, there were no schools, stores, or parks visible. Nor were there any churches or synagogues. Had the Polish people all fled for their lives? Were they divided into two groups—non-Jews and Jews—with the latter deported to camps of some kind? Had partisan Poles been killed when Germany first invaded?

"Welcome to Poland," Klaus said as if reading her thoughts. "We crossed the border about an hour ago. These useless, rutted roads are slowing us down." He huffed. "At least our panzer divisions have successfully navigated these sorry excuses for traveling."

Roads that, Anna thought, had probably become hard to drive on because of the German panzers, though she wouldn't voice her opinion with Klaus. Her list of things she couldn't talk to him about was growing so much that it was choking her speech. She considered asking why he hadn't woken her earlier but decided it was better not to seem like she was interrogating him. "I'm surprised I didn't snap awake at the checkpoint."

"After I informed the guards who I was and who my superior was, they waved me through. Clearly smart men who don't want any trouble."

"They had no questions about me?"

"I mentioned that you were a liaison for the Lebensborn Society, recently appointed by Max Sollman, and that I could wake you to get your identity papers, even though you were sleeping off a cold. Believe me, they never gave you a second thought."

"Sollman? Not Himmler? I don't believe you've mentioned Herr Sollman."

Klaus shook his head. "I meant to say Heinrich Himmler."

"Who is Sollman?"

"He isn't a concern to you."

The one thing Anna easily recognized was when someone rudely dismissed her. When it came to Klaus, she knew better than to mention the mystery man, who she suspected would not be a kind or good-hearted person. Was there such a thing among Nazis?

Not for the first time since waking from that terrible nightmare about coming home to a distorted mother and twin daughters, Anna noticed a change in Klaus. At first, she thought his behavior might be due to a sulky mood or possibly his recent head wound. Now, she wondered if this was how Herr Agers truly acted in a Reich role, carrying out official Nazi directives on behalf of the Fatherland. Or had he lied to her from the moment they met, twisting things to suit himself, and now the truth was catching up with him? Then again, maybe she should soften her attitude toward him—the man who likely prevented her rape by the Wehrmacht soldier, as well as the louse in the woods near his parents' house. Several times now, he has asserted that he would always be her protector. While she struggled with growing indignation at his self-appointed role, she had to admit that she had no one else who cared enough to look out for her. With each new day she faced, she learned that the world was too vast and frightening to face alone.

On the other hand, if she kept Klaus as her only protector, she would be admitting that, as a woman, she couldn't take care of herself and had to rely on someone else, which she didn't believe. Sure, she was young and lacked experience outside her very strict family home, but, for better or worse, she had never felt intimidated about stepping out on her own. Not even bombs dropping from planes had stopped her before. Additionally, as more time passed with Klaus—head injury or not—she became acutely aware that she needed to phrase each of her thoughts shared with him in a way that would benefit her, meaning she couldn't afford to antagonize him. For her peace of mind, she especially couldn't risk bringing up the subject of Rosa. If her daughter were miraculously alive, she needed to avoid putting her in danger from a ruling government determined to conquer and control the world, willing to eliminate anyone, like Rosa, seen as harmful to the Aryan race.

"Where in Poland are we?" she asked, a reasonable and fair question.

"We're approaching what used to be called the city of Łódź—now named Litzmannstadt after a German general from the Great War. Under no circumstances should it be referred to by its original Polish name. We'll reach our destination just before noon."

"Where in Łódź… sorry, I mean Litzmannstadt, are we going?"

"To an orphanage. It's adjacent to the ghetto."

"A Jewish ghetto?"

He diverted his attention from the road and fixed his gaze intently on her. "Were you expecting any other?"

Despite a surge of fear, she willed herself to keep her eyes on him, trying to overcome self-doubts about feeling young and foolish. "*Nein.*"

"It was mainly aimed at Jews. Any Roma captured were thrown into the batch of *Untermensch.*" He tapped his temple. "And, you know, anyone who didn't have much upstairs."

"You're phrasing things in the past tense."

"That's right. For your sake, you won't have to see any of these sub-humans."

When does a person cease being a human? Her stomach knotted. She was afraid of what he might say next and concentrated on not throwing up.

"The ghetto," he continued, "was liquidated starting this spring and continued into August. However, there are still about nine hundred Jews remaining in the camp to clean up the mess left behind. We all expected a disaster, but not to the extent that it's taking all this time to clear out. Do not interact with them. No matter what."

She wanted to ask what would happen to these nine hundred *people,* but also held back those words.

Liquidate—one of the strangest words she had ever heard used. Originally, it was intended to eliminate spoilage and prevent contamination. Leave it to the Nazis to give it a new meaning when it involved removing human beings from the face of the earth. Now that the Polish city had a German name, what had happened to its residents? Were most of them Jewish? Did the men, women, and children of Łódź try to escape during the German takeover? Could they not have had a chance, and along with those living in neighboring towns, been rounded up like animals and shoved into this ghetto? Anna wanted to scream, curse, sob, or do all three. Instead, to placate Klaus, she sighed. For now, she was trapped in a vehicle he was driving, under his protective care in a country not her own, about to aid a nation that was increasingly one she did not want to call her own. And she knew full well that he carried a gun, one he would not hesitate to use against her if she revealed her true feelings toward the Reich.

"Heinrich issued the liquidation decree himself," Klaus added. "So, no worries, Anna. There are no sorry sights to see. Believe me, before the last of the deportations, the terrible views and smells were... well, let's just say you should consider yourself lucky that you're seeing this place now and not a few years ago, let alone during its heyday of chaos this past summer."

Was that supposed to make her feel better? He had no right to dismiss the sights and smells of people as *terrible,* especially when they were victims—held as prisoners by those who wouldn't care for their needs—and never given a choice about their living conditions, and barely able to hold on to life before being taken away for elimination.

Then, reality hit her again. Since he had the sanctioned approval to criticize anyone who wasn't a full-blooded Aryan and a member of the Nazi Party, he felt justified in saying whatever he wanted about anyone unlike himself in thought, deed, and heritage.

"Now, listen up," Klaus continued. "We should reach the children's camp—Kinder-KZ Litzmannstadt—in just a few minutes. Originally built for orphaned Polish Christian children between the ages of eight and fourteen, we've taken in younger children who are especially suited for loving German families eager to raise children in the spirit of promoting the goodness of the Fatherland." He inhaled deeply. "I need to tell you about your duties. But before I do, you are to report only to me. If you have any questions or conflicts, see me. Do not avoid me by taking matters into your own hands. Do not talk to anyone else. Understand?"

She resented his condescending arrogance. Her feelings were

made worse by the fact that she was in no position to challenge him. Once again, she said what she knew he expected to hear. "Clearly."

"Heinrich Himmler created the Lebensborn—meaning *spring of life*—program. Since the Łódź Ghetto's liquidation, we have been seeking out and encouraging Aryan women, whom our experts identify as racially pure, to come to designated nurseries where they can give birth to perfect babies, and then surrender them for adoption to caring, loving German parents."

"Why couldn't these women care for the babies themselves?"

"These are women who might lack the financial means to give a proper upbringing for a master-race child suited for Germany. Many of them were pregnant outside of marriage, a disgrace to the Reich."

Yet, when they met, he wondered if she might consider contributing to the cause, knowing she wasn't married. Goosebumps dotted her arms. Why was he giving her a scrutinizing look, eyebrows furrowed and all? Could he possibly know about her past pregnancy?

He made a right turn and drove deep into the city. Passing some still-standing churches and a few destroyed ones, she saw the remains of a synagogue, with rubble revealing its once-glorious size, likely cherished dearly. Several intact houses stood out proudly, almost like they were participating in a pageant to show the ruined world around them that beauty and a semblance of family life persisted despite the cruelty that had existed in the ghetto for an unimaginably long time. They passed schools and other institutions, and Anna could not tell whether they were in operation or, if so, to what extent.

"Don't be surprised if you hear Kinder KZ mistakenly called a children's concentration camp," Klaus said. "KZ, as I mentioned, was designed for poor, orphaned Polish Christian children, not Jews. Their young age makes it easier to shape their minds to all that Germany stands for."

Klaus slowed down as they approached what appeared to be a main gate on Przemyslowa Street. After driving about six more meters, he turned into a smaller gate manned by one guard. Anna took a deep breath to hold back a wave of dizziness—the main gate they had just passed was for the ghetto. The ghetto, where thousands of Jews likely died from starvation and disease or were rounded up and sent off to who-knew-where during liquidation.

"You're about to meet some beautiful children who match the criteria of Nordic-looking kids with fair features, blond hair, and striking blue eyes—a close fit to native-born Germans. I'm sure you're aware of the shortage of German-born babies that occurred once Germany began to implement its global expansion. Just think about what you personally will be contributing to your native country—with your help, these little ones will become Germany's new Aryan children."

Liselotte gave birth to her twin girls in May 1942. Before that, her mother forbade her from going out onto the streets of Berlin while she was pregnant, leading Liselotte—now Anna—to believe her mother was ashamed of her. After Regina and Rosa were born, and Rosa showed signs of physical and mental developmental issues, her mother became even more watchful over her daughter and granddaughters. Looking back at the recent past, she could now see that her mother had been right. There were solid reasons why she shouldn't have risked traveling the streets of Berlin while expecting her babies; as an unmarried young woman, she might have been taken into Nazi custody by eager German SS members seeking a better home than she could provide, and as soon as she had given birth, the babies would be snatched away from her, and who could tell what they would do with her? Had her mother known then? And after the twins were born? While the Nazis searched for individuals who might weaken their racial stock—whether adults or children—Rosa would have been *disappeared* and healthy Regina, with an unwed mother, would be given up for adoption for the greater good of Germany.

Now, because Liselotte left her home, her daughters' lives were at risk. She was the one who tore her family apart and destroyed any chance they had for a future together. Acting as Anna, she had to do whatever it took to reunite with her family, even if it meant tricking Klaus into thinking she was on his side. However, there were obstacles.

"You still haven't told me what my job duties are. How can I possibly help, Klaus? You know I don't speak Polish."

"Your language abilities are not a problem." Klaus gently squeezed her hand, and it took all her strength not to pull it away. "That's why you're perfect to help with the Germanization of these young minds. They are absolutely forbidden to speak their native tongue—not even in a whisper to another child. They must become German. They must think like Germans. Under no circumstances are they allowed to behave like Polish children. If they are caught speaking Polish, celebrating Polish customs or traditions, reminiscing about their families, or even playing a Polish game, they will face serious punishment. Once they have completed the Germanization process, you will help bring them home to Germany and into the welcoming and loving arms of their new German parents. The new German children will be happy, making Germany happy."

"And who will be the one to discipline the children with the punishment you mention?"

He looked her directly in the eye and smiled. "You are, my dear Anna."

"Are there any needy ones?"

His cheeks flushed a reddish hue. "Needy?"

For the life of her, she couldn't tell if he was angry or excited. Which would trouble her more? She had to swallow twice before she could speak. "Children who need help every day. You know, those who can't speak, hear, or see… maybe some who can't walk or eat on their own—"

"Do you mean imbeciles? Why would we spend our time and resources on them?" He narrowed his eyes sharply at her. "You do realize how children like this could harm the Aryan race, right? That they have the potential to tear apart the strength and unity of Germany?"

She had become so distressed about her own children and family situation that she only now realized she had confused Germany's obsession with perfecting the German race. She must have appeared foolish to Klaus. Now, she needed to correct her words, even if she despised each false statement she was about to make. "Of course, Klaus. I got carried away by these worthless children. I can see how giving these valuable, deserving Poles a good German home is the best thing for them and for Germany."

He stared at her intensely. She fought the urge to flinch.

"You won't have to deal with these lesser beings—they've been culled from the stronger parts of society who deserve to live and thrive. Even those who were able-bodied and capable-minded but showed signs of delinquency have been removed. I'm sure we prevented many criminals from growing up and becoming a tragic hardship to society. You will only help the loveliest of them. It's exciting and most rewarding—you'll see."

The more Anna learned about the German occupation of Poland, the more surreal it sounded. Jews were rounded up, either killed immediately or pushed into camps associated with death, or—if luckier, depending on one's perspective—into ghettos filled with squalor and longing for death. Then there were the non-Jewish Poles. Like parts on a conveyor belt in a factory, they were moved out for having undesirable traits and either disappeared suddenly or became slave laborers. The children, considered racially pure Aryans, had all traces of their Polish backgrounds systematically erased. The newly Germanized children were then transported to Germany and handed over to individuals who believed they were adopting exceptional German children.

"There's one more thing I can't stress enough," Klaus said.

She looked up.

"The Germanization of these Polish children must never be made public—neither in Poland nor in Germany."

So, Anna thought, the Nazis were deceiving not only the families from whom they were taking the children but also their own German citizens. For now, acting as Klaus's associate, she nodded.

"They are to be explained as German orphans from the regained German territories," Klaus added. "This is not a stretch of the truth, as there have always been many ethnic Germans in Western Poland. Do you fully understand?"

"Ja," she said without hesitation. Yet, she struggled to understand and knew she would always find it hard to accept how others could not only consider one child's life more valuable than another's but also give the child to strangers. Human beings are not commodities like potted plants that only need watering and sunlight.

"So, can I count on you, precious Anna?"

Precious? If he only knew what she was thinking and scheming, he would probably put her on the next transport to the nearest extermination camp. For now, as part of her deception, she smiled. "I can tell you're positively excited and honored to do this work, and I'm happy to help you."

"That's what I was expecting to hear from your sweet lips. You won't just be a *Brown Sister* working with our SS men while they abduct a child..."

"Abduct?" No wonder he had trailed off. He had been slipping up a lot lately. What else might he reveal? It made her wonder again if his muddled mind was a lasting side effect of his head injury or if it stemmed from a deeper physical or mental abnormality. Maybe he was the one with faulty Aryan blood.

"I meant to say," Klaus said, "while our men rescue these orphans in need of a home."

"I understand," Anna said, offering him a kind smile, though it was the last thing she wanted to do.

"You're my assistant now. I need you to help accelerate our process and make sure that the properly selected children leave this Kinder-KZ camp as quickly as possible."

"Why is that?"

"Time isn't on our side. The Red Army is advancing through Eastern Poland, so we must accelerate our Germanization efforts and send these children to Germany quickly."

"I'm ready." And Anna was prepared—prepared to never see his face again, or anyone else connected to the Nazi party.

15

LISELOTTE/ANNA

"Obey or else."

Klaus's whispered, concise warning as they entered the Kinder-KZ camp jolted Anna. She swiftly shifted back on her heels, almost losing her balance, but she hid her stumble by smoothing her jacket.

The SS officer sitting behind a simple oak table, no bigger than a basic sewing machine stand, peered over his silver-rimmed glasses. "Shut the door. Tell me who you are."

Klaus took the initiative to attend to the door, which squeaked like a cabinet with rusty hinges that shouldn't be opened. He then approached the officer. "Klaus Agers reporting with my new associate."

The gray-haired man stood and gave the Sieg Heil salute. Klaus quickly returned it, and to avoid drawing attention, Anna also performed the expected gesture, keeping a neutral expression.

"Ah," the officer said. "Of course, Herr Agers. I have heard about you."

"I haven't met you. Your name is?" Klaus asked.

"I am Hans Muller, Herr Agers. I've been working here for a week now."

"Very good, Herr Muller." Klaus glanced at the door on the right. "May we go in?"

Deep furrows lined the officer's forehead. He looked at Anna then shifted his attention to Klaus. "I must ask you and your associate to pledge loyalty to the Führer and the Reich."

Klaus nodded.

"I will be most happy to," Anna said.

Klaus swore his loyalty first. Officer Muller then faced Anna.

"Raise your right hand and repeat after me." He waited until she obeyed. Then he asked her to state her name. When Anna did—using her alias, Anna Bauer, not Liselotte—she felt a sense of relief, knowing she wasn't about to truly pledge her allegiance to Hitler or his supporters.

"I, Anna Bauer, swear by God this sacred oath, that I will promise unconditional obedience to…" She concluded with the expected words, "So help me God." Although her childhood was marked by a lack of church attendance with her mother, or anyone else for that matter, she could not help but believe that the all-powerful creator and ruler of all life would do anything short of shedding tears upon hearing such a pledge of respect for a man and a government intent on controlling a world comprised of those they deemed worthy of life, by taking the lives of others. She could only pray that this God would understand her false vow of allegiance to Hitler and the Reich, viewing it as just another step toward escaping Poland, fleeing Germany, and running from, not toward, evil, which was destroying the lives of innocent human beings.

"Good, then," the officer said. "I'll show you around the children's area where they spend their days before returning to the separate quarters for boys and girls. After that, I'll take you to your accommodations until your departure. Lunch is served for everyone at precisely noon." He glanced at Klaus. "Will you be accompanying Fräulein Bauer?"

"I expect to," Klaus replied.

Officer Muller nodded and motioned for them to follow.

"The children's day area," the officer said over his shoulder as he led Anna and Klaus, "is at the end of this hallway. We currently have ten children—four boys and six girls. The youngest is three. The oldest is eight."

Anna's curiosity was piqued. "Given how valuable the Kinder-KZ is to the Reich, I expected more children."

At the entrance to the children's area, Officer Muller paused and turned. "Our last transport of children departed for Germany just last Tuesday. We aim to move the children out two to three times a month, depending on their readiness."

"Their readiness?" Anna asked. Catching herself, she added, "I mean, of course, the children need to be ready, but—"

Klaus raised a hand to stop her. He also offered her a warm smile before turning to the officer. "Pardon Fräulein Bauer. While she is eager to work with us, she is also committed to being as efficient as possible. That's why I've asked her to join us. Not only has she supervised the operation of three nurseries, the last of which was in our occupied Amsterdam, but she is excited about this new opportunity to help the Fatherland."

Anna had given Klaus the benefit of the doubt, believing that his previous lying—exaggerations—she'd caught him at had stemmed from health issues. But now she wondered if he had lied his way into his key position with Himmler—or if it was that other person, Max Sollman, whose name had slipped from Klaus's lips a bit too easily. Gaining power in the military was probably similar to advancing in any other company—either you worked hard or you fabricated falsehoods to reach your goals. With a blank expression, she accepted her cue to stay quiet and let Klaus do most of the talking.

"I hope you find this facility to your satisfaction, Fräulein Bauer."

"I'm sure I will be impressed, especially based on what Herr Agers has told me."

"This particular group of children needs a bit more work in their studies," Officer Muller said. "Fortunately, aside from the occasional spoken word of their forbidden Polish, they have become much more assimilated and adjusted than when they first arrived here two weeks ago."

Just when she hoped to stay quiet, with Klaus's watchful gaze on her, it was clear that, of the two, she was the one expected to respond.

"What is the preferred punishment if I should hear a word of Polish?" she asked, feeling like a hideous monster. She may not have been the type of mother who cuddled her daughters or used sweet endearments, but she certainly never resorted to a firm hand or physical discipline.

A lopsided grin spread across the officer's face, distorting his features and making him resemble the male version of the neighborhood shrew from her childhood—the one she and the other kids deliberately avoided. "Humiliation works wonders. Sometimes, even a threat alone is enough to change a behavior quickly. When it comes to the two oldest—an eight-year-old and a seven-year-old boy—pull down their trousers and undergarments, spank their bottoms in front of the other children, and let them walk around without their clothes for hours. For the youngest ones, take away their play privileges and dessert." After a brief pause, he added, "I trust you will have your own system of punishment."

"I do, but I believe I should be cautious about food restrictions." The two men looked at her. "We need to fatten them up for their prospective German parents. We want to make them appear healthy and adoptable, and nothing less."

"You certainly understand what to do when it comes to children and bettering Germany," Officer Muller said, admiration in his tone. He looked at Klaus. "I will note that your associate is already fitting in well with our group."

"Very good," Klaus said, stunning Anna by not adding anything more.

The officer pushed open the door. The noise of children playing and talking quieted instantly. A blond boy playing with a toy Third Reich soldier—probably made in the early 1930s since 1939 marked the end of toy production for war materials—threw his toy onto the center of the red and gold diamond-patterned rug. He ran straight toward Anna and wrapped his arms around her legs. His touch left her flustered, and as if she was suddenly airborne, she ricocheted off the walls of her memory…

Regina ran to her, wanting to know where her twin sister Rosa was, wanting comfort from her mama.

Liselotte ignored her daughter, accusing her mother of handing Rosa over to the Gestapo.

Her mother told her to pick up the hysterically crying Regina and calm her down so they could talk.

Instead, she threatened to leave her mother and Regina for the only person who accepted her for who she was—flaws and all—Gerhard. Her lover. The father of her two girls. The man she wanted to marry.

She would never come home again.

Gerhard, a traitor to the Nazi Party, was killed by the Nazis.

Ten months ago.

Officer Muller lifted the boy off Anna and then set him down on the floor, bringing Anna back to the present. "That's enough, Gunther." He clapped his hands twice and called the other children over. "Line up." Without hesitation, a line formed from the smallest boy—Gunther—to the largest boy, followed by the same formation with the girls.

"Everyone, this is Fräulein Bauer." The officer pointed to the youngest. "Tell Fräulein Bauer who you are and what you want."

"I'm Gunther," the little boy said in Polish. He shrugged. "I miss my… mat—"

"*Nein, nein,*" Officer Muller said, his neck turning pink. "Who are you? Who do you miss?"

"Mutti," he said in German, adding his name. He sniffled and wiped his nose with his finger. "But she now lives in Germany. I want to go to Germany."

"Very good, Gunther. And soon, you shall. Fräulein Bauer will see to it that all of you get to see your mothers and fathers. The sooner you all behave and learn your lessons, the quicker you will leave this lovely camp and go to your families. Won't that be nice?"

Anna thought the children would definitely smile from ear to ear, maybe a few bouncing with excitement or even shouting out in joy. Instead, an eerie silence settled among the children until it was their turn to introduce themselves to Anna.

"Carry on with your playtime. In a few minutes, Fräulein Bauer will gather you for lunch. Afterward, you will go to the classroom for your next lessons."

A girl, about six years old, raised her hand. Anna took the initiative and called on the child. From the corner of her eye, Anna noticed Klaus gave a small nod of approval.

"I want to know what is for lunch."

"You're Gisela, right?" The reddish-blond girl nodded, and Anna stepped toward her, kneeling at her eye level. "I'm not sure what we'll have for lunch, but I'm sure it will be tasty. What's your favorite German dish?"

Gisela lowered her chin and fiddled with her skirt pockets. "I think it's called... I'm not sure... wurst?"

The poor child was likely struggling with the German word for sausage compared to the term in her native language. "Let's hope! Wurst is also my favorite."

Klaus offered her a hand up, murmuring into her ear, "You're doing quite well."

At first, she was surprised by his rare praise and blinked in confusion. He nodded, seemingly confirming what she had heard.

A gray-haired woman entered the room. Officer Muller introduced her as a temporary attendant for the children until Anna settled into her new position. He then gestured broadly toward the door. "I'll show you to the dining room and then to your rooms." He glanced at his wristwatch. "Lunch will be served promptly at noon. Afterward, it will be time for the children to enjoy some fresh air and sunshine on the patio. Fräulein Bauer, will you attend to that while Herr Agers and I speak?"

"I would be most happy to."

"Fräulein Bauer and I have had a long journey," Klaus said. "Lunch sounds promising."

Officer Muller held the door open for Anna as they entered the hallway. "Oh, it is. Our meals are one of the many advantages of working here. The cook and his staff excel at making sure we receive wholesome meals."

Anna was certain he spoke in earnest. She quietly sighed, holding back her frustration. From the viewpoint of those in charge, it was better to give kidnapped children a proper diet before placing them with a new family in a foreign country.

At the end of the hallway, they turned left and passed a closed door. Anna heard a woman crying and instinctively stopped.

"Inconsequential," Officer Muller said sharply, more like a warning than a dismissive remark. He jutted his chin to quicken their pace away from the door.

Klaus placed the palm of his hand on her shoulder. "This way, Anna."

She narrowed her eyes at Klaus. She would not be fooled; she knew what she heard. Klaus, however, ignored her, keeping his gaze fixed on the officer's back.

They reached a pair of double doors. Officer Muller pushed both open to reveal the dining hall. Two women wearing white aprons bustled around the large room. One arranged silverware and plates on long rectangular tables, each seating eight. The other woman mirrored this setup on round tables, which were smaller and seemed to accommodate children. No matter their size, each table had fine linen cloths and, for now, unlit candles. As Anna scanned the rest of the room, she noticed that potted plants decorated tables in front of each large, curtained window. A second-story balcony overlooked the hall; beyond its sparkling glass doors were a few tables with lamps and a desk. A library or office? Anna would find out soon enough, especially since she was responsible for teaching the children about what it means to be German.

"Unfortunately," Officer Muller said, "there will be no wurst today. Potato and vegetable soup for lunch, and a meat stew for dinner. With the children in mind, we always have plenty of bread, cheese, fruit, and raw vegetables with each meal. We make sure they get the best nutrients we can provide." He motioned for them to leave. Once back in the hallway, he added, "I'll show you to your rooms. The men are quartered in a building behind this one, which Herr Agers, I'm sure, is familiar with." Klaus nodded. "For you, Fräulein Bauer, you will be in Room Two upstairs. I suggest that ten minutes before the hour, gather the children and bring them to the dining hall. Starting tonight, for dinner, you will be entirely on your own with the children."

"No worries, Herr Officer Muller," Anna said. "I will be with them all afternoon and will have them ready promptly for dinner at..." She let out a little laugh. "Well, I'll have them ready once I know the time for dinner."

"At seven."

"Excellent," she replied.

"You've been very helpful, Officer Muller," Klaus said. "There are a few things I need to discuss with my associate, and then, if you don't mind, I will show her to her assigned room."

The officer agreed and left to return to his desk.

"I'm confident I can find my way, Herr Agers," Anna said.

Klaus pulled her close to his chest and held her tightly enough that she couldn't pull away. He twirled one of her curls around his finger. "I'm impressed by your quickness to accept your new role as my associate, expressing eagerness to work with the children. It takes a beautiful, good soul to care for another person."

He slid his hand down, cupping her backside. She tried to squirm away.

"Don't," he murmured into her ear, his breath hot and sickening. He held her tightly against him. "I like you right where you are—in my arms. Don't you want to be here?"

She couldn't breathe. Her only thought was that if she stayed still, he would loosen his hold on her, and she could escape.

"If you keep up the good work and let me have my way with you, Anna, I might ease up on investigating your background. Trust me, I ultimately control all the information I gather, and if your situation is not in your favor, you won't like what I do."

Heat surged in her chest, but not from passion. This vile creature claimed he would protect her from all harm, yet he would not hesitate to eliminate anyone the Reich considered unworthy of life, including herself. Then, with a snap of his mind, he effortlessly transformed into a disgusting rat that forced himself on her, spewing threats about conducting background checks on her if she failed to cooperate, both at work and now in the bedroom, and warning she wouldn't like the results. Who exactly was Klaus Agers?

The answer became clearer with each second she spent with him: he was a man who exploited others to reach his goals, whether as a Nazi—though she was starting to wonder if he was deceiving the Reich as well—or acting in his own best interest. Clearly, he relied solely on manipulating people to satisfy his desires. Perhaps he had met his match, though she did not support the Nazi regime. She had, unfortunately, only thought of herself until recently, but she was growing and changing. She could only hope it wasn't already too late for her to reunite with her children and her mother.

Klaus lowered his hands to his sides and stepped back from her. "The previous children's attendant left behind a detailed list of lessons and preparations for these little ones that will become Germany's newest, delightful children as soon as you Germanize them."

He had made his threat clear and had returned to business?

And there was that word again—*Germanize*. Anna had never heard of the term until Klaus explained to her that many children from other countries now needed a home. Never mind that the rapid pace was linked to Nazi Germany invading and destroying other nations and tearing families apart. Now, she couldn't escape that one word—Germanize—defined everyone's sole purpose under this Kinder KZ unit.

"You will not be disappointed in me," she said, uttering false words in the hope of escaping from him, at least for now, until she could figure out what to do next. Believing the conversation was over, she turned away, but Klaus stepped in front of her. She was startled when he brushed his fingers across her right cheek. So, he'd returned to acting as if he had the right to physically *handle* her?

"One more thing," he said.

Stay calm, she repeated to herself. *Show no fear*.

"Under no circumstances, Anna, will you explore or inquire about that room where you may have heard a woman cry out. If you see any officers enter that room, immediately turn away and go elsewhere. Understand?"

No, not at all. Where she *may have* heard a woman crying? There was no doubt in her mind about what she heard. For now, as his captive, she gave a nod.

"I'll show you to your room now." He stroked her cheek again. "I'm quite pleased with you. You're proving to me that I made the right choice in bringing you here. I'm looking forward to seeing what else you can surprise me with."

"On behalf of Hitler, I will not disappoint." With the lie just spoken, she pardoned herself, emphasizing that he needed to trust her to find her own room. Without waiting for a reply, she walked away.

She could swear her life on it that what he hoped for in the surprise department didn't match what she had in mind. However, while away from him this afternoon, she had to quickly think of clever ways to avoid becoming yet another woman locked behind a closed door, waiting for a visit from one officer after another. Most importantly, she needed to plan how not to surrender to Klaus's fancy.

SLEEP ELUDED Anna that first night as she struggled to settle down in yet another bed not her own. She tried several tricks to calm her mind —counting forward, counting backward, imagining herself floating on a raft in a peaceful lake, placing herself in a perfect, make-believe future, and thinking of a favorite food then using the last letter of that food to think of another, and so on. She avoided dwelling on escape possibilities—too overwhelming since she was unfamiliar with the grounds, the city of Łódź, and Poland itself. It was useless; nothing worked. When she first looked at the bedside clock, it was one in the morning. An hour later, it was two. She flung off the blanket from her sweaty body, slipped into the clothes she had prepared on the desk chair to wear when she woke the children for breakfast, put on her cold shoes without socks, and hurried to the door. She planned to walk the halls in search of water and maybe find some relief from her anxiety through mild physical activity.

The logical choice was to go into the kitchen, which was accessible through the dining hall. She saw no harm in doing so, though she carefully descended the stairs to the first floor to avoid stepping on a dry, creaky step. At the end of the first-floor hallway was the forbidden room, whose occupant she had heard crying earlier. This time, she only heard silence.

The door to the mysterious room suddenly swung open. Like a captured mouse, Anna backed into a corner. She faced a straight-haired blond woman who wasn't much older than herself. However, unlike her, she wore a buttoned black tunic over black trousers and rugged high-top shoes—a woman who was clearly prepared for action.

"Are you alone?" the stranger whispered.

"Right now." Unsure of what else to do, Anna raised her hands in surrender. "I'm unarmed. I won't hurt you." She introduced herself and explained her purpose at KZ.

"I'm Magda," the woman said, fixing her gaze firmly on Anna. "In their minds, I'm the new camp breeder. But no longer."

Anna had heard plenty of stories about women who willingly—and often, unwillingly—obliged soldiers' desires. In fact, in the early days of living on the Berlin streets, a few women she met strongly suggested she consider offering her *services. It's good money—comes in handy for your next meal.* One of these women had offered to connect her with an organizer so she could start right away. Anna moved away from these street women as quickly as she could, but with the sour taste in her mouth that if her bad luck continued, she might have had to reconsider.

Feeling rude, but curious, Anna glanced to see if Magda showed with child.

"Hold back your snooping eyes—I'm not pregnant." Magda took two long strides toward her and pressed a knife to her throat. "I'm leaving right now. I take no chances—you must come with me. If you refuse, you'll meet your Maker now rather than later."

"But... how?" Despite the cold blade against her skin, Anna patted her skirt and focused only on practicalities. "I may not have my night clothes on, but these shoes aren't made for any kind of trip."

"You must trust me."

Every time Anna trusted others, it backfired. Besides the woman's name, she had no idea who she was, nor her plans. Then again, despite the risk of getting caught, this might be her way to escape from Klaus. "Won't we be seen?"

"Only if you delay us another second. There are arrangements in place," Magda swore, her accent now more noticeably different from German or Polish. "I'm not giving you a choice."

16

AUDREY, NOVEMBER 1944, US-BOUND

Audrey shifted in her seat on the US transport as the plane hit a patch of turbulence. She would first arrive in Greenland, then board another plane to Grenier Field, the US Air Force base in New Hampshire. From there, she would travel to Boston for a domestic flight to Milwaukee. Accustomed to being transferred from one Red Cross post to another by ship, she had almost forgotten what it was like to fly in what now felt like a sardine can tossed into the air, hitting steady areas of turbulence.

"You're looking a little green," her seat partner said. He wore camouflage battle fatigues and looked as if he had been pulled out of combat and dropped into their plane without a chance to change. He nudged a pack of Wrigley's chewing gum toward her arm. "This might help. Cuts down on ear clogging. Might also take your mind off your gut."

She nodded, pulled out a piece of gum, chewed it a few times, and rubbed her ears before glancing at the sandy-haired American soldier. "Thank you. I was trying to ignore my body doing somersaults, but obviously, I was failing miserably. By the way, my name's Audrey."

"Jacob, from Kansas. Call me Jake. Nice to meet you, though I'm sure you're thinking there are better ways to meet than during wartime and sitting on a plane we're hoping to God doesn't crash."

She closed her eyes tightly and heard Jake sigh.

"Me and my big mouth," he murmured. "My wife, Barb, always says that I don't know when to quit."

Audrey opened one eye. "She thinks you say too much?"

Jake chuckled. "Yes, ma'am. That's my honey, all right."

His grin quickly disappeared as if he had never joked. It was her turn to offer comfort. She touched his arm. "Is Barb okay?"

Jake shrugged. "That's why I'm heading home. She lost the baby, four months along. She barely pulled through. The doctor thought I should come back—Barb has no family to speak of unless you count a ninety-nine-year-old great-grandfather living in a California old folks' home." He turned away and stared at the back of the seat in front of him.

"I'm so sorry about Barb and the baby," Audrey said, silently praying for the couple's strength. "How are you holding up?"

"Trying not to think of myself. I just want to get back to my wife and take care of her." He straightened up but then sank back into his seat.

Nerves, Audrey concluded. She fully understood where he was coming from. It was one thing to be in combat, or, in her case, helping others who are serving, but having a loved one ill and in need of help just made things more complicated with sadness and added responsibilities. This, she unfortunately now knew from experience.

"I'm sure your presence will be just what Barb needs."

He nodded. "I hope so. The strange thing is how sorry she is. The couple of times I talked with her on the phone, she kept crying and apologizing. Says we're young. Says the doc tells her she's in good enough shape to have more kids. But then she says she can't even think about losing another child. I told her not to worry about that right now. One thing at a time. She needs to recover physically, and you know, from the mental loss of..." He leaned over and scrubbed his face with the palms of his hands. "Gads, I'm babbling again."

"You're probably nervous, especially talking to a complete stranger about personal, emotional issues, particularly in the middle of a war. It's understandable." Audrey wanted to ask many questions out of curiosity and a need to engage in conversation. However, she also understood the importance of letting him lead in this vulnerable situation. "You two have been through a lot. It's good you're going home to your wife."

"And you, Miss Audrey? Are you headed home?"

Home. The one place she never expected to see again, at least not for a long time. The one place she never thought she would be welcomed back to.

"Yes," she said softly. "My mother passed."

"I'm so sorry to hear your unfortunate news. Was it sudden?"

Startled as tears suddenly streamed down her cheeks, she pulled a handkerchief from her gray skirt pocket and wiped them away. "She died in an accident, but I'm unsure of the details. I've been out of touch with them ever since I left home after the Pearl Harbor bombing to work for the Red Cross. My parents and two siblings have stopped communicating with me." Aware that she was now babbling, the need to talk to someone and get it off her chest kept her from stopping. "I've always been close to my mom. Although I wasn't surprised by my father's initial disapproval of my choice, my mother's silence when I wrote home hurt like nothing else."

"Maybe it came down to your father's influence over your mom and your whole family—not that I'm trying to be nasty about it. I just know how fathers can be sometimes."

About to voice her thoughts, Audrey's insides flip-flopped as the plane hit more air turbulence. She gripped the armrests. "This never gets easy to handle."

"I hear you loud and clear on that one." He also pulled out a handkerchief and wiped his forehead. "You were saying?"

"I suspect you're right about Pop's control over Mom, though I find it all confusing. Just before Pop learned of my decision to work for the Red Cross overseas, Mom shared family news about how my paternal grandparents had barely escaped Europe and made it to America. If anyone, you'd think my father would welcome any effort to help win the war against the Third Reich and the prejudiced hatred it spreads."

Jake shook his head. "People don't remember their pasts… they don't want to. That's why hatred festers like a nasty infection and wars begin."

"I'm afraid you're right. Well, now that Mom's gone, I might never find out." Audrey thought more about this, her shoulders relaxing as a memory resurfaced. "When I was a kid and had my tonsils removed, my parents gave me a get-well gift. It was a ceramic owl bank with wise sayings carved all around it. The only one I remember, though, is the classic *let bygones be bygones*."

"Reconciliation. Forgiveness." Jake whistled softly. "That's got to be the rarest but most necessary two things to happen between human beings."

"Definitely. Especially with Mom's passing, I guess it's time to let go of any grudges against my father and the sadness connected to leaving home."

"Time to move on?" Jake asked.

She eyed his uniform, imagining that Jake's experiences on the battlefield must have taught him many life lessons. "Yes." It wouldn't be easy, but it was truly time to stop mourning what she had lost in family life over the past few years and, instead, focus on carrying her mom's beauty and good memories in her heart.

"If you don't mind me asking, when did your mom pass?"

"About a month ago," Audrey said. "They tried to reach me, but it seems like I'm a tough one to track down. As I mentioned, I don't know the details, like what time of day or whether she passed immediately or was hospitalized for a while, but apparently, she was struck by a car while crossing the street right in front of the house."

"Oh, how sad."

Feeling her family's pain and fully aware that her father and siblings would forever relive her mom's death every time they faced the road, Audrey sniffled. "As soon as I read the telegram, I phoned home. My father was the one who actually answered."

"How did that go?"

"I apologized for the delay in contacting him, saying I had just received the news. When I told him that I'd just made arrangements to fly home immediately, I held my breath, waiting for him to explode in anger." She glanced out the narrow side window, feeling relieved that the turbulence had subsided. When she faced Jake, she welcomed his gentle smile.

"I bet you a piece of gum that he wasn't nasty, and said he was happy to hear that you were traveling home."

"Yeah," she said, nodding her head while recalling her pop's relieved tone of voice. "How did you know that?"

"A father would have to be incredibly callous not to feel happy that his daughter is coming home. Based on what you've shared about him, he seems more like someone who got caught up in a tough moment than a cruel dad, and he never had the courage to say he was sorry, regardless of the long time that passed between you two."

"I think you're right. I'll visit for a while, but then I will need—and want—to return to London, where I've been working with Tracing Services. Something tells me that he'll understand this time."

"He might knock your socks off and say he's downright proud of you—and that your mom would be too."

Both happy and sad tears streamed down her face, and she wiped her face again. "Look what you did," she said with a fixed smile. "You got me crying like a little girl."

"No, ma'am," Jake said. "I know you're joshing, but crying over family is absolutely fine. No shame in that."

"Thanks, Jake. I've needed a kind listening ear."

"Right back at you for listening to me about my wife and all."

Just then, the pilot announced they were about to land in Greenland, where they could transfer to their next flight.

"Almost home," Jake said.

Audrey leaned against the cold passenger window. "Sounds wonderful to me."

In some ways, General Mitchell Field—the local airport, renamed in 1941 from Milwaukee County Airport after Milwaukee native General William Mitchell—never felt particularly welcoming until Audrey arrived to see her family. In other respects, it also seemed intimidating, given all the changes since she last saw the place. The anxious knot twisting inside her loosened as she suddenly understood what many combat personnel, like Jake, must feel when they first return home, no matter the reason.

Toting her carry-on duffel bag, she made her way to the baggage claim area to meet her father as planned. As she entered the busy space, she saw him immediately. Although his back was turned, she quickly recognized his tall height of six feet two inches, slim build, and his usual choice to skip a jacket against the November cold in the Midwest.

Nervous like a child expecting a negative reaction, she slowed her step toward him. Aware she was being foolish, she mentally tested different names for him. Pop. Dad. Daddy. Father. At some point, she had called him all of those. She chose the one she last used for him, despite the heavy feeling of the now unfamiliar word.

"Pop," she called out from about three feet away. He didn't turn to face her. Thinking the noise in the low-ceilinged department drowned out her greeting, she tapped him on the shoulder, ready with a smile for when he turned.

A much younger, mirror-image of her father pivoted around.

Audrey dropped her duffel. She palmed her cheeks as if that would prevent the squeal from escaping her lips. "Pete!"

Her now mature-looking, acne-free brother, sporting a mustache, picked her up and swung her around. "It's about time you're home, Audrey."

Tears welled in her eyes.

Pete swore. "I didn't mean to make you cry."

"I know… I know." She let out a soft groan. "I'm a bag of mixed-up emotions, that's all. Don't mind me." She craned her neck to see if her father was standing off to the side, maybe smoking a cigarette. "Is Pop here?"

Pete's smile faded. He shoved his hands into his trouser pockets. "Nope. Said he had a lot of work to do and gave me the car keys to pick you up."

"Well, look at you," Audrey said cheerfully. "You're driving—guess you've finally proven yourself trustworthy."

Pete crossed his arms, his muscles more defined than the last time Audrey saw him. "Lots of things have changed. We didn't have a choice."

She stepped back. "I'm sorry. Did I—"

"Oh, no, sis. I know you were just joking, but I also know what you're thinking—it's written all over your face. None of this is your fault. Don't you dare blame yourself." He glanced over his shoulder at the conveyor belt that now stood still and empty. "You didn't have any other baggage?"

She picked up her duffel. "Just this."

Pete took the bag from her hand. "Let's go. We'll catch up in the car."

"Okay. Hey—does Pop still have that burgundy Ford Deluxe?"

"Of course, and I'm driving it. Forget the war and the national money crunch. You know he won't replace any vehicle until it rolls over and kicks up its four tires."

Despite the solemn reason for her return to Milwaukee and her nervousness about seeing her father, she couldn't help but giggle. "That image of the car on its back takes the sting out of things."

They weaved among families, couples, and more solo travelers than Audrey had imagined. Her heart lurched when a man with an amputated leg hobbled by on crutches and met a weeping woman and a young girl carrying three balloons—one red, one blue, and the third white. The woman ran to embrace the man as the girl jumped up and down, calling out, "Daddy… Daddy… Daddy…"

Audrey stopped in the middle of the busy pedestrian crowd. A gentle, steady hand held her upper arm. "Sis? Are you all right?"

No, she was not. But she wasn't about to tell her brother. If sadness pierced her heart, she was sure that her brother, sister, and father were also caught in the clutches of grief. She lifted her gaze to meet her brother's. "I'll be fine. Let's keep going." She forced a grin. "I can't wait to feel that familiar chill when we step outside."

"Brace yourself. It may be November, but it feels more like mid-January. At least, there's no snow yet."

"That's one good thing," she mumbled, and they continued walking for two more minutes in silence to the parking lot.

Despite the brisk wind that whipped through the wide lot, the cold air felt refreshing, invigorating Audrey's senses. She was delighted and touched when Pete beat her to the passenger door and held it open like a true gentleman. She slid in and watched through the side mirror as her brother tossed her duffel into the trunk.

"What's her name?" Audrey asked the moment Pete squeezed into the driver's seat.

He shot her his notorious stink eye.

"The one who taught you all these lovely manners," she said, teasing. She drew a breath audibly, keenly aware that it might very well have been their mom who instilled Pete's gentlemanly manners. The last thing she wanted for her brother was to evoke feelings of sadness.

"Relax," Pete said. "Mom would have loved to see my rise from the lagoon of a male teenage creature, but Sally gets all the credit."

"Sally?" Audrey said as Pete started the car. "I don't recognize that name."

"That's 'cause my secret weapon is safe and sound at the University of Rochester. New York, that is."

"Aren't you graduating from high school in June?"

"Done and did that last year."

She rubbed at her tight neck. So many changes. "A year early?"

"Sure did. Your bratty brother has grown up." He laughed. "You're looking at an honors student who received a full scholarship as a biology major and was accepted as a freshman a year early. And that's where I met Sally."

"Oh my, Pete." She rubbed his arm. "Congratulations. I bet Pop and..."

Pete made a right turn. "It's okay, sis. To say, Mom, that is. It's not like it's a dirty name or conjures up lousy memories."

Audrey wrapped her arms around her middle. "I know. I'm sorry."

That's another thing—stop apologizing for everything. You won't even get through a full day at home if you're sorry-faced or weepy."

Aware that he meant well, she nodded. "So, tell me about Sally. Then, Caroline."

"Ha. I wondered when you'd ask about sis, who misses you lots. But first, Sally. She's beyond hot—"

"I kind of figured that, but spare me the details."

"Honestly, I was going to say that she's hot, not just in the looks department but in every way. She's smart—much more intelligent than I am and anyone else I know—charming, hilariously funny, and she loves my cooking. That's a good thing since her only culinary skill is burning toast. You won't meet her unless you come to visit at school —she couldn't make it here with me for the funeral. As it is, I'm only here for two more days before I head back. Hey—how long are you staying? Is this a permanent return?"

"Return of the prodigal daughter? Oh, no. And I truly hope Pop doesn't see it that way. I'm here to pay my respects and will return to London, or wherever they need me, afterward. That's where I'll be until this bloody war ends. I will, though, make it my priority to visit you—wherever you may be—when I return home. Hopefully, the next time will be for a much happier occasion, like your wedding."

"That would be my number one dream come true," Pete said, his tone so mature, sweet, and sincere compared to when Audrey had left for the Red Cross. "We talked, though. Both of us agree that it would be best if we graduate first and get our feet cemented in our work."

Audrey believed it was best for Pete to stay in college and avoid the draft. She could only hope and pray that by the time he graduated, the war would be over. Maybe people would finally be able to enjoy life instead of destroying it worldwide. However, this was his decision to make, his life to live. So far, so good.

"Now, tell me about our darling sister Caroline."

"I love your dedication to sticking with your questions, sis. No sarcasm, by the way."

"None taken," she replied with relief. In the short time she had spent with this new, wonderful version of her brother, she had come to respect him and did not want any ill feelings to develop between them.

"It's Caro, by the way. Don't call her Caroline, or you'll never hear the end of it."

Audrey clapped her hands together. "I love it."

"She's sassy, smart too, for an eighth-grader, and controls Pop with her puppy-brown eyes. The kid doesn't even have a pimple on her face—just tons of drooling guys hanging out, escorting her home from school, and calling her left and right. Pop is close to fit-stage each time the blasted phone rings, but I swear, all Caro has to do is blink, and he melts faster than butter." They both laughed hard, then sobered just as fast. "Caro took Mom's death pretty badly. By the time I arrived from Rochester—two days after the accident—she was a wreck. When I wasn't with Pop at the funeral home making arrangements, I spent time cuddling with her. Or, maybe she cuddled—calmed—me." He sighed. "It's all a blur now. It's been three long weeks."

"I would have gotten here sooner if I could."

"I know you would. And don't let Pop fool you—he knows you would have, as well."

There it was, the segue into the elephant-in-the-room topic.

"How's Pop taking things?"

"He's hurting, but he won't talk about it. You know how he is—probably like many fathers, taking things on the chin for their kids. Just call him Mr. Stoic." Pete grunted. "I'll probably be like that one day when I have my own brood of kids. It's genetics, I'm sure. Speaking of which, I'm a biology major. I want to explore the role of genetics in impacting human-social life, but that field is still in its early stages. Maybe one day soon, it will be recognized as its own subject, likely becoming the next major frontier for humanity, one that we cannot turn back from."

"You've always been a science buff. Do you want to become a physician?"

He shrugged. "Or go into research. I'm not sure. I have a little time before making the big decision."

She wanted to ask about Sally's studies, but needed to learn more about their father. Since they only had about three minutes until they reached home, she should ask without hesitation. "How's Pop dealing with the subject of me when it comes up?"

"We're practically home."

"That bad?" she asked, feeling the gooseflesh return to her arms.

"He has his good and bad days."

She hoped today would be a good one. "Any hints on how to deal with him? Sorry to say, but I've grown rusty."

"Ride with the breeze if you can."

That was good advice for getting along with just about anyone, though her father might be an exception. Hopefully, the tension between them remained in the past. She was willing to take a chance on mending their relationship and hoped he felt the same. If anything, the passing of her mother, his wife, might serve as a constant reminder to both of them that time is a precious gift between two people. Taking a deep breath, she said, "I will surely try."

"Good timing." Pete rounded the corner. "And here we are, home sweet home. And look at that—a nearby parking spot." He pulled into the diagonal parking spot in front of their father's shoe repair shop.

Audrey looked at the store's front window, which displayed old-fashioned repair equipment and 1890s white kid leather lace-up women's shoes. "Not much has changed," she said, painfully aware that any differences she would see would be upstairs, in the family's apartment above the shop. She decided to handle her approach like a bandage: rip it off quickly, get the pain over with fast. Without delay, she pushed open the car door and got out, practically jumping out of the vehicle.

"Go for it, sis!" Pete called after her.

Audrey didn't need to ask what he meant. They both understood that confronting Pop would be difficult, but it was necessary. Still, she didn't expect her father to open the side door leading upstairs to their flat, step out, and look her in the eyes.

17

LISELOTTE/ANNA, OCTOBER 1944

Uncertain which was darkest—the moonless night or the sewer beneath the former Łódź ghetto where they were trudging through—Anna followed Magda. The only thing she was sure of was that Magda was leading her away from Klaus. At that moment, that was all that mattered, and she was willing to tolerate wet, damp feet, a constant chill, and the fear of being caught by anyone who saw her as disposable.

Magda quickly moved to her right, causing the water to ripple. "Don't look down."

Anna had to trust this woman, whose reasons for escaping the camp were kept secret but strong enough to make her take the same risks Anna faced. If Magda warned against looking in a certain direction, there was probably a good reason—perhaps a dead body or what was left of one. From overheard conversations, many people—especially Jews and POWs—used the sewers to hide and escape from the Nazis' confinement. If she and Magda spent much time together, they would have plenty of chances to talk about their lives and what brought them to this point in their journey.

Anna shifted her dim *latarka* at Magda's back, then lowered the light to the water. Despite the dimness, she stepped aside as Magda had done. A cold, watery mixture that looked and smelled like a combination of acrid and rotten waste, soapy substances, and unknown chemical sludge rose above her shoes. Fortunately, just before leaving the camp, Magda relented and gave Anna a pair of high-ankle boots and socks. Although they were soaked seconds after entering the sewer, and her feet felt as if they were swimming, she could walk better than in the shoes she had left behind.

A memory of her life when she was still Liselotte, before meeting Gerhard, flickered before her. Seeing her younger self was sad: a bratty, demanding teenager who constantly whined to her mother when she did not get her way, accusing her of playing games by taunting her with the supposed dangers Hitler, the madman, inflicted upon Germany and the rest of the world. Too bad her younger self believed she knew better than an adult. Too bad she refused to see that her mother loved her. In a series of precious life moments, after falling madly for Gerhard, Liselotte had gone from a self-centered child to a mother of twin girls, one with serious developmental issues, living in a country determined to dominate the world without hesitation to kill anyone who did not meet the Aryan standard of the human race. To make things more complicated, she was now trying to escape from a man who wanted to keep her captive, telling her how to serve him better in the name of the Third Reich.

"We don't have much further to go before we make our exit," Magda said softly. She had already warned that any conversation between them would need to be in whispers. "Are you holding up, Anna?"

"I'm looking forward to getting away from this moat."

"If only it were a moat surrounding a fairy-tale castle. It could be worse, though."

Magda's reply helped put their current situation into perspective. "You're right."

"When we exit," Magda continued, steering their conversation in a different direction, "we will walk about five kilometers through very dense woods. This won't be the time to worry about wolves or other creatures of the night." She swore. "Especially when the real beasts wear a uniform and won't hesitate to kill you."

Anna nodded, grateful for their conversation, which slightly improved the atmosphere and helped calm her anxiety, which she had tried to hide from Magda. "No worries about me. I've traveled in the dark plenty of times, both in Berlin and in rural areas." Anna thought about the men she had encountered in two separate situations, both with malicious intentions toward her. "And I agree with you about the true beasts. I'm all too aware of the dangers posed by animals versus humans. I'd take a confrontation with an animal any day." She did wish she were equipped with at least a knife, but she focused her mind on escaping from Poland and their shared goal of reaching England.

Magda let out a muffled snicker. "That's for sure. If we had to make a run for it, at least it's autumn and we don't have to worry about the weather making our walk more dangerous than it already is."

Anna was about to ask for more details about her travel plans, but Magda pointed ahead.

"We're almost done here." Magda fell silent again.

Anna's thoughts quieted as well, offering a calming numbness. The faces of Klaus, her mother, and even her children faded away. The tension in her knotted muscles surprisingly lessened, giving her more energy. She knew this would not last, but for now, it ironically pushed her to keep moving forward.

Anna guessed that thirty minutes had gone by since they entered the sewer. Just as she was starting to daydream about places she might escape to with Magda, a light flickered ahead. She looked down at her arm wrapped around Magda's. Who had gripped the other first?

"You are?" said an unmistakable male voice in French. Luckily, Anna's past language studies did not fail her now, and she could understand every word he uttered.

"The trees are swaying," Magda replied in French, surprising Anna. Or was Anna more amazed that Magda was seemingly ready to speak in code?

"Katerina?" the man asked.

"*Non*. Magda."

"*Très bien*. Follow me."

Magda looked at Anna and signaled her to continue. Anna, both curious and cautious, had no choice but to follow this man. Magda brought up the rear. The three of them trudged through the dark tunnel for about fifteen minutes, with only the constant dripping of water for sound. Suddenly, the stranger stopped. Anna would have bumped into him if Magda hadn't extended her arm in time. "Up there," the man said, shining his light on a rope ladder that led to a square wooden hatch. The mushrooms growing on the surface suggested that either the hatch hadn't been used in a while or the wood was rotting. Possibly both.

Anna pushed aside her squeamishness about mushrooms in anything other than her dinner dish and followed the man up the ladder, hoping the battered doorway to the outside world would hold as he tried to open it. When he pushed open the hatch and the red, orange, and pink of dawn shone brightly, Anna squinted so hard she wobbled and reached out for anything that might give her support.

"Let me help," the man said, offering her a hand. "You need to quickly get your sea legs back."

"Thank you…" She wanted to ask him for his name and tell him her real name, but the way Magda stared at her, tapping her pursed lips with her index finger, warned her to stay quiet. She inwardly sighed and let the others continue.

Magda reached into her tunic and pulled out a fistful of Reichsmark. She handed the man the payment and then nodded toward Anna. "There's a little extra for her."

The man smiled in appreciation. "Do you know what to do now?"

"Yes," Magda said.

"Good." Without a word more, he darted off.

Magda grabbed Anna by the elbow and spun her around in the opposite direction from where the man was headed. Pointing toward the dense woods, she said, "Let's go before brighter daylight exposes us."

The two hurried away and walked in silence for what had to be at least an hour. Anna, wanting to end a barrage of scary what-if thoughts, cleared her throat in the hope she could get Magda to talk. "Please, it's time you told me about yourself. Where are you from? Why were you in that camp?"

Magda grunted. Anna understood her unspoken question: Where do I begin? Anna hoped Magda wasn't debating whether she could trust her with personal details. Although, to be fair, they both had reasons to be curious, let alone suspicious of each other. For all Magda knew, Anna might be a German woman with fake documents that appeared convincing, yet she was fleeing from Klaus, a Nazi who wouldn't simply sigh and let her go without consequences. As for Anna, she was running away with a woman she knew nothing about, a woman who was clearly being held against her will at the former Łódź ghetto camp, making her seem like someone who probably knew too much and would be hunted.

Above, a pair of geese honked. Anna thought to use the noisy birds as a means to wedge back into the conversation. "At least it's only geese. I've heard that Poland has bison roaming its woods—do you think that's a concern for us?"

"I've heard those large animals roam in far eastern Poland. Ack. Maybe it's the Soviet Union now? Maybe Germany has claimed that land... stupid war. Who knows? I don't think we need to worry, at least not about bison—we're heading south."

"Ah, so we're passing through Poland. There must be concerns about the Nazis stopping us, no matter which route we take, right? So, tell me our exact destination and your plans to keep us safe."

"You ask a lot of questions."

"And you don't answer any of them."

For several more minutes, they wove through thick brush, stepped over fallen logs, and if Magda was anything like Anna, she also ignored the burning stitch in her side.

"You know me by the name I gave you," Magda said, stopping Anna in her tracks. She gestured for Anna to keep going. "Do not expect to hear my last name. I might be French. Or not."

"Interesting way to put it. Then again, I might be Anna or not."

"You're funny," Magda said, though in the first light tone Anna had heard her use.

"During my school years, my friends said my humor was a strength of mine," Anna said. "Honestly, most of the time it's a clumsy attempt to hide nerves."

"I think everything will turn out fine."

Magda *thinks*? Anna didn't like the sound of that. Then again, the last thing anyone could demand during wartime was a sense of certainty.

"Do you handle cold weather well?" Magda asked.

"I'd prefer sunny and warm days, but yes, I can tolerate the cold."

"We have about an hour's hike ahead. When we leave the woods, we'll still be in Poland. A man and his young daughter will be waiting for us. Don't be alarmed by his German uniform. At this point in the war, many of us aren't who we seem to be." Magda narrowed her eyes at Anna. "I'm sure you understand why."

Anna nodded.

"Good. This man will help us get our new travel documents and reach Kraków. You are German, right? Besides speaking it fluently, you wouldn't have been with that German you showed up with if you were Jewish or Roma, that's for sure."

When the war officially began on September 1, 1939, with Germany's invasion of Poland, Anna was Liselotte, a thirteen-year-old. All she wanted was to focus on defying her mother, having a fabulous time with her girlfriends, and attracting boys' attention. She had vaguely heard about the social differences among Germans, Poles, and Jews. Even then, she found it was odd because Germans and Poles followed different Christian denominations. The citizens of these countries strongly identified with their nationality—German Lutherans, Polish Catholics. However, Jews remained Jews regardless of the country they were from; only their faith, not their nationality, defined them. The start of the war resulted in the loss not only of their citizenship rights in Germany or Poland, but as the war progressed, Jews were also stripped of their right to practice their faith. They were a people forced to lose all sense of identity, as if they were not human beings. No country to belong to. No God to recognize.

Anna glanced at her fellow fugitive… runaway… escapee. All negative words reflected how Nazi Germany saw her and Magda. She swallowed hard before speaking. "*Ja.* I am German, not Jewish, nor Roma." She wanted to ask Magda the same question. Her instincts told her to hold back and respect her boundaries. Magda would reveal what she wanted when she wanted.

"Excellent. I'm not sure how long our stay in Kraków will last, but the plan presented to me is to get to Zakopane. From there, we'll eventually move from place to place into the Low Tatras, where we'll either wait out the winter or the end of this miserable war, whichever comes first."

Apparently, this escape plan was not put together overnight but instead involved a few—maybe many—people secretly plotting. Although Anna was eager to learn all the details, she accepted that now was not the time to press Magda for specifics. "Then what?" she asked simply.

"First things first," Magda said over her shoulder as she started walking again. "Let's get there—in one piece—and then you will learn more."

What other options did Anna have besides trusting a desperate woman with a getaway plan who was waiting for a specific time to carry it? She took a deep breath, exhaled loudly, and hurried to catch up with Magda.

They moved swiftly through the woods, slowing only when they faced two steep inclines. Without a compass, map, or guide, Anna pushed down any anxiety threatening to surface. One day, in the hopeful near future, if she ever needed to teach her daughters or anyone else about the meaning of blind trust, her escape story with Magda would serve as the perfect example. Maybe by then, she and her daughters—perhaps her mother as well, if their relationship could be healed—would have plenty to celebrate. Rosa's surprising health improvement. Regina's acceptance of why Liselotte had to leave when she did. Liselotte's mother's forgiveness of Liselotte leaving the family. And, especially, the hope for an end to this dreadful war, with Hitler and his Nazism wiped out, never to threaten again. Was this all a child's fantasy? Or just a desperate woman's hope? What would she do with her time besides loving and caring for her family? Become a history teacher and share vital lessons about the horrors of war? Maybe she should attend college and pursue journalism, reporting on how some truths of life are not all shiny and glittery. There were many possibilities if she kept holding onto her dreams.

A touch came to her arm. She glanced up at Magda.

"Are you okay?"

"I'm as fine as anyone can be, all things considered."

Magda huffed. "I called your name a few times."

"Oh? Pardon me. I was lost in my daydreams."

"Daydreaming is for a woman sitting at home on an overstuffed sofa, eating dates and not thinking twice about what's happening outside her parlor window. Not for people like us marching through the woods to save ourselves."

Anna thought it was best not to argue this subject. "What did you want to tell me?"

"I believe we're almost to the point where we'll meet that man and child."

"That's good news. Although I wish a child weren't involved."

"He might not have a choice but to bring the little one along. Let's hope we seem less suspicious with a child—maybe we'll be mistaken for two aunties." Magda pointed at another incline, mumbling that she hoped this was the last one. They kept hiking, glad to reach a flat area of open land.

Anna exhaled loudly. "I hope I never see another hill."

"This place does look like the location that had been described to me," Magda said. She stopped and shielded her eyes with her hand. "Over there. See that vehicle? That's our contact."

"How can you tell?" Anna asked, trying to ignore her pounding heart.

"By the child standing beside the man wearing an SS uniform, exactly what I was told to look for."

Just as she was about to respond, Anna grasped her throat, feeling like her words were getting stuck. She stepped back.

Magda seized her arm. "What's wrong?"

Anna wriggled free from Magda and dropped to the ground. "See that other person, the one not wearing a Nazi uniform? Tell me when he's gone."

Magda must have sensed her panic and crouched down next to her. After a few minutes, Magda propped herself up on her elbows for a peek before lowering herself back down beside Anna.

"No worries—the lone man is gone. It's just the man and child now. One vehicle as well."

Anna craned her neck for a look. Seeing only the two people Magda mentioned, she stood cautiously and reached out her hand to help Magda up.

"You don't think that was your friend from the Łódź ghetto?"

"If it was, he's certainly no friend." Anna slapped her hand over her mouth.

"Steady, now." Magda rested her hand on Anna's shoulder. "Are you feeling queasy?"

The last thing she wanted was to seem weak and unstable to Magda. She couldn't risk the other woman leaving her behind. She shook her head, pretending her stomach was calm, not upset, as Magda rightly guessed. "This doesn't make sense… how is he following me, already?" She closed her eyes tightly, forcing the images of Klaus out of her mind. When the nausea subsided, she faced Magda. "Tell me exactly where we are."

"We've traveled about two hours south of Łódź. Can't say exactly by kilometers."

"Well, that might be him," she replied, not wanting to say Klaus's name. "I don't know how he would have known to come here. Or why he suspected we would travel this way—I didn't leave any clues."

"Neither did I," Magda said, her tone sharp, matching the scrutinizing look she gave Anna.

Anna's stomach twisted again. "Magda, you do believe me, right? I wouldn't put us in harm's way."

"I believe you wanted to escape him as much as I wanted to get out of that horrible place, and that means doing whatever it takes to make it happen." Magda crossed her arms. "We'll talk more about this later. Would you like to stay here while I meet with this man, who is apparently waiting for us? I can ask about the other man, then signal to you that all is good, and then you can join us."

Fearing she would be left behind, Anna had only one reply. "I'm staying right beside you."

18

AUDREY, LATE NOVEMBER 1944

Sitting across from her father at the kitchen table, Audrey almost felt like she had never left home. Her pop's unlit pipe rested in an ashtray, waiting for his first smoke of the day, which usually followed their breakfast of scrambled eggs and white, buttered toast—his favorite. With him as the main breakfast cook, Mom had always enjoyed a few extra minutes to relax in bed or in the tub before starting her day of cleaning, cooking, and running errands before her family returned from school or work. Audrey, with her breakfast cooling on her plate, looked toward the hallway, expecting her mom to walk into the room.

Pop set his fork loudly on his plate. "I'm still doing that too."

Audrey shook her head as her cherished memories conflicted with this now surreal childhood home of hers, where everyone and everything had changed. She looked at her father, silently questioning why they were all alive except for Mom. After three weeks of visiting her family, she was still expecting to see her mom walk into the kitchen, her sweet smile lighting up the room.

"Does it get any easier?" she asked.

"Not fair—you're leaving today," Pop answered indirectly.

Despite the heavy subject of losing her mother and the fact that

Audrey was about to leave to return to Europe, once again putting too many miles between her family and herself, she recognized her pop's attempt at humor. "Audrey saves the world, you know."

His slight smile faded. "I cannot say it enough, but I'm so proud of you, hon."

Maybe the only quirk about losing her mom was that it made her father, siblings, and herself realize they needed to get their act together—to forgive, overlook, and love, love, and love each other. It might have taken them this long to drop the awkwardness between them, but she'd come to accept her pop's expressions of appreciation for her as if it were a warm quilt on a cold day. There was a reason why the saying 'better late than never' existed.

She smiled. "Keep talking like this, Pop, and I might not go anywhere."

"That's my intention," he said in his most deadpan tone. "I'd take you up on that, but I know that's not what you truly want to hear."

"Don't," she said, and looked at the clock over the sink. Her cab would arrive in thirty minutes. "It's difficult enough leaving—"

"We'll be okay."

"I'm sorry. My dedication to helping war victims find missing family members is once again disrupting my own family—talk about irony." She stood and grasped her father's hands. "I should be here with you, Pete, and Caroline… I mean, Caro. I'm not sure I'll ever get used to her new nickname."

"Don't apologize. What you're doing to help others is vital during this terrible war. I just wish your mom were here—she would be so proud of you."

Audrey couldn't remember the last time she hugged her father, but she took three steps around the table and pulled him into her arms. "Will you… you know, hold up?"

He glanced at the untouched food on her plate. "Most definitely. After I get over you rejecting my cooking, I'll be as good as my old gruff self."

"Oh, dear." Audrey glanced over her shoulder at her breakfast, which was congealing into a mysterious blob. "Before a flight, my tummy treats food as an enemy target. Don't take it personally. I would even turn down one of Mom's homemade pies..." She groaned, turning away as her eyes brimmed with hot tears.

"It's okay, Audrey."

"No, it's not."

"It has to be. As we discussed, it's best not to leave your mom out of the conversation, tiptoeing around this place as if mentioning her name might disturb her peace and quiet. We'll honor her more by sharing our memories of her." He tapped the side of his head. "In all honesty, I was a mess during that first week after her death. Here's the thing—I learned that by including her in my daily life, at least in thought and heart, I started to think outside of myself. Mildred Wilson was a real person, a saint in my book. I'm still her husband. I'm still a father, a businessman, a friend, and a good neighbor. I need to keep giving to others. Your mom would be quite sad if I got trapped in my grief and forgot about those I care about."

A sense of comfort wrapped around Audrey, chasing away the last of the heavy blues that had been weighing her down since she learned about her mother's passing. "Pop, that's a good way to think of it."

"She'll always be with us." He leaned away. "Finish getting ready. The cabbie will be here soon—I doubt he'll wait."

Five minutes later, as she headed toward the kitchen, she remembered the last time she left this house three years ago to train with the Red Cross, convinced she was doing the right thing by helping her country. One lesson after another in the field showed her how much more she needed to learn about how life unfolds. Now, at age twenty-four, the only truth she knew was that some lessons waiting for her would be good, and she would cherish them. Still, much of reality would be tough, probably testing and shaking her to the core. She had to keep moving forward because the alternative, being paralyzed by fear, would accomplish nothing.

"Pop," she called out. Not seeing him or hearing the usual sound of his shrill whistle, she looked around the kitchen and then the living room. Her large duffel was missing. She figured her father had taken it downstairs to watch for the taxi. She slipped her small carry-on bag and her purse over her shoulder and headed toward the stairs, calling out once more.

"Down here," Pop replied.

"I didn't miss him, did I?"

"No. I'm keeping an eye out, though. Do you have everything?"

"Everything but you," she said, not caring how mawkish she sounded. When she reached him, she looked at her watch. "Best if I stand outside so the cabbie doesn't do a U-turn." She bent down to clutch the duffel, but her father grasped the bag and stepped outside with her. Fortunately, yesterday's cool breeze was gone. The morning's sunshine carried a pleasant hint of warmth.

She thought her words would surely bring a smile to his pursed lips. "What's wrong, Pop? Maybe I can look into getting another flight if you would like."

"Nah. I'm just thinking, that's all." He half chuckled. "We all know how dangerous that could be."

"Is it about tracking down Babenko family members? I promised I would."

He pointed at the yellow cab that stopped at the stoplight. "Yes, and I know you'll keep your promise. Call me nervous, that's all."

"About whether I might not discover news about our lost family?"

He shrugged. "Or, what you might learn about them."

While working at the Red Cross, Audrey faced the daily uncertainty experienced by people missing their family members. She understood how this fear could influence each individual, either helping or hindering their efforts on the research horizon.

She placed a hand on her father's arm. "Facing change, Pop, is never easy. When it comes to unknown family roots, the firm soil we've always stood on suddenly feels loose and slippery. Our grasp on life becomes shakier, and we realize how tiny we are in this huge world."

He nodded. "And the solution, my wise daughter?"

If only she had the right answer. "We readjust, a specialty that humans have practiced since the days of Adam and Eve."

A car horn blared, and they both jumped.

"Your limo has arrived," Pop said. "Time to go, sweetheart."

"Yes, it is." It was time for her to readjust once again.

19

LISELOTTE/ANNA, KRAKÓW TO ZAKOPANE, JANUARY 1945

Anna woke up on New Year's Day in the host family's home, where she and Magda had been staying since arriving in Kraków after fleeing from Łódź. The Janicki family included Pani and Pan Janicki, and their daughter Klaudia, who was the same age as Anna—nineteen—though Anna told everyone she was twenty. The family opened their doors and hearts to Anna and Magda. Would they have done the same if the two were Jewish or Roma? Publicly, the Janicki family supported the Third Reich, but privately, they condemned Hitler's hatred of every non-Aryan. Was it an act to trap them? Magda was reserved around their hosts. Anna was also cautious, but she grew more trusting as the weeks went by.

The rare peaceful night's sleep Anna had enjoyed was shattered the moment she opened her eyes on that New Year's Day morning, glanced at the cot just a breath away from hers, and saw that Magda was gone. Propped up against her pillow, a note begged to be read.

Dear Anna,

This is both a difficult and joyful letter to write. First, the good news: my pre-arranged contact arrived for me as planned, and I had to leave in the middle of the night. I didn't want to wake you because I know how precious and rare sleep is to you. And, honestly, I didn't want to see your teary eyes or hear any cries of 'no, not without me,' because soon it will be your time, and I did not want to upset you.

It may have taken me some time to reveal my true identity and how I ended up in the ghetto, where the only bright spot was meeting you. I shared all this with you just yesterday out of safety concerns. Leaving you behind is difficult for me. I will never forget you. I hope you will always remember me.

Please don't be upset with me for not telling you that this city would be our separation point. Risks should not be taken during this terrible time.

Now, do not delay—destroy this note. I can't specify the exact time you leave, but you will know. You won't be forgotten. I will always remember you and pray that you are reunited with your daughters and mother.

M

ANNA REREAD THE MESSAGE, tore it into tiny pieces, and then stuffed the fragments into her pocket to toss into the privy. She was genuinely happy for Magda but also upset that Magda had left her behind. Having no other choice, she was on her own in finding a way back home and continuing her search for her family. Since leaving her childhood home, she had to adapt to whatever life threw at her. Though she couldn't single-handedly harm the Third Reich, she believed she had caused enough concern for Klaus and those working at the Kinder-KZ children's camp, and likely, Klaus was pursuing her. Since escaping his clutches, the fear of someone discovering her was as real as the ground beneath her feet. This fear, as unavoidable as it was, became her constant companion. She learned to use it wisely, sharpening her senses for potential danger, deciding whom to trust—if anyone—and improving her decision-making.

The major lesson she learned, which she believed helped her grow from a bratty, selfish teenager into a more mature adult, was that she was better at adapting than she had thought. Each new day brought a fresh life lesson. During her lowest moments, she had raised her hand, shaken her fists, and mouthed the words: Just how much do I really need to learn? And in her happiest times? She was grateful for a new day, a new chance to reconnect with her family and improve her life.

The more time she spent in Kraków, the more she realized she had met her match: the relentless cold of winter. Her days in Berlin might have also been cold and snowy, but nothing compared to the bone-chilling frost of this Nazi-occupied capital of the General Government, which supplied the Third Reich with agriculture and light industry. So far, the city had avoided the brutal mass destruction of war. That was, if one was not a Jew. About 16,000 unfortunate people had been rounded up and placed into the Kraków Ghetto. The ghetto was dismantled between June 1942 and March 1943, before she and Magda arrived in the city. The forced ghetto residents were deported to either the Belzec extermination camp to the east of the city or Auschwitz, sixty kilometers to the west, by train. When Anna learned about these people and the suffering they endured at the hands of many who followed orders without resistance—even participating in killing people for their different faith, culture, and heritage—she decided that, in some way, she would spend her post-war years helping to spread love and respect, two things that were scarce these days. Whether this war would end with only white Aryans living and controlling the world was yet to be seen. For now, instead of questioning the Supreme Being's intentions, like many have since the war began, she spent her days praying for an end to this madness and seeking guidance on what to do next.

In a state of chaos over Magda's sudden departure and the frenzy that comes with oversleeping, Anna threw on a blouse and skirt. She slipped into shoes—thanks to the Janickis' daughter, who had been generous and caring to Anna from the very moment she and Magda arrived at their home. Thinking of Klaudia, she wondered if she knew about Magda leaving. If not, should she tell Klaudia and her family? For now, since she was running late, she skipped breakfast. Walking through the kitchen, she exited the small house near the Vistula River to go to work.

A strong wind blew north from the Tatra Mountains, which loomed in the south. Her hood flew off her head, and, as if someone had shoved her, she was pushed back against the front door. The doorknob jabbed into the small of her back. Usually careful not to draw attention, she gritted her teeth and held back a yelp. After the wave of pain subsided, she straightened and took a deep breath. "I can do this," she whispered, remembering that, even though many had surrendered their will to live and millions had been killed in this ruthless war, she wanted to survive, and a gust of wind would certainly not defeat her like an army. Again, Anna faced the wind, and this time, she managed to step outside.

Klaudia walked up the snow-covered path toward the house and waved at Anna. "What is meant to hang, won't drown, Anna," Klaudia said in Polish, a language she had been helping Anna learn beyond the simple basic words she had used at the Łódź ghetto. The saying implied that certain things in life will happen, and that one cannot escape fate. Though Anna was uncertain why her friend would say these words now.

"Another Polish…" Anna glanced quizzically at Klaudia. "What's the word I'm looking for?"

"*Przysłowie*," Klaudia said, the Polish word for proverb. She spoke it more slowly and waited for Anna to repeat. Then she shifted the hemp satchel from her shoulder to the floor and pulled out some mail.

"You're an early riser," Anna said.

Klaudia straightened Anna's hood. "In all seriousness, there's a reason why we Poles have a saying about choosing action instead of filling your mind with negative possibilities. Would you like a quick lesson on how this German occupation is not the first for Poland, though we all hope it will be the last?"

"So, you're saying that what the Germans did to Poland and its people might be fate that can't be changed, but taking action is better than worrying?"

Klaudia nodded. "Yes. You're a good learner."

"The proverb you shared is a good enough lesson for today." Anna regretted the abruptness of her words and mumbled an apology for her rudeness.

"What's troubling you?" Klaudia reached for Anna's arm. "How can I help?"

"Magda is…" Anna glanced around to see if anyone was walking up the street or watching from a front yard. In a whisper, she added, "She's gone. She left a note."

"She's carrying out her plan?"

Anna rocked back on her heels. "How do you know about a plan?"

Klaudia offered a gentle smile. "Does not everyone during these troubling days have a plan of escape, especially strangers who seek emergency shelter like the two of you?"

A flood of tears filled Anna's eyes. Ashamed for not appearing stronger, especially since she expected this time would eventually come for Magda, and she should not be so emotional, Anna wiped her eyes instead, happy for her friend. "I can only hope she'll stay safe and…" She sniffled loudly, silently cursing her emotions she tried to restrain, and pushed out the single word she hoped would comfort her friend. "At peace."

Klaudia pulled Anna into a gentle hug. "Yes, I wish her these things too. From what I've sensed from the little I've learned about her, she may have been a strong woman, but she definitely didn't have it easy."

Aware of how Magda remained reticent about her past, Anna doubted Klaudia knew even half of the abusive horrors she had endured—the mistreatment Anna had only recently learned about.

"Let's believe," Klaudia continued, "that Magda is on a quick trip home to her family and will always stay safe."

Magda's dream was to return to her homeland of Belgium and help other women overcome the same hardships she endured during the war. Anna would greatly miss her friend. Selfishly hoping Magda would join her on the next part of her journey, Anna wished her the best as she returned to her mother, grandfather, and her two nieces. For now, she needed to change the subject quickly, or she would never leave the house without crying all day in front of too many curious people.

She watched the handful of mail Klaudia was holding. "See any dashing men while you were out?" An innocent question between two young women, except Anna was not ready for Klaudia's serious expression, complete with a furrowed brow.

"Yes. While waiting in line at the *poczta* for the mail, I overheard a dark-haired man with intense brown eyes and a slim build asking if anyone had seen a woman named Liselotte, though he warned she might be using an alias."

Klaudia studied Anna's hair so closely that Anna wondered if the girl had become suspicious of her fading dyed blond hair. Then again, throughout history, women have always done whatever was necessary to survive or, at the very least, to keep up their appearance. Surely, Anna wasn't the only one in war-torn Poland with dyed hair. "Did this person say anything else?" she prompted.

"He went on to describe this Liselotte."

Anna swallowed hard. She was certain this man was Klaus. But how did he know her real name? What else did he know about her, her family? How did he figure out she was here? Was he searching every Polish town or city until he found her? And then what? How and why would he conduct a personal search for her during a war, especially one that would take so much time from his work? It was not as if she knew his most personal feelings that she could use to betray him to the Nazis. All she wanted was to be rid of him, but for some reason, he wanted her. Why couldn't he just forget about her? If he wanted revenge, then her escape from him, from Poland, was in jeopardy.

Her crashing thoughts coalesced into a single realization: there had to be more to Klaus Agers than just the Himmler-obliger on a relentless quest to Germanize the world. The way he guided her out of Berlin, convincing her to follow him in ways she now saw as desperate and naive. Despite everything, she had never revealed her background, especially regarding her daughters.

And the uncomfortable times he had touched her?

The man either wanted something from her or wanted her for himself.

To control her? Was he so infatuated with her that he saw her as a romantic conquest? He was a strange one—dangerous, especially if he was after her. No, not if. She was now sure she hadn't imagined seeing him when she and Magda came out of the deep woods after escaping the ghetto. He had to be hunting her like a prized trophy. She pressed her lips, fighting back a scream. Why in the world did he want her? She was no one to him.

Anna looked toward the Tatras. It was time for her to move on. Staying in place would only put her and possibly the Janicki family in danger. But venturing into unknown wilderness, especially during the harsh winter and a war, was extremely risky.

Her lower back throbbed from hitting the doorknob, and she rubbed it, stumbling a little. She groped around the doorway to try to steady herself.

Klaudia grabbed Anna's arm. "What's wrong, my friend? You don't look well. Are you dizzy?"

Anna nodded, flinching from both the terrible situation she was in and how she was feeling physically. She clutched her middle. "My stomach is somersaulting."

Klaudia touched Anna's forehead. "You don't feel especially warm. Let's not take any chances. I'll help you to your bed. When *Mamushka* comes home from work, I'll tell her what's happening. Should I go to the factory and tell them you won't be in today?"

Although Anna was nervous about facing disciplinary action if she failed to show up for work at the textile factory—possibly even losing her job—she wanted to avoid the greater, more costly risk of running into Klaus. Whatever his motive, he could easily sabotage her plans to get back home, find her family, and start her life anew. With his word against hers, and leveraging his Nazi allegiance and connections, he would almost certainly seem more credible. He could send her to a work camp, accuse her of being Jewish or an enemy of the Reich, and send her off to nearby Auschwitz. It was not unheard of—Magda had experienced it herself. Her unfortunate friend had become a victim of vicious men driven by their sexual desires and power while working for Hitler. She had miscarried once and hadn't conceived since. Magda was only lucky when she met a man from the Polish Resistance who, disguised as a Nazi officer, visited the Łódź ghetto and promised to help her escape. Her planned departure coincided with the day Anna and she met.

Anna searched Klaudia's eyes. "When is your father arriving home from work today?"

"The usual time—right before supper."

She weighed the risks of not raising suspicion about her absence from work at the factory versus avoiding Klaus. Staying out of Klaus's sight won. "Yes, I think it's best if you report me as ill at work. Tell them I'm sick with the flu that no one would want to catch. I'm going back to bed."

"I was hoping you would say that. Now, do you need my help getting back to your room? Would you like me to bring you something to eat?"

"No, thanks," Anna said, rubbing her belly, which was genuinely upset from anxiety, not about food. "You're going to my workplace, which is plenty of help, and I—"

Klaudia retraced her footprints in the snow toward the road. Glancing over her shoulder, she said, "Go and rest. I'll take care of things for you at the factory."

Following the Janickis' family's recent practice during the German occupation, Anna locked the front door. However, since secured doors wouldn't keep out military fighters, resistance members, or anyone else trying to enter, the locked door didn't ease her stress and made her even more anxious. She shuffled through the small kitchen, only stopping to pump water from the sink for a drink. Carrying the glass, she went to the room she had shared with Magda until last night.

Oh, my friend. Where are you? Are you thinking of me? Do you only think about returning to your family, which I can't blame you for? Stay safe. Be well.

Taking the pillow that Magda had used and scrunching it up behind her own, Anna leaned against the rough cushions. Feeling woozy from the fight to stay alive, from becoming a person without a home, whether by her actions or the result of war, and living in a foreign country that was besieged by her homeland, she closed her eyes. Determined not to fall asleep, she mentally listed the first things she would do upon returning home… wherever and with whoever.

The sound of a door slamming woke Anna from a dreamless sleep. Jolting upright, she turned toward Magda's bed to find it empty. Where was her friend? And more importantly, where was she?

The bedroom door opened. "There you are, sleepyhead. I knocked, but I thought something was wrong when you didn't answer."

Klaudia? Anna rubbed the side of her head. "Sorry. I must have fallen asleep."

Klaudia waved her hand to dismiss Anna's awkwardness. "No worries. I'm glad you're fine. My mother's not home yet, but Tata is. He would like to speak with you. Do you need help to go downstairs?"

Testing her feet and balance, Anna stood. Without swaying, she said, "Looks like I just needed some rest." Worry gnawed at her inside, but she fought the urge to rub her stomach. "Is your father upset with me?"

Klaudia's right brow lifted. "No. Why should he be? I did tell him that this stranger was asking for Lissel…Lissy…"

"Liselotte," Anna said, surprised at how unfamiliar her name now sounded.

"Yes, Liselotte," Klaudia repeated. "A pretty name, isn't it?" she asked, but her eyes flickered nervously. She fumbled for an excuse to leave, deciding she needed to tend to the chickens.

Anna shrugged off Klaudia's nervousness, the first she saw between them, and watched her leave. Slipping out of bed, Anna straightened her lopsided skirt and blouse, brushed her hair, and, inhaling deeply, headed downstairs. Pan Janicki sat at the head of the plain oak kitchen table, cradling a mug of tea that carried a minty aroma through the low-ceilinged room.

He tilted his chin toward the empty chair across from him. "Have a seat, Anna. Would you like a cup of tea? The kettle's still hot—help yourself." After she declined, he added, "My daughter says you've been unwell."

"I'm feeling better now. Nothing to worry about, or catch."

"That's good. It would be bad timing for everyone if you were sick."

Unsure of what Pan Janicki might mean, Anna sat cautiously, forcing herself to look directly at him instead of averting her gaze out of nervousness.

"My wife and I welcomed you and Magda into our home without question."

"I'm very grateful, Pan Janicki. We—I don't know what I would've done without your help."

"Anna, you're a strong woman who doesn't give up easily. Strength and determination are necessary traits these days."

Surprised by his praise and assessment, she was about to thank him, but he continued.

"I can't—won't—say much about my… let's say, activities. I will say that I do what I can to help those in need."

"There are so many who need help," she murmured. Her daughter Rosa's eyes flashed before her. Her mother's voice echoed around her, warning her to fear those eager to snatch up twins and make them vanish. The burnt smell of not only Gerhard's body but also his loving parents, who cared for her unconditionally. The sunken-eyed, despairing look of the starving as they stared at the rotund guts of men welcoming gluttony for Aryans. Jews, Roma, the mentally ill, and anyone labeled *Untermenschen*—subhuman—were taken from their homes, towns, and countries and thrown into camps where no human should be kept. Children were torn from their families, conditioned until they broke, and forced to forget their birth identities, reprogrammed to become someone else. Would these horrors ever end, or were they all living in hell on earth now?

Anna lowered her gaze to her lap. "I assume you know about Magda's sudden departure."

"Yes. I arranged it."

She swallowed hard and peered directly into his eyes. "Pardon?"

My wife and I are Catholic Poles. We assist the Resistance and other underground activities. That's how you came to stay with us." He leaned forward. "You are not to speak of this to anyone." A command, not a question or plea.

"I won't, but…" Her hands shook so much that she clasped them together on her lap.

He raised a hand to stop her. "I will not tell you more than you need to know. You will not tell me more than I ask of you." He gestured between the two of them. "We understand each other, right?"

"I trust you."

Pan Janicki gave a slight nod. "With a stranger in town asking for a woman who matches your description, it's time for you to leave. This is sooner than we expected."

"But how?" She licked her dry bottom lip. As eager as she was to go home, leaving now in the middle of cold January without Magda—her only confidant, like a sister—felt daunting and dangerous. Then, the truth hit her. "I've put you and your family in danger, haven't I?"

"Not yet. But it's time to act for our mutual benefit. We've learned the Red Army is advancing west. We hope they will liberate most, if not all, of Poland. Still, it's best to get you out quickly. I'm sorry it couldn't have been with Magda." He leaned back and crossed his arms. "This is what I've arranged for you. You need to pack your clothes. Klaudia was told to give you extra items for the snow and cold. However, we deliberately haven't told her any details—she's young, too trusting, and my wife and I will do what we must to ensure that she's not held accountable."

"No wonder she seems a bit shaken," Anna said softly. "I promise you that I won't slip details out to her."

"We'll give you some cash and food. You leave tonight, at midnight."

"By myself? How? Where?"

"You will follow my instructions to meet a man and a woman here in Kraków. They are also on the run. You're all young—about the same age—and in relatively good health. The three of you are fit to make this journey—don't worry. First, go to Zakopane, south of here. Three others will be waiting for you. From there, you will go into the

Tatras, traveling from village to village until the war ends or another country is deemed safe. The journey is tough, but you should be fine if you stay alert and listen for instructions."

Should be fine. Yet, what other choice did she have? As much as Klaus seemed ready to trip her up by hunting her down, she doubted he would trek into the cold, mountainous Tatras. He could easily wait her out in the comfort of his parents' house, enjoying everything good Nazis tend to indulge in, whether it's the delights of food or contributing to the deaths of countless thousands or perhaps millions of people. She was the one who needed to be brave and make this challenging trip.

"Yes, I'll do what you say."

"Excellent. There are a few more things you need to know. First, these people you will be traveling with are Jews. Do you have a problem with that?"

"No," she said without hesitation.

"They have obtained Aryan documentation to help cross the borders. They are determined to pursue freedom. Do you?"

"Yes."

"Good," Pan Janicki said. "Then, together, you will stay strong and support each other. However, as you know, not many want to help Jews escape to freedom."

She held back a sigh as a memory of a secondary school classmate came to mind. They had both enjoyed their Gymnasium classes until Hitler came into power, when he restructured education mainly for boys. At the same time, the curriculum for girls shifted to focus on how to be proper wives and mothers. The classmate's father had briefly taught history in the United States. Sympathetic to the idea of opportunity for all, he traveled to the U.S., expecting most citizens to respect the civil rights of Black Americans. He was shocked to find that not only were textbooks promoting *The Lost Cause* narrative, claiming the Civil War was fought over state rights rather than slavery, but society also harbored a lot of prejudice against Black Americans—prejudice that was often expressed in cruel ways, sometimes resulting in death. Here was someone expecting to see empathy and understanding. Instead, he witnessed the opposite: a belief that Black people did not deserve the same freedoms as White Americans. He returned to Germany, learned of Hitler's new decrees, and gave up his teaching license.

"Pan Janicki, I know this, but honestly, I don't understand why. The Jews didn't attack Germany or any other country. They became victims, along with many others of different faiths and backgrounds, who are often wrongly regarded as unworthy of life, as if they should be blamed for all the world's wrongs. Why wouldn't others be cheering for their victory?"

"Correct. As you know, that kind of thinking will only lead to danger, most likely the loss of your life. From the perspective of the Third Reich, freedom and rights are only for the Aryan. In their view, if someone thinks *liberally* like that, it proves they are not Aryan, whether German-blooded or not."

Despite chills running down her arms, she looked Pan Janicki in the eyes. "To be bold, I still fail to understand why more people refuse to help the Jews or anyone in need."

"Many people are hesitant to take the risk of being arrested, deported to a camp, or killed on the spot for helping the Jews. That is why this work is carried out secretly. No one wants to become the next target of hatred, imprisonment, or murder."

She smiled. "I'm thankful for your work. You have a golden heart."

He shook his head slightly. "I appreciate that, but I'm not innocent either. I admit it took me a while to figure out my role in this war. It also took me some time to recognize my prejudices against Jews and others, and that it was wrong. I then had to swallow my shame and help those in need."

"I understand," Anna said. "I've had many lessons—the hard way—these past few years." She averted her gaze. "I'm ashamed to admit that not too long ago I was a self-centered teenager who had a lot of growing up to do." Her breath hitched at the thought that these life lessons had come at the cost of her broken family and her separation from them. She needed to ask her mother for forgiveness, not the other way around. And one day, when they were mature enough to understand, she also needed to explain to her daughters her foolish naivety and ask for their forgiveness for leaving them behind. That is, if she could find both Regina and Rosa... and if Rosa could understand. If not, she could still give her the love she deserved to receive over the past few years. "Anna, it's never too late to renounce a wrong and to change. You're a different, better person now. Isn't that what truly counts?"

She pressed down on her lip.

"What are you thinking?" he asked.

"I'm curious about how you've been managing to avoid Nazi attention?"

Pan Janicki rubbed his hands together. "Due to my soil and crop production management skills, I've avoided the scrutiny that most Poles face. However, what hasn't escaped *my* notice is that, war or no war, people tend to think of themselves first, their families second, and sometimes friends and neighbors. Sad to say, this war won't end anti-Semitism or hatred in general. Sorry to be so grim."

"We all have to do what we can to make it to the next day, right?"

"Yes. You will be fine. One warning, though: never strap on a pair of skis if you don't want to be mistaken for trying to escape from the Nazi eye and get shot at."

She could tell that, unfortunately, he was not joking. She swallowed back her nervousness. "I will remember this advice."

"You need to get ready now. I will talk to my wife and daughter. Remember, you must never confide in anyone."

In gratitude, she hurried over to Pan Janicki and embraced him fiercely. She then excused herself to freshen up and pack for what she knew would be the longest trip of her life. A life! She still might have many more years ahead. She could help someone else get a chance to live. She might even be reunited with her family.

Anna headed toward the stairs leading to her bedroom. Despite the cold and the howling wind, it was best to use the outhouse before packing her personal belongings, few as they were, which was a good thing. The fewer she had, the easier it would be to escape in just a few hours.

She cautiously opened the front door and almost tripped over a tan fedora. Recognizing immediately who likely owned this Bavarian-style Tyrolean hat, she covered her mouth to hold back a scream. Bending down, she picked it up, stepped back inside, and quickly locked the door. The note pinned to the hat drew her attention.

My Liselotte,

I have found you. You are mine. I will continue to track your every movement. You will not escape my devoted attention. We were meant to be together forever. Take care of yourself, for me. I will see you soon.

Klaus

She collapsed onto the hand-woven brown and tan braided rug and leaned against the door for support. A pair of notes. First, upon waking this morning, a farewell message from Magda was written with words of friendship. Now, this evening, she received a warning from a madman in her pursuit. Threatening, fiendish, and ruthless. She quickly ran upstairs. With no time to spare, she shoved both notes from her mind. She had a journey to make.

20

AUDREY, VERSAILLES, FRANCE, 1945

On April 30, 1945, Audrey believed that, like her, everyone else in the world vowed never to forget the day Hitler killed himself. However, she also sensed the collective breath being drawn as people around the world wondered whether they could trust the news and if this meant the war was finally over. Was it safe to rejoice, or might someone worse take control? Would Germany surrender—and when? Signs pointed to a complete victory for the Allies—peace, the return of civilization, and the end of barbaric cruelty—being within reach. Spring had indeed arrived. Grass turned green. Trees leafed out. Flowers bloomed, and birds sang. Blue skies and bright sunshine warmed bodies and spirits.

And then it happened: Tuesday, May 8th. V-E Day.

On that glorious day, the joyful shouts outside pulled Audrey away from the paperwork scattered across her desk, reminding her to help find someone's lost brother, another's husband taken as a POW, a daughter stolen in the middle of the night. So many people missing. She had helped locate several and reunite them with their loved ones; yet, with the thousands—if not millions—unaccounted for, she felt no peace.

Audrey hastened to the double doors of the SHAEF office. During the liberation of France from Germany in August 1944, the Supreme Headquarters Allied Expeditionary Force established a registration and tracing service in Versailles for missing and displaced people affected by the war across Europe. Less than forty-eight hours after Audrey returned to London from visiting her family, she accepted the transfer to France, moved into a modest apartment above the office, and quickly fell in love with the country and its people. She hoped this would be her final move during the long, wretched war.

On the stone step in front of the office, as she saw the wide smiles on the men, women, and children stepping lively past her and continuing down the narrow cobblestone street, she knew the war had truly ended. Her gaze followed the crowd to the intersection of Avenue de Paris, where she observed a larger group of people. The joyful sounds streamed toward her: hurrahs, shouts of pure jubilation, the clap of improvised cymbals, whistles, and groups singing "La Marseillaise," the national anthem. All the sights were spectacular! She would never forget them. French flags, American flags, British flags—all waved by spectators as well as parade participants. No wonder people of all ages were running past her, eager to join the celebration. The long-awaited and well-deserved extravaganza would be even bigger in Paris. She could only hope that, despite the loss of so many lives in Poland, the heartbreak of destruction, and the uncertainty under Soviet rule, the Poles knew the war was over and that their hearts were once again full of hope.

Then why was she struggling to breathe? She leaned heavily against the doorframe. Closing her eyes, she pushed aside the guilt that haunted her daily for not finding news of her paternal family as she had promised her father. With no clues, her father's disappointed face flashed before her every day. Then in her mind, she saw her mom, brother, and sister. Heard their laughter, their sorrow, and their expectations of her. Her life was quite different in her youth, but unlike many who survived this war, she understood she had no reason to complain. Still, sadness had carved itself into her heart.

It felt like ages ago when she was a high school freshman that she had daydreamed about marrying the world's best man and honeymooning in Paris. Back then, as a newly turned fourteen-year-old, she heard talk of Germany having a new leader... a never-smiling man called Hitler with the title of Führer. Who cared? That was in some country far away across the Atlantic Ocean. That leader could give himself any name and do whatever he pleased as long as he did not interfere with her batting her lashes at the boys in her class, her mom cooking a big Sunday meal, or the family taking their annual summer vacation in Michigan's Upper Peninsula, where they feasted on Cornish pasties filled with beef and potatoes, laughed over bad jokes, played pranks, and stayed up past normal bedtimes.

"Mademoiselle Wilson?"

A gentle touch on her arm drew her attention. She blinked Henri into focus. "I'm fine," she told him in French. She had learned enough of the language to hold polite conversations and gather information to help others when they visited her office.

Henri's eyes twinkled. "The Germans signed the papers. They have surrendered. If it pleases you, would you join my *maman* and my brothers as we celebrate the end of Nazism? Good reason to rejoice, *non?*"

"Oui," she said with a smile, praying to God that this was really the end of Nazism.

Although Henri was eight years younger than her and very attached to a blond beauty named Charlotte, he maintained a self-appointed, genuine big-brotherly watch over her. Audrey found this charming. Truth be told, it made her feel like she had family to rely on, rather than feeling alone. Maybe this end of the war—a victorious time—also signaled the next phase of her life, which she had been avoiding thinking about. For now, though, it wasn't the right time to focus on herself.

She looked at Henri, her friend. She was among others she cared about, and they cared about her. She glanced toward Avenue de Paris and smiled. She was one of countless people in this spinning world who had survived the war and did not need to worry about her life because she was alive, not suffering. She could look forward to a bright future and didn't need to act woe-is-me negatively. It was safe to count on the churches holding masses that day, and she planned to attend, expressing her gratitude.

"Let's go join the others, Henri." She grasped his hand, and they joined the celebration.

21

LISELOTTE, LYON, FRANCE, JUNE 1945

After a six-month journey, as planned, Liselotte's traveling companions parted ways as they left Switzerland. The group of ten split into two. Six members of a Polish family, including two parents, one grandmother, and three children, traveled south to Spain. She and three others headed north toward the hilly city of Lyon. Sadly, this meant Liselotte had to say goodbye to the one child she had grown closest to, Rutger. When she first met Rutger and his family, she forced herself to stay away from the boy, even avoiding eye contact with the two-year-old who could not walk and spoke only a few random words. When they entered the Tatra Mountains, Rutger's mother gently but firmly questioned Liselotte's attitude toward her son. Liselotte collapsed onto the snow-covered ground and, through her sobs, begged for forgiveness for her distant and indifferent behavior.

"Is it because we're Jews?" the boy's father asked, his piercing gaze narrowing at her.

"No... no," she had said, trying to reassure this man but fearing she had failed. The father stood with clenched fists, staring at her, daring her to give him a reason to show how he would protect his youngest child. She could not blame him. This family had barely escaped

Poland and had come too close to losing their little boy several times because of prejudices against his disabilities. They would not be stopped by her. "It is the honest truth," she said when her breath briefly steadied.

"How can we believe you? You refuse to look at my son. You won't speak to him. Why is that? Is he not good enough for you, as he is for us? Are you of a Nazi heart, wanting our child dead?"

"Rosa." The lone word escaped her in a cry.

Both parents exchanged glances. The man's mother placed a hand on his shoulder. They waited in silence for Liselotte to continue.

"I miss my little girl so much… It's because of me that she's gone, possibly dead." It was the first time Liselotte had spoken the word dead in connection with her daughter. "And it's all my fault." She continued to tell the full story of her twin girls, Rosa's complex developmental challenges, and how, while she was out of the house, her mother had turned Rosa over to the Gestapo agents during their house search.

She peeked at Rutger, held tightly in his grandmother's loving embrace. Rutger's family saw him as beautiful. Liselotte had seen Rosa as damaged. She had hurled that awful D word at her mother like a destructive grenade. Ultimately, she was the one who caused ruin in her family by seeing her daughter as broken. Not the damning Gestapo. And definitely not her mother. Liselotte should have seen only Rosa's beauty. She should have been the one to stand up for her. Instead, she focused on herself, narrowing her goals to marrying her boyfriend, Gerhard, and starting a new life that would surely bring happiness.

"And here's another way to know I'm telling you the truth," Liselotte said. "Something you can use against me if you suspect I mean harm. My true name is Liselotte Kellerman, not Anna Bauer." The moment she had confessed her identity, a weight lifted from her entire body as if she had been cleansed of filth. "I would like for you to call me Liselotte, now."

While she had made her confessions to Rutger's family, a truth overwhelmed her senses. "I was terrified. Not of my baby, but of myself. Of knowing that I couldn't possibly know what to do for Rosa… that I might cause her suffering with my own hands." One by one, she met each of Rutger's family members' eyes. "I was the real terror. Not my child."

"You're not a terror." Rutger's grandmother stepped beside Liselotte, gently placing Rutger on Liselotte's lap. "You were afraid to love. Love is a gift to be used, so don't worry if you're loving correctly. Love helps you grow into the person you need to be."

Liselotte feathered her fingers across Rutger's soft cheeks. From that moment on, for the rest of their journey, she looked after the little boy as much as his mother permitted. Fortunately, that was often. Now, as she traveled toward Lyon, she missed Rutger more and was reminded of her twin girls… and her mother.

Liselotte and her Lyon-bound companions, two brothers in their thirties and a man in his late fifties, walked about two kilometers when a medium-sized truck pulled up beside them. The driver, a bald man with bushy white eyebrows, leaned toward the open passenger window and exhaled a cloud of cigar smoke. Speaking in French, he said he was heading to Lyon and asked if they needed a ride.

Liselotte could only recognize a few words in French, none of which he mentioned, except for the city's name. She immediately looked at Anton, the youngest of the two brothers, who spoke not only their native Polish but also German, Italian, and French fluently. Anton was already smiling.

"*Oui,*" Anton said. He gestured to Liselotte and the others. "We… pardon us… must stay together."

"That will be fine," the driver said. "My old truck looks rough, but it will hold up with you and your few belongings." He eyed them, then muttered a word that Liselotte suspected was a curse. "The four of you are skin and bones. War does that." Without warning, he shoved open the passenger door. "You," he said directly to Liselotte, gesturing to her and the truck's cab. "Get in here. The men can hop into the back."

Although Anton translated, Liselotte understood the driver just from his motions. Her eyes searched Anton's. *Do you think this is safe?*

His facial expression might have been blank, but it was indisputable: Not any more dangerous than walking that entire distance.

With their limited belongings packed into worn-out rucksacks, including Liselotte's bag, the men climbed onto the truck bed. Liselotte accepted the driver's help and settled into the passenger seat. The man then shifted the truck into gear, and they continued down the road.

The man stayed silent. His firm grip on the wheel and intense focus on the road made Liselotte uneasy. Wondering if he was nervous too, and hoping to help them both relax with conversation, she asked if he spoke German, instantly regretting mentioning the language of France's recent occupiers, worried it might increase his anxiety.

"A few words," the man said in German, relaxing his shoulders.

After exchanging names—his was Georges—she asked, "Do you live in Lyon?"

Georges nodded. He raised three fingers and then indicated three levels of steps.

"Your children?" Liselotte asked.

He smiled. "Three boys. Grown men."

Although she was curious if he was married, she thought it would be impolite to ask. His smile reassured her that his family probably survived the war. She was happy for him.

"Your sons…" She lifted three fingers just as he had minutes ago. "Do they live in Lyon?"

"Near me." He signaled the number one with his index finger. Lifting his hands off the wheel, he rocked an imaginary baby before quickly putting his hands back on the wheel.

"A grandchild?" she asked.

Georges exuded a grandfatherly pride.

Liselotte winced as anguish engulfed her soul. Her surroundings suddenly shifted. France disappeared. Her unplanned, unwanted journey from Berlin to Poland to the Tatra Mountains also vanished, as if it never happened. In her mind, she was propelled back to a past that felt like yesterday…

"I appear healthy," she told her mother, repeating what the doctor had told her. "And pregnant. Probably with twins."

The pain and panic of childbirth. Her firstborn was a beautiful, healthy girl whom she named Regina. Then came the birth of her second twin. She had grown suspicious when the doctor stopped looking at her and when her mother glossed over details of this baby… of Rosa.

Losing sleep. Losing herself. Being a mother every second of the day and night to one active baby and another who struggled to thrive. She was just a caretaker, barely eating or speaking adult talk. She craved love and attention, something to chase away the overwhelming fears each day brought from caring for twin babies during wartime. Her mother warned her never to take the twins outside because eager Nazi-pleasing neighbors were always ready to snitch to the Gestapo that Rosa was someone who weakened the Aryan race and therefore needed to *disappear*.

Gerhard re-entered her life and the lives of his children.

And then, her nearly normal life ended. One day, she returned home after visiting Gerhard. Rosa was gone. Her mother failed to save her baby from the claws of Nazi forces, claiming she was helpless to rescue her granddaughter and had to surrender Rosa. In response, Liselotte did the only thing she could think of—she ran from her home, ran from her remaining family.

Over and over again, this replayed in Liselotte's mind every day since she left the only home she'd ever known. No matter how much she tried to rein in her thoughts, she couldn't escape this endless loop, no matter who she met, talked to, or saw from a distance. Would it ever stop? Or was this a punishment she was meant to endure every day for the rest of her life? With the war over, people had a chance to start fresh. But how could she? Was there any point in living?

"Mademoiselle?" Georges said, switching back to French. He shook her shoulder.

Liselotte hugged her middle. Slowly, she lifted her gaze to his.

He pointed at her. "Good?"

She nodded slightly. She had two choices: end it all and say goodbye to life, which meant giving up on trying to find her family, or courageously face the coming years, knowing that starting over involved small steps and never giving up. Most importantly, she had to stop replaying all that sadness in her mind. She needed to work harder to control her thoughts, not let her thoughts control her. The entire world had been profoundly affected by this devastating war, and the horrors were still ongoing in Japan. If she looked closely, every face she saw was haunted by some tragedy—war is never kind. She looked at Georges, the kind driver who had offered the four of them—complete strangers— a ride.

She was as good as she could be—and would dedicate her days to staying as optimistic as ever, hoping that the future she dreamed of would become her reality. That's why she asked this kind stranger her next question. "Red Cross office? In Lyon?"

"Red Cross," Georges repeated, furrowing his brow. "Family? Missing?"

"Oui," she said. "My family. I need to find my family."

"Train. Lyon to Versailles. Look for Red Cross. Good?"

She smiled. "Very good."

Georges squeezed her hand. He then flexed his right hand four times. "To Lyon."

Twenty minutes until they arrive in Lyon? She would soon board the train, locate the Red Cross office in Versailles, and seek information about her mother and two daughters' whereabouts. With images of her family flashing before her, she smiled at Georges.

"You're a kind man, Georges." *And I must be kind, too.*

22

LISELOTTE, VERSAILLES, FRANCE, 9 JUNE 1945

According to Georges, the Lyon-Perrache train station opened in 1857 in the Perrache quarter of Lyon and emerged from the war with minimal structural damage. Its classical-style architecture reflected the designs of ancient Greece and Rome and featured a double rooftop. Fortunately, the tracks between Lyon and the Paris station, Gare de Lyon, covering about 500 kilometers, suffered little damage from the French Resistance against the Germans.

The station's wide, arched doors welcomed Liselotte into a spacious, comfortable passenger terminal. She had never traveled by train, let alone gone any significant distance alone. She looked around the waiting area for a possible seat. A few benches had vacancies, but men of different ages sat there, and she felt nervous about joining them. On her far right, two women kept a careful watch over a handful of active children. To her left, she noticed a woman whom she doubted was much older than she was. The stranger lifted her head, and her black hat with a brown fringed band reminded Liselotte of riding hats from before the war started. It fit her updo hairstyle perfectly. Liselotte blinked as the poised woman picked up her purse from beside her, patted the now-empty space, and nodded for

Liselotte to sit next to her. Before anyone else could take the seat, Liselotte grabbed her belongings and hurried over.

"*Bonjour*. I'm Louise," the woman said in French. "Please have a seat. I speak German as well, if you prefer."

"My name is Liselotte," she said as she sat. "German is best. Danke."

With an hour's wait for their train and eager to pass the time, they exchanged introductions. Liselotte began, cautious about what she would share with a complete stranger.

"My family is from Berlin, though I've recently been living in Switzerland." Thinking of her mother and daughters, and remembering that she had promised herself she wouldn't get caught up in the details of what had happened to them, she took a deep breath, sat up straighter, and told herself to focus on Louise. "We've become separated, and now I'm heading to Versailles to find out more. And you?"

"I'm sorry to hear this," Louise said. "We'll part ways then, in Paris. You on one train to Versailles and I on the other, heading further north to home."

Liselotte waited to see if Louise would explain further. She didn't, and that was okay. Like herself, the woman might be grappling with the truth or choose to keep her private life guarded. Who could blame her? The war might be over in Europe—and hopefully soon in the Pacific—but the past few years had taught family, friends, and strangers to be cautious about what they shared in conversation. Reflecting on her past, she wondered if anyone would ever truly trust again. It had become a changed world.

After two announcements over the loudspeaker, Louise cleared her throat. "France is still navigating through the impacts of Hitler's reign of terror and inhumanity. I don't believe one aspect of everyday living hasn't been touched, including the country's train system."

Liselotte nodded, quietly relieved that Louise subtly shifted away from personal topics. As Louise continued, Liselotte found it oddly fascinating. During the war, France lacked autobahn-style expressways for rapid public transportation. The petroleum shortages only worsened the situation. This was a major problem for Germany. Because they needed to move troops, Panzers, and supplies to build the Atlantic Wall along the northern and western coasts to defend against the Allies, as well as transport goods from Portugal and Spain to Germany, and then ship thousands of Jews east to Poland's concentration camps, Germany relied heavily on the French Railroad, SNCF, the government-owned rail system.

While Louise continued about the rail system, Liselotte's thoughts drifted back to what the woman had told her about the helpless men, women, and children riding what had become known as death trains. Now that the war was over, the world was slowly learning through the revelations shared by the survivors of the notorious camps the conditions, experiences, and the massive transports of millions of people to these hellish places.

What was it like to live in your own home, practicing your family's faith and customs for generations, if not centuries, only to suddenly be ripped from the roof over your head, taken from your community, separated from extended family and friends, and crammed into a train car barely meant for animals? Some of these cars were so crowded with people that everyone had to stand hour after hour as they traveled east to an unknown destination, which, given the circumstances, couldn't have been even halfway good. No food. No water. One or two communal pots to relieve themselves. And what if someone died while standing? What if an elderly person couldn't endure the ride, or if a child had disabilities?

The drumbeat of guilt echoed again in her mind.

Once again, she restrained her runaway thoughts. *I'm in control of myself. I don't have to subject myself to a lifetime of sadness.*

A gentle touch came to Liselotte's arm. She looked into Louise's eyes. "Pardon me, Louise. I was thinking of the many unfortunate who rode the trains to the camps."

Louise sighed. "Camps? What a poor choice of words we've come to use. It's not like anyone was taken to a park for a picnic lunch and a game of chess."

"Yes, you're right."

Their train to Paris was announced. Standing, they smiled at each other, silently communicating: *This is exciting. Finally, a step closer to our destinations.*

Since seating wasn't assigned on board, they took the first two available seats next to each other. Louise graciously suggested that Liselotte take the window seat.

"I live in France and have often seen the countryside," she said. "You're passing through, Liselotte. Enjoy."

"Will you be my guide and point out sights of interest?"

"Of course." Louise rifled through her purse, pulled out a tube of lipstick, and applied the soft pink color to her lips. "We'll be passing mostly through wide-open farmland, with a few villages here and there. The war hit this area hard. They're pretty much empty now due to food shortages, Parisians leaving the city and moving out to the countryside, infrastructure damage, and especially the brutal control of the Vichy regime."

About fifteen minutes north of Lyon, the green fields began to give way to rolling hills. If Liselotte ignored the war's brutal effects, she could lose herself in the untouched beauty of this land. That's when it hit her.

She immediately turned to Louise and offered a bright smile. Playfully, she said, "I've figured you out. You are either an author of French history or a professor of this very subject."

"Not both?" Louise said.

Liselotte recognized the tease. Chills ran up her arms when Louise's smile suddenly disappeared. "What's wrong?"

Louise leaned toward her, even though the car wasn't full of travelers. "I'm coming out of hiding," she whispered. "When Germany invaded France, I could no longer teach at the university. I was..." Tears rolled down her cheeks, and she waved her hand, unable to speak.

"It's okay," Liselotte said, hearing how absurd those words sounded. It was not okay for one country to attack another and take away its chosen way of life and beliefs. It was not okay for one government to decide how another country should be run, and who gets to live and who gets to die. "That's not what I meant. Everything about war is wrong, each and every time."

"You speak passionately," Louise whispered, still keeping her voice low for only their ears to hear.

Liselotte looked around. No one appeared to be listening. And if they were, the war was already over. How long would it take for each of them to stop living in fear, even for a moment? Or was this the new way of life? "I... I am..." She swallowed convulsively. "I, too, have come out of hiding. I'm trying to find my family."

Louise patted Liselotte's hand. "Pardon my forwardness, but I suspected so of you. And I'm sorry for whatever you may have gone through."

"As I am sorry for you."

They didn't need to ask each other about their faiths or heritages. They were simply two strangers in a vast crowd of millions who were now homeless, estranged, or without a country of their own. The criteria the Nazis once used to divide people now united most of the world.

"We will get through this, yes?" she asked Louise.

"Ja," Louise said more firmly. "We will. We have no choice but to move forward." She fussed with the clasp on her purse. "Now tell me, do you have family in Versailles? Is that what brings you to that town? Maybe I can offer some guidance."

Liselotte's cheeks burned as she remembered how little she had told Louise earlier about her family there. She quickly pushed aside her embarrassment—victims of war do whatever they must to survive. Louise did not seem upset by this, so Liselotte decided to let go of any misplaced shame. "Honestly, no family there, at least none I know of. I was told about a Red Cross office where they can help me find missing relatives."

"Ah, yes. I understand. We all have missing people in our lives now." She pulled out a slip of paper and a pencil from her purse, jotted down a name, and then handed it to her.

"Audrey Wilson?" Liselotte asked. "Do you know her?"

"We met a few months ago. She's very kind, compassionate, and eager to help anyone in need find a loved one. I'm confident she'll be instrumental in helping you."

Liselotte felt her mouth drop open. Could everything really be this easy from now on? "Louise, I'm unsure how to thank you."

"You just did, my friend." Louise smiled. "Settle back in your seat and rest. Sleep, if you must—I'll wake you when we get to Paris so you can transfer trains on time. Do not worry."

For the first time in a long while, Liselotte was truly not worried.

AUDREY WILSON WAS GONE. The Red Cross office was shut down, as if it had never operated at this location. When Liselotte asked the landlord where Audrey had gone, she was told Bad Arolsen, Germany. She had left her home country what felt like years ago, and now, Liselotte Kellerman, no longer Anna Bauer, was heading back to Germany. She would find Audrey Wilson. She would search for her mother and daughters. She knew she would find peace by making peace among them all.

23

AUDREY, BAD AROLSEN, GERMANY, 1946

Finally, having just connected with her brother by phone, Audrey would have squealed with joy if it hadn't been for her two other officemates, one busy assisting a Polish-speaking, haggard man, the other reviewing her notes.

"Pete, I'm not sure whether to stare at the phone like it's a toy and I'm hallucinating or to babble nonstop. My goodness, it's wonderful to be talking with you again. How are—"

"Sis, calm down. Before we get disconnected again, let me squeeze in a word or two."

"Talk away. Just know I'm smiling at every word you say. Ha. You could probably get away with one of your boyhood insults, and I'll just say you're my best pal, ever."

"Gads, Aud." Pete chuckled. "You must be awfully lonely, wherever you are."

She pressed the receiver more firmly against her ear and sniffled. "I'm missing my family, that's all. I'm in Bad Arolsen."

"Did you say bad or bat? What's so bad about that place?"

"No, silly. Bad in German means spa. Arolsen is a spa town—think mineral springs."

"Cool."

"Well, its history is… let's say colorful, not really cool stuff." Not wanting to get into the town's Nazi involvement, especially hereditary Prince Josias of Waldeck and Pyrmont's rise to power and his appointment as an assistant to Heinrich Himmler, she told her brother she would update him when they saw each other in person.

"Are you calling today to tell me the good news that you're coming home?" Pete asked in a cheerful tone.

Audrey glanced at her two teammates, a man and a woman. When she arrived in Bad Arolsen, she quickly began her work at one of the two palaces where the United Nations Relief and Rehabilitation Administration—UNRRA—operated. Sometimes, she worked with nearly 1,000 military personnel, civilians, and displaced persons, all focused on helping displaced individuals return to their home countries. Her specialty, tracing the missing victims of Nazi oppression, proved to be essential. Even though she learned every day about the terrible ways people had become separated during the war, she remained passionate about her work. Unless ordered to return to the United States, she was not yet ready to leave.

"Not quite, Pete. Soon, I hope. I just wanted to say a quick hello." She had to steer the conversation away from herself. "Listen, sport. With my time limited, tell me about Pop, Caro—are we still calling Sis by that name—and you. Still in school?"

"Pop's doing okay—you know, as good as he can be. He's always asking me if I've heard from you. He tells me about the letters he gets from you. Between you and me, Aud, he reads them over and over. Yep—Caro is still Caro. She's dating a senior, which Pop isn't too happy about. She's not exactly making things peaceful around here, if you catch my drift."

"I can just imagine. And you? How are you and Sally—are you two still an item?"

"Nah," Pete said, his voice suddenly serious. "Just engaged."

This time, Audrey squealed. She looked around the office, but if anyone was bothered, they kept quiet. "Wow. I'm thrilled for you. Congratulations. Do Pop and Caro know? Have you set a date?"

"Hold on, there, Sis. Yes, Pop and Caro know—I'd sworn them to secrecy until I told you myself. Wanted to surprise you."

"That you did!" Audrey eyed a young woman walking into the office. Wearing ragged clothing and with her hair unevenly cut and disheveled, she resembled many who had come looking for help to find loved ones. Audrey smiled at the stranger, motioned for her to have a seat, then partially turned to face the wall to provide a shadow of privacy. "Listen, Pete, I have someone in the office to help. Tell me, though. Have you set a date yet?"

"We're waiting until after graduation to settle down, hopefully in Rochester. It's a great place to live—different, in a good way, from back home. Why don't you consider moving here, when and if you ever return to the U.S.?"

She thought of Private Joseph Campanili and smiled. He lived in Rochester. He told her to look him up. "Yes, I will return. I have some loose ends to finish up here first." *Joe.* She hadn't stopped thinking of him. Had he thought of her? "Rochester sounds very promising. Listen, I have to go. I'll try my best to give you another call shortly."

After saying goodbye, she faced the woman pacing instead of sitting calmly. "Hello. Do you speak German?" Audrey asked in German. "Or English?" She looked at her colleague, Maja. "Polish?"

"German."

Audrey smiled. "Then I can help you. My name is Audrey Wilson—"

"*Gott sei Dank.* I found you." The stranger brushed away tears streaking down her face. She pointed to herself. "My name is Liselotte…" She rubbed her cheeks, which had a slight blush. "Pardon. I've used too many false names over the past years. My family name is Kellerman, which still feels strange to say right now."

"Many have sat in that very seat where you are and have told me the same."

"Oh?" Liselotte said, then sat on the wooden chair. "To think that I've wondered all this time if this uncomfortable feeling of using my real name was my personal punishment that I would always carry."

"I understand. Each one of us carries self-blame."

Liselotte moved to the edge of the chair. "I'm lost from my family. I need help."

Audrey smiled. "Then I'm glad you came here. Would you like some coffee or water?"

"No thanks."

"All right, then," Audrey said. She grabbed a pen and a notepad. "Tell me everything I need to know. Take your time, though. I'm in no rush."

Liselotte fingered the off-white shirt hanging loosely on her. "I am German, born in Berlin. I am not Jewish."

"Your faith and nationality don't matter here at UNRRA—we help any displaced person return to their home countries." Audrey reflected on the many people she had met since the war ended. She had no doubt that she had helped several individuals who had once openly shown loyalty to the Nazi Party in their search for missing loved ones. Whether right or wrong about their beliefs—hopefully, their former convictions—they also endured the pain of loss.

Audrey gently looked at Liselotte, whom she guessed was a few years younger than herself. She suspected that the woman's lack of confidence was surfacing again. Could her family be adding to this self-doubt? War, with all its fears, might be a factor. Audrey imagined that many issues and events in Liselotte's environment made her uneasy. Carefully, she said, "The past few years have brought much uncertainty to how nations and individuals will endure."

Liselotte worried her bottom lip.

"Let's stick to the basics." Audrey noted down Liselotte's answers about her mother's name, her exact Berlin street address, and asked a few other key questions. Still, when it was time to tell when and how she and her mother were separated, the younger woman dropped her gaze to the floor. Something didn't quite add up. Audrey suspected that shame and guilt—two emotions that often go hand in hand—played a big role in Liselotte's silence. Trusting her instincts, she gently asked, "Liselotte, were you the one who ran off from your mother, losing sight of her? I ask not in judgment. If it helps, I also know what it's like to get separated from family."

Liselotte fixed her eyes on Audrey as if she had resolved to confront her problems directly. "I haven't been a good daughter."

Although Audrey's curiosity was piqued, she maintained the professional and objective stance she had taken since starting her work with the tracing services. "That doesn't matter, nor is it up to us to decide. Our goal is to reunite you with your family, as you've stated you want to do. Correct?"

"*Ja*, though I was the one who left my home," Liselotte said. A few seconds passed, and she added, "There's more."

Again, Audrey waited for the woman to speak when she was ready. Over the years, she had heard many sad, tragic stories that she doubted would make it into the history books, although they should. Older siblings who felt powerless after losing younger brothers and sisters to kidnappings. Parents forever tormented when authorities forced them to surrender their children to the enemy. Families witnessing the torture and/or death of other family members and friends. The Nazi concentration camp stories of women, children, and the elderly sent to immediate death by gas, while younger men were herded in a different direction like animals. And, of course, no matter who—since death is not partial—those who lost loved ones due to illnesses that, perhaps if during a time of peace, medical attention might have prevented.

"My mother was right—I was too young when I had my twin daughters. But it happened. I was only interested in myself."

Audrey stood and moved her chair beside Liselotte. "This is not the time to be hard on yourself. You cannot change what has happened, but you can move forward. Let me help you search for your family. The results will be your best medicine to heal." She only hoped for Liselotte's sake that it would be because of good news. If not, perhaps it would be a closing, and healing might happen slowly over time.

"Okay, then," Liselotte continued, eyeing Audrey as she picked up her pen and moved the writing paper closer. "I keep telling myself the same things you speak of, but when I'm especially tired, like now, this personal war inside me still controls my mood. However, since this isn't about my inner demons but information you might need to know, I'll continue. My daughter Regina was born healthy. Not Rosa. She had health problems that the Nazis saw as harmful to Aryan survival. My mother warned me not to take the twins out of the house… she warned me about many things. I could only think about my boyfriend and left the girls home with my mother while I visited him. One day, when I arrived home, Rosa was gone. My mother said the Gestapo came to the house and took Rosa. I… I…"

"Take a deep breath, Liselotte. Exhale slowly. You're sitting beside me… the war is over. Let's try to make things better, together, shall we?"

After a moment to gather herself, Liselotte gave a slight nod. "I walked out of the house. I left my family and stayed away. Berlin was bombed. I met a seemingly nice man who turned out to wear different stripes, as the saying goes. He worked for the Nazis—I guess most Aryan German men worked for the Nazis in one way or another. Anyway, he took me to Poland on business, and I fled as soon as I could. Last summer, after the war ended, I was in a group that made it to France. Although you came highly recommended, I panicked when I discovered that your office was now in Germany, actually delaying setting foot in my homeland."

Audrey had heard many stories about desperate people searching for lost relatives in their homeland. The irony was that, when it came to returning to the place they had been separated from and longed to go back to, they experienced the same anxiety that Liselotte was going through.

"Well, I'm glad you're here, Liselotte. I'll be happy to help you search for your mother and daughters." Audrey settled back into her chair. "I will tell you how I can help, and what the two of us can do together. I'll inform you of our resources and other possibilities. Then we will develop a detailed plan of action."

For the first time since arriving at the office, Liselotte smiled. "I appreciate how you've used the word *together*. This search is sounding less scary and overwhelming."

24

LISELOTTE, GERMANY, AUGUST 1946

Liselotte told Audrey everything about her search for her family, except what she encountered in Atton, France. That was when she visited the stone cottage that had once served as a safe house, a place where she hoped to find her daughter, Rosa. When she found the building empty, with no sign of where anyone had gone, all her hope was shattered like a target hit by Allied bombs in Berlin during the war. However, unlike the many people she had come to distrust by the time she arrived in France, she trusted Audrey, the American woman. Through Audrey, she secured a file clerk position at UNRRA. This was her first paid job, and by helping others, she gained the confidence she needed to keep searching for her own family. The one nice surprise was that she and Audrey had become friends.

While Audrey stayed in her dorm-like room provided by the UNRRA, Liselotte rented a room in town. A few times, their search for her family involved walking, taking a taxi, or riding trains, and once, they made an overnight trip to Belgium. Sadly, when it came to her mother, whom she had started to think of as the more endearing term, Mutti, no trace of Helene was found. Regarding her daughters, who would have turned four this year, not a single mention of Rosa or

Regina appeared. They had all vanished, as if they had never existed—gone as quickly as Liselotte had exited their lives. Alone in her room, more thoughts of her family flashed through her mind. Trying to stay strong, she mostly managed to overcome what she thought of as mind visits. When she least expected it, the heartbreaking darkness seized her with the relentless force of a predatory bird circling above its next target…

Had Rosa grown any stronger by now? Could she sit up? Babble any words? Interact with others? Had anyone adopted her, seeing past her physical condition and recognizing her as beautiful? And Regina? Although Rosa's hair was thin, precious Regina had thick blond hair. Had it darkened like her mama's by now, or even become more beautiful with a reddish-brown shade like Liselotte's grandmother's? Did she still live with Grammy, happy to play outside now that the war had stopped? Did she help Grammy bake cookies? Pick bouquets of yellow, red, and orange flowers from the garden?

Had Regina stopped asking about her sister? Did she remember having a sister? Had she forgotten her mother?

Liselotte ordered herself to rein in her wandering thoughts before she became emotionally paralyzed, as she had been when she left the Atton safe house without Rosa. Thank God she'd met Audrey, who helped her accept she had two options: surrender and fade away, or move forward in life. One way or another, everything would work out. If not right away, then eventually. She would never give up again.

Now, as she pushed open the office door, she heard the whir of a fan. Across the room, Audrey searched through a filing cabinet. Seated at his desk, Daniel, one of Audrey's colleagues, presented information to two women. Liselotte gulped. The women, both fading-blonds in their fifties with identical facial features and petite builds, appeared to be twins. Daniel and the two clients stood and shook hands. The two women walked past Liselotte and exited the building.

Her heart started pounding. She backed up to the door and leaned against the dark, varnished surface. Air left her lungs, and she couldn't cry for help.

No more attacks of anxiety. There are plenty of twins born every day. Yes, I have the right to be concerned, but anxiety will only weaken me. There's no reason to compare everyone's family situation with my own. Put things into perspective.

A wave of calmness started to settle over her. Relieved, she took a deep breath and looked around. Now that the twin female clients had left, it was just Audrey and Daniel. The office, filled with shelves and cabinets cluttered with files and documents, gave her a feeling of belonging, perhaps because of its purpose to help find lost loved ones. The tension that had knotted her shoulders and made her breathe harder just moments before eased even more.

Audrey's phone rang, and after a quick wave to Liselotte, she went to her desk and answered the call. "My stars, Joe." Audrey's face lit up with delight. "Finally, it's really you." With one finger raised, she signaled to Liselotte to sit down and mouthed that she would be just a moment or two. "So, tell me, Private, when are we going to see each other again?"

Feeling like she might be intruding, Liselotte shook her head, thinking it would be best to step outside. When she heard Audrey ask Joe to hold on for a second, everything came back to her. Audrey had met Joe during her early Red Cross days when she was stationed in Trinidad. Although Audrey never said much, Liselotte could easily see that her friend was smitten with this former Army member who had returned home because of an injury.

"Wait," Audrey called out to Liselotte. "Please stay." Audrey continued talking with Joe. "Are you still in Rochester?"

Still feeling a bit awkward as she leaned on the doorjamb, half inside the building and half outside. Rochester must be a place in America—a big city? A town? She couldn't quite remember where Audrey said she was from, though, of course, Joe could be living somewhere else. What was life like in the United States? Thinking about the glamorous movie stars, plenty of food, and the strong job market and opportunities for both men and women, all these mental images she'd gathered over the past few months made emigrating to the US sound tempting. She let out a soft sigh. Those fancy dreams weren't realistic, especially since her mother and daughters might still be in Germany. Reuniting with her family was all that mattered, not chasing illusions in faraway lands.

"I see," Audrey said, drawing Liselotte's attention back into the office. "Are you sure?"

Liselotte smiled at Audrey, who she hadn't seen this excited in a while. She appreciated the friendship of this woman who radiated joy to others, no matter what had happened in her life. Liselotte knew she needed to apply this very lesson in her own life.

"It's a good possibility," Audrey replied to Joe. "I still haven't learned anything about my missing Babenko relatives, though. Maybe just a little more time?"

Liselotte couldn't help but raise an eyebrow in curiosity. What was this? Audrey had never mentioned that she also had missing relatives.

"One moment, Joe." Audrey mouthed to Liselotte that she would be right off the phone, then resumed speaking with Joe. "Okay. I'll do that. Give me a day or so, and I'll call you back with an answer."

Aware that Audrey was finishing her chat with her special guy, Liselotte hurried toward the door to give them more privacy. But when she heard Audrey squeal, she turned around just in time to see her friend standing behind her desk, with one hand pressed to her head and her eyes fixed on the phone.

"With that amazed look on your face," Liselotte said, "you must confess everything to me."

Audrey slipped her hand from her head to her side and glanced at the clock on the opposite wall. "Daniel," she said to her coworker, "do you mind if I step out for a bit? I promise I won't be gone for long." After he reassured her that it was okay to leave and to take as much time as she needed, she turned back to Liselotte. "There's something we need to discuss."

"With this nice weather, would you like to sit over there?" Audrey asked, pointing to a bench. "If not, I'm up for a walk."

Whenever Liselotte grew nervous, her legs felt rubbery, and she would become unsteady. Without hesitation, she said sitting would be fine, and they chose the first empty bench. As much as she wanted to hear what Audrey had to share, a wave of uneasiness clouded her mind so strongly that she was tempted to look up, fully expecting to see a cloud hanging directly over her head. What she saw around her didn't help her relax. Tired-looking men and women moved about as if they had nowhere to go. Probably, their home, let alone their family —their way of life—had become casualties of war. Gone. And what about the once-beloved family pet? She had seen many stray dogs roaming the streets and skittish, and far-too-thin cats. These poor animals all deserved to be tucked into homes, enjoying the comforts of food, warmth, and love, just like the homeless people wandering the streets, searching for a way to start over after devastation.

"Liselotte?" Audrey said gently. "You're so quiet. I'm nervous for you."

"Pardon." Liselotte paused to gather her thoughts. "I was taking a walk down bad memory lane—thinking about how Germany and its people were before the war, compared to now."

"The war may be over, but memories continue to haunt us all."

Liselotte faced Audrey and nodded. "Is it possible the world can ever fully heal after the destruction from this war?"

"I believe so. Like illness, recovery time will differ by individual and country. Some will recover more quickly than others."

"I think…" Liselotte gasped, startled by the thought that had just raced through her mind.

"What is it?" Audrey asked.

"I think the key to recovery is forgiveness."

"I agree," Audrey said. "To forgive and to accept being forgiven."

"For sure." Liselotte looked down at her lap. "Sorry. I don't mean to always be lost in my thoughts. There's definitely more to life than just me."

"No need to apologize. I'm your friend, and I care about whatever's on your mind."

"Friend," Liselotte murmured that beautiful word. In a world with more than two billion people, having one true friend was to be rich. "Thank you for caring. I'm not sure how my life might have turned out if I hadn't met you."

Audrey gently squeezed her hand. "You would be fine."

"Let's move on, though, because I don't want to keep you from your work. I'm curious about the urgency and excitement I heard in your voice just a few minutes ago, back in the office. I hope it's good news." Liselotte smiled at her friend, though any news might mean Audrey's departure, which would mean working with another UNRRA worker. While they were all professional and knowledgeable, she was unsure how effective her search would be without Audrey. "Has your Private Joe asked you to join him? You know, we may not have known each other since our school days, but I want you to be happy."

"That's very sweet of you. Whenever Joe calls, I tend to act like a schoolgirl excited just to hear from him." Audrey leaned back against the bench and crossed her legs. "But Joe isn't the person I want to talk to you about."

"Oh?" Audrey's news could be either good or bad. "Hearing about your special man asking you to marry him and sweeping you back home might be easier than not having you by my side while I search through Germany for my missing family. I mean, I'm sure the other staff members would help me in my search for my family, but honestly, I'll be at a loss without your always-available shoulder to lean on."

"Where do you stand in your commitment to find your family?"

For a moment, Liselotte's mind went blank. She wrapped her arms around her waist and narrowed her eyes at Audrey. "I don't understand this sudden question. I thought you understood my wish to find my mother and twin daughters."

"A few developments have popped up."

Liselotte held her breath as panic overwhelmed her. Opening up to Audrey—or anyone—was never easy, but she had just shared her raw feelings about what their friendship meant to her. Now she felt more vulnerable than ever.

"The two leads I told you about last week…"

Why had Audrey stopped talking? This was probably a bad sign. Liselotte's eyes welled with tears. To hide her emotions, she looked away.

"The information I had hoped to rely on for your search went nowhere," Audrey said softly. She pulled a handkerchief from her purse and handed it to her. "I'm sorry."

Liselotte accepted the pink-and-white flower-printed cloth. She nodded and dabbed at her eyes. "Me too."

"The first lead, a woman who lived on your Berlin street, had fled the city just before the last major bombing raid. When she returned, she said most of the buildings were destroyed, and if there were any survivors, she hadn't met or heard about them."

Liselotte gripped the bench slots on both sides of her. "Tell me more—I'm prepared. I'm not expecting a pretty picture."

"Then, the official report from the local authorities confirmed the woman's observation I just mentioned. It stated that most of the houses in the neighborhood and surrounding areas—including your family home—were completely destroyed." Audrey touched Liselotte's arm. "Most of the deceased were accounted for. A few were not. I'm sorry to say nothing was said about your family, good or bad."

No matter which country Liselotte traveled through while fleeing from Klaus, she saw many women crying while holding the hands of children, whether it was their own child or an orphaned one. "Did this neighbor say, if before the bombing, my mother might have mentioned going somewhere else?"

"I'm afraid not."

"Any other leads?"

"Yes—it came from a man. At first, I was hopeful because I thought he was searching for you."

"For me?" Liselotte wiped her suddenly damp hands on her sides. "Why... would..." Why was it hard for her to speak? She tried again. "Why would he look for me? Do you have... his name? A description?"

"Actually, I do." She pulled a card from her skirt pocket. "I have this information—a name and phone number. However, when I received this card, his last name was already smudged and unreadable."

"His first name, then?"

"Klaus." Audrey's eyes widened. "Are you okay, Liselotte? All the color has drained from your face. Do you recognize his name?"

Taking in as much breath as she could, Liselotte shook her head. "*Nein*. I thought you would say a different name, someone from my old school I never want to see again."

Audrey looked at her for several seconds longer than Liselotte thought she could handle. Finally, she half-smiled. "I guess we all have former classmates we wish would disappear and never bother us again."

Although Liselotte had despised herself for keeping quiet about certain incidents—and people—even to Audrey, she still couldn't talk about Klaus at that moment. Still, she was curious. She aimed for a casual tone. "Although it's clear that this lead has also gone nowhere, I'm intrigued. How did you find him? What did he say?"

"He found me. Well, I should say he found the UNRRA agent in the Berlin office, who then contacted me and sent me the card. He said he was looking for a Liselotte, a young woman possibly with a daughter." Audrey narrowed her eyes. "Honestly, this has me quite disturbed and nervous for you."

Did he know about her children? She was certain she had never shared that information with him. Still, a Nazi in his position—someone who tore families apart by kidnapping children and bringing them to Germany under the cover of Germanization—could easily have her real name and address. Those damn Nazis kept lists of everyone and everything.

"Please, tell me anything else you learned about this man."

"At first, he inquired about Anna Bauer, not Liselotte, and definitely not Liselotte Kellerman. He mentioned he wasn't sure if you had a child. Without saying another word, he left the Berlin office and never returned."

Liselotte told herself to stay calm and keep a neutral face, but she wondered how much longer she could. She remembered how, back in

Poland, when she still went by the name Anna Bauer, Klaudia had told her that a man named Klaus was in town asking for her. Then, Liselotte found Klaus's note, addressed to her, on Klaudia's family's doorstep, saying that she belonged to him. It was painfully clear that Klaus Agers was following her. For some reason, he wouldn't be discouraged.

"Audrey, did the Berlin agent give my full name to this stranger?"

"No. As we discussed in our first meeting, we do not disclose our clients' names or other identifying details. This man may have asked for Liselotte by name, but your name was not provided to him. Even though the war has ended, it doesn't mean there aren't people out there trying to hurt or take advantage of others. We would need your full consent to share any of your information, though we strongly advise against it. The Berlin agent wasn't even allowed to reveal my name as the primary contact for this search or which office I work from. I believe you don't need to worry about this agent."

Liselotte straightened up when a sudden thought crossed her mind. "How long ago did you find out these leads were flops?"

"They were both just confirmed earlier this morning."

"What do we do now? I'm not ready to give up, Audrey."

"That's good. Neither am I."

Liselotte placed her hand over her heart. "That's a relief. After hearing you on the phone with Joe and how happy you sounded, I thought you had asked me to step outside, not just for fresh air but also to say goodbye. Like you wanting to return to your country, meet up with Joe, and the two of you would continue your next chapters in life, together."

A smile returned to Audrey's serious face. "As much as I like the idea of seeing Joe again, I want to continue helping you. However, based on this information, you have a decision to make: keep pursuing or call off the search. Whatever you decide, I will respect it."

"What's this about you having lost relatives that you mentioned to Joe?" Liselotte cringed, feeling her cheeks burn with heat. "I'm sorry, Audrey. This is not my concern—I'm intruding, let alone admitting to eavesdropping."

"It's okay." Audrey sighed. "Joe asked me to come back to the States, to the city of Rochester, where he lives." She surprised Liselotte by taking both of her hands in hers. "I am dedicated to my work. My commitment is to find your mother and daughters. Just because these leads panned out badly, it doesn't mean that we need to cancel the search."

"Your commitment," Liselotte said, "is to live the rest of *your* life as you want. You have a family, a man I suspect loves you, and you love him. And all this is in a different country, far away from Europe."

"I truly want to help you, so please don't try to persuade me otherwise. If anything, it motivates me to find my grandparents' extended family, which I promised my father I would."

"Did you? That's interesting."

"Yes," Audrey said. "But sadly, I haven't found any answers."

Liselotte lowered her chin. "Maybe some dead ends in life are permanent, no matter how much we wish otherwise."

"Tell me how long you want to continue your search *here*?" Audrey asked.

"Here?" Liselotte echoed.

"Yes, in Germany… in Europe. No sign of Helene Kellerman or her granddaughters has been found here."

Liselotte's mouth dropped open so abruptly that she felt her jaw click, and she rubbed it. The thought that her mother or her daughters might have died in the war was too overwhelming to contemplate. But this new possibility, one she had never considered before? "Are you now suspecting that my mother went outside of Europe? Maybe to America?"

Audrey shrugged. "Maybe. Maybe not. She either wants to be found or not… if she is alive."

"*Ja*," Liselotte said to all those possibilities. "Is giving the search here, in Europe, one more full month, foolish?"

"Not at all."

Liselotte stood. "Unless you have another appointment, would you like to return to the office and plan a new approach?"

"Yes, let's. There's nothing better than a plan of action to help tie up loose ends. One thing, though."

Liselotte might have tugged on the bench earlier, but now she pretended to yank it, grinning like a fool. "Okay. I'm ready."

"I have one condition—that you accept that my helping you is something I truly want to do."

For the first time that day, Liselotte relaxed fully. "*Ja*. I accept."

25

AUDREY, GERMANY, SEPTEMBER 1946

For the first time since joining the Red Cross and later becoming a tracing specialist, Audrey could understand why people felt like losers and carried guilt for failing themselves and their loved ones. If her mother had never let slip that little piece of information back in 1941—which now seemed like decades ago instead of just five years—there was a good chance Audrey might never have learned about her father's relatives. Sadly, both Pavlov and Olena Babenko died at the age of forty during the 1918 Spanish influenza pandemic. The few remaining family members, aside from her father, had passed away without recording or sharing information, which did not help answer the growing number of questions. It was both frustrating and sad. Similar to Liselotte's heartbreak over a missing mother and twin daughters, and the turmoil of all the emotions tied to her specific situation with no resolution in sight, Audrey could understand why it was hard for Liselotte to move on.

What other options were available? For herself, Audrey might consider finding more work in tracing or other dedicated supportive services for those searching for loved ones and displaced people. Realistically, though, this would mean she would have to stay in Europe longer. Sure, she could, in theory, settle down and live many more years in any of the countries she had come to appreciate. However, that also meant traveling back to Milwaukee to see her family, which made her feel like just another guest rather than a part of it. Yet, as each day dragged on and she saw one person after another without any closure about family news, the one thing she did not want was to lose her immediate family, especially to become strangers because of the distance. When she talked to her father on the phone, he would joke that he missed her because no one else cooked like her mom, except Audrey. When Audrey confessed to her brother, Pete, that she was burning out from her Red Cross position, he said she needed a break from Europe with its war memories that still had repercussions on daily life for many. He also mentioned there were many classes she could take at the University of Rochester and that she was overdue to meet Sally, his fiancée, and that he could see them becoming the best of friends. Then, there was her baby sister, Caro, who would be graduating from high school in another two years. It was bad enough that Audrey had missed out on seeing her mature the past few years, but if they did not reconnect soon, it would be like not having a kid sister at all.

What choices did Liselotte—her client, her friend—have? She could also remain in Germany, her homeland, look for work, find a place to live, and reach out to others, eventually making new friends. Would that mean giving up her goal to find and reconnect with her mother and daughters? Not necessarily. In her attempt to escape the war, her family might have dispersed across Europe. On the other hand, war destroyed not only family and friends but also towns, cities, traditions, and memories. Could the sole survivor move forward? Did they all face a future that once promised brightness but now darkens the day, turning hope gray?

The brick clock tower of the Rathaus Bad Arolsen, the town hall, and part of the tracing services complex chimed noon. Audrey took a deep breath and looked up. Sure enough, as punctual as ever, Liselotte hurried over.

"Hello," they greeted each other at the same time.

Audrey patted the empty space on the bench. "Have a seat. Have you had a good morning?"

"Yes," Liselotte said. Although the word *Yes* was spoken worldwide, Liselotte had been practicing speaking more English than German this past month. Audrey was happy to help her by offering tips on navigating confusing rules. Continuing in English, she said, "And that's one of the things I would like to speak with you about."

"I always have two listening ears for you."

"Don't I know it?" Liselotte grinned. "Did I say that correctly?"

Audrey nodded. "You sure did."

"Okay. I will begin. I want to go to America with you. What do I need to do? Where in America can I live? What work do I do?"

"Let's start from the beginning. What about your search for your family?"

Liselotte removed her sunglasses to show reddish eyes. "I've cried enough. How do you Americans say this… no medals?"

"Some say, I don't need a medal," Audrey said. "Although I don't like to brush off—dismiss—the very real need to find loved ones, or how much it hurts when they can't be found."

Liselotte waved her hand. "No, no. I understand. I would never think that about you. Your talent is finding people. Anyone can see how much you care about others." She briefly lowered her chin, then lifted her gaze to meet Audrey's eyes. "I'm glad you've helped many people. But for me, it's time to accept that my family is either happily living in heaven or…" She took a deep breath. "Or they don't want to be found. At least, not right now. It's time for me to stop… what's the word… guessing. Yes, that's it. It's time for me to stop guessing which is which. I can't go on if I'm trapped. I'm twenty years old now. No more little baby."

And I'm twenty-six, Audrey thought. She was old enough to know not to deprive herself—or others—of the personal life desired, to allow for the grace to change plans, and not to feel guilty about it. "I understand what you're saying. Making an either-or decision is unnecessary in both professional and personal situations. These strict choices—without room for flexibility—might bring you more guilt than you bargained for."

"What is *bargained for?*"

"Anticipated... usually, something you never wanted."

"Like a headache?" Liselotte pointed at her temples. "This I have plenty of."

"Exactly. I can help you gather the necessary documents and make arrangements if you want to emigrate to the U.S. It might take some time to get everything in order. I might leave ahead of you to set up living accommodations and find work in Rochester—"

"Pardon?" Liselotte said, appearing confused. "You are also ready to return home?"

"Well, not just yet. Let me clarify. My father and sister live in Wisconsin, a state in the Midwest region of the country. My brother studies at a university in Rochester, New York, in the Northeast." How could she say she was more interested in meeting up with Joe Campanili than in moving back with her pop and sis, and express this to a young woman who cannot find her mother and daughters?

"Ah, I understand. Rochester is the city where Private Joe lives. Yes?" Liselotte reached for Audrey's hand and gave it a little squeeze. "It's okay to tell me this. It's okay to want a man in your life."

Audrey rubbed her mouth to keep it from falling open in amazement. Before she could respond to Liselotte's apparent reading of her thoughts—and confirm her feelings about moving on in life sooner rather than later—she watched her friend stand up.

Liselotte extended a hand. "How do you Americans say about getting things moving?"

"Moving?" Audrey mused. "Oh. Do you mean it's time for us to get the ball rolling?"

"Yes, yes. That is the saying."

Audrey jumped to her feet. "It is, indeed, time for both of us. I'll look into matters for you as well. Maybe it won't take long. Here's another saying, though not exclusive to the United States, for my soon-to-be American pal—just maybe, Lady Luck will shine on us."

"That sounds wonderful."

26

LISELOTTE, ROCHESTER, MAY 1952

"Thank you for calling Rochester Haven House, a boutique hotel with a big heart. How may I assist you?" Liselotte said in her best General American English. Although she had taken many night classes to study English since arriving in the US in the spring of 1947, the variations in how Americans pronounced their vowels and the many dialects not only within the United States but also from people calling from outside the country, speaking their own accented English, still tripped her up now and then. "Yes, we have a room available for this weekend. How many guests will there be?" The lobby door opened, and she waved hello to Audrey as she approached the front desk

"Don't rush," Audrey mouthed and took a seat in one of the plush mauve armchairs by the fireplace, which hadn't been lit since the end of March.

"Your daughter's graduation? Oh, how nice," Liselotte said to the woman on the other end of the phone. She had quickly learned that the key to the receptionist job at this historic hotel on Broadway was to listen carefully while sounding genuinely interested in what the potential guest might say. The rest of her time was spent following efficient hotel procedures. However, when the caller mentioned her daughter, Liselotte's attention began to drift. Next week, on May 15th, her daughters would turn ten years old. Was Regina living with her grandmother? At forty-nine, was Helene often mistaken for being her mother? Where were they living? Italy or Scandinavia? Somewhere closer to Rochester, like Pennsylvania, or across Lake Ontario in Toronto? Could it be possible that now, with the war over, Helene might have taken Rosa in, and the three of them were living together again? Liselotte could even find some peace of mind and accept that her little girls were not with her if it meant they were well, happy, and living as best they could. But this not knowing? Her growing English vocabulary, not to mention her native German, failed to give her the right words to describe the emptiness in her aching heart.

"Very good," she said into the phone. "We look forward to seeing you and your husband this Saturday morning at eleven o'clock. I'm sure you will enjoy your room. Have a nice day, and once again, thanks for considering Rochester Haven House."

"My, my," Audrey said, approaching Liselotte. "You're sounding more American each day." Although Audrey said this in an upbeat tone, Liselotte recoiled inwardly, with shame and guilt once again shaping her mood.

Audrey leaned across the desk and touched her arm. "Liselotte? Have I upset you? I didn't mean to. I'm sorry if—"

"No, you're fine." Yet, with only the two of them in the lobby, Liselotte couldn't help but avert her gaze to the desktop. "It is me... my twin girls are turning ten next week. When this caller said her daughter was graduating from nursing school this weekend, my thoughts jumped to my own daughters." *Guter Gott,* she thought in German, then pressed her index finger to her lip. *Move on,* she told herself. *You're getting stuck in the mind again.*

Liselotte took a deep breath and continued. "When you walked in here, you had a mile-wide smile on your face. Don't let silly me ruin your joy. You must have had an excellent workday." In need of a break from the intensity of working for the Red Cross during the war, Audrey had accepted a library assistant position at the Central

Library of Rochester and Monroe County, located at 115 South Avenue, near their downtown apartment.

"Well, I'm happy, all right. I just received the big news that I was accepted into the University of Rochester's new School of Social Work."

Audrey had become like the sister Liselotte never had, and her wonderful news eased her worries and sad, drifting thoughts. She jumped to her feet. "I'm so happy for you. I say this from the bottom of my heart."

"Yes, I know. Thank you. And I'm glad you're sounding good, again. You have a way of making me worry about you."

"We must celebrate."

"That's why I'm here. Joe and I are going out for dinner tonight, and we want you to join us." Audrey glanced at the lobby clock on the stand behind Liselotte. "You're off in half an hour, which gives you plenty of time to go back to the apartment and refresh yourself. Joe will pick us up at 5:30 for a 6:00 reservation at Zachary's."

Liselotte patted her white work blouse tucked under the navy blue blazer. "What's that saying… three's company?"

"Here's another saying for you—balderdash! Nonsense, my friend. I won't accept anything but a sure-will-join-you guys. That's because both Joe and I very much want your company tonight."

Liselotte released a playful sigh, then immediately narrowed her gaze at Audrey. "Wait a minute… are the two of you…" Learning new social phrases had proved more difficult than learning the essentials of English. She supposed that this was true for most languages. "Will there be a gentleman at the restaurant, arranged specifically for me to meet?"

Audrey snapped her fingers. "Darn. A blind date! Why didn't I think of that, roommate?"

"Excellent. I'm not ready to meet a man right now." Or, perhaps ever. The few she had met definitely did not end well. Klaus's words cut through her thoughts. *I'll look out for your safety. Always.* She had run from him for many reasons, none of which she had told Audrey.

Some things were better left alone, even if they could not be forgotten. "Please be respectful of my wishes."

Audrey flinched.

"Oh, dear," Liselotte said. "Pardon. That was forceful of me."

"If you're not ready to date, you're not," Audrey said delicately. "It's your choice. I didn't mean to put you on the spot. Please, though, don't think you'll interfere with Joe and me. We do want your company tonight. So, yes? You will join us?"

Mentally drained from thoughts of the men from her past, Liselotte pushed them out of her mind. She wanted to be with her friends. She wanted to have fun. "Yes. Of course, I want to celebrate with you."

LISELOTTE RETURNED to the apartment shortly after Audrey. A good find, the two-bedroom apartment featured a cheerful yet claustrophobic kitchenette, a small living room with leftover 1930s-style pale pink posy bouquets and tan stripes, and an adequate bathroom with a dull black-and-white color scheme. Strangely, it seemed to shrink when they were both home and needed privacy. Fortunately, they were rarely home at the same time, except during bedtime or when getting ready for work in the morning. Recently, Audrey spent more time away with Joe, including overnight stays, though it was not Liselotte's place to comment. Actually, she was happy for her friend. She believed it was only a matter of time before they celebrated Audrey and Joe's engagement. Liselotte's breath hitched when Audrey walked into the room. "Wow—look at you. A new dress. You look amazing!"

"Look who's talking! Goodness, Liselotte—I love your new hairstyle. Do they still call it a bob these days?"

Liselotte tousled her hair. "The hairdresser calls it the Italian Cut. I call it relief from fussing with longer hair. A last-minute impulse—I barely had time to leave work today, get it cut, and return home on time."

"It's cute—quite you!" Audrey twirled in her new full-skirted floral dress in blue, pea green, gold, and mauve. The cotton material billowed out gracefully. "Like it?"

"It's beautiful, but you look lovely in whatever you put on." Liselotte winked. "As long as Joe thinks so."

"We'll find out soon. I'm glad you like it, sweetie. It comes with a matching bolero jacket, but I might leave it behind since it should be warm tonight." Audrey glanced at the antique Art Deco mantel clock on the end table beside the sofa, a moving-in gift from her father. "Will you be long?"

"Okay. I get the hint." Liselotte hurried to her bedroom. She kicked off her blue flats, peeled off her work clothes, and slipped into her old but favorite rust red skirt and a tan blouse. After putting on fresh makeup and fussing with her hair, which, in its shorter length, took no time to tidy, she put on shoes that matched her outfit and grabbed a black purse. "I'm not as glamorous as you are," she said as she entered the living room, "but you're the star of tonight's show."

"You look fine," Audrey said. A car honked. She leaned over the steam radiator in front of the window. "There's the cabbie. Let's go and knock socks off, shall we?"

"Do I have time to scribble that saying down before I forget it?"

"Not now." Hooking her arm with Liselotte's, Audrey winked. "Don't worry. I'll remind you later."

THIS WAS Liselotte's first time dining at Zachary's, or at any fine-dining restaurant in the States. With its off-white walls decorated with bronze-colored sculptural reliefs from Greek mythology, tables covered with white linen tablecloths set with white china trimmed in red, wine glasses, and elegant silverware, red carpeting matching the red-painted ceilings, and large vases of red roses placed in front of the off-white floor-length curtains, the atmosphere conveyed to patrons that they could expect an exceptional meal. However, while this was a special celebration for Audrey's acceptance into university, even Joe, who owned a car repair shop and made a modest living, caused Liselotte to suspect he was planning something even more special for Audrey. Although the evening would soon reveal the mystery, Liselotte's uncertainty grew. She felt both excited for her friend and like an intruder, despite Audrey telling her she very much belonged beside her tonight.

"Everything looks wonderful," Audrey said as she looked at the menu. "I'm having trouble deciding. What are you two ordering?"

Liselotte examined the menu. Unfamiliar with such fancy choices, she struggled to choose between the shrimp cocktails and Oysters Rockefeller for appetizers, and the Steak Diane and Trout Amandine for the main dishes. Although she doubted she'd have room for dessert, the Lemon Chiffon pie and Bananas Foster were quite tempting. "It all looks scrumptious to me."

Joe, dressed in a soft brown suit that complemented his charming personality, looked pleased. "That's what I was hoping to hear, ladies. I'm glad the menu is appealing. It's a special occasion, and I wanted everything to be memorable."

"That it is," Audrey said, squeezing Joe's hand. They held each other's gaze so intensely that Liselotte had to resist fidgeting.

"The shrimp cocktail and the trout sound lovely," Liselotte said, wondering whether the other two were paying attention, though she could not blame them for focusing on each other. This was obvious love in action, something she truly desired for her friend.

"Shrimp Cocktail for me, too," Joe said, not taking his eyes off Audrey. "And I'll order the steak."

"I thought you would," Audrey said cheerfully. "I'm ordering the same."

The waiter, dressed in black pants, a white shirt, a dark red bow tie, and a black vest, approached with the bottle of red wine that Joe ordered when they sat down. After pouring their drinks, the waiter then took their orders.

Joe raised his wine glass. "A toast to my wonderful companions, to my love, Audrey, on her acceptance to the University of Rochester, and to the success of turning your dreams into reality."

After sipping her wine, Liselotte excused herself to the restroom, declining Audrey's offer to join her. "No worries," she said, winking at both of them. "I don't want to miss a thing and will be back in a hurry."

The hallway to the restrooms was at the far end of the dining room. As Liselotte was about to enter the corridor, a group of men and women exited and briefly blocked her path. She stepped aside to let them pass, accidentally brushing against a chair. She immediately turned around to apologize to the diner.

"I'm so..." The room spun wildly. Stars burst around her head. She stepped back, reaching for anything to hold onto to regain her balance.

"Let me help you," the man said, as he stood up from the chair she had bumped into.

Klaus? How... it couldn't be... here in Rochester?

"Please sit for a moment," the man said. His three companions at the table also extended an invitation.

Liselotte straightened up. "I'm so sorry."

"That's all right." The man turned slightly to his left, revealing his full face. His bright blue eyes contrasted with Klaus's brown eyes. His height and round gut—she could not imagine Klaus overindulging—also did not resemble her nemesis's. When he further expressed his concern, she detected a Southern American accent rather than German one. This was not Klaus but rather her overactive imagination. She apologized once more and hurried to the women's room.

Secured in a stall, she patted herself as if checking for wounds, aware that the pain was in her mind, not in the rest of her body. She felt justified in her fears about Klaus, especially her worry that he might track her down like a hunter pursuing a wild animal, whether for fun or revenge for her leaving. This incident deepened her sense of exposure. Klaus was a disturbing person. He might have promised her protection, but only if he controlled her every move. After all these years of running from him, she still had to remain vigilant. Weak-kneed, she leaned against the partition of the next stall and struggled to breathe. It had been nearly eight years since she last saw him. Considering his abilities, if he truly wanted to find her, he would have done so by now. She was just beginning to stop obsessing over him… had even ceased having nightmares about the shady man who hides truths more than she does.

Aware that she was alone in the restroom, she whispered, "I vow that on this night of celebrating with my friends, I will refuse to believe that this man is pursuing me."

Stepping out of the stall, Liselotte washed her hands and checked her hair and makeup. *As good as I can be.* Thinking about enjoying her friends' company and this lovely restaurant and its promise of a delectable dinner, she hurried to their table, careful not to bump into any tables, patrons, or waiters carrying trays of elegant meals.

Just before she reached the table, she stopped abruptly. Why was Audrey crying, frantically wiping tears from her eyes and cheeks? Yet, Joe was beaming?

Thinking about giving them privacy, she asked, "Shall I come back?"

"No," Audrey and Joe said simultaneously. Audrey sniffled. Joe continued grinning.

Confused, Liselotte sat. "What's happening here?"

Audrey kept her gaze on Joe but reached out her left hand to show Liselotte a sparkling, large diamond engagement ring. "Joe has asked me to become his wife, and I said yes. This is the happiest day of my life."

Joe leaned over to kiss Audrey. "If this is happy, I'd hate to see you on our wedding day."

"Oh, my goodness," Liselotte said, and began to weep. They were not only tears of joy for her friend but also thankfulness that she had made it this far in her journey of escape and starting over while avoiding the horrors of war. And, as she had just learned, it was also relief from avoiding an unpleasant encounter with someone who needed to stay in her past. "I am so happy for you two. Congratulations!"

Joe sighed. "Liselotte, you're sobbing too? Do I really have to watch over you as my bride-to-be walks down the aisle?"

Liselotte hugged Joe. "Good thing I know you're just joking. I'm glad you're marrying my best friend. Do you have a date in mind yet?"

"No," Audrey said, then looked at her fiancé. "Although I'm thinking that after I graduate from my studies, any time we marry is a perfect time for me."

Not caring if she was causing a scene, Liselotte pretended to cry dramatically.

"What's wrong?" Joe asked, his smile quickly fading.

"I'm going to lose the best roommate I've ever had," Liselotte said, then laughed heartily. She looked back and forth at the two of them. "I knew this wonderful time might happen tonight, and for once, I'm glad I was right."

Audrey grasped her hand. "I am, too."

27

LISELOTTE, ROCHESTER, MAY 1956

May began spectacularly, especially after a winter that felt particularly miserable and seemingly endless. The late-season storms brought the total snowfall to nearly 107 inches, making it the third snowiest winter on record for the area and causing many people to worry about disruptions and delays in daily life. Fortunately, the gentle breezes of May blew away the last snowstorm from April. The longer, sunnier days gave way to trees leafing out, and the blooming of magnolias, rhododendrons, and dogwoods added brightness to the city of over 300,000 residents with their pale purple, yellow, pink, blue, and scarlet hues. Not a day had gone by since Liselotte settled in this American city nine years ago that she had not felt thankful for becoming a citizen in 1952 after a five-year process.

Now, at thirty years old, she had no regrets about not earning a university degree, having a prestigious career, or finding a husband to start a new "second family." Instead, she wished she had reconnected with her mother and two girls. Every day, she obsessed over their ages. This year, her mother, Helene, would be fifty-three, and on May 15th, her twin girls would have turned fourteen—if they were alive. Liselotte shuddered. She could not afford to think of Rosa and Regina as anything but happy and healthy. Actually, she could not handle the worry about many things these days. She had a job that gave her exactly what she wanted: commitment, good relationships with co-workers, stability, and, recently, a promotion to assistant manager, which meant better work hours and vacation pay. Plus, she had made new friends at the Readers-For-Life book club held at the library where Audrey worked. These positives made her willing to finally tell Audrey what she had kept hidden—something that could backfire on her and those she loved.

Seated on the sofa, she checked her wristwatch. Good, Audrey should be back from her last exam any minute now. Even though she was graduating in a few weeks and she and Joe had set their wedding date for the autumn of '57, she still hadn't moved into Joe's apartment. Although she spent more time at his place than at their shared apartment, she hadn't yet made the move. Audrey didn't see herself as old-fashioned, and she wasn't worried about what others might think if she moved in with Joe as his fiancée but not his wife. It was more that she was so busy with her studies, her job, and precious hours with Joe that she hadn't taken the time to pack her belongings and move. The two of them even planned to skip a honeymoon and buy a house instead.

"Don't worry," Audrey told Liselotte. "Come the first of October in 1957, when I become Mrs. Joseph Campanili, I'll be living with my new life partner every day of our lives together."

The sound of a key slipping into the door lock relaxed Liselotte but also sparked a nervous energy. She smoothed her navy-blue, red-polka-dot culottes, tugged down her blue blouse, and moved the vase of pink and yellow daisies she bought after work to the center of the coffee table. She and Audrey adored vivid colors, laughing and falling in love at first sight with their apartment when they first saw the lipstick-pink living room walls and green kitchenette.

"Hello, Roomie," Audrey called as she stepped into the apartment. Liselotte, continuing their new routine, returned the greeting with a 'hello, soon-to-be-graduate.'

"Oh, oh," Audrey said, staring at the flowers. "What's up?"

Liselotte jutted out her chin toward the chair across from her. "Please join me."

"Okay." Audrey sat, rubbing her hands. "This sounds serious, like Mom leading up to an interrogation, like the one and only time I ever snuck home after curfew."

"Nothing like that."

After a few moments of silence, Audrey scooted to the edge of the chair. "You're not smiling... please don't tell me you received bad news."

"That's the one problem I have with you as a friend—I can't keep my expressions from giving me away." Liselotte smiled to put her friend at ease.

"Is it about me graduating—don't you dare throw a surprise party for me." Audrey kept such a serious face that Liselotte knew right away she was joking.

"You're funny. If I were planning such a surprise, I would have just ruined everything." Liselotte nervously clutched the collar of her blouse. "Did you want a party? I should have thought to—"

"No, please. No parties. No guilt. Okay? Just continue because I hate suspense."

"Okay, then," she began, but she paused again. When she saw Audrey's narrowed gaze, she ran her fingers through her hair and sighed. "Over the years, I've shared most everything about myself."

"Most?"

"Yes, about my mother and daughters—from Rosa's tragic condition to her sudden disappearance and the subsequent breakup of my family that I initially blamed on my mother, but really, it was because I left them to—"

"Please," Audrey said so softly that Liselotte had to strain to hear. "We've gone through this many times. You were a teenager thrust into single parenthood in the middle of World War Two. Your mom was also a single parent. You both had a lot to handle, and it's no surprise there was significant tension between you two."

Liselotte gave a small nod. "I've also shared with you how I managed to escape working in Poland and hid in the Tatra Mountains until after the war, when I then went to France and finally returned to Germany, where I was fortunate enough to meet you."

"Yes. That's resilience for you," Audrey said gently and sincerely.

"There's more you need to know—something I worry might someday cause problems for you and Joe. I admit I should have told you earlier. Still, on this perfect spring day, as nature comes alive after months of hibernation—ironically, when everything is going beautifully for both you and me—I feel compelled to share this final piece of my history."

"A secret?" Audrey wrung her hands. "Talk about a slow build-up of suspense... or is it that you're stalling?"

Liselotte met Audrey's gaze. "It's more like an omission. Secret… omission... call it whatever you like. It's something I neglected to tell you because I don't want to worry you." Liselotte appreciated Audrey's nonjudgmental expression. Her intuition told her that Audrey wouldn't run for the hills to escape her, as one of the new American expressions she had recently picked up went.

She inhaled deeply. "When I told you that I found work in Poland and left because the job was not only dangerous for me but also linked to the Nazi regime, which I fully opposed, I was telling the truth."

"Yes, I believed you. Knowing you, I don't expect you to now deny the truth and tell me you were a Nazi."

"I'm definitely not a Nazi, nor have I ever been. However, I was deceived by one. His name is Klaus—"

"Klaus?" Audrey paled. "The same Klaus whose card I received through the Berlin office, the one with the rubbed-off last name?"

Liselotte nodded. "Yes, I'm quite sure that was him. Klaus Agers is his full name. He was a fellow German I met when we literally bumped into each other while rushing to a bomb shelter during a raid in Berlin. At that time, I was living on the streets with no other options to escape the bombs and the chaos that followed. One thing led to another, and I realized he was a dedicated Nazi. Through subtle coercion and manipulation, he took me to Poland until I couldn't tolerate another moment of his presence or follow his work ethics."

"What finally pushed you to leave him?"

"I was horrified that he wanted me to Germanize Polish children—kidnapped from other countries—so they could be brought to Germany and raised as Aryan Germans by Aryan parents. But what drove me to flee that night was meeting another captive woman, whom I later learned was a sex slave to the camp's officers. Magda and I met just as she was leaving, and as a witness to her actions, she left me no choice but to run for my life with her."

"It's a good thing you did leave." Audrey leaned forward. "Sorry for my bluntness, Liselotte, but had Klaus ever forced you to have sex with him?"

"Here's the thing about Klaus," Liselotte said, pausing as more painful memories washed over her. "He had threatened me a few times. He tried to control me, claiming he would always watch out for me to keep me safe. As for forced relations, no. He never made me, nor did I volunteer—not that I was attracted to him. However, on a few occasions, he hinted that he was attracted to me, and that I was his—as if he owned me—making me believe he would push himself on me sooner or later."

"Deciding to run from a Nazi who wanted to keep you under his watch forever was a wise choice. I hate to think about what else he might have had in mind." Audrey got up and moved to the sofa, sitting next to Liselotte. "Do you think he's followed you across Europe and now into the States?"

"I wouldn't doubt it."

Audrey raised her fingertips to her bottom lip, seeming lost in thought. "Have you seen him since? After all this time, is that why you now feel he might be a concern to Joe and me, let alone you?"

"When Magda and I exited the tunnel that we used to escape from the camp, I was pretty sure I saw him standing by a parked car, talking with the man we were supposed to meet. It's one of those things, though. One second, I'm sure it's him, and the next, I don't see him, as if he vanished into thin air."

Audrey's brow furrowed.

"What is it?"

"I understand what you mean. It's a common experience, especially after losing someone close. I went through it when my mother passed, practically seeing her everywhere. At the time, because of my Red Cross travels, that meant in the Caribbean and across Europe. Setting aside the fact that the world was at war, Mom would have loved visiting foreign places, but she never left the country. Who or what I thought was Mom was definitely not her."

"Yes, it's very unsettling. But I'm now wondering if it really was my overactive imagination—and with everything in life falling into place for both of us, I wouldn't want to be careless. See, in addition to just after my escape with Magda, there were a few other times."

"Yet, each time, if indeed it really was Klaus, he didn't take any step to talk to you or to hurt you?"

"That's correct," Liselotte said, nodding for emphasis. "That's mainly why I shrugged it off all this time. I probably should have mentioned this a long time ago, when I first started *seeing* him. But then you and Joe got engaged, and I didn't want to ruin your happiness. Now that you're about to graduate, I realize that the longer I wait to tell the people who matter most to me, the more I might be putting you in danger. That is, if the crazy person is indeed following me." She lowered her chin in shame and huffed. "If anything, I think I'm ruining my own life."

"Clearly, Liselotte, you're upset, and you have every right to feel that way."

"Yes. Thank you," she murmured, taking a few seconds to compose herself. "The last time I thought I saw him was at your engagement dinner, but fortunately, when I got a better look at the man, it was clearly not Klaus." She leaned forward and buried her head in her hands. When she felt Audrey gently massaging her tense shoulder muscles, she pushed her thoughts onward. "I've been afraid of this person for years. I've dreamt about him and mistakenly seen him on many street corners and in dark alleys—it's like I can't leave home without thinking of him. The thing is, he could very well be out there to hurt me. I can't understand why, after so many years apart, he would want to spend his time and resources chasing after me for no reason. There's nothing for him to gain, unless it's an awful case of revenge."

"Maybe he's the one truly obsessed." Audrey lifted her hand from Liselotte's back and grasped her hand. "Sick people do sick things. Dangerous people do dangerous things. You have valid reasons to worry, especially since there's always a chance you're not just imagining this—that it's really Klaus following you. Do you want to involve the police? Do you want to press charges? As you know, Nazis are still being hunted down and charged."

"The thing is, no one in a position of power, like the police, would consider helping me if I'm unsure whether I've seen him. To them, I'd only appear as a walking case of paranoia. Listen to me—I sound crazy, at least to anyone who doesn't know me—"

"You're far from crazy," Audrey said softly. "You have every right to be concerned... he's a dangerous man. If anything, if he collaborated with the Nazi Party in kidnapping children, I believe he might be wanted for international crimes and should be taken into custody. You would be helping many people, Liselotte—not just yourself."

"But it's not like he has walked into my workplace, called there, or even at the apartment—not even a ring followed by a hang-up after hearing my voice. He's probably still in Germany... maybe he's already been arrested for war crimes... maybe even executed for all I know. Maybe all I need is a therapist to help me get over this person whose name I don't even want to say anymore."

"Are you telling me this because you're nervous about living on your own soon?"

"Not really, believe it or not. I worry that if he finds me, he can also find you and Joe and cause trouble for both of you. He knows how to emotionally manipulate me into doing whatever he says."

"To some extent. He couldn't fully control you, as you proved by escaping from him."

When Liselotte didn't reply, Audrey added, "Would you mind if I share all of this with Joe?"

"Of course not. Please do. You know, I've started to think of Joe as the brother I've never had."

"That's sweet. I'm glad. He's fond of you, too. He enjoys playing the older, protective brother. Audrey chuckled. "His own sister... let's say, a sweet challenge... he says he appreciates your mature insight on life."

"Mature insight…" Liselotte mused. She turned to look out the window behind the sofa, parting the curtains slightly. How she wished she had more maturity and insight years ago. She never wanted her past to unfold as it had; no one welcomes sadness. If she ever had a chance to rebuild her relationship with her mother and daughters, she would seize the moment and, this time, hold it so close to her heart that she would never let go again.

"Liselotte?" Audrey touched her arm. "Do you want some time alone?"

"No, no. Please stay." She faced Audrey. "I escaped from Klaus—this miserable person—years ago. These sightings of him are probably either in my head or of people who look like him, at least at first glance. However, he hasn't shown up in person or made direct contact." She took a deep breath. "For the record, I'm no longer a naive or desperate kid. It's likely he's not targeting me, but since many other people in this world could cause trouble for me, I can't be scared of everyone. I have to live and enjoy my life, and I don't need another war to teach me that. I'll be careful, and I'm telling you this because I want you to be careful too. You mean a lot to me, Audrey Wilson—soon to be Audrey Campanili. I don't want any harm to come to you. But we can't live in fear of what tomorrow might bring."

"You're exactly right. Fear only paralyzes us, turning us into stone statues, making us unable to respond properly to situations and even preventing us from seeking safety or helping others. I want you to promise me that you will tell me the next time you experience a Klaus-sighting. Agree?"

Liselotte looked around the small but charming apartment she had shared with Audrey since arriving in Rochester, a home in a city that had treated her well. After Audrey and Joe married, it would become her own place. She was looking forward to another new beginning—

stage—in her life. No one would ever hold her back from all the positive possibilities she might enjoy.

She met Audrey's gaze. "Yes, I agree to tell you if I see him again. I also agree not to live in fear."

"That sounds wonderful, my friend."

Liselotte smiled. "It does."

28

LISELOTTE, ROCHESTER, SATURDAY, SEPTEMBER 28, 1957

Under Liselotte's management at Rochester Haven House, numerous weddings and receptions unfolded like pages from a storybook, full of romance and elegance. Today promised nothing less for her dear friend Audrey—if not more. She glanced at her friend's reflection in the mirror of Audrey's father's hotel room. "Poor Joe. Everyone will keep their eyes on you and ignore your groom."

Audrey fussed with her pearl drop earrings. "I'll keep my eyes on him and make sure he's not getting too lonely."

"And that's all that matters, my dear. Now hold still," Liselotte said, pinning the lace veil on Audrey's head. She glanced back at the mirror and saw her friend's smile. "Beautiful, that's what you are."

"You're sweet—and that's why I keep you as a friend." Audrey laughed. "I'm glad we were able to secure Haven House's reception room despite having to adjust the ceremony date at the church—who would have imagined so many couples vying for an autumn wedding?"

"The fall is a beautiful time to get married… any time you marry a wonderful man is the right time," Liselotte sighed dreamily. "I'm thrilled to be your maid of honor." She glanced at her wristwatch.

"Your dad will be out front with his car in ten minutes to take us to the church. Now, stand, and let me see you billow."

"Billow?" Audrey quirked an eyebrow. "People swirl; dresses billow."

"No grammar lessons today." Liselotte motioned with her palms up for Audrey to stand. "Come. Stand and billow."

Audrey giggled, stood, pulled her chair back from the mirror, and slowly turned around. "Good enough?"

"Once more… perfect. You are the perfect bride about to marry the perfect man."

"And you're the perfect friend who gushes too much, though I love it." Audrey grabbed her slim purse adorned with tiny faux pearls and crossed the room to the door. "Ready, Liselotte?"

"Okay." Liselotte glanced at her to-do list. "Looks like everything is good. We can go now."

"Ever the executive manager," Audrey said playfully, though Liselotte appreciated the recognition of her recent promotion. "Oh, my gloves are still on the dresser. Could you grab them for me?"

"Of course."

THEY ARRIVED at the church with fifteen minutes to spare—just enough time to breathe, but not enough to worry. Liselotte sniffled when Audrey's father, Hank, hooked his daughter's arm.

"Are you ready, honey?" he asked.

"Oh, I am, Pop. The only way today would have been better was for Mom to be with us."

Hank patted Audrey's arm. "Oh, have no doubt she's with us." He glanced over his shoulder at Liselotte and smiled. "Are you ready, Miss Maid of Honor?"

"Yes, and I promise no more crying until the pastor pronounces you man and wife."

When the string quartet played Wagner's "Bridal Chorus," the flower girl, Joe's cousin's seven-year-old daughter, Maisy, walked down the white-papered aisle runner, scattering rose petals.

"Ready," Liselotte winked at Audrey and Hank before facing forward. Behind her, she heard Hank say a quick 'I love you, Audrey,' more than enough to motivate Liselotte—and keep her from weeping —as she began her walk into the church.

Each step brought her closer to Joe's best man, Maisy's father, Douglas Littleton. Liselotte had met Doug—he preferred the short version of his name—at the wedding rehearsal two days earlier. He seemed nice, but they hadn't had much chance to talk beyond a casual remark about the soon-to-be bride and groom and the delicious dinner. Audrey mentioned him very little, except to say he had become a single parent after losing his wife, who tragically drowned in a boating accident when Maisy was a year old, and how Doug had raised her as a devoted, loving father ever since, never marrying or even dating.

Standing next to Doug was the only other groomsman, Audrey's brother Pete, who, two years ago, married his steady girlfriend Sally, whom he met when they were students at the University of Rochester. When Pete was not working in a pioneering Rochester DNA research lab, he was at home with Sally, playing with their one-year-old daughter, Pamela. Liselotte looked forward to getting to know Pete and Sally better, especially once Audrey and Joe returned from their honeymoon in Quebec City. Liselotte mentally patted her heart, feeling relieved that those two had finally agreed on a honeymoon instead of forgoing a once-in-a-lifetime romantic getaway.

Hank kissed his daughter on the cheek and handed her to Joe. Then he sat beside his daughter, Caro. At twenty-six, Caro had come a long way from her older siblings' view of her as temperamental. Like her brother, she graduated early from college and became an elementary school teacher in her hometown of Milwaukee. Watching Audrey's family, Liselotte couldn't help but feel happy for her friend, who had lost her mother but had grown closer to her dad, brother, and sister. Liselotte's thoughts wandered to the realization that she and Pete were the same age. In their own ways, Audrey and her family were moving forward, overcoming sorrows, and choosing new paths… and she was too. Once again, Liselotte's eyes brimmed with tears, but this time she felt happiness as well and wanted to cherish the beauty of love, whether between a couple or family members. Life often does not turn out the way a child hopes for the future, and certainly not in the way a teenager—headstrong and determined but not always sensible—romantically sighs about her near-future adult years. Learning that she could live in both realms of joy and grief, she had also learned to move on, and she wasn't about to let anyone take that away from her.

When Joe began to recite his vows, Liselotte, standing beside Audrey, cleared her mind and focused on the bride and groom, where it belonged—in the first place. Today, their wedding day was all about them. They had decided to exchange the traditional wedding promises, which Liselotte had no doubt the couple would honor forever through their years together. Cheers erupted, and the quartet played Mendelssohn's "Wedding March." The wedding party started the recessional with the newlyweds leading the way, followed by the bridal party. Under a canopy of pink roses scattered across white-painted trellises, they gathered outside in the fresh, crisp autumn air to greet their guests as they exited the church for the reception.

Liselotte fought the urge to excuse herself and rush back to the Rochester Haven House to oversee the reception dinner. She had appointed her second-in-command to handle the celebration festivities, giving herself the day off to relax and enjoy. The first thing she did after the guests greeted Audrey and Joe was to pull them into a hug. "Congratulations, my friends. I'm so happy for you."

"But you're crying," Joe teased. "I'd hate to see what you do when you're sad."

"Never you mind." Liselotte sniffled and stepped back. "Now, Mr. and Mrs. Joseph Campanili, put on your biggest smiles for the photographer, and head to your wedding reception while I slip away from the spotlight. It's your day to shine brightly."

"They are a handsome couple," a voice came from behind her. Doug?

She turned around, surprised but happy that Doug was talking to her. "Yes, they are. From what Audrey has told me, this was a union in… in… What is that common American saying you have?"

"American saying?" Doug repeated. "Oh, right. You're German."

"By birth, yes. By choice, I have been a citizen of this country since 1952. Occasionally, though, I still get stuck on some typical American expressions."

Doug grinned, a handsome look on him. "Well, I was born in Boise, Idaho, thirty-five years ago, and I still scratch my head wondering about certain phrases." He tapped his right temple twice. "I think the term you're looking for is 'in the works,' as in, Audrey and Joe have been a union in the works for a while. From what Joe has told me, ever since he set his eyes on Audrey helping him in the military hospital, he could not take his eyes, nor his mind, off of her."

"Daddy," Maisy called. "This is so much fun! Everyone looks beautiful."

With his eyes locked on Liselotte, he said, "They sure do, honey."

29

LISELOTTE, ROCHESTER, AUGUST 1961

"Oh, Maisy, honey, what's wrong?"

"Nothing. Don't come in here."

At age ten, Maisy was usually not a child to worry about. However, as Liselotte got to know her and her dad, Doug, she realized that when a child denied that something had happened after shouting "oh-no," followed by a warning not to check the situation, it meant that the adult needed to go straight into the kitchen without delay.

Liselotte swung open the kitchen door, immediately understanding why Maisy was upset, and probably mortified, knowing her. A puddle of spilled chocolate milk was on the table, dripping onto the floor, and the girl's new white dress was splattered. The poor darling. No wonder she was upset. Liselotte kicked aside the shattered glass pitcher on the floor.

"Dad's never going to forgive me," Maisy said, choking back a sob. "The pitcher was Mom's favorite thing in the whole wide world."

Liselotte grabbed a sponge and a basin from the storage area under the sink. Getting on her knees, she began to wipe up the mess. "Here's the truth, Maisy. While I never knew your mom, I'd bet a lifetime's supply of chocolate milk that *you* were her favorite in the world, not a glass pitcher."

"Are you just saying that to make me feel better? I'm not a little girl anymore. If Dad wants to punish me, I couldn't blame him."

Where was this coming from? She was way too serious, considering the three of them would be leaving on vacation as soon as Doug arrived home from an early morning house showing to potential buyers. Leaving the spilled chocolate mess alone for now, Liselotte playfully booped the child's nose.

"Stop," Maisy called out.

"Not until you start smiling." She began tickling Maisy's belly, which finally made her laugh. "That's better. Believe me, your dad can't wait to see your face when you see the pink-hearted bridge into Snow White's Grotto at Disneyland."

"And I can't wait to see Dad's face when he's with you, all day long."

"Me?" Liselotte asked, playing innocent. She and Doug had hit it off so well during Audrey and Joe's wedding reception four years ago that they've been steadily dating ever since. Since they were only dating, she lived apart from Doug and Maisy, as it should be. If marriage ever came into the picture for the two of them, that would, of course, change their living arrangements, but for now, she still lived in the apartment she once shared with Audrey. However, discreetly, she and Doug had occasions to share their passion away from Maisy's young eyes, and had happily discovered that they were a great match in that area of their lives.

"Okay, Maisy. I admit—I think I'm more excited than you are about not only visiting California and seeing the Sleeping Beauty Castle, but I'm also counting down the seconds until the three of us leave New York and spend two wonderful weeks together. Oh, the fun we'll have! With your dad coming home soon, why don't you go change your dress while I finish cleaning up the spill."

Maisy looked at the floor, half cleaned up. "That's still a lot of chocolate milk. Want me to help with the rest?"

"Nah, I have it." Liselotte watched Maisy leave the room, then sighed. "That's enough milk to quench the whole state's thirst," she mumbled, and then continued to clean up the spill. After the mess was cleared, she glanced at the clock and was surprised to see it was ten o'clock. Goodness. Although Doug was one to adhere to punctuality when meeting potential customers, whether at his growing realty office or in showing properties, he was a master at making Liselotte sweat with anxiety by not calling to explain his circumstances.

If she were honest with herself, trusting Doug wouldn't even be a question. In the first few weeks of getting to know each other, she shared not only her upbringing—such as giving birth to twin girls at the young age of sixteen, with one of them in poor health—but also the disappearance of Rosa, which led her to leave her mother and Regina, regrettably. She even admitted how she had helped Klaus before painfully discovering his dedication to the Nazis and how she fled from him, though she still harbored guilt for not rescuing the kidnapped children awaiting transport into Germany for fresh beginnings with new families. Since she no longer saw Klaus randomly once she and Doug became a couple, she saw no reason to upset the man she loved or scare him away by telling him about how she used to catch glimpses of Klaus here and there.

Doug was a patient man, slow to judge, which meant a lot to Liselotte. He also opened up about himself, including the fact that now that she had entered his life, his sadness over the tragic loss of his wife no longer haunted his days. Without a doubt, he was the man meant to be in her life. It was only a matter of time.

Time. Where was he? They both needed a break from work, and with Maisy on summer break from school, they had spent many evenings planning and booking this special trip. Whether it started or ended with a marriage proposal wasn't her main concern. Right now, she just wanted to be with the two people she loved, to have fun and share smiles. And yes, she also looked forward to enjoying the California sunshine that everyone she knew raved about.

On her feet, she stuck her tongue out at the silent phone, thinking Doug simply never called because he was on his way home. She'd just turn on the radio on the kitchen shelf above the sink and catch up on the news, something she usually avoided during a typical workweek.

"Reporting live from Berlin," the newscaster said, introducing himself by name and the radio station. "We are witnessing a wall being built in Berlin, which has significant global impacts. If concrete could speak, it would reveal how Germany is now divided into two halves—West and East. Many German families and businesses are now torn apart, separated on opposite sides of a once-united country. Throughout the day, we will provide live updates to keep you informed."

Liselotte might have turned off the radio. She might have groped the sink as she collapsed to the floor. She was unsure. Her world had once again become a blur. Time had once again stopped. Had ten minutes passed, or ten hours, when she felt the gentle tug pulling her into a hug?

"Sweetheart?"

She licked her dry lips. Keeping her eyes closed, she murmured, "Doug?"

"I'm right here. I rushed home as soon as I heard the news, but apparently, you heard about what's happening in Germany too."

"Berlin…"

"Yes."

She gasped and opened her eyes. "Where's Maisy?" She tried to stand, but feeling the uneven weight of her past burdens piling up on her shoulders, she tilted to the left. Doug grabbed her arm, stopping her from falling.

"Maisy's fine," Doug said, kissing the top of her head. "She met me at the door, saying you had everything under control in the kitchen. When she said she didn't want to bother you and that you've been very quiet, I ran right in here, especially knowing the breaking news. Did you pass out? Are you hurt?"

"What time is it?" She sat up, pressing her hand to the side of her head as if her disorientation could be contained. "I'm not sure if I fainted or just kind of caved in on myself. I don't think I'm hurt. Have we missed our flight?"

"There's plenty of time to reach the airport—it's the least of my concerns. Right now, you're what matters most. You'll see—this whole Germany situation will be taken care of. It'll be okay, honey."

Based on her experiences from the last world war and what her mother mentioned about her parents' time during the Great War, events at the national level in Germany did not always go smoothly. "I have my doubts it will be okay," she said, and tried to stand. "For all I know, my mother and daughters might be on the wrong side of that idiotic wall." With the harsh reality of the reporter's words echoing in her mind about how her birth nation was dividing, she leaned heavily on Doug and started to cry, not caring how she sounded.

"Many say this will all be forgotten in just a few days."

Liselotte thought about how Hitler declared that his new policies would become the law across all lands and that only the Aryan race was destined to enjoy the Earth. The leaders of the rest of the world might have initially dismissed his claims, but they soon realized how mistaken they had been about this evil dictator and how much his actions would forever change the world. She shook her head firmly. "No, it won't be over quickly. Maybe not ever."

"Come on now—where's your American spirit of never giving up?"

Doug cared more about her than about the world situation, and she loved him for that, among other things. Truth be told, he—and many other Americans—probably didn't even see this as a major global concern. When she remained quiet despite his gentle teasing, he drew her into a tighter hug.

"You're with me, honey," Doug said. "I will make sure you're fine, always. I understand your concern about your mom and daughters, but as we've discussed, you've been apart for eighteen years." His voice grew gentler than she had ever heard before. "You were only barely seventeen years old when you left your home. That's fewer years together than apart. If your mother hasn't tracked you down in all this time, sweetheart, you must keep moving forward in your life, concerned only about making yourself happy." He cupped her face, kissed her deeply, then smiled that sweet look of his that she adored. "I can only hope that your happiness includes Maisy and me."

Was he still talking about building the Berlin Wall or again suggesting that she forget about her supposed family—the ones, in his view, who never tried to reach out to her? Or was he referring to something different?

"Doug, what exactly do you mean by my happiness tying in with you and Maisy?"

He reached into the inner pocket of his black business blazer and pulled out a red satin ring box. He opened it to reveal the most beautiful, sparkling diamond ring Liselotte had ever seen. "I was going to surprise you with this at our first dinner tonight in California, but it seems to me that this is a much better time." He kissed her, then knelt down before her. "Will you marry me, Liselotte? Together, we can dare to make a new, better tomorrow."

30

LISELOTTE, ROCHESTER, FEBRUARY 10, 1962

Right before Liselotte was about to press the door buzzer, she pulled out her compact from her black-beaded shoulder purse to check her hair. A carry-over from the war days of poor eating, her hair remained thin, and no matter how well she ate afterward, she was always self-conscious about her appearance. Holding back the silliness of growling at her reflection, she shrugged. "I can do this," she whispered, and then rang the bell.

"Perfect timing, as always," Audrey said in greeting. She craned her neck to look over Liselotte's shoulder. "Just you? Not that I'm ever disappointed to see you."

"Since I was running late at work, I phoned Doug to tell him that he and Maisy should meet me here. I'm surprised they haven't arrived yet."

"Brrr, I'm cold." Audrey opened the door wider and gestured her inside. "Come in where it's cozy and warm. Don't worry about those two—they'll be here any second. Let me take your coat—Joe's making hot apple cider toddies to warm us adults up. Maisy will have to settle for hot chocolate or plain apple cider."

"She won't fuss."

Audrey closed the coat closet. "I know. She's such a good kid."

"That she is. I'm lucky to have her in my life."

Audrey sat in her favorite platform rocker, which she had inherited from her grandmother when her pop sold his Wisconsin house and moved into an apartment. Liselotte sat across from her on the sofa. They looked at each other silently.

"This is not like us," Liselotte said after a few minutes of uncomfortable silence."

"I know," Audrey said, eyeing the kitchen where Joe was fixing the drinks. "And to think that we girls actually have a few minutes to catch up with each other." She grinned. "I guess we can always start with compliments. You look lovely in that brown corduroy skirt and white sweater. Then again, you always dress nicely."

"Thanks. Is that a new Pendleton pantsuit? I love the ivory and brown blend." Liselotte laughed. "Good. We got that out of the way—let's talk about something better, perhaps deeper. I thought for sure that you would have good—"

"Good news?" Audrey asked, finishing Liselotte's thoughts, which she always did well. "No news here. But sometimes in married life, that's a good thing."

Especially since Doug wasn't yet present, Liselotte decided to jump right to the subject she knew Audrey was eager to hear. "Okay. I'll start. Doug and I…" It pained her to see the corners of Audrey's lips curl into a hopeful smile. "Sorry, but no. We haven't set a wedding date yet."

With a sudden downturn of her mouth, Audrey leaned forward. "How do you feel about that?"

Her friend's non-judgmental ways were one of the things Liselotte always trusted. "It's more me than Doug."

"Meaning?"

"Doug is a sweet, wonderful man—and I adore Maisy."

"I'm not hearing the L-word."

Liselotte pursed her lips and nodded. "Oh, I do love him… love them both. But it's me. If I were ready to marry, I would marry Doug without a second thought." Believing that leaning back into the sofa and relaxing would make it easier to talk, she shifted, but her lower back pinched. Imagining the grimace she just made only tensed her more. She straightened, clasping her hands and then releasing them. "You know of my history with men, Audrey. None of it is good. I've spent years trying to heal from a lot of heartbreak. The closest I've come to it is learning to live with my past rather than escape it. Know what I mean?"

"Yes, I can relate, though not exactly when it comes to enjoying a loving relationship," Audrey said carefully. "For me, it's more about learning how to live with old family wounds while moving on at the same time." She gasped and covered her mouth. "I'm so sorry."

"Yes, that's also my thing—committing to a man and dealing with family hurts, as you say." Liselotte twisted her mouth to the right and wryly said, "No man in his right mind would want to marry me. I'm what Americans call someone who carries too much emotional baggage."

"How does Doug feel about this?" Before Liselotte could answer, Audrey reached for a tissue from the box on the side table, hurried over to Liselotte's side, and gently dabbed her face free of tears. "Oh, dear. I'm so sorry—I had planned a happy evening tonight, not a sad one."

"I know. No hard feelings." Liselotte sniffled." To answer your question, Doug is an amazing, wonderful person. He says he wants no one else but me as his wife, and he's willing to wait. And if I never want to marry him—and believe me, there is no other man—he's perfectly happy just the way we are."

"And Maisy?"

Liselotte sensed the discomfort in her friend's question. "The two of us share a very close relationship, and Maisy seems perfectly fine and accepting of what we have rather than what we don't." She looked straight into Audrey's eyes. "Doug and I keep our intimacy private from Maisy. And, one good thing from that tumor I had a few years ago is that it led to the surgery I had... well, at least Doug and I don't have to worry about our passion for each other resulting in a baby out of wedlock." She sighed. "I'm beyond exhausted with the whole wedlock issue—once was enough."

When more tears started falling down Liselotte's cheeks, Audrey squeezed her hand. "I can only imagine." After a moment, Audrey offered a little smile. "Well, I have some good news, and no, it's not what you're thinking."

"Drats." Liselotte had hoped to hear about a baby on the way for Audrey and Joe, but seeing her friend's smile, she knew her good news was indeed good, and that was plenty for her. "Go on—don't leave me in suspense."

"Well, my news takes on a new meaning when it comes to never giving up. After years of searching for my missing Odessa relatives, I heard from Oksana Babenko, a second cousin living in London. Despite her thick Russian accent—thankfully, she speaks English well —I understood her just fine. I thanked her for putting up with my American twang, which she said she adored. We talked and talked—she's married and has three daughters, all of whom are married with children and live close by. The best part is that, even though Oksana couldn't tell me what became of our past relatives, she was able to share some anecdotes about several family members from her childhood. She was such a pleasure to talk to. We exchanged addresses and promised to stay in touch."

"That's wonderful news. I'm so happy for you. Did you get a chance to call your dad?"

"You bet! I ended up catching Pop right after he settled into bed for the night, so the first thing he thought was there had been an accident or some other horror. After we got past that, he expressed tons of gratitude that I never gave up my search for family news. I have a feeling he's just pleased someone from the family is still around." Audrey dropped her gaze. "I didn't confess that I all but gave up."

"Sounds like you've inherited that hope that keeps you going all these years from your dad."

"You're right. And to put your mind at ease about what you see as a baby dilemma, honestly, Joe and I are fine either way." Audrey winked several times. "We haven't given up trying."

"What haven't we stopped doing?" Joe asked as he entered the living room, carrying a tray of cheese and crackers. Instead of waiting for a reply, he set the food on the coffee table. "Should we be concerned about Doug and Maisy, yet? I wonder if I should turn down the oven temperature so our chicken doesn't become barbecued."

"I like barbecue," Liselotte quipped, then jumped when the door buzzer sounded.

"It's about time," Joe said as he headed toward the door and swung it open.

"Is Liselotte here?" a man asked in German-accented English. "She uses several last names. I need to speak with her."

"And who are you?" Joe asked.

"An old friend. I've come back for her. She needs to know this."

From the sofa, Liselotte craned her neck and wished she saw anyone but him.

"I followed her to this house. She must be here."

"Hey," Joe said, holding out a hand as the stranger tried to enter the house. "Stop."

"Move aside."

From her seat, Liselotte mouthed to Audrey, "Klaus. Police." She watched Audrey hurry out of the living room. She should have left the room too, but as if frozen, she couldn't move. Klaus looked worn in his middle age. His hair, now silver, and his face deeply etched, enhanced his withered, wasted appearance, as if he had suffered greatly during the years after she fled from him. Although she did not enjoy revenge, she somehow couldn't feel sorry for this man who broke up families and shattered lives in the name of conquering the world for the Third Reich.

Joe grabbed Klaus's arm. "I said stop. This is my house, buster. You can't just—" Joe began to shove him outside.

Klaus pushed his way back into the house, punching Joe in the face and knocking him to the floor. Voices came from behind Klaus. Maisy asked who the man was. Doug grabbed Klaus by the arms and pulled them behind his back as if handcuffing him.

Maisy! Liselotte would never allow a child to be in danger. She quickly rushed toward the commotion. "Get out, Klaus. Stay away from us." She grabbed Maisy, who was starting to cry. "Honey," she said as calmly as possible, "Go to Audrey in her bedroom and lock the door."

"Do as she says," Doug ordered his daughter.

Liselotte helped Joe stand. Unsteady on his feet, he leaned heavily against the coat closet door.

Klaus, struggling to break free from Doug's grip, looked Liselotte in the eyes. In German, he said, "After all these years searching for you, I'm not about to turn away. I told you that you're mine. I've come back for you."

"Never," Liselotte said, continuing in German. She stepped back.

"I have some important things to discuss with you, Liselotte, that I'm sure you won't like. But it will have to be my way, not yours."

"I don't care what you say. Leave. Now."

Klaus broke free from Doug's grip and yanked a knife from his back pant pocket. He hooked an arm around Doug's throat and pressed the blade to his neck. "I swear," he said in English, "if you don't shut up—all of you—and let me talk, it's the end of Dougie for you."

He knew Doug's name?

This was unacceptable. With her loved ones in danger, Liselotte refused to give Klaus even a second more of her attention. Knowing Joe kept several guns in the house—one of which was in the hall table drawer—she would distract Klaus and grab the gun. A faint sound of sirens swelled into a roar.

"Go away, Klaus," Liselotte shouted, purposely in English. She was sure he understood her, and she wanted those around her to witness what she said. Slowly, she stepped backward toward the table with the hidden gun. "I don't care what news you have."

Doug shifted, and Klaus slashed his neck. Then he shoved Doug to the floor.

"This is your loss, Liselotte," Klaus said, "Not mine."

"I want nothing between us," she said in a clear, level tone. From the corner of her eye, she saw Joe frantically shaking his head at her. "Whatever you think was once between us was only in your imagination. The reality was that every second I wanted to get away from you, forever."

Outside, tires screeched to a halt.

Audrey stepped into the entranceway. Liselotte had to act now before anyone else got hurt. Too late. Klaus grabbed Audrey and, holding her captive, shoved her out the door.

Joe pushed Liselotte aside and grabbed the gun from the drawer. Unhampered by his prosthetic foot, he chased after Klaus. Without considering the likely outcome, Liselotte stepped outside and shouted at the two police officers running toward the house. "He's taking her hostage."

Klaus shoved Audrey to the ground, then pulled a gun from another pocket and pointed it at Liselotte. "Fine. I'll take you to hell with me instead."

Three shots sailed through the air.

Liselotte collapsed to the ground.

"Liselotte," Audrey yelled. "Oh my God..."

Liselotte's world turned dark.

THE ONLY THING Liselotte remembered when she first opened her eyes in her hospital room was that Klaus was dead. Whether she recalled this from the memory of Klaus unexpectedly showing up at Audrey and Joe's doorstep, or if someone had told her while she was unconscious in the ICU, she couldn't say. As other thoughts flooded back, she clearly understood that she was alive, having survived a three-hour surgery to remove a bullet from her shattered right femur, and facing about six months or more of grueling rehab. Blinking her vision clearer and seeing her loved ones gathered around her was all that mattered.

Doug kissed her cheek. "Rise and shine, my lovely."

Before she could reply, Liselotte felt her hand being squeezed and looked up to see Audrey.

"Is Joe okay?" she asked her dear friend.

"Yes, hon," Audrey said, tears streaming down her face despite her smile. "He's—"

"I'm right here," Joe said, stepping out from the side and more directly into Liselotte's view. "If it weren't for you alerting the cops, I would have been a goner. They shot and killed Klaus, and..." He swallowed multiple times. "I wish I could've gotten you out of harm's way before that bastard shot you."

Weakly, Liselotte lifted a hand and waved away Joe's apology. She forced herself not to focus on her right leg, heavily cast and suspended in some type of traction device. "All that counts is that we're all alive."

"And Klaus will no longer try to harm you, or anyone," Doug said. A heavy silence spread between them.

Liselotte looked at her loved ones around the bed. "Thanks for visiting me the past few..." She squeezed her eyes shut. "Has it been days or weeks since..." She shot her eyes open, too afraid to keep them closed. "Since this horror happened?"

Doug leaned over the bed and gently took her hand. "Three weeks, darling."

She sighed. "Three long weeks. I've been in a coma for that long?"

"Actually," Audrey said. "You've been in and out of a sleeping state. Let's think positively—you're still with us."

"You're right," Liselotte said. Gratitude filled her. She had wonderful people supporting her, who loved her, and she loved them. She would recover. And, Klaus was now past tense, where he would stay.

A clatter came from the corridor.

"What in the world?" Doug said as a bed tray wheeled into the room.

"Oops. Sorry." A thirty-something-year-old, dark-haired man stumbled into the room, grabbing the runaway tray before it could collide with Liselotte's bed. Beaming, he pointed at himself. "My name is Kenny. My wife had twins two weeks ago. Today, I'm taking my family..." He stopped short, staring at Liselotte. "Helene," he called repeatedly over his shoulder. "Come. Look. This woman looks just like you."

"Wait a minute, guy," Doug said, stepping toward the stranger. "We've had enough intruders to last a lifetime. Leave this room immediately."

"Kenny," a woman called as she entered the room. "Let's not disturb these nice people. I've fixed things in the hallway if you'd like to keep wheeling Gina and my grandbabies…" She fixed her gaze on Liselotte and grew pale.

"Mutter?" Liselotte murmured, trying to lift herself up by reaching for a metal triangle hanging from a chain above the bed, but Doug helped her lie back down, telling her there would be plenty of time to practice sitting up soon.

"Helene?" Another woman, roughly Liselotte's age, entered the room. "Is everything okay?"

Kenny pointed at Liselotte and Helene. To the woman who had just entered, he said, "Fanny, I don't know if they'll ever stop looking at each other."

Helene approached the bed. "Liselotte?"

Liselotte wiped away a fresh round of tears running down her face. With years of words stuck in her throat, she could only nod.

Helene faced Kenny and the woman Kenny called Fanny. "This is my daughter, Liselotte." She grabbed a few tissues from the box on Liselotte's bedside table and gently wiped Liselotte's face. She looked at Liselotte's legs, noticing the pain and emotions visible in her daughter's eyes. "It's been too many years since we parted. I'm unsure what misfortune has brought you here to the hospital, and I hope to God you're okay. We've found each other." She glanced at her companions and smiled, then looked back at Liselotte. "This is Kenny, husband to Gina—your daughter Regina—who gave birth to a boy and a girl two weeks ago. And this fine woman is our dear friend, Fanny." She looked at Audrey, Joe, and Doug. "I apologize for the intrusion."

Doug ran his fingers through his hair. "Sweetheart," he said to

Liselotte, "something tells me this is more a miracle than an intrusion, right?"

Liselotte opened her mouth to agree that he was absolutely correct, but before she could say a word, a voice carried into the room from the corridor.

"Hello, does anyone remember me? I have two tiny newborns nestled in my arms, and if I'm hearing correctly, the mother I can't remember is in that hospital room. If someone doesn't wheel me in soon, I'm going to go crazy."

"Enough with separations," Helene said. She strode out of the room and, within seconds, wheeled Gina and the twins to Liselotte's bedside. "My dear daughter, this is Regina—Gina—your daughter, and your grandchildren, Thomas and Rosa."

Helene took Thomas out of Gina's arms, and Fanny picked up Rosa.

Liselotte's gaze shifted from Gina to Thomas, to Rosa, and then back to Gina. "My little girl… who is all grown up now."

"And with a family." Without waiting, Gina lifted herself from the wheelchair, sat beside Liselotte, then leaned over to slip her arms under Liselotte and hugged her. "Sorry," she said, mumbling around the tears streaking down her cheeks. "I'm not good with formalities."

"I was never good with those kinds of things, either," Liselotte said. She sniffled and moaned.

"Am I hurting you?" Gina asked.

Liselotte sniffled. "No… no. I've missed so much in your life. I'm the one who has hurt you." She looked at her mother. "And you. I'm so sorry."

"All that doesn't matter now," Helene said. "Two weeks ago, my family grew with two new arrivals, and now, once more, with you. My heart's big enough for this."

"Family," Liselotte murmured, testing the word aloud. "Is Rosa named after my other daughter? Is she alive?"

Gina held Liselotte's hand. "Right after the twins were born, Fanny—our amazing attorney, whom we'll tell how we became acquainted with another time—received a phone call from her assistant, who was traveling throughout Europe looking for my sister. Sadly, we just learned last night that she passed away just after her eighteenth birthday a few years ago. Likely, from a suspected heart ailment... she passed in her sleep." Gina pressed a finger against her mouth, looked away for a moment, then looked back. She took a deep breath as Kenny placed a supportive hand on her shoulder. "She not only survived the war but lived wonderfully, better than expected. During the war, with help from German nuns in the resistance movement, she was placed with a loving family in Switzerland, who helped her strengthen her legs, sharpen her motor skills, and taught her basic speech. They had two other daughters who doted on Rosa. Together, this family made sure Rosa grew to be a happy young woman, despite the odds." She glanced at the baby in Fanny's arms. "It was my honor to name my daughter after her."

Liselotte placed a hand over her heart. "It hurts to know Rosa's gone, but she'll live forever within me." She began to sob. "If I could go back in time and change things, I never would have left you and your sister... how I wish I were a better, more loving mother instead of only thinking about myself." She glanced at Helene, who stepped beside her.

"My dear daughter," Helene began, "there aren't enough words to express how horrible the war was... no one escaped heartache. Both you and I did our best, yet we fell short in several ways. What we can't do is wave a magic wand to make what happened and how we reacted vanish. We must live with this." She squeezed Liselotte's shoulder. "There's a solution to this past mess, though. One, I'm sure you're thinking along the same lines as I am. Yes?"

Liselotte nodded. "To move forward—as a united family—from this day forward," she said, liking the certainty in her tone. One by one, she lovingly looked at her mother, her daughter, her grandchildren, then at Kenny—a son, if anything—and Fanny, someone she reasoned would become a great friend. "If you all will have me in your lives?" She scanned her gaze over each of them, nodding and smiling.

Liselotte then locked eyes with Doug. "Between a man I love with all my heart, someone I want to marry as soon as I'm discharged from here, and my dear friends and growing family, I'm truly happy."

"Liselotte," Kenny said softly, sniffling. "If you don't stop crying, I'll cry. Ask Gina—my crying is not pretty."

Chuckles spread through the room of friends and once-lost, now-found family.

Family. Liselotte loved how that word, which had eluded her for years, now appeared clearly before her. It took her many painful days —years—more than it should have—to accept that she had made a terrible decision to rashly leave her family based on her then-naive idea of romantic love, putting herself before her children and her mother, and then dealing with the guilt and regret that followed. Back then, she definitely needed to grow up and learn how to prioritize others. The price—with too much time taken—had been steep. Yet, she had *found herself*, as the kids these days like to say.

She wanted to burst out laughing in joyful shouts for everyone to hear. She wanted to cry away her sins of poor decisions and impulsiveness, as a final act of forgiveness.

"You're beginning to tremble," Gina said, tucking the bedsheet around Liselotte's neck. "What can I do for you to make you more comfortable? Another blanket, perhaps?"

"Can you call me Mom?"

"Well," Gina said with a smile, "can you say you've found home now?"

Liselotte grasped her daughter's hands. "Absolutely."

Gina brushed the tears from her eyes. "Then I'm happy, Mom."

Reader Group Guide for ***Coming Back To Home***:

1. The story opens with Liselotte coming to terms with a weighty decision. If you could reach out to this character in real life, what coping strategies would you suggest?

2. While traveling to Klaus's parents' home, Klaus and Liselotte talk about the author Johann Wolfgang von Goethe's work. Can you relate to his quoted words: "Know thyself? If I knew myself I would run away"?

3. As Liselotte drives Klaus to his parents' house, she wonders about the people who had once lived in the elegant apartments they were passing, and who would be able to live there post-war. Are you a daydreamer? Do you wonder how people have lived during various times?

4. Have you ever known of any civilians who went missing during a war?

5. Have you had to navigate carefully among family and friends to learn about your heritage?

6. Several reasons had caused Liselotte to leave behind her mother and daughters, plaguing her with guilt that haunted her daily. Has guilt ever obsessed you? Were you able to overcome it?

7. While talking with Audrey, Liselotte realized that forgiveness might depend on accepting that someone else has already forgiven you. Have you ever been in a situation where someone says they forgive you, but you do not easily accept their forgiveness?

8. Liselotte and Audrey agree that fear can paralyze one from seeking safety and moving on in life. Have you had to overcome your fears to resolve an uncomfortable situation?

ABOUT THE AUTHOR

Photo: @ElaineStock

When Elaine Stock penned the novel, We Shall Not Shatter, inspired by her paternal heritage from Brzeziny, Poland, she discovered her passion for writing what she loved to read: historical fiction. It became the first of her bestselling Resilient Women of World War II Trilogy. What pleases her the most is that readers have reached out to say her books have encouraged them to face their tomorrows. Born in Brooklyn, New York, she lives in upstate New York with her husband and enjoys long walks down country roads, visiting New England towns, and, of course, a good book.

Visit with Elaine at: https://elainestockbooks.com

Most of all, please recommend this novel to others.

www.ingramcontent.com/pod-product-compliance
Lightning Source LLC
LaVergne TN
LVHW020705110826
845149LV00012B/2110

* 9 7 8 0 9 9 9 5 7 6 3 5 9 *